SURVIVOR

Out of the Wild

Diane Mayer Christiansen

ISBN-13: 978-0-578-79992-6

Cover design by: Art Painter
Library of Congress Control Number: 2018675309
Printed in the United States of America

To Jackie, a true survivor.
Be Brave.

More care is put into the characters than many books of its ilk. The disconnect between the two protagonists--one still carries a flame, one still carries regret--is compelling, and the emotional anguish of characters in a sinister and traumatizing position is realized effectively.

--BookLife Publisher's Weekly Review

CHAPTER ONE

Wren

Tap, tap, tap. I hear my mother's knuckles rap gently on my bedroom door before I can even open my eyes. My head is thick with sleep one second and then flooded with the anxiety that today will bring. I roll over in bed, throwing the cover off so that I won't be tempted to stay safe and secure under the warm blankets.

"I'm up," I say. I can hear my mother's footsteps as they fall upon the stairs leading down to the kitchen. I hesitate to leave my bed, my mind working a mile a minute. Today is the beginning of my future. The assembly hall will be crowded as those who have finished their secondary school, and have received their qualifying letter, will come to apply for their choice of universities. As much as I can feel a flutter of excitement, my stomach is also churning regrettably with what the outcome will mean for Aiden. I glance over to my nightstand and see the silver ring resting next to my tablet. A sweet gift from a sweet boy, a token that I'm not ready for and a reminder of the pain that I've caused. As I slip the ring onto my finger, I think today will most likely be the hardest day I have ever experienced.

I sit up and pull on my simple gray pants and matching light-weight shirt. We all dress simply in Sector Three but soon that will change. Once I am accepted into the university, my clothes will become a deep shade of green, the color that indicates learning and tells the world that I will do great things with my life. My uniform may not have the gold and black Sector Two emblem stitched onto the breast pocket but I'm okay with that, at least I think I am. As I pull my hair up into a high ponytail, I can imagine how those new clothes will look, dark and formal to set off the fiery red of my hair. Aiden will look so handsome, too, with his slender build and tall stature, he will be an impressive figure in his new green uniform even if he isn't standing next to me. I take a deep breath and steady my nerves before joining my mother in the kitchen.

Sun shines through the small window, reflecting off the four foil-ware containers sitting on the counter: two for the morning meal and two for the evening. The house is set up simply and is like every other house on our street in our sector. A large kitchen opens into a family room with tall windows surrounding the space. Upstairs there are three bedrooms and a bathroom plus a storage area. I like our home, but I wonder if Aiden is right that the houses are bigger in Sector Two. The thought brings another pain of guilt into my heart.

"Hi, Honey," says my mom as I enter the kitchen. "Did you have a good sleep?"

I nod as she begins to fix the morning meal. She opens the lids from two containers and pops them into the heater. I catch a glimpse of eggs mixed with potatoes and vegetables. My stomach gives an involuntary growl.

"So, made up your mind yet?" She gives me a sideway glance. Within hours she will know what I have decided.

"Wren, you couldn't ask for a better partner than Aiden."

"I know," I say. "I know he's perfect. He's kind and caring and loyal. He's great."

"And that's bad?"

"No," I reply, not able to meet her eyes. "I just think that maybe it would be better for me to stay here, you know, attend the university and continue to live at home."

"Wren," she replies as she looks at me lovingly. "I gave up the chance to go to the best schools because your father wanted to start a family. I don't regret that part," she adds hastily. "but you deserve the best, Honey, and just so you know, I'll be okay." She hugs me and I cling on a little longer than usual, breathing in her familiar scent of oranges and honeysuckle. "So, you follow your heart, okay?" I nod and smile. If only my heart wanted what Aiden wants. For some reason that I can't explain, whenever I think of my future, I don't see him in it. I want to feel passionate about someone. I want to look into his eyes and just know. Maybe that doesn't happen in real life. I know I should just take what's in front of me and be happy. I just can't, not right now.

"Will you be going to the banquet with Aiden?" asks my mom as she busies herself with napkins and cutlery. She looks up at me when I don't answer and notices the ring with a smile. "When did you get this?" she asks, touching it gently.

"Yesterday," I reply, trying to hold back the tears and the memories that go with them.

"Well, that's nice," she says, her eyes delving into mine questioningly.

"We broke up." I blurt it out before my voice chokes up. My mother comes around the counter to hug me.

"Oh, babe, I'm so sorry." I sob into her shoulder keenly aware of my runny nose wiping against the fabric of her shirt. "Maybe you can patch it up today, before the ceremony."

"No," I say pulling back. "No, there's no fixing it, at least not today." She doesn't press me, but I'm sure that she knows what's going on.

"Listen Wren," she says as she rubs my back. "I know that four years seems like a long time to someone as young as you, but it's really not. If you really do want to stay here and Aiden loves you, and I'm sure that he does, then you can be together after graduation."

"I don't think so, Mom."

"Love doesn't just go away, not true love. It wouldn't be the worst thing if you both ended up working closer to home. The capitol has its perks but his father and yours managed to get good government jobs while not living in the capitol." I smile at her and she takes my hand to get a better look at the silver band on my finger. "This means something."

What does it mean? What do I want it to mean? Maybe Aiden's right. Maybe one day years from now, once the university is far behind me, I'll look at this ring and see what could have been. Aiden will never be happy until he has his great job, his big house and all of the other luxuries that money can buy, and it's more than that. He wants to do something big in the world, something important. I feel that pull too, just not in the same direction. I want to ask my mother what it was like for her when she fell in love, how she knew that she loved my father so deeply that she gave up her own dreams for his.

I want to ask her if I'm crazy for giving up a great opportunity, attending the university in Sector Two, something that I've worked for all my academic years. I want her to tell me that she needs me and that she's happy that I'll be here and not miles away. But there's no time for any of these questions, there's no time for anything at all. As the buzzer goes off indicating that our food is ready, another sound breaks through the air. A loud siren, echoing off the houses and penetrating through my skull like a hammer. My mom's eyes are wide with fear as she shoves me to the front door. I swing it open and see a bright ball of fire in the distance, red, like the sun has begun to hurl itself through the sky. Red like my flaming red hair, bobbing along the tree-lined path by the lake where I jog with Aiden. Red-hot, like the pain I know Aiden will feel when I tell him that I cannot commit to him, not yet. It's not the sun, no way. It can't be! Without warning, without an explanation, without any time to react or plan, it's here. It is the most unreal moment of my life and, unfortunately, I can't move.

Oh my God, Oh my God! I stand awestruck as the blazing ball of light penetrates the sky, lighting it up like the whole world is on fire, expanding out like a golden umbrella. I'm panicking, I can feel it. The shaking begins deep down and works its way to the surface. The drills come back to me in an instant: leave all your belongings, head directly to the shelters deep underground or to the cryobanks, run as fast as you can. My instinct is to run but Aiden pops into my head, his golden hair and those chocolate brown eyes. Where is he? Will he be okay? Will he make it to his cryotank? I dash away from the open door just as my mom runs through it and I get to the halo screen and punch in his name, Aiden Veka.

"Damn it!" I stumble over the keypad until I get it right on the third try. I can hear the halo screen trying to connect and then I see his face and I take a deep breath.

"Wren!" he exclaims. "Go to the cryobank. I sent a car. It should be right outside!"

"Aiden," I say, staring into his eyes that look as afraid as I feel. His mouth is a straight line, his brows are furrowed and there is a hint of stubble covering his chin. I see him glance behind and hear the chaos outside that must mirror my own. He is panicking too, but not for himself. Of course, in the worst possible moment, when our lives are hanging by a thin thread, Aiden thinks of me first.

"Go!" he yells, sharply. I push back from the halo screen but then turn back, grasping for the edge of it.

"Tell me you're going, Aiden. Don't do anything heroic. Promise me." He nods, frantically. He leans in closer until his face fills the screen.

"I love you, Wren, I've always loved you and I'm sorry," he says. I hesitate, knowing what I should say but unable to say it, and in that moment of hesitation the screen goes blank. I don't waste another second and hurl myself out of my front door. Where is my mother? My eyes scan the scene quickly, searching for her. The light is blinding and the sudden heat oppressive. I cup my hands around my eyes, and I see her in the crowded street in front of our house. Everyone is panicked and running for their lives. The constant siren adds another layer to the terror while my once-civil neighbors push and shove their way through the street, running to the rail trains or to the underground. I can just make out random shouts through the noise.

"They did it! They sent their nukes!"

"This is it! I hope we gave them more of the same!" It's everyone for themselves, all our nation's ideas of systematic conformity out the window. All the peaceful care that our citizens are encouraged to show for others and the idea that, at least here in our nation, we take care of our own, are all trampled over like ants on the sidewalk. Everyone runs except my mother who has stopped to help an elderly woman who has fallen and is in clear danger of being stomped on. I recognize the gray-haired bun perched on top of Mrs. Connor's head, the widow who lives next door. My mother pulls her to her feet and whispers something in her ear, calming words, I'm sure, words that will do absolutely no good here. Useless words. The light is blinding, and I can see small fires beginning to catch. A tree, a fence, a house, all begin to smoke and burn. My skin feels the prickle of heat, it's hot and the intensity is growing by the second. Luckily, the electric car that Aiden ordered pulls in and blocks the street. The mass of crazed people notices it too. A man points to the car and shouts to the rest of those surrounding him. There's no way I'm letting them take my ride to safety. I won't make it to the cryotanks on foot, not with this mob.

"Mom!" I call. "You have to come now!" I run to the car before someone can hijack it and place my palm on the lock pad. The door snaps open and I throw myself inside. My finger hovers above the closing switch as I scan the street once again for my mother. There she is, only feet away, her arm around Mrs. Connor, pulling her gently toward the car. My mother's eyes are wide with fear and shock as she drags the old woman faster. Her hair, like mine, is a flame mixing with the world around us, wild, untamed. It strikes me at this moment how much we are mirror images of each other. Her deep green eyes, like moss, beg me to be safe, her full bottom lip quivers as I'm sure mine does, and her small willowy frame and delicate hands struggle to keep Mrs. Connor upright.

Suddenly, a man bursts from the crowd, heading toward the car. His face is twisted with rage, his thick arms bulging with taut muscles, ready to mow down anyone in his path. He plows into my mother, causing her to lose her step and fall. She brings down Mrs. Connor who looks like she might not recover from the impact. I let out a cry as the man locks eyes with me and I know in an instant what his intentions are. It's either me or him and, without another thought, I jam my finger onto the closing switch and the car door snaps shut, leaving my mother abandoned along with the man. I press my face against the back window as the car begins to lurch forward, screaming for my mother to run. Our eyes lock one last time and I see her nod and release Mrs. Connor who does not move. *She'll make it*, I think. She has to. She will make it to the underground and find her way to the cryobank. I'll meet her there.

As the car weaves through my neighborhood, heading to my cryobank located a few miles to the north, the streets are packed. More running people, the sky ripped with explosions as gold and white-hot chunks of something burst out like fireworks, hitting the ground with sizzling force. Just as I decide to lock myself into the safety harness, there is an even bigger explosion of glass and metal. Two rail trains have collided, and I watch as they fall from the track, landing ten stories below in a mass of debris. There are other electric cars like mine speeding their way to wherever they have been programmed to go. I worry that, with all the foot traffic, mine may hit someone. It jostles back and forth using avoidance technology, making me nauseous. The continuous siren is joined by a symphony of shouts and screams and cries from my community in panic. If I could fly up into space, I wonder if this is what I would see covering the entire planet: a messy end-of-the-world movie scene. But this is not a movie and my gut clenches with the pain of it. All I can do is press my forehead against the window and watch in horror, trying to control my rapid breathing and my limbs that won't stop shaking.

Aiden has programmed the car controls to take me directly to the cryobank where both of our families own tanks. After decades of advancements, the science of Cryogenics has advanced. My body will be suspended, frozen in time to be revived in the future, perhaps at a time when the world has replenished itself, when this nightmare is all over. There are banks located all over the country, gathered around the bigger cities and spreading out into the farming communities. The tanks are expensive, though, and very few can afford them. What will happen to those people now, those whose only chance are the underground bunkers? I continue to watch out of the windows as my car hurls me forward, quicker than I've ever traveled. The hideous ball of light is spreading, getting closer. The thing is so bright that I can't look into it. The clear reality hits me hard that this is the end of everything. This is it! And what is even worse is that no visions of my life flash before my eyes, no memories that I'm thankful for, only complete and utter terror as my mind and body race for self-preservation.

CHAPTER TWO

Aiden

The image of Wren's face is burned into my mind as I race for the door. All of my anger has evaporated at the thought of losing her forever, like this. My father is waiting, the outside world rushing past.

"Let's go!" My voice sounds crazy and my heart feels as if it will explode out of my chest. But my father is calm, I see it all over him, and his hands are steady as he rests them on my shoulders.

"I'm sending you to the government bank," he says with composure. "You'll be safest there. I've sent word that you'll be coming. There's space for you. Compartment number four. Go now, lock yourself into the car and don't get out until you reach the bank. Do you understand, Aiden?" My eyes flick to the government issued car waiting in the driveway. All hell has broken loose as every citizen in my sector races for safety. The siren blocks out the screams of terror but, I can see it on every face that passes my door. Women are dragged by their husbands as children are thrown over shoulders. The elderly don't stand a chance. Even as I watch, I see a man fall to the ground, trampled by the horde. Fire lights up the sky in a beautiful deadly array of reds and oranges.

"Aiden," says my father, shaking my shoulders. "Do you understand?" I don't understand. What is happening?

"Dad."

"Go!" His voice commands and I search his eyes for answers. "I have a job to do and then I'll meet you there."

"Come now," I say, taking a deep breath, trying to calm my nerves. It's impossible, an impossible nightmare.

"I have to put a call in to the Secretary of Defense. We have to coordinate our next move. I'll meet you at the bank."

"Is that what's going on here? Is this a war?"

"I don't know, but I have to make sure." His rough hands push me toward the door. I hesitate, searching the crowd for familiar faces, but they all look distorted and unhuman. The touch of my hand on the window unlocks the car door and I throw myself in. Instantly the siren and the screams and the noise of all the destruction around me is silenced. I lean back in the leather seats and close my eyes, allowing my brain a few precious seconds of relief as the car glides forward. It will be a long trip, but this government-issued car is designed to withstand any element that's thrown at it, including the fireball that is now propelling itself across the sky. I wish I could have sent Wren this car or one like it. I still love her, even after my disappointment and anger.

"She'll make it," I say to myself. She's smart and strong and resourceful. She'll make it. It's true what they say, in moments of extreme danger that your life passes before your eyes. As I watch all the bodies rushing toward the hope of survival, I see everything I am, being flushed down the toilet. The years of hard work, the networking, and the countless extra projects, all designed to get me to the top, to create the best life possible not only for myself but for Wren. What was it all for? It's all gone in an instant of fire and smoke. I think about last night, her words and all my anger. Even now, I'm pissed. I'm angry and hurt and even a little indignant thinking about her lies and her promises. We had a better chance than most to get a foot into Sector Two with our academic achievements and our family connections. Why throw that away?

"Damn it, Wren," I say out loud. It's like that nice, neat little box of plans that I had

she dumped and scattered across the ground. Was I that self-absorbed, that selfish? The answer is yes. Maybe what I'm seeing outside of my window is not as bad as it seems. Maybe there's still a chance. But as my car eases onto the highway, away from the crowds, I know that it's far worse. The ball of fire in the sky begins to erupt, spewing its contents to earth. The trees along the highway begin to burst into flames. The fire leaps onto anything that will catch; the rooftops of businesses dotting the road, human bodies running out of them, and even my car. I feel the heat as the blue flames lick at windows, trying to catch. Sweat begins to trickle down my back and the seat is becoming uncomfortably hot. I'm not sure how long the car will continue to be safe. The heat alone might kill me.

"Come on," I hiss. "Increase speed," I command into the car's sensor controls. I feel a jerk as the vehicle tries to accelerate.

"Acceleration function disabled due to hazardous conditions." The AI voice is irritatingly familiar.

"Fuck!" I slam my fist against the seat. "Increase speed, you stupid piece of shit!" This time the vehicle doesn't even attempt to speed up.

"Acceleration function disabled due to hazardous conditions." I take a deep breath and try to get myself together. The panic and realization of my situation are hitting me hard.

"Engage cooling system," I say a little more calmly now.

"Unable to engage cooling system due to drained energy source."

"Damn it!" *Think, think, think.* Come on, Aiden, get it together.

"Estimated arrival to destination."

"Estimated arrival at Government Cryobank Three in approximately forty-eight minutes and seventeen seconds."

"Energy level stats."

"Battery charge at seventy-eight percent, Five percent depletion due to extreme heat. Exterior heat peak at thirteen-thousand-fifty degrees Celsius and lowering."

"Okay, engage cooling system for two minutes."

"Unable to engage cooling system due to drained energy

source."

"Override."

"Override complete." With relief, I feel the cold air hit my sweating skin and I wipe my face with the hem of my shirt. My eyes scan the car and I remember a small compartment near my feet. I open it and take a bottle of water from the supply, guzzling it. The flames are no longer licking at the windows and I see the road stretched out before me.

"Energy level at seventy-two percent, external temperature seven-hundred twenty degrees Celsius and lowering. Continue override?"

"Continue override for one minute and then recalibrate." I sit back on the seat that has cooled considerably, watching the world pass by. The sky is filled with a painting of orange and yellow overtaking any other color. A haze is beginning to cover everything as fire and smoke billow from the inhabited areas along the highway and charred remains scatter like dust. The cool air shuts off.

"Energy level sixty-seven percent. Exterior temperature two-hundred sixteen degrees Celsius and dropping." I'll be okay. If another fire-bomb doesn't hit the car, I'll be okay.

Time passes slowly, inching along in a blur. Today could have been the day that Wren decided to come with me to Sector Two. Right now, at this moment, I might have been the happiest guy in the world. I shake my head. No, that wasn't going to happen. She was struggling with something, maybe with her feeling towards me. Now none of it matters: our argument, our choices, even the love that I have for her doesn't matter. It's all meaningless in a sea of fire. There's no time left to wait for her to fall in love with me, really fall in love with me. I must not have done enough, said enough, to let her know that it was her, always her and nothing else mattered. And then I stop myself. This isn't true. I wanted things. I wanted a big job, high up, a powerful position. Deep down I know that I would have sacrificed anything for that, even her. She must have known that too. What a fucking idiot I've been. Now all that matters is survival.

"ETA?"

"Estimated arrival at Government Cryobank Three in approximately six minutes twenty-three seconds." I glance out the window that has blackened around the edges from the fire. The seat is cool again and as my hand presses against the door panel, it feels warm but not hot. The area leading up to my exit is deserted except for a scattering of small fires and smoke. The car veers to the right, off the highway and onto a side street. All around me are ruins. Every home in this sector has burnt to the ground and are smoldering in their bones. Fallen trains block the road as my car makes the necessary maneuvers to navigate me to my destination. There are no people, no movement at all but for another government car that I see heading in the same direction. Another survivor. I can't see their face, the car is too far away, so I look ahead to the round titanium carbide structure built to withstand any disaster, Government Cryobank Three. The car slows as we make a sharp turn, taking a ramp that will lead underground. The heavy metal door staggers open and we enter the structure. The generators must be working. The car drives deep below the main building and comes to a halt next to a loading platform.

"Destination reached." With a hiss and the scrape of metal, the door panel opens. I waste no time and launch myself from the car and run in the direction of my cryotank compartment. The air is stale and warm on the platform but once I pull open the door leading to the tanks, it feels fresher and cool. The hallway is deserted and still, but I know I'm not alone, I can feel it. Number four flashes before my eyes and I press my palm onto the door, hearing a series of beeps as the door slides open. The room is large and posh, all things considered. Everything is streamlined from the sleek black leather sofa to the rectangular glass table and pale plush carpet. The only sore thumb in the room is the imposing presence of a large green, metal tube in the corner, the cryotank. I know what I'll have to do, and I only hope I'm brave enough to go through with it. Now I wait for my father.

CHAPTER THREE

Wren

I see the round building of the cryobank in the distance, an unassuming structure built of deep red fiberglass sheets, one story high, curved and smooth. I know that beneath the outer structure there is reinforced steel and stone, all designed to keep out heat, radiation, and toxins. Deep below the ground, where the cryotanks are located, is the safest place in the world. My car comes to a stop just in front of the building. As I remove my restraints, I can feel my hands trembling. I fumble with the release on the harness buckle until I hear it snap open. Launching myself out of the car, I run full force to the front glass doors, joining the pack of others trying to get in. Turning back to the car briefly, I look up into the fire. The heat rushes toward me like an evil wind, sucking the life out of me. Everything is burning now. Most of the trees in the distance have charred, more homes begin to ignite as fire jumps from rooftop to rooftop like a wild rabbit. Smoke and ash add themselves to the hot wind, stinging my eyes. A man runs, covering his mouth with his shirt, not wanting to breath it all in, but he falls, and I don't see him get up. *Oh no, oh no! That can't be me!* The front doors are heavy and with so many of us trying to get through, I feel smashed between legs and arms. I notice a small opening near the bottom of the entryway and I'm able to squeeze through with the other children and parents and grandparents.

I waste no time, pushing myself through the front door between an old man with a cane and his young granddaughter. I take the stairs two at a time to the lower levels, my feet banging on metal stairs as I go lower and lower, deeper into the core of the earth. I can hear the siren even down here, but the air feels clean and cool, for now. Once I hit the bottom, I wrench open the heavy metal door that leads to the tanks, sweat running down my back, my heart racing out of control. The circular hallway where my cryotank is located appears in front of me and I slow. *Breathe, breathe.* The place is eerily deserted. The dim blue glow of track lighting across the floor gives me an ominous feeling of dread. With more than one hundred cryotanks located here, including mine, I should see someone. And then I hear a stampede of feet, pounding hard down the stairs behind me. I don't have time to think. I run the long hallway until I see number fourteen and quickly place my shaking, sweaty palm on the identification pad located in the center of the door. The blue light scans my fingerprints and then turns green with a beep. The door slides open with a hiss, bathing me in synthetic light.

As I enter, I hear the door close behind me and the click of the lock trapping me inside. I stand and breathe, unable to focus. There is an immediate feeling of relief, but it's short-lived. I can't stop the panic and the fear and the shaking. I let out a sob and try to stop the flow of adrenalin that is making me nauseous and turning my body to mush.

I begin to sob harder, tears running down my face and into my mouth, and I can't stop. I crouch to the ground, crying like a child, feeling empty and terrified and so alone. On and on I cry and sob and choke on the snot running from my nose. I'm breaking down and who the hell cares? Not me and not the guy in the chamber next to mine. I start to hyperventilate, unable to control my breathing. I want my mother here with me, I want Aiden. And then the thought of the two most important people in my life makes me stop. What if they didn't make it?

I am safe here in the bowels of the building. I close my eyes and think of Aiden. Is he safely tucked away down the hall? I think about my dad and the huge chasm between us. We could have had a great life if he had stayed, the best of everything. Maybe then I wouldn't have questioned my university choice. Maybe then mom would have been happy and perhaps even made something more of her life. Maybe then I wouldn't have had to hurt Aiden.

I wipe my eyes on my sleeve and glance around the small space. The tank sits in the far corner, a human-sized thick plastic tube encased in dark green steel, on a platform with three stairs leading to the top. It looks the same as it did last year when I came with my mother for my annual what-to-do-in-case-of-an-emergency drill. I should have listened better to the procedural lecture. To the left of the tank is a shelving unit with various supplies. I take a bottle of water and leave the food. It's the freeze-dried junk that's guaranteed to last forever. I'm thirsty and I quickly down the bottle of water. I search the space for more usable inventory. There's a small sink with a green hand towel next to the shelves and, as my eyes travel upwards, I notice air vents that are now pumping in clean air. Then, suddenly, the siren stops. Instantly, the lights go out and I'm plunged into complete silence and darkness. Before renewed terror can overcome me, I hear the buzz of the generator system kicking into life. The lights flicker and then turn on. This can only mean that the city has been destroyed and my panic begins to rise to the surface again. It's too late. If you haven't made it to safety, there's no more time. I curl myself up into a ball, my back against the hard, cold wall, my face buried in my arms. I don't want to see, I don't want to be here, so I press my eyes shut. I'm way too afraid for tears now. How long can I stay here? How long will the generators last? *Breathe, breathe, breathe.* Just as I tell myself to calm down, that soon we will be cleared to exit our rooms, I smell something rancid. Burning, something's burning. As I glance up to the air vents, I see it, deep gray smoke slowly entering the room.

"Oh my God!" What do I do? What do I do? I know the answer, but I'm terrified to go through with it. My lungs begin to sense the danger and I cough and cover my face with my sleeve, remembering the man outside who collapsed. The smoke and ash envelop the room quickly. If I stay out in this room, I will die. Survival mode kicks in again and I run to the tank and pull open the heavy lid. It's made of a clear material so at least I won't be in total darkness. Without hesitation, I climb into the tank. The thick billowing smoke streaming into the room makes the decision easier, but I don't remember the procedure. *Damn it!* I pull the clear lid down over my head and it fits like a helmet. As I find the latch, just under my chin, I pull it shut and hear a click as I am sealed inside. The room is filling fast. All I can see is dense smoke, invading the clean air. I know that fresh air is being pumped into the tank, but I still feel suffocated, claustrophobic locked into this small tube. I take gulps of air into my lungs and, once again concentrate on breathing. I have to get this going. When the cryo-fluid enters my tank, it will preserve my body, my organs and my tissue. I will be injected with a drug to slow my heart rate and my oxygen consumption. I will myself to continue with the procedure. This is life or death. I squeeze my eyes shut, forcing my brain into recall. The doctor's words come back to me.

"The procedure is simple. The medication will slow your heart rate to a

basic minimum for the preservation of brain function. Once you are sedated and your systems have slowed down, you will be injected with a glycerol-based substance called cryoprotectant. This will allow the body's cells to survive the freezing process. The bank's computer system is programmed to begin the warming process at the fifty-year mark. This process takes several months but the system is guaranteed. Nothing can interfere."

Okay, step one, slow the heart. Right now, that seems impossible, considering the wild tattoo that my heart is hammering on my ribcage. Injection. Yes, that's the first thing. I feel to my right and as my hand runs over the cool, smooth surface of the encasement tube, I feel the small button that will release the needle filled with the medication used to put my body in a relaxed state. I press against it with my elbow and feel the sting as I'm injected. The medication rapidly takes effect, my movements slow as I search with my hands for the small ledge that will hold my arm in place. I strap my arm down so that my veins are visible. The movement of the straps triggers a red light to scan for the best insertion point for the IV fluids. Like a warm blanket, the calm begins in my feet and moves its way up until I feel as if I am floating. It's bliss but even as I feel my pulse slowing, my mind still races. Taking deep breaths helps to calm my mind and it wanders to Aiden, to my life, all seventeen years of it. I think about my mom and how much I love her and about my dad who left when I was eight. We were never able to put the pieces of our family back together after that and I feel the sting of regret for not trying harder. Just as my thoughts become fuzzy and I feel myself drifting into nothingness, I dimly hear the cryoshute open and liquid begins to pour in.

CHAPTER FOUR

Wren

"We're going to have a great life. You know that, right, Wren?"

"Yeah," I reply softly as I feel the cool river water splash against my legs and envelop my feet. "Yeah, I know, Aiden." He chuckles softly as if he really believes it and my heart drops a little, wishing that I could too.

"So we have a plan?"

"I guess so," I reply. There's a twinge of uncertainty in my voice but I smile it away and gaze up into his chocolate brown eyes. I've always loved the contrast there, the deep dark eyes and his fair blond hair that's trimmed short in preparation for the university.

"Do you want to go together?" he asks. "We could turn in our applications at the same time."

"No," I reply too quickly. "No, my mother wants to take me. It's kind of her last adult gesture before I go away." He smiles knowingly and nods. The truth is, there haven't been many adult gestures in the past ten years, not since my dad left.

"Sector Two will be so great!" says Aiden with relish. He reaches out to capture a loose strand of my hair and tucks it behind my ear before pulling away. "I love your hair," he says softly, his mood changing to something romantic. "I love that fiery red head of yours, it's different, unique, just like you, Wren." I look away, embarrassed. I can't handle compliments, not from anyone.

"Thanks," I reply blushing. I get another chuckle from Aiden.

"It's a good day," he says, trying to lighten the mood. "Not too hot, not too cold. I can't believe that everything will change tomorrow."

"Yep." I splash the water with my feet and feel the warm sun against the back of my neck. It's beautiful here, the gentle sound of the river is calming and the echo of birdsong cheerful and light. We sit side by side on the small peer that's been here forever, a place that's ours, and even though my brain is telling me that this is a dream, a distant memory, it feels real, so real. Aiden rattles on.

"I hear that the housing in Sector Two is much more spacious than here in Sector Three and the food is served on real china plates not in foil ware containers."

"It sounds fancy," I reply, my nerves beginning to tighten.

"It is, but that's the kind of life we can get used to," he says happily. "Attending the university in Sector Two is only one step away from the Capitol and Sector One. I'm positive we could get great apprenticeships there." I drop my head so that Aiden can't see the confusion in my eyes. He notices, though, and lifts my chin gently with his hand.

"What's wrong, Wren?" I take a deep breath.

"What if I don't get in?" He lets out a bark of laughter.

"What are you talking about? Of course, you'll get in."

"I don't know. I haven't taken as many advanced classes as you have, and my skill set is limited. They might not need aspiring botanists, but they'll always need engineers." He knows that I'm right. He has done all the right things, met all the right people and still been able to follow his dream of creating something out of metal and wire. He takes my hand and rubs the back of it with his thumb, moving in small circles.

"They will need botanists and especially students like you. Your hydroponic work was at the top of the class. And..." He turns his eyes to mine, and I melt just a little bit. "And there's your dad," he continues. "Both of our fathers have government jobs that the university won't overlook." I force a smile and nod. "So, you're good?" he asks earnestly, and when I nod again, he smiles widely, causing the dimples in his cheeks to appear. It strikes me how handsome Aiden is, how lucky I am that he chose me. "I have something for you," he says slyly. I glance up and see him reach into the pocket of his trousers and pull out a small package tied with a pink ribbon.

"What is it?" I ask. Aiden often brings me small gifts: bouquets of wildflowers gathered in the fields beyond the river, smooth stones carved with our initials, but never something wrapped up hidden in his pocket.

"Here," he says, placing the package in my palm. The ribbon is so beautiful, I don't want to open it, but I gently tug at the silk, hoping to save it as a keepsake. As I slowly remove the top of the delicate box, I see a glint of silver and hurry to pull out what lies inside. A silver ring falls into my hand and I stare in awe at the lovely gift from a boy who always thinks of me. It's a simple band, smooth and shiny with a tiny red stone embedded onto the surface.

"It's, it's wonderful," I exclaim. "It's too much, though." I know that this must have cost a lot and I feel guilty.

"Here," he replies ignoring my protest. He takes the ring and holds it up to the sun so that I can see the stone better. I smile up at him as he slides the ring onto my finger.

"It's perfect," I say a lump forming in my throat.

"I just want you to know," he says, his voice husky with emotion. "You're more to me than just a girlfriend. You're the person I want to be with forever, the person I want to share in this amazing new life that we're going to have." He pauses and leans in to kiss me tenderly, first on my cheek and then on my lips. "We've both worked so hard. We both have what it takes to make the best life possible. And I love you, Wren, I really love you." I don't know what to say as I feel the tears begin to well up in my eyes. I glance down at the ring, and a tear drop jumps onto the silver surface.

In this perfect world our government is set up for the good of all. The sectors are run by a group of ten men and women. No one knows their identities, but each representative is responsible for speaking for each sector and all decisions are made through debate and compromise. It is set up under a shroud of mystery but each of us know the same thing, we will be taken care of, we will be protected. I want to tell Aiden all the things that he wants to hear. I want to reassure him that I'm right there with him, but I can't. There's still a question mark somewhere deep in the back of my mind. I know how our lives are supposed to look. We go to the university, we are assigned good jobs, we are expected to get married and produce children, all set in stone to assure the stability of our world. To deviate from this is insane and reckless but there's a part of me that wants to be reckless. How could I ever explain this to Aiden? I can't. So instead, I just meet his gaze and say, "Thank you." He stares at me long and then drops is eyes.

"Something's wrong," he says not missing a beat. His voice is soft, little more than a whisper.

"No," I counter and then I let out a deep sigh that I've been holding in. "I just, I just..." I stutter. "I'm worried about my mom," I say, not able to meet his eyes this time. It's a half-truth but, of course, not everything. I see Aiden's shoulders relax and he takes my hand again, running his finger along the silver ring with the scarlet stone.

"Your mom will be okay," he reassures me gently. "My dad's here a lot of the time and he'll look out for her." He smiles and adds, "I promise." When he notices that I'm not returning his grin he asks, "Is it something else?" I don't answer, I can't. Aiden has been with me through so much. Through the gawky adolescent days when I felt like I didn't have any friends to the overwhelming job of helping my mother cope in her deepest depression. He's seen it all, tousled, wild hair in the morning, no makeup on those days when I just didn't have the energy to make an effort. He's been by me, telling me that he loves me and what have I done for him?

"Look, Wren," he says, the patient edge beginning to dissipate from his voice. "I've told you that I love you every day for the past two years and before that when we were just friends. It isn't lost on me that you've never said it back, but I always thought that you just had a difficult time putting your feelings into words." He softens his tone before continuing. "I know it was hard when your dad left. I get it, but if you're afraid of me leaving, if that's what's holding you back, I'm telling you, you don't have to worry about that. I'm here."

"It's not that," I say shaking my head. "Really, Aiden, you're great, perfect." I take a deep breath and try to sort out the emotions going around in my head like a crazy carousel. "I'm worried about my mom, Aiden, I am, but I'm just not sure about anything. I'm not sure if Sector Two is right for me, if I'd even be happy living in the Capital someday." He opens his mouth in surprise and then shuts it again, shaking his head back and forth in disbelief. "I know it's what you want. I know it's all we've been talking about for close to a year, but now that it's time to choose, I just don't know if it's right for *me*." I see the hurt in his eyes and my eyes sting with fresh tears.

"Maybe it's me you don't know about," he replies.

"No," I say, desperately trying to put a cheerful vibe back in my voice. "I just need some space, that's all, some time to figure out where I want to go. I can do that here in Sector Three and be with my mother and see you from time to time..."

"See me from time to time," he echoes bitterly. He moves to stand up, rolling down the legs of his trousers that stick to his wet skin. "We had a plan, Wren. We talked about it over and over again: go to the university in Sector Two, compete for Capitol jobs and have our own place, get married, have a couple of kids. What were you thinking during all those conversations? Seriously, if you think that I'm going to give all of that up to stay here, you're crazy."

"I would never want you to do that," I say softly.

"Oh, yeah, that's right, you need some *space*." My heart breaks at his pain and it's worse because I know that I'm the cause and I could make it all go away if I decided to. "It would have been nice if you would have spoken up sooner," he adds. "It's a little late for me to just drop everything and change my plans." I take the ring from my finger and hold it out to him. His deep pools of liquid chocolate gaze at it intently.

"No, you keep it," he says, roughly. "You've still got twelve hours to figure out what you want. If you decide that it's not me, then keep it as a reminder of what you could have had and what you lost." I don't have the heart to argue and I slide it back on my finger as a gesture that says, I don't want it to be over. He turns and walks away, jumping off the pier, his shoes hanging from his hand.

"Aiden," I say but he doesn't hear me and the memory begins to fade replaced by complete confusion.

Where am I? I am floating, falling through space. Slowly, so slowly, the haze begins to clear, and my body immediately starts freaking out. Even before my thoughts can catch up, my body is responding to medications running through my veins like an electric shock. My heart begins a rapid rhythm and my arms flail into what my mind perceives as open space, only to hit something hard and metallic.

"Ouch!" I whisper. My voice is strange, my throat raw and dry. I hear a buzz and then feel the sting of a needle pinch my arm. The antibiotic solution that the doctor explained would help my body defend itself from illness after being so long in suspension. My heartbeat begins to steady, and I take a few deep breaths. My eyes are heavy, but the floating sensation is wearing off. I can feel the weight of my body, the warm air blowing onto my skin, and sense close walls surrounding me. Slowly, my eyes flutter open. All at once, the reality of what I've been through rushes over me and I stare wide-eyed through the plastic helmet into the small room beyond the tank. My breaths come fast, causing light fog to mark the thick plastic in front of me.

I let out a small sob. So, I've made it. A click by my ear verifies my survival and indicates that the tank is now open. I push the helmet up, taking small breaths of air to make sure that the biochemicals or smoke or ash or whatever have dissipated.

It's difficult to get out of the tank. My limbs seem to have a mind of their own and I feel weak. I can tell that I've lost some weight. Or maybe I've just shriveled in the solution like a dried prune. It's been a long time. My heart beats a steady rhythm now, but I take my time, moving inch by inch. The platform steps are cold under my wobbly, bare feet and the floor below is smooth. I see a pile of clothes on one of the shelves along with food. It's some kind of granola cake wrapped in airtight plastic. Someone has entered the room while I slept, and it's slightly disturbing to think that a stranger has seen me unconscious in the tank. There must have been staff maintaining the building after everything settled down. The doctor never mentioned that.

I sit on the hard floor and start with a bottle of water, taking small sips. Once I've downed two bottles, I take a granola cake and bite off a corner. My taste buds explode and my mouth immediately waters. The cake is salty and sweet and dissolves on my tongue. Even though my stomach is screaming at me to shove the entire thing into my mouth, I go slow. I don't want it coming back up.

Standing back up is a challenge. I take a few steps around the room. I'm wobbly but I feel good, better and better each second. The gray pants and top that took me through the horrific end-of-the-world nightmare are in bad shape, so I turn my attention to the clothes on the shelf. The fabric of the tan jumpsuit is strange but so incredibly soft, like liquid air. Once I slip my legs into it and zip it up, I find that it is completely comfortable. There are several pockets, one on each hip as well as one on the side of my leg. The two breast pockets have zippers and are lined with a water-resistant material. I can feel my ginger hair tangled all around my head and I know that I must look feral. I take a minute to run my fingers through and braid it in a long plait down my back. Now I wait. I sit down on the sterile-looking bed, letting my legs dangle as I scan the room. The tank on its pedestal takes up most of the space. It's hard to believe that I've been incased in its metal womb for fifty years. My eyes flick to the door. A light crisscrossed in heavy metal bars illuminates red. It's not safe out there yet. Still, someone has been here. The jumpsuit wasn't here when I locked myself in and I also spy more water and more food, different from the freeze-dried stuff. I'm alive but I'm alone. *Aiden, where are you?* All I can do is sit here and think about my life, my seventeen years of existence. I would be sixty-seven if the world hadn't burned. It's more than mind-blowing. What would life had been like. Everything seems stupid now, my need for independence, my worry that maybe Aiden would stop me from having the life I really wanted. My thoughts are interrupted by a loud blaring alarm and suddenly I see the red light flash green.

I slip my feet into the sport shoes next to the door. My touch activates the door and it slides open. Hesitation. I take a steadying breath, remembering that last day, the day of fire. Is there any way my mom made it? My heart breaks at the thought. What will life be like without her or Aiden? Could he still be alive tucked away in this compound wondering about me? That thought is enough for me to take the first step out of my room.

The circular hallway is filled with the sound of shoes hitting the concrete floor. I also hear noises coming from the stairwell. I step out and look to my left where a man stands taking it all in.

"Are you all right?" he asks in a husky voice. When I nod, he walks slowly towards the stairs. Others follow, leaving their rooms, walking slowly, passing by with a nod. Faces full of confusion, dazed, none of us fully comprehending what we're dealing with now.

I follow and pull open the metal door. Feet pound up the stairs passing by a girl who sits alone on the bottom stair sobbing into her hands. She is wearing the same tan jumpsuit that I was given, but she is smaller than I am and younger, I think.

"Hey," I say softly and, though I don't mean to scare her, she jumps and looks up. Her cheeks are streaked with tears, her face a blotchy mess of pale hues. Her long white-blond hair is pulled back in a tight ponytail, making her delicate features prominent against her alabaster skin. She gives a loud sniff and wipes the tears away with a swipe of her hand. Our eyes lock, her large kaleidoscope pools of blues and grays so different from my own forest green.

"Sorry," she says in a hushed voice. "I'm just...I'm just scared."

"Yeah," I reply. I take a seat next to her and she moves over to make room.

"My name's Wren," I say softly.

"I'm Gemma," she replies with a half-smile.

"Well, it's nice to meet you, Gemma," I say. "Did you come here with anyone else? Your mom or dad?" She shakes her head wildly.

"When the fire came, there was no time. My mom put me in a car and sent me to the bank. My sister, Jewel, was staying with my grandparents and my mom went to make sure they made it to safety. It's in the next sector." She looks into my eyes and I see the fear there, the same wild fear that I feel. "I'm not sure if they made it." Fresh tears begin to streak down her pale cheeks.

"Don't worry, Gemma. We'll be okay." I don't believe my own words yet, not really.

"There's a chance that your family made it or that there's someone that you might know up those stairs," I say, trying to sound hopeful. "But we'll never know unless we go up and see what's going on." She gives me a slight nod and we slowly walk up together.

I push the door open at the top of the staircase. As the great room comes into view my eyes quickly scan the area. There are groups of people, some young and some older, sitting in the various chairs and sofas lining the walls and forming clusters in the center. It's like a sea of dark tan blending in with the brown and cream-colored upholstery, all of us in our jumpsuits; all of us labeled survivors and none of us knowing what to do next. There is a hum of chatter and I catch a sentence or two. Where did you live? Do you have family with you? What do you think we should do? Can we get outside? I search each group looking for my mom but there are no other gingers in the room. My heart sinks and I feel like the granola cake may come up. I put a steadying hand on Gemma's shoulder, and she covers it with her own.

"My mom's not here," I whisper in a shaky voice. I take a few deep breaths to calm my panic and step into this new arena. I think this is the beginning of many things or maybe it's the end, I'm not sure. My eyes glance to the front doors, to the long windows that years ago let bright light filter through. All the glass is obstructed with thick steel covers, blocking out the world beyond. We have no way of knowing what, if anything, is still left.

The room is lighted by synthetic bulbs high above on tracks, and the air is being pumped in by some generator somewhere. But it's a comfortable space, even if everyone in it has confusion and fear written all over them. In the center of the room is a circular desk where a large halo screen rests. I scan the area again, quickly, searching for strands of red or blond and though there are many fair-haired people, none of them is Aiden and none of them are my mom. I will never see my mother again, never be able tell her that I know she did the best she could, that I love her and am sad that she gave up so much for me. Her warm arms will never embrace me again and her calming words will never reach my ears. And Aiden. I'll never again see those deep brown chocolate eyes gazing at me with longing. I'll never hear the words, I love you, not from him; and I let him down, in the end, I hurt him. My eyes look down at my hands which are clasped into fists. The sliver ring with the crimson stone presses against my skin, still shiny, still encircling my finger after all this time. Aiden was right about the ring. It will always remind me of what could have been.

"I'm sorry," says Gemma. I nod and try to get myself together. My shoulders are heaving with the sobs I force to stay inside. I run for the stairs and take Gemma's spot there, as I sob for everything that I've lost. Gemma comes to sit with me, rubbing my back and saying kind things in my ear. She shouldn't be doing this, comforting me. I'm older, I should be the strong one. Every one of us is feeling this keen sense of loss.

"What's going on upstairs," I ask, trying desperately to push all my sorrow away. I gently take my grief and close it up in a box a tuck it somewhere in the back of my brain, stored away for later.

"Some of the adults found a kind of halo screen program.

They're trying to figure that out," she says. "Some girl found a storage room. There's food and supplies." I look up quickly.

"How many supplies," I ask. "Did she say?"

"No," replies Gemma. I see the fear in Gemma's eyes as she waits for me to tell her what our next move is. I want to know the truth of what has happened. How long has it been? What is going on outside of these walls? Were there other survivors out there? At the very least, I need to know what plan is next and maybe help Gemma find her family. Even with my own complete devastation and loss, I still want to know. Maybe helping Gemma will keep me going.

"Okay, Gemma," I say as I gather myself. "Let's go back upstairs and try to figure out what to do next."

CHAPTER FIVE

Wren

Almost every survivor is already huddled around the circular desk with the halo screen, waiting. Gemma and I find a spot in between a father and his young son and another young woman. The boy looks up at me and gives me a half smile. Two men stand in the center of the desk pushing the halo buttons. At first nothing happens.

"Try rebooting the computer," says a tall olive-skinned man. He looks older, maybe in his forties. "The system may be jammed after so many years on the same frequency." One of the men flips a switch back and forth and immediately the halo screen pumps on like a living creature. There is a ringing of shouts and a wave of fist pumps across the crowd. One of the men raises his hand to quiet everyone.

"I'm going to run the program now," he says. The man is

tall and balding with wisps of fair hair laying across his head. He instantly reminds me of my science teacher in school: old, monotone and nondescript. "Everyone quiet, please. I'm not sure how long the program will work. We have no idea how the system is even running or who might be running it, so pay attention." He looks around at the crowd until there is total silence. The huge screen projects against the wall, filling it from top to bottom, the familiar green background with a three-dimensional black United Nations emblem rotating across it. Everyone seems to hold their breath. The emblem fades as lines of text begin to scatter across the screen. The words, Sector Data from Solar Flare, runs as a banner across the top. It is an inventory of each sector, a list of what is left. My stomach churns as I read it.

Sector Five: Destruction Rate: complete devastation. Air Quality: unsustainable. Renovation Plans: none.

Sector Four: Destruction Rate: complete devastation. Air Quality: poor. Renovation Plans: none.

I hold my breath as my eyes travel down to my sector, the place where we are at this minute.

Sector Three: Destruction Rate: 80% deviation. Air Quality: fair. Renovation Plans: Phase Three.

It's not as bad as the sectors further out but it still hurts.

Sector Two: Destruction: 50% devastation. Air Quality: good. Renovation Plans: Phase Two.

Sector One: Destruction: 20% devastation. Air Quality: optimal. Renovation Plans: 90% complete.

A palpable excitement begins to shoot around the room though no one seems concerned at the missing data from the outer sectors. The father next to me begins to hug his son and, as my eyes flick around the group, tears are replaced by smiles. There is hope in learning that at least one place has survived and is waiting for us. Will they come to get us now, take us to Sector One? Gemma glances up to me questioningly and I shrug. The banner at the top is replaced by a new one, this one reads, Squad Detail. The sector data disappears, and new words slide into place, a list of names, divided into groups.

"This must be a division of those of us in this bank," says the balding guy who seems to have taken charge of the halo screen now. He's right. Those of us who have survived here have been divided into squads and I search frantically for my name. It's there near the top, under the heading: Survivor Squad Two. I breathe a sigh of relief when my eyes flick down the list and I see Gemma's name at the bottom. There are six names in all, three men and three women and a murmur goes through the group as people begin to search for their squad members.

"There are documents coming," says the man and I can hear the hum of a printer that must be located under the circular desk. "Hey, everyone…quiet down! I've got something here, some information to read," For a moment the air quiets and we all stand still, waiting. There are so many questions left unanswered, especially what we're all supposed to do now.

"Okay…Survivors," reads the man in the loudest voice he can muster. "In accordance with the new government laws, all those who have taken refuge within a cryobank are required to leave and make their way to one of the three hubs located on the boarder of Sector One." The man pauses and swallows hard before continuing. "The government does not have the resources for a rescue mission but have instead reviewed all personal data and have made a fair division of the population, keeping in mind, age, mental capacity and strength." The man looks up again, his face a mask of shock. I glance around and see that everyone seems to be overwhelmed by this information, everyone but a tall slim woman who stands next to me. She stands with her arms crossed over her chest, her abundance of black curls bouncing against her deep chestnut skin as she nods, unfazed.

"There's more," continues the man. He clears his throat. "It is considered unlawful to remain at the bank for an extended period of time due to the limited supplies. Please follow the directions below to ensure everyone's safety. Number one, only one squad may leave the bank per day. The larger the group, the more difficulties there will be when trying to maneuver through the wild areas. A smaller grouping allows for consistent movement so that no one is left behind. Number two: Follow your squad map to your designated hub. This will limit overcrowding within each hub." The man holds up a pile of maps that have been printed along with the paper that he is reading now. "And number three: be vigilant. The world that you once knew has changed. There are unknown dangers, especially in the lower sectors. Be watchful and travel smart. Once you arrive, family members will be reunited, and job details will be assigned. We here in Sector One, look forward to your arrival and to your input into our new government. Good luck.

As the maps are laid on the desk, I feel a rush of those behind me, pushing in, anxious to get a good look. Suddenly, another man shouts from behind.

"I don't give a damn about those squad lists," he says angrily. "Who's to say we won't die within seconds once we leave this compound? The idea of trekking across who-knows-what kind of landscape, is pure stupidity. I'm not going so you can just shove that list." The balding man looks up, his mouth hanging open in surprise. The group is quiet, no one knows how to deal with this kind of dissention.

"I would think that you would want to go, you may have a family member

out there waiting for you," replies the balding man. "There might be others who need our help. I want to be a part of the fabric of the new world and…"

"Well, that's you," says the angry man. He's stocky and rugged looking,

and I think that if anyone would want to tough it out here, it would be someone like him.

"In my mind the risk doesn't outweigh the reward. I've got no one left. There are supplies here. That girl found a whole storeroom of food and water." The man points to the woman standing next to me. Her dark curls frame her face and her pale blue eyes form a huge contradiction to her brown skin. She can't be much older than I am but there's something fierce in her features, something angular that makes her seem like a fighter.

"I'm going to sit back and wait for the military to get its act together and find the balls to come and get us," continues the man.

"And if they don't…get the balls? You heard the letter; it's forbidden to stay here." The balding man tries to match the man's aggression but fails.

"Well, what are they going to do? If they can't get here to rescue us, then I'm pretty sure they're not going to be able to do anything to stop me from staying." The murmuring begins again with some people agreeing with the stocky man and others arguing against his point. I feel the tall woman next to me stiffen and then hear a deep sigh.

"Hey," she says to the group. "Hey...HEY!" she says again, jumping on a chair that rests next to the desk. Her curls frizz out all around her head and her steely blue eyes are wide with disbelief as if she can't understand how anyone would be stupid enough to stay here. The crowd quiets again. Gemma glances up to me and I arch my eyebrows in wonder. "Look," the woman continues. "I know it seems crazy to go out into the wild without really knowing what we're up against, but I'm sure we aren't the first people to leave their compounds. The military wouldn't send us out if the air were still too contaminated." The stocky man begins to grumble again, and the girl rolls her eyes. I'm liking her more and more. "Look," she continues. "We all knew that this was a possibility, that the opposing team might send their nukes over and that we might send ours back. That's not what ended it all but it's why we all bought into the cryobanks, right? I know that I, for one, did not give up fifty-thousand credits just to say that I owned my own tank." Many of the people in the group gave subtle nods. "So, it's time to suck it up, put on your big boy pants and do what it takes to make this land our home again. It's that simple."

"Okay, sweetie," says the stocky man with a sneer. "If it's so easy, you can be the first one out. Then if you die from the poison in the air, we'll all know how safe it is and we'll suck it up and stay where we are." The woman cringes at the word "sweetie" but doesn't miss a beat.

"Okay, genius, no problem. I'll be leaving the compound tomorrow morning with or without my squad, and I suggest you all do the same when it's your turn. This cryobank can't be as safe as you think, especially if we are being told to leave. I've seen the storage room and you'll eventually run out of water at the very least." She returns the stocky man's sneer. "Then I wonder how tough mister-I'm-staying-right-here will be." She leaps from the chair after a final clap of her hands. I'm amazed at how confident she is and how strong. It's everything I want to be but fail at miserably. The balding man gathers the printed list and clears his throat.

"I think it would be best if I hand out the maps. You can then decide on your course of action and we can put together an evacuation list so that we're not all leaving at once," says the man running the halo screen uncomfortably, trying to avoid more arguing. There is a mass of nods in agreement. I grip Gemma's shoulders and she leans into me.

"Okay," shouts the girl next to me as she glances back to the wall where the squad names are still viable. "I'm looking for Ian Winter." A dark-haired boy comes to stand next to her. He smiles extending out his hand. He's tall and I can see the hint of a muscular build beneath his jumpsuit. I notice Ian's name on the wall just above my own and I feel a sense of relief. Ian is young, maybe close to my age, seventeen, or a few years older, and that gives me hope that our squad is built for what lays ahead. If anyone can make it out in the wild, Ian and Briar can.

"I'm Wren Johns," I say, introducing myself. "And this is Gemma Marks." Gemma is too shy to step forward, but I can sense relief in her as well.

"I'm Briar, Briar Simpson and so far, it looks like we have a strong group. Only two more to go." As other survivors move towards their squads, I notice that they are as diverse as our community: old, young, and somewhere in between. It does seem as if care was taken in dividing us up. A short, stocky boy joins us as Briar calls out for Rory Rickman. He has a pinched face, his nose turning up at the end, and a head full of thin wispy dirty blond hair. His small sharp eyes dart from my face to Briar's to Ian's. It's like he's sizing us up. Since I've got at least an inch on him, I'm not too worried. An older man comes to stand in our group. He is lanky and tall, sporting the epitome of nerd-like glasses which are thick and ginormous.

"Hi, I'm Arick," he says extending a hand me. I take his hand. He is different from the others, forty-something, clearly the oldest in our squad. He seems calm, his handshake soft but firm. His brown hair is dusted with gray. The thick brown-rimmed glasses perched on his long nose tilt awkwardly, making his face seem tilted as well. Maybe he's smart. His brain may come in handy, who knows. Still, if he loses those glasses, I think he'll be in trouble. With this group, we'll make it to a hub, I know we will, at least most of us will.

CHAPTER SIX

Aiden

"Fifty years is a long time," he says as if I couldn't possibly understand the significance of it. Commander Rob leans back in his chair creating distance between us. The white jumpsuit that he wears makes his skin pale, almost sickly but his sturdy build tells a different story.

"Yes, Sir," I reply. "Fifty years is a long time." I think back to the night of the solar flare, the complete and utter chaos, the destruction and the death. I feel like I've actually lived those fifty years not been asleep in a cryotank waiting it out. The Commander notices my sadness and leans closer, saying in a low voice,

"My condolences on your loss, Aiden." He means it, they are not just empty words. "Your father was a good man. He did good work here, government work that no one else had the balls to do. He was tough as nails and I'm sure we'll see the same determination in you." It's a compliment but the words still come out cold. That's the world we live in now, cold and hard with only the strongest surviving. Our conversation is interrupted by a knock on the door.

"Come in." My two squad members enter, each taking a seat next to me. Raven's jet-black hair is pulled back from her face, her steely gaze shifts to the Commander, challenging him, I think. He doesn't know her well enough to understand that she will never back down from a challenge.

"You asked to meet with us...Sir?"

"How are you all getting along here at the hub? Are your sleeping quarters..." His attempts at small talk are completely ridiculous, especially to Raven. She's business first.

"Good," she replies quickly cutting him off.

"Excellent, good," replies the Commander with a nod. He leans back in his chair once again, rubbing his chin in relaxed contemplation. "As you are well aware, the three of you were assigned to this hub for a reason. It's true that each of you has had a family member who has worked in an upper government position but you're here because of what you bring to the table." Spencer glances to me, his eyebrows arched questioningly. He's never been able to see the thing that makes him stand out, his unwavering ability to problem solve on the spot. "You've been watched," continues the Commander. "All though your academic careers and you were flagged as having great potential as future government employees."

"Okay," says Raven again, as if she's been aware of government spies lurking around the corners, watching her movements her entire life. As if she's always known that she would one day be at the top.

"Thank you, Sir," replies Spencer. He gives Raven a side-ways glance of annoyance. "I think I can speak for each of us in giving our appreciation for this safe haven. I hope not to disappoint you." Commander Rob gives a chuckle.

"Oh, I am certain that I will not be disappointed. You've already proven yourselves out in the wild. You arrived safely just as we hope all the survivors will. And that brings me to the reason for this meeting." Raven sits up straighter, more than ready to get to the point. "I realize that you've only had a few weeks to recover and begin training, but we have a problem. Something has come to my attention and I need help."

"What is it?" asks Raven.

"One of the government's smaller cryotank compounds was revived several days ago. This compound was the resting place for a handful of high-ranking officials, three in fact. We have intel that they did indeed leave the compound heading towards this hub, but somehow we lost them." My heart begins to race. I know in an instant what the Commander will ask of us. I've been waiting for this moment since the day I awoke and found myself alone within my tank.

"So you want us to go back out there and search for them?" asks Raven.

"Precisely," replies the Commander. "It shouldn't be difficult. They know their way around the area even as demolished as the world is now. I'm sure that they just got caught up in some unforeseen obstacle. A few extra hands will get them home safely." I feel Spencer deflate next to me. His auburn hair sweeps across his eyes as he leans forward in his chair. I know he doesn't want to go. The four days we spent in the wild, trekking through the gray sand and rough terrain took its toll on him. Spencer's tough, tough as any soldier mentally, but soft too. His body just wasn't built for physical endurance even if his brain was. He glances up at me with his hazel eyes, eyes that have just enough green to remind me of someone else. He gives a sigh.

"I wouldn't ask this of you if it weren't necessary," continues the Commander. "The compound isn't far away. It shouldn't take more than a day to get there." Why not just send out a solar vehicle? I think to myself. If it's that close, it doesn't seem right to risk human life, our lives. But I already know the answer and I don't want to voice my thoughts because I want to go. I've been waiting for my chance to go back and search for the one person that matters to me, the one person that I cannot live without, Wren.

"You'll go on foot. We can't send a vehicle with you," says the Commander, confirming my thoughts. "On foot you'll be able to get to places that a vehicle can't reach. Load up and you'll head out first thing in the morning. With any luck we should see you all back here in forty-eight hours." He pauses and looks at each of us in turn. A light smile plays around his lips, a smile that resembles pride. "If you pull this off, the three of you will be given your choice of any government job."

"When we pull this off," replies Raven with the extreme confidence that she always shows. As we exit the Commander's office Spencer's face is covered in dread.

"Back out into the wild," he says with a shaky voice. "God, that's the last place I want to go. It was bad enough the first time. Dehydration, rough terrain and who knows what else." Raven gives a huff of disgust.

"Suck it up," she says. "It's two days." She's practically bouncing on her feet with excitement. "It will be worth it once you're choosing your upper-level tech job." She's right, though I think with Spencer's knowledge on all things computer related, he would have gotten that job either way. But it will be worth it, so worth it when I find Wren.

CHAPTER SEVEN

Wren

"Okay, okay, simmer down," says the guy behind the desk. "I think the best thing to do is to figure out the supplies that are available." Mister-I'm-not-going-out-there pushes through his squad, who eye him warily. I can see that they're not overly excited to have him.

"Yeah," he says. "I want to be there for that!"

"That's fine. I think each squad should appoint one person to come with me to the supply room. We can divide up any resources together to make sure we keep it fair." He directs his words to the man.

"Great," replies the man. "I appoint myself." The rest of his squad look too afraid to argue, but they mumble to each other. I turn to my group. It's a no-brainer. Briar is the one who discovered the supply room in the first place. She already knows what's there.

"The first thing I need to know from each of you is, are we all in?" she says as we huddle together.

"Yeah," I reply a little too quickly. She smiles at me and winks. We are all on board to leave in the morning, though the short blond boy with the sharp eyes, Rory, seems a little hesitant. He keeps glancing around at the other squads like he wants to commit mutiny already.

"Look," says Briar. "The supplies that I saw could last all of us a month, maybe. Staying here is suicide, but I'm not going to be responsible for any quitters along the way. You have to be sure." Arick lays a hand on Rory's shoulder. "I don't see any quitters here," he says softly. Rory shrugs him away.

"I just want to make sure that we get our share," he says. "That crazy dude who refuses to leave is going to try to hoard stuff, just wait!"

"Well, I won't let that happen," replies Briar nonchalantly. "While I'm gone why don't you guys go check out the map. We need to figure out the quickest course."

"I'm going with you, Briar." Rory crosses his arms and I can tell there's no way he's budging. Briar could turn this into a power struggle but she's smarter than that.

"Fine," she concedes. "And Wren can come too. I'll need help carrying the supplies."

"We'll see if we can take a look at the map," says Arick. He extends his arm around Gemma and gives the tall, incredibly good-looking guy, Ian, a nod. Ian's body is strong, but I'm not sure yet about his temperament. He's probably used to getting what his wants with those awesomely deep blue eyes.

"Let's go." Briar pulls me gently by the arm, leading me in the direction of the storage rooms. Rory follows behind, his arms still crossed. I'm worried he'll be difficult. I just hope we can make it to the hub quickly.

We form a line with the other squad members and enter the supply room eagerly. As I stand in the cool space of the room, I'm amazed at the volume of things. Shelves hide the walls and are stacked to overflowing. One wall's shelves are stocked from floor to ceiling with cartons of bottled water. I also notice the now-familiar granola cakes piled high in boxes, along with foil bags of freeze-dried meals. One of the shelves holds bottles of pills and medications and there are some supplies I don't recognize at all. Tubes and tins and bottles of so many things.

"Let's gather in the center of the room," says the man who I now accept as in charge. He seems to know what he's doing as he begins to take inventory of each shelf. The supplies can be divided up evenly but there is still the very real fact that we can only take as much as we can carry. After loading up the pile of backpacks that were set aside for each squad, there is a noticeable dent in the supplies. Briar was right, even with the cases of water left, it won't last forever. Every squad is given tablets that can help purify biohazard toxins from small water sources. All the medical supplies are also handed out to the leaving squads. This includes medications, bandages, and ointments in case of injury. Obviously, we will need them more than any slackers staying behind. As I glance around at the different teams sorting through their supplies, I notice the angry man leaning against the doorframe. He doesn't seem as sure now. I see him eyeing the depleted water. Most of the granola cakes are gone as well. Briar is right, this guy's committing suicide. At least he won't care that we're taking the camping stuff. The tents are incredible light and lined with some kind of silvery material. Briar says that they will be warm. Will we need them to be warm?

"Did you count the water?" asks Rory as he heaves two backpacks over his shoulder and picks up another by the sturdy loop on top. For a short guy with a little extra weight, he seems strong enough.

"Yes," she replies with some irritation. "We each have ten bottles." She gives a sigh. "The only positive thing is that at least our loads will get lighter as we empty the bottles."

"I'm not sure that's a good thing," I retort with sarcasm.

"We'll be okay," says Briar. "We're young and determined." I nod but then think of Arick. "Plus, we know the atmosphere is safe and even if we can't find water right away, there's always rain." There is a hint of uncertainty in Briar's voice.

"I watched some stupid survival show once when I was little," chimes in Rory. "You know, it's perfectly safe to drink your own urine." I wince at the thought.

"Yeah," says Briar as she swings a backpack over her own shoulder. "That works great if you've got urine in the first place."

"Whatever," he replies with a grumble. "Let's get on with it." The storage room begins to empty and the three of us begin to walk back to the main room, anxious to see what Arick and the others have discovered. Just as the hallway ends, Briar pulls me back.

"Wait," she whispers. "I want to show you something." Rory doesn't even give us a backward glance, so I follow Briar back down the hallway, this time passing the storage room. At the end of this hallway is another hallway that I didn't notice.

"This way," and with another pull of my sleeve I follow her. She stops at another door, a heavier door made of steel with a keypad lock. Quickly, Briar types in a four-digit code and the latch clicks open.

"How did you do that?" I ask in amazement. She glances at me, a smile playing on her lips.

"I was the first one smart enough to go exploring," she replies. "I had an hour to snoop around. Let's just say that I've got skills and leave it at that."

"Well, I'm glad you're in my squad." She pushes open the door as it squeaks on its hinges. Even though there is no one in sight, we tip toe inside and close the door behind us. I turn and peer into the dim light. And then my breath catches when I see what's there. A long table covered in maps and cabinets filled with weapons. I'm not sure what some of the stuff is though I can certainly distinguish the rifles from the knives. Briar walks over and takes a small handgun from the shelf, cocking it back with a snap.

"Come on," she encourages. "Pick something out." I hesitate. I've never held a gun or even a knife like these. The blades are thick and serrated and very scary. I'm just clumsy enough to fall down and heave that blade deep into my gut. Or cut off an appendage.

"You just never know, Wren. We might need to protect ourselves out there. I'm not saying we will have to use them but it's better to be prepared for everything."

Briar notices my hesitation and hands the gun to me. I take it. It is heavy, but not as heavy as I thought it would be. The weight of it and the smooth, cool metal feels good in my hand. It fits.

"Don't worry, it's not loaded." I nod and aim the weapon and then try to hand it back. She shakes her head. "Keep it." Briar hands me a box of ammunition and an extra clip. Back before the flare, I would have never even touched something like this, but now, I have to admit, it makes me feel safe.

"You need a knife too."

"I don't know," I reply. A gun is easy. Aim, shoot and run. Defending myself with a knife is something completely different. I'm not sure I'm capable of that kind of savagery.

"We might need it for hunting or cutting firewood." The statment is made in an offhand way. I'm thinking that Briar is as squeamish as I am until she adds, "If you have to use it to defend yourself, go for the gut, okay?" She shows me a jabbing motion and I feel my stomach turn. I nod, not wanting to open my mouth. I step up to the cabinet and scan the array of knives. Some are long like swords while others are compact and deadly. I choose one of the smaller knives for two reasons. First, it has a thick sheath to protect the blade and me. Second, because I don't want to add too much weight to my pack. The gun is heavy enough. I see Briar stash several knives into her bag as well as two guns like mine. As we turn to leave, I ask, "Who else knows about this room?"

"No one yet," replies Briar. "I wanted to get first pick before the masses invade. I have a feeling that this room will be wiped out in minutes once everyone knows about it." She pauses, thinking. "I wouldn't want these weapons used on anyone here." She is thinking of the man who insists on staying behind. Rory is so sure that the man will stash away supplies, and Briar must think that he would use force to get what he wants. They may both be right. In this new nation, if you can even call it a nation anymore, people will change. The thought of starvation and death will make a man do anything to survive. They'll become barbarians.

Arick, Rory, Ian and Gemma are waiting for us when we get

back. Ian holds the map with our location marked in red and the hubs marked in blue, dotting around Sector One. We find a corner to sit away from everyone else. As I glance down at the map, I am disheartened by the distance we will have to travel. The hubs are far to the north, farther than I have ever traveled let alone walked. I squeeze my eyes shut and try to snap out of the depressed cloud that hangs over me. Why even bother, a voice says in my head. Everyone you love is dead. But there is more than just me to worry about. I don't want to give up. Aiden wouldn't want me to give up and neither would my mom.

Ian is pointing to the map, dragging his finger along a line from our cryobank to the hub outlined in red. I shake my head to clear my thoughts.

"We should follow the river," he says, his eyes meeting Briar's. It's clear that they will be the leaders. The river is winding and veers away from our destination briefly. That's concerning.

"That will take too long." Rory's squeaky voice is already becoming annoying. "The river goes completely out of the way. A straight route north is the best course." He draws his own line with his finger. "We'll save days." Days?

"How long will we be out there?" I ask. I can't tell the distance just by looking at the map.

"It looks like this hub is about two hundred miles due north, maybe a little more." says Ian. "If we average fifteen miles a day, we could potentially get there in a week. I wouldn't want to attempt more than that. We have to be cautious. We'll have to take time to find secure places to rest." I can feel my mouth hanging open in shock. I think of the supplies that we just stuffed into our bags and know that there's no way we'll make it with what we've packed. Not enough water. Even if we allow two bottles a day, that's not nearly enough especially if it's hot out there. I've never in my life walked more than a few miles at a time and by the looks of Rory, he's walked even less. As if reading my thoughts, Ian continues. "I know it seems like a lot and we may not be able to achieve that goal. We aren't sure what the landscape will be like." I look away, briefly. It's too much.

"Like I said, we can save days going in a straight line," adds Rory again. Arick leans over the map to evaluate while Gemma watches everyone intently. She looks nervous. It's not a good omen that our squad members are already arguing.

"Hmmm," says Arick. "We have limited water...any game for hunting will probably be found near water sources, especially if there's little water out there. The river seems like the right choice. There's no sign of water out west, at least not from this map." He pats Ian on the back, causing Rory to scowl.

"Yeah," adds Briar. "What's a few more days if it means water and, potentially, food?" Rory gives a huff and retreats. Briar gives an eye roll. "Look, we all have to work together, Rory. We're a democracy here. I'm not saying that your idea isn't good, but we need to talk out all of our options."

"Whatever." Since I'm sitting right next to Briar, I easily hear her whisper to Ian,

"I'm not babysitting this one."

CHAPTER EIGHT

Wren

The plan is set. We leave at dawn and try to get out before the other squads even wake up. Briar doesn't want to deal with any drama from those who might have decided to stay. Before we break up for the night, I notice that she doesn't mention the weapons room and keeps the extra knives to herself. I'm assuming she wants to figure everyone else out before she puts a sharp weapon in their hands. I wonder why she trusted me. Our group is diverse. Gemma is quiet and shy and young, while Rory is completely outspoken and kind of annoying, actually, very annoying. Arick seems to be solid, level-headed and laidback. Ian is the tall, quiet type, the kind of guy that always felt unapproachable in school. I wonder who he lost, maybe everyone like me. Briar is my favorite in the group and I already feel a connection with her. I think I'd follow her anywhere. She's a tough chick and fearless. So, where do I fit in?

I'm not brave like Briar and I'm completely void of self-esteem. But I'm smart, the top in my class. I can figure out problems and make solutions, especially when it comes to growing food. But none of us knows what is out there. My skill set might not matter when it comes down to it.

I walk back to my tank room after tucking in Gemma. Her room is identical to mine, with a pull-down twin bed that can be used as a shelf when not sleeping. I tell her to drink plenty of water and eat a granola cake or two. I can see the fear in her eyes, but she puts on a brave face. This journey will be hardest for her and, as I think of her, I feel heat creep up my face. I'm pissed. I'm pissed at the stupid sun for exploding and taking my life away. I'm pissed that Gemma was left all alone. I'm pissed that, now, I have to be brave when all I feel is afraid. I'm not ready. I sigh heavily and take a cake and try to eat but the crumbs get stuck in my throat. I know that it's important for me to rest but when I'm finally alone, stretched out on my bed, my mind wanders. I just can't shake the reality of everything: the mass destruction of the earth, the loss of so many, the passage of time. It's been over for so long. That realization frightens me the most. Hot tears begin to burn my eyes and I let them stream down my cheeks and moisten the thin pillow tucked under my head. It's not fair, so not fair. I cry for everything I was supposed to be, for the choices that were difficult but that were mine. I cry for Aiden, dead now, snuffed out like a candle. I cry for the fact that I'm still a virgin and I've only ever had a handful of kisses. The thoughts of all the things that I'll never do now rush over me. I'll never have that great university job. I'll never be that young innocent child again. My tears flow harder and I sob into my pillow. I let them go, knowing that this will be the last time I will allow myself to feel anything. My throat is dry, and after what feels like hours, I sit up, hugging my knees to my chest. I take a bottle of water and drink slowly, wiping my tears away. I get myself together with one last deep shuddering breath. I have to let my mom and Aiden go. There's so much regret that I'll have to live with and it's heavy.

There's nothing left to do but try to rest. All the crying has exhausted me. I close my eyes and think of Aiden. I couldn't say the words I love you, to him, even though he said them to me daily. If I could see him again, what would I say? If he were here with me would things be different now? Would I somehow find the words to tell him that he means as much to me as I do to him? My heart gives an uncomfortable shutter. Even now, the answer is no.

I wake up the next morning way too soon and I can feel the tired grit behind my eyes. But I can also feel adrenaline running through my limbs. The sooner we take off the sooner we get to the hub. My backpack is zipped and ready. The knife I put well concealed, in the outside pocket, just in case I need it in a hurry. The gun is further down in my pack, buried. I tiptoe out of my room and silently wander to Gemma's. She left the door open knowing that I would be by to get her in the morning. As I enter, she is curled in a ball under the thin sheet, but her eyes are open, focused on the doorway.

"Are you ready to go?" I whisper, and she sits up and nods. I check her backpack and add in another bottle of water. As she jumps from the bed, I put my hands on her shoulders. "Listen, Gemma, I want you to stay close to me, okay?"

"Okay," she replies and leans in for a hug. I return her hug, smiling and then push her gently away. It's time to get serious.

"I don't know what we'll find outside. I have a weapon, but

I don't want anyone else to know, okay?" Her brows furrow in confusion but she agrees not to say anything.

"Do you think there are bad people still out there?" she asks with a trembling voice. I don't want to scare her any more than she already is, but I have to be honest.

"I don't know, Gemma," I reply, smoothing a few loose strands of her silky blond hair behind her ear. "Honestly, the only people I trust right now are you and Briar." I give her a smile and strap the backpack over her shoulders. "Everything will be fine. In a few weeks we'll see if we can find your family. We'll make plans to start over and I'll make sure that whatever those plans are, we'll be together, okay?" She hugs me again and I reach into one of my jumpsuit pockets and pull out an extra granola cake.

"Put this in your pocket, just in case something happens to your pack." She follows my instructions and we leave the room and walk quietly up the stairs to the main area. Of course, Briar is already waiting. She paces the small sitting area next to the circular desk.

"Where is everyone else?" asks Briar eagerly as she sees us. Gemma is holding tightly to my hand but releases it when she sees Briar. I give Briar a shrug.

"I don't know but I'm sure they'll be here soon. It's early." She sighs and takes two giant determined steps toward us, planting herself inches away.

"Look, I don't want to say this to anyone else, but I have a gut feeling that I can trust you." I glance to Gemma and she nods.

"You can," I reply. Briar nods back.

"This whole mission is questionable," she says. "I don't know why I feel this way, but things just don't make complete sense."

"Well, we've been through a natural catastrophe. Nothing is

the same," I retort. Her eyes narrow.

"It's more than that," she says in a hushed voice. "It's been fifty years. It just doesn't make sense that a plan wasn't put in place to transfer the compound survivors to the hubs long ago."

"Well, we've all been in cryo-hibernation. I guess it takes time," I say.

"I like you, Wren, and I like the Devil's advocate approach. It helps me think through things. But I've got news for you, not everyone was in hibernation for fifty years." My mouth opens and closes. I don't have any comeback for that. Briar continues, "I'm sure you noticed the neatly folded jumpsuit that appeared in your room since you're wearing it." She smiles darkly. "Some of the supplies in the storeroom can't be fifty years old. And there's something else."

"What?" I whisper. I feel Gemma take my hand again and squeeze.

"I found another working halo screen in one of the offices. I couldn't call out from it, but I could see several messages being transported from hub to hub. I hacked into the hard drive on the computer and I saw something."

"What?" I ask breathlessly.

"I saw images. Other people like us but it was weird. I'm not sure what it was, it could have been some video clip from before the flare or possibly other survivors, but the outside looked bad, wild, basically uninhabitable. The thing that bothers me though," she continues, "is that, according to the data, the images originated from somewhere outside of the immediate area, I'm talking outside of the sectors."

"Oh my God," I say, covering my mouth in shock. "There is nothing outside of the sectors." We grew up learning about the history of our government and the sectors that make up the United Nations. Back in the early years of our country, the land was divided up into fifty sectors called states. After years of famine, drought and natural disasters caused by an unstable environment, the government began to salvage what land they could. The nation reformed itself and those states that would not join, were cut off and left to obliterate themselves. The west coast was the first to succumb to disease and then the rest of the coastline states followed. Only one strip of land could be saved, the central axis that once made up sectors with names like New Mexico, Colorado, Nebraska and Kansas. This viable land was cultivated by us. Nothing else survived. The insight of our government saved us and hopefully they are saving us once again.

"There must be more," continues Briar. "What have they been doing for the past fifty years? Have some of the survivors already started over somewhere else, away from the hubs, away from the government, away from the sectors? Have they found new viable land or are people forced to live in unlivable conditions? That's what I've been asking myself. Just promise me something you two," she adds.

"What," I ask curiously.

"Don't trust anyone yet, not even in our squad. And keep this information between us."

"Okay." Just as Gemma and I both agree, Ian and Arick arrive, backpacks slung over their shoulders.

"I guess this is it," says Ian with confidence. His hair is slightly tousled, but it only makes him look hotter. I run my hand self-consciously over the frizzy ends of my braid. I have to remember Briar's words not to trust anyone yet. Sometimes the nicest guys turn out to be serial killers.

"Has anyone seen Rory?" There is a hint of irritation in Briar's voice. "I really want to get out of here before the others are up." No one knows where Rory is or where his tank is located, so Ian pulls out the map and we do a quick review. Getting to the river will be our target for today. Ten miles north-east. Briar thinks it will be a good test of our endurance. We do a sweep through our packs one last time. Arick pulls out a compass that causes Briar to nod in approval. I glance to Ian. I study him, wondering if I can trust him. His dark hair falls across his eyes and he sweeps it back, revealing the square jawline and high cheekbones of his face. His deep blue eyes meet mine and I quickly look away, embarrassed. I feel rather than see him smile and my cheeks burn.

"I'm only waiting five more minutes for Rory. If he doesn't show, we're out of here," says Briar. Arick decides to go and search for him as Gemma, Ian and I take a few more sips of water and zip up our supplies. As Briar approaches the front doors leading to the unknown, Arick returns with Rory in hand. He is disheveled and groggy and barely has his jumpsuit zipped up.

"I think we are all accounted for," says Arick with a laugh.

"Why the hell do we have to leave at the crack of dawn," says Rory with a yawn. "God, we've got all the time in the world. It'd be nice to at least be able to sleep in."

"You've had fifty years to sleep, Rory," yells Briar in disgust. "You may not be anxious to see your family again, if they're out there, but I'm not wasting anymore time. Do what you want but we're leaving now."

"God, chill, Briar. I'm ready." Briar cranks the door handle in front of us, removes the three latches and pushes.

CHAPTER NINE

Aiden

We eat a big dinner at one of the many restaurants within the hub. When we're done, we load up our packs with everything that we'll need for the next few days.

"Here." Raven tosses me a handgun from the cabinet. I pull out the clip and load it. I'm surprised at how easily I hold a gun now, how natural. Spencer powers off his communication device. We'll be off the grid most of the time, but the GPS components will help locate us if we end up in trouble.

"Commander Rob sent this over," says Raven as she takes her tablet from her back pocket. "We should probably go over it now." She holds her tablet flat in her palm and taps the screen lightly. Instantly a hologram appears haloed in green light, showing us details of the mission before us.

"God, I love technology," exclaims Spencer as his eyes scan the information. The first image is of a map. It's familiar, showing our hub and the distance to the compound in question. The commander was right, the distance seems short, maybe fifteen miles out. It isn't unrealistic that we should reach it in a day. Now I can understand the urgency to find the missing officials. Something must have happened. It's been two weeks since they left their cryotanks behind. The map evaporates as three faces appear before us, each with names and bios beneath. A woman and two men.

"Second in Command Brent Woodman, Dr. Sylvia Bell and Professor Dominick Donavan..." says Raven.

"Dominick Donavan?" interrupts Spencer. "*The* Dominick Donovan? The tech genius who developed the whole halo system?"

"It says here that before the flare, Mr. Donovan was working on a special project," I add as I read the short bio. "It must be something that the government is interested in."

"The guy is amazing," gushes Spencer. "He single-handedly revolutionized cyberconnectivity, not to mention his role in cyber strategic weapon control..."

"Listen, Spenc," interrupts Raven. "Once we find them you can get all freaky with Donovan, maybe talk tech, share personal cyber-stories, even move in together, but for now let's keep the enthusiasm to a minimum. We have a job to do, right?" Spencer turns his blushing face away.

"Second in command," says Raven under her breath. "I'd say that's important."

"I wonder why they chose us for the mission," I ask. "Why not send seasoned soldiers?"

"We're fresh out," replies Raven as she shuts off her tablet. "We are the last squad to come out of the wild, so they probably figure our memories of the area are still vivid." She tucks the tablet back into her pocket and adds. "Anyway, it's a great opportunity for us. In and out and then we can sit back and plan out destinies." I nod but I don't say what's really on my mind. It won't be a quick mission for me. I'll help our squad find the three officials and then I'm AWOL. I've already decided not to tell them. The less they know the better once the commander begins to question them. Hopefully he'll be so happy to have his Second in Command back that he won't care that I'm missing.

"We better get some rest," says Raven as she zips up her pack and slings it over her shoulder. "Meet you at the tunnel exits at zero-eight-hundred." Spencer gives me a wary glance as Raven heads in the direction of her sleeping quarters.

"She's intense," he says, making me laugh. "I mean it," he continues. "I'm terrified of that girl. We already know that she won't hesitate to take someone down who gets in her way and she's becoming a real soldier, a part of their wheel." I pat him on the back reassuringly.

"That's probably the real reason why they chose us to go back in," I say. "Come on, it's Raven. After everything we've been through together, does it really surprise you that she's trying to fit in?" He looks down at his hands in defeat.

"I'm not like her," he says softly. "The training isn't easy for me."

"Like Raven said, when we're done with our little trip, you can do whatever you want. Maybe you can work with your new love interest Donovan." He glances up hopefully.

"Okay, just to make it clear, he's a genius and I'm only interested in his brain." I laugh.

"Okay, okay, I didn't mean to challenge your manhood." Spencer smiles.

"One more trip in but you have to make me a promise," he says.

"Okay."

"Protect me from Raven if she goes all militant on us."

"I think I can handle that."

When I get back to my room, I grab my tablet from the charging dock. Raven has sent me the hologram with our mission details, and I waste no time bringing up the map. I can see my old sector, so far away, and the cryobank where Wren's tank is located. I won't have to go all the way back, just far enough to trace her steps. In the weeks that I have been here, I've been able to dig up a few facts. Wren's bank should have been reactivated twenty-four to forty-eight hours ago. They were divided into squads and each given directions to one of the three hubs located roughly one hundred miles apart along the border. I have to assume that she wouldn't stay at the bank long. My heart hurts at the sorrow that must be eating her up inside, at how alone she must feel. I need to be there for her, help her through what will be a horrible journey. My best plan is to walk a horizonal line east from the western edge of the wild, until I am perpendicular to our old sector and then walk south, looking for signs of others traveling. It will take her much longer than four days to reach her hub. She'll make it, I'll make sure that she makes it. I open my pack and tuck in the tablet. My supplies are meager, really only enough for four, five days tops. I'll have to figure something out once we find the officials. I'm confident that at the very least, I'll be able to reload on supplies at the government cryobank. We'll have to make that our first destination. If we find the officials before that, well, I can hit the bank once I part ways. For now, I need to try to sleep. If I learned anything from being in the wild, it's that sleep may be hard to come by.

CHAPTER TEN

Wren

I don't know why, but I hold my breath. The heavy door makes a loud grinding sound as Briar pushes, leaning the weight of her body into it. It's thick metal, clearly an emergency exit and I'm sure it hasn't been accessed in a long time. A sliver of light filters through the edge of the door, growing bigger across the floor. Before even witnessing the remains of what used to be my city, I feel the heat, damp and stifling. The door swings open with a resounding bang, and we all stare motionless.

"Shit!" exclaims Briar. "I...I didn't think..." I can feel her shock because it's mirrored in my gut. I slowly step out into a gray world, followed by my squad. Old photographs of the moon's surface pop unwelcome into my head. That's where we are, the moon. Everything is gone. The train system with electric tracks that sat high above the city, gone. The homes that dotted the streets and the streets themselves, gone. The electric car that brought me to this place, gone. No trees, no grass, no sidewalks or squirrels, there is nothing but a vast steely desert of ashen sand. Remarkably, the sun is there, a former shadow of itself and it beats down through a kind of dingy smog that is little protection. Once a giant golden ball of light, it now appears like a reflection of the earth, gray like another lunar body.

"This is stupid," says Rory. "What the hell has been going on for fifty years?" Briar comes to stand next to him. She rests her elbow on his shoulder.

"Well, when you think about it, we couldn't expect much more." Rory shrugs her arm away. "A giant ball of fire ripped from the sun and tore into our atmosphere. I mean, come on, everything was bound to burn." She bends down to run her hand over the ground's surface. She scoops up a handful of sand and lets it run through her outstretched fingers. "It's soft, kind of like a beach." I turn in a big circle looking out as far as my eyes will go and see nothing. The cryobank looks like an alien of glass and steel sunken into the sandy ash, the only visible sign of life.

"The silver lining is that we're all still breathing," chimes in Arick. "I guess the atmosphere is compatible for life." Gemma takes my hand and I see the tears streaming down her cheeks.

"Well, I guess we better move out," says Briar. Ian takes the lead, reaching for the compass from Arick and marking the north-eastern path that we must take to reach the river, if it's still there. Rory walks behind us and eventually Arick falls back too, listening to Rory's complaints of the weird terrain and his worries of running out of water. It is difficult to walk in the ashen sand at first. My shoes sink down every time I take a step and quickly cause my ankles to become sore. Looking out at the horizon, it's all the same: gray and barren, a field of nothing. I can feel sweat trickling down my back as soon as we're five minutes into it. This steamy heat is like a sauna, the air is thick with moisture that we can't drink. None of us speak for a long time. Even Rory is silent as we walk like robots, one step at a time, our only haven, the compound, falling far behind us. After about an hour, my throat is so dry that I can't even swallow my own spit. I don't want to tap into my water supply, it's too soon for that. I don't want to be the first one, either. I let my mind go, wandering back to Aiden. From as far back as I can remember, there has always been Aiden.

On the first day of primary school he simply walked up to me, stuck out his hand and said, "Hi, I'm Aiden. Do you want to be friends?" and even at seven years old, with his baby face and hair that was always too long and unkept, how could I resist those puppy eyes? As we got older, he became my rock, the one person I knew I could count on and when we crossed that line between friends and something more, it felt right, natural. I couldn't imagine my life without him back then, couldn't imagine him with someone else. What changed? When I think of him now, I miss him, I miss him so much that it feels like a fist squeezing my heart. The pain of losing him is almost unbearable, like suddenly losing a family member, but not like losing a lover. Not at all like that.

"Wren...Wren..." Briar's voice cuts through my thoughts and I immediately feel the heavy heat and my aching feet. And then Aiden is gone. We have all come to a stop and Briar's eyes watch me carefully.

"Okay?" she asks.

"Yeah," I reply. I glance around to the group and everyone looks worse for wear, even Ian. We're beginning to blend into the gray background, as the humidity helps the sand stick to us.

"I think we could all use a break," says Briar. Without hesitation, Rory plops to the ground in a heap and pulls out a bottle of water. His sharp black eyes dart around the group as he guzzles his water greedily. I don't trust him. All it's going to take is one catastrophe and he's going to lose it; I can feel it. My feet are sore, and I can feel my delicate, pale skin begin to burn despite the hazy sky. The back of my neck is wet with perspiration and the fringes of my unkept hair stick to my face. I screw off the cap of my water and take small sips. Immediately I feel the water absorb into my tissues and my thirst intensifies. I want to drink down the whole bottle in one big gulp, but I know I can't. I have to go slow. I look up to the sky as I sip. The gray ball of the sun is higher now and that means we've been walking for hours. It must be close to noon. Gemma, Ian and Arick are also sipping slowly from their water bottles, but as I turn to Rory who is spread out on the sand, I see him toss his empty bottle aside and dig into his pack for another. Briar follows my gaze.

"Hey, Rory," she says. "Slow down." Rory's eyebrows raise, questioning her. Briar takes a step closer. "I just think it's better to error on the side of caution when it comes to food and water."

"I don't see what you're freaking out about," he replies flippantly. "When we get to the river we can fill up." He begins to twist off the cap. We watch him with wary eyes.

"We don't know what we'll find at the river," continues Briar. "It could be dried up or polluted. We can't count on anything." Rory gives a snort.

"Yeah, well, we all have a limited supply of water so let's be honest. If we don't find water in a few days, we're all dead anyway." Gemma lets out a small sob and I see Arick pat her back gently. Rory takes a swig of the newly opened bottle of water and wipes his mouth with the back of his hand. "I might as well not be thirsty now because if that river is dry it's game over anyway."

"Listen, Mr. Bundle of Hope," says Briar, her brows furrowed in anger. "Conserving our water could be the difference between life and death in the long run. It could mean the difference between dying on day eight or surviving to day nine when we find a water source. It's not rocket science, Rory." Rory gives Briar a scowl, but I see him recap the bottle and put in back in his pack.

"We have to be smart about this," continues Briar to the group. "We don't know what is ahead of us and we have to conserve resources. Survival 101, okay?" Everyone nods except Rory who gives an eye roll that Briar misses. Ian pulls the map from his pack and we all gather around. He gazes at the sky and then runs his finger across the map, along the river to the east.

"It looks like we have plenty of time to reach the river before dark," he says. "I'd say that we've been walking for about four hours."

"Four Hours! We should be there by now," says Rory exasperated.

"It's been slower than I anticipated because of the sand," replies Ian. "With that in mind, we should reach the river in, roughly, two more." I can't believe how relieved I feel that there are only two more hours left of this walk. How stupid. We have days left, maybe weeks. God, how will I get through this? Ian gives me a small smile as we begin to pack up and start again.

"It's not too bad for our first day out," he says softly.

"I guess." All I feel is hot and sweaty and in dire need of a shower that I know isn't coming any time soon. Plus, it's only the first day. As I think of this, I see Gemma loading her pack onto her back with Arick's help. If she can do it then so can I.

"Okay," says Briar. "Let's go. When we get to the river, we can set up camp and dig into those meal packs."

"Great," replies Rory, sarcastically. "Can't wait."

CHAPTER ELEVEN

Wren

Arick and Briar take the lead this time while the rest of us follow behind. I feel better after the water break, my throat isn't on fire anymore, just scratchy. I'm slowly getting used to the sweat and grit that cover me but not the monotonous scenery. My eyes are continuously searching for color, anything to make this all seem normal.

"How's it going?" asks Ian as he steps next to me, his feet shadowing mine in the sand.

"I don't know," I reply honestly. "I'm tired like everyone else, I guess."

"Yeah," he says solemnly. "But at least we know the air is breathable. We'll get to the hub as long as we're smart about it."

"I guess," I say half-heartedly. I wonder why he's choosing me to talk to when Briar is so much more interesting. I can understand him steering clear of Rory because he's kind of a jerk, but me, I'm so basic. I sneak a side glance at him. Perspiration glistens on his temples and the back of his neck. I can see the line of his muscles as the jumpsuit sticks to his broad chest. Even as I watch, he reaches up to unzip it, pulling the sticky fabric away from his skin.

"It's hot," he says. I catch a glance at his bare chest and quickly look away, my cheeks hot from more than just the environment. I can feel my own sweat trickling down my back and pooling between my breasts.

"Yeah," I reply with a gulp. "It's hot." I look behind and see that Arick has moved to the back of our pack and walks with Gemma, both speaking in low tones. Rory lags behind, muttering complaints. My foot lodges itself in a particularly soft patch of sand and I stumble. Ian reaches out to steady me, grabbing my arm.

"Whoops," he says. "Careful, Wren. We can't have any injures out here."

"I'm good," I reply embarrassed. His hands are large and strong and surprisingly gentle on my arm, steadying me. I feel a pang of loss as he lets go.

"What are you thinking about?" asks Ian as we continue our trek.

"Oh, not much, just pizza and ice cream and soda, nothing important." He lets out a short laugh.

"We'll have to see if there's any freeze-dried pizza in our rations."

"Yeah, well, I'm not holding my breath." He turns to me with a dazzling smile.

"How about when we're out of this desert and safe at the hub, I make you a pizza?"

"If there are enough supplies at the hub, I'll make everyone pizza!" I say. He smiles again but I see sadness behind those intense blue eyes.

"Deal," he replies and then adds, "We'll be okay. Once this hike is over we can get back to our real lives." I turn to him in wonder.

"How?" I ask. "How will we ever get back to our real lives? This is what our lives are now." His expression becomes dark.

"I didn't mean that things will be the same as before. How could they? I just meant..."

"I know," I reply, softly. "I want to see what's waiting at the hub too." Ian turns away, the corner of his lips turned down in a frown. He is hot and cold, one minute flashing his brilliant smile and the next making me feel like a silly school girl with a huge crush. I try to give myself a quick whiff to see if my BO is as bad as it feels but out in the open it's hard to tell.

Time, once again, seems to stand still as we traverse the mundane terrain. Nothing changes, just more gray sand stretching out as far as the eye can see. The silence around us is eerie. Only the sound of our feet grinding into the sand as we walk can be heard along with soft talk that comes from Gemma and Arick behind me. I slow my pace so that they are closer. When I'm close enough to hear their words, I fall into stride.

"She is the beautiful one," says Gemma, softly. "Jewel is good at school and has tons of friends and has always been my parent's favorite child. I wonder if they are alive...if Jewel didn't make it and they see me at the hub, will they wish it was her?" My heart sinks. How could she think something like that?

"Well," says Arick. "I know that this may be difficult for you to believe, but I have found that parents don't usually have favorites. You have your own gifts, Gemma, and you are special in your own way."

"That's always what adults say," she replies with doubt in her voice.

"Is it?"

"Do you have children?" she counters. I notice his eyes flick to the ground.

"No," he replies softly. "I was never fortunate enough to meet the right person and then work was so demanding that there was never time." He glances to Gemma. Realizing that his tone has turned somber he adds brightly, "But I know that if I had been lucky enough to have a daughter like you, I would have been your biggest fan and I would have said the same thing and meant it."

"It's just that I've never had anything to brag about. I'm shy around people I don't know and I'm not smart like Jewel. It's always been her award ceremonies and her university acceptance letter and her invitations to special events. I've always felt…left behind, unnoticed."

"Hmmm," says Arick. "Sometimes it takes us a little bit longer to find the thing that we are good at. You're what we call a late bloomer if that's possible at your young age." I can almost hear her smile at his words. "Your parents love you, Gemma, I know they do. When they rest their eyes on you again, they will show you just how much."

"I think I see something just ahead!" shouts Briar and we all stop in our tracks and search frantically into the distance. There's something there that looks different, like a slope off the edge of the world. I'm guessing that slope leads to the river.

"Finally," says Rory in an annoyed voice. We all quicken our pace and within a few minutes we reach the river's edge. My heart sinks when I see what's at the bottom of the shallow gorge. There is no sound of rushing water, no fish bobbing their open lips just above the surface, no cool glossy stones lining the bottom. The river isn't completely dry, but it might as well be. The gray sand has slipped into the bottom of the river painting it the same color as everything else out here. It's murky and it's doubtful that it's drinkable even with filtration. The sand is too fine.

"Well, we still have water left so..." says Arick. Ian comes to rest his hand on Arick's shoulder.

"It's okay," he says. "As long as we follow the river north, we should hit on something. There's some water here, as spoiled as it is, it had to come from somewhere."

Briar has made her way down the slope by sliding on her butt. She pulls an empty bottle from her pack and fills it with the filthy water. As she holds it up, it looks more like spoiled milk than water.

"Ian's right," she says. "As long as we conserve what we have from now on, we should find water eventually." She gives Rory another annoyed glance but either he doesn't notice, or he just doesn't care. He throws his backpack down with a grunt. We're all exhausted and one by one each of our packs drop too. We decide to make camp several yards away from the river.

"Let's get our tents put up and get a meal in us," adds Briar. "We can start again first thing in the morning."

I've never been camping in my life and there's a reason for that. Sleeping outdoors in a flimsy tent isn't my idea of fun. Gemma and I pull out the small compact sacks that hold our tents. Along with the tent are several folded-up poles attached to each other by stretchy cording. I dump everything out in front of me and stare at it in confusion. This is so not my forte'. Gemma gives me a smile and takes one of the poles, expanding it.

"It's easy," she says with a laugh. She feeds the poles through openings in the fabric and before I know it a small tent pops up in front of me.

"Wow, thanks Gemma. You're really good at this," I say with enthusiasm. I open the front flap of the newly constructed tent and crawl inside. It's small and cozy. There's no pillow in my backpack but there's a glossy, silvery blanket that feels like liquid when I let it fall over my hand. This is something made with new technology. It's another unnerving reminder that though we've been out of circulation for fifty years, others have not. The other tents pop up to form a circle creating an open space in the center.

"I'm not sure about making a fire," says Briar. "Doesn't seem like a good idea if we really don't need it. Plus, there are no building materials. I don't feel like using any of our resources for fuel and hunting down a tree would be impossible."

"Yeah," retorts Rory. "It's only a hundred and ten degrees out here. I'm sure a fire would help." But as he says this, I notice a change in the air. The sun is slowly sinking, and it seems to be taking the heavy heat with it. It feels good. The sweat sticking to me begins to evaporate. Rory pulls his pack in front of his crossed legs and pulls out a freeze-dried meal pouch.

"Ooh, yummy, mac and cheese!" Briar gives him a frustrated glare.

"You'll be begging for that mac and cheese in another week," she says. I search through my rations of food and see that my options are limited. There's only mac and cheese like Rory's or spaghetti with meat sauce. I pull the spaghetti out and read the pouch. The package says to add water, so I open a fresh bottle of water and pour in a little, stirring it all together with the attached plastic spoon. I close the pouch and can feel the contents expand and become warm. As I take a bite, my tongue explodes with the flavors of tomatoes and basil and my mouth begins to water frantically.

"Wow, this is actually good!" I say, watching Gemma pour water into her pouch. Everyone else follows along, everyone but Rory, that is. He's already scraped the last of the cheese sauce from the pouch and has tossed it aside as he gulps down the last of his open bottle of water.

"Mine's good too," says Gemma. She's eating the Mac and Cheese and it does look good. I finish up my bottle of water and though I'm not full, at least I'm not as empty as I was. Rory leans back against his tent, patting his belly as if he's just eaten the meal of his life. Briar gets up and stretches. I can tell she's stiff and sore just like I am. She walks over and extends a hand to me. I take it and she pulls me up from the sand.

"We better get some rest before we head out in the morning," says Briar.

"Do you think we need to keep watch," she asks, more to Ian than to anyone else.

"I'll stay up," replies Arick with a grin and I'm relieved. "I'm not sure that it's necessary but I'm just one of those people who doesn't need much sleep, always have been."

Rory and Ian retreat into their tents and I turn to Gemma and ask, "Will you be okay?"

"I think so," she replies. "You're right next door." I smile at her and push a loose strand of blond hair back from her face.

"If you need anything, just knock," I reply, knocking on the flimsy material that is my tent. I climb in, pulling my backpack with me. The lack of a pillow and sleeping bag is concerning but I must make do. I find a soft spot in my pack and put it behind my head, lying on my back. I stare at the tan fabric of the ceiling. Why does everything have to look the same? It's becoming difficult to remember what a colorful world looked like. My muscles feel tense with the strain of worry and there's a dull throbbing in the back of my head from all the walking in the heat. I concentrate on my breathing, slow and steady. I relax each muscle of my body in turn. As my eyes close, my breathing takes over and my body and brain begin to finally relax completely, I feel myself drift away. For some reason, my last thoughts are not about my mother, or even about Aiden. I think about Ian and wonder if he'll walk with me again tomorrow.

CHAPTER TWELVE

Aiden

"Hey, where's Spencer?" asks Raven. She's fidgeting with her pack as she stares around at the empty space by the tunnel doors. She's ready to go and already looks aggravated.

"I'm only two minutes late," replies Spencer as he comes up behind me. "I think I know better than to keep you waiting." His hair is disheveled, and his backpack is open, a gun in danger of falling out. I smile because we look like our old crew dressed in the tan jumpsuits that are at least clean now. I honestly never thought I'd put it on again. Raven glances at her tablet and gives Spencer a nod.

"Okay, are we ready then?" she asks.

"The sooner we get out of here, the sooner we get back,"

chimes Spencer. He looks like he could use a second cup of coffee. Raven gives him a sideways glance.

"Remember, we have a job to do. I want us all going by the book." Spencer glances at me, his eyebrows arched.

"Yes, Sir," he replies with a salute.

"All I'm trying to say is, it's different this time. We're smarter and we know what to expect. Commander Rob is counting on us."

"We know, Raven," I say. "Let's just not forget who we are."

Raven looks down, contemplating something. As she meets my gaze she replies, "I know who I am Aiden. I'm a member of this new government." Her eyes flick to Spencer who is watching us closely. "I might have been a scared, weak girl a few weeks ago, but I'm not that girl anymore."

"I don't think…I never thought…," stammers Spencer.

"I want to do this mission by the books, okay? When I choose a military career, I want to have something to back my choice up with. I don't want it to be just handed to me." I nod. Raven was never a scared little girl. She may have felt like that a few weeks ago when we woke up in our cryochambers, but she never allowed us to see it. At eighteen, she has government official woven into her DNA. She had to learn the hard way, like the rest of us, but she stood her ground in every challenge and there were many. She is the brains and the muscle of our small squad and her greatest attribute is her unwavering ability to make a decision and stick to it. If it weren't for that ability, Spence and I would have sat around for days analyzing the pros and cons of every choice our first time out. Her words make me wonder if she really doubts herself, if deep down she's insecure.

"Okay, then," says Spencer, bouncing on the balls of his feet. "Let's head out."

The wind hits us hard as the automatic steel doors open. It's cool and crisp and takes my breath away. That should give Spencer a jolt. We won't feel cold for long, I'm sure of that. A handful of electric vehicles sit waiting at the loading dock of the tunnels entrance, charging, ready for their next task. My hands itch to rest on the side panel of one and jump in. It would be so easy just to haul ass out of here, but it's not my choice to make. The Commander has his reasons. These vehicles look sturdy enough, but they can only make it a few miles out in this kind of terrain. Still, if it becomes the difference between finding Wren or not, I'll come back to hijack one. Raven pulls up the hologram of the map and we get our bearings.

"We'll take the most direct route south to the government compound," shouts Raven over the wind. It howls through the tunnel like a trapped ghost trying to find its way out. "There's no need to mess around with directions. We have the supplies that we need and it's really just a matter of getting there or finding the officials first." Our footsteps echo off the concrete that makes up the tunnel floor and we lean our bodies into the wind. I can see the exit, a circle of golden light illuminating the end of our dark pathway. All at once we step from the hard, cold floor onto soft gilded sand, the wind dispersing around us in an instant.

Flecks of sand reflect from the mountain ridge like sequins, stars far away in the distance. Soon we will leave it behind to skirt around west of the ridge, missing most of the difficult terrain. A hazy sun begins its ascent into the sky casting sparkling light on the sand at our feet. I instinctually make a mental note to keep my eyes open for water supplies just in case. One thing that I've learned out here is that it's better to plan ahead. Goosebumps play on my arms and the back of my neck as the heat from the sun warms away the cold from the wind. I know what I'm in for; more heat, sweat and sun.

"So what job are you going after?" asks Spencer as our shoes dig into the sand.

"I don't know," I reply, my mouth already feeling dry. I've always been an overachiever. My dreams before the flare were all about rising to the top, an upper level position with the government, like my father. My life revolved around it, but now...? I pause to think about it. After everything we've been through, those dreams seem ridiculous, almost meaningless. "I guess I would like a job where I can really make a difference, some place that really needs my skill set." Raven gives a snort of disbelief and I nudge her playfully.

"Well, you've got mad skills for computers and technology and building stuff out of nothing," says Spencer.

"Yeah, right," I reply laughing. "Compared to you I'm a complete moron.

"That's not true," he counters. "Anyway, you shouldn't compare yourself to me. It's not a fair evaluation." He gives me one of his crooked grins.

"Maybe something in engineering, something mechanical."

"You'd be a great leader," says Raven.

"No, that's you," I say.

"I mean it," she continues. "There's something in the way you are, the way you talk to people. You take the time to look at every side and always come up with a solution that will make everyone happy." She pauses for a moment, considering. "I'd make a good leader too, but only in a military setting."

"Yeah," agrees Spencer. "You're great at giving orders." She rolls her eyes and gives an exasperated sigh, but I know she finds him as endearing as I do.

"Well, I think we all know where I'll end up," adds Spencer.

"Where? The CEO of government tech?" I ask.

"No fricken way," he says. "I don't want some high-power job, on call twenty-four hours a day, constant complaints and always a fire to put out somewhere. No, I'll do better tucked away in some closet working on cyber security. It's a big job, searching out invaders, but calls for ambiguity. I like that." Yeah, that suites him. He's a genius but he's also shy and insecure especially in social settings. I think about Raven's words and wonder if I would be a good leader. As long as I'm doing something productive, something to help our new world get better, then I could lead. Wren would like that, the idea of working for the betterment of the world and not the betterment of myself. A knot forms in the pit of my stomach as I think about her, my lost girl with fiery red hair and endless emerald eyes. She never really knew me. She thought she did, but I worked hard to never let her see that side of me, the selfish side, the side that wouldn't stop until I reached the top of the pecking order. I was hard. I would have stepped on anyone. But there was something about Wren that made me soft. She brought out the best in me but gave me way too much credit. I wasn't the caring, kind guy she thought I was, but I could be. I could be that guy for her, especially now.

We walk on through the endless golden sand, Raven leading the way and Spencer bringing up the rear. It's beautiful out here, a real desert, possibly an area little affected by the flare. One hour, two and then Raven stops.

"What the hell is that?" she asks, sheltering her eyes from the bright sun. I follow her gaze into the distance, and I see it, several structures dotting the area up ahead. From this far away it's hard to tell what they are but, as I squint, I make out at least eight of them, eight dark marks breaking up the horizon.

"Break time," says Spencer unconcerned. He drops to the sand and pulls out a bottle of water. My throat is so dry that I'm not sure I'm capable of swallowing. I steal the bottle from Spencer's hands and take a gulp.

"Hey!" he exclaims grabbing it back.

"I'm not sure what that is," I say to Raven. "They don't look big enough to be buildings. Maybe some kind of gate system?" I feel my jumpsuit sticking to my back and the edges of my blond hair curling up from the heat and humidity. Raven's pale cheeks have gotten some color and I'm hoping that she remembered to put on sunscreen.

"Well, there's only one way to find out," says Spencer as he gulps down the rest of his water. “Let’s go.”

CHAPTER THIRTEEN

Wren

I wake up sometime in the night, shivering from the cold. I can see my breaths in small puffs of white as I grope for the silvery blanket that has slipped off me in the night.

"Oh my God," I hiss as I pull it back over me, shaking uncontrollably. Hours ago, it was scorching hot and now it's barely above freezing. Maybe having a fire would have been a good idea after all, and I make a mental note to push for that once we find wood. My body is stiff and screaming in pain. I roll onto my back and once again try to control my breathing. The thin blanket does help a little and, in a few minutes, at least my teeth have stopped chattering. I'm still cold. I nudge the opening of my tent with my foot and see that it is still dark. I'm still exhausted. I've barely caught a few hours of sleep but, as tired as I am, my mind won't shut off. Time seems to pass slowly out here but I finally see the sky lightening and a hazy yellow begins to lift over the edge of the horizon. As tired as I feel, I have to get up before I freeze to death. I rub my exposed skin with my hands. My face is dry, almost as dry as my mouth. I take a few minutes to reorganize my pack and sip some water. I take out all my meal packs and granola cakes and set them aside. The bottles of water weigh down the bottom of my pack and so does the gun that is hidden underneath. The knife is still tucked in the outside pocket. I reach in and feel the cool handle. It comforts me to have the weapons, but I'm not sure if I can ever use them. I run my hand across the back of my neck and feel a layer of gray dust and sand. Along with the tiredness pressing behind my eyes, I feel grimy.

I take out my small toiletry bag. Reaching in, I find a small cake of soap, several individually wrapped squares labeled Insta-cloth, a disposable toothbrush along with a small tube of toothpaste, tiny plastic bottles of shampoo and an assortment of bandages and antibiotic ointment. It's not much but I'm grateful. I'm hoping that soon I'll find enough water to break out the soap. For now, I can spare one of the Insta-cloths, even if all it does is make me feel a little cleaner. I rip one open and pull out a thin washcloth that smells slightly of lavender. It's bigger than I imagined and wet. I wipe my face and neck luxuriously. It's nice and the scent of wildflowers cuts away the bad odor that's starting to become noticeable. I don't know why I really care. We're all developing layers of filth. I guess I just want something normal, something positive. Maybe it also has something to do with Ian. As I pull the cloth away and see the change in color from white to almost black, I'm horrified. I don't care. I take a swipe under my arms and down my cleavage with the dirty cloth.

"Gross," I hiss in disgust, as I wad up the used cloth. Still, that little Insta-cloth has made me feel better. Not exactly clean but I smell better. Next, I open the small tube of toothpaste, disregarding the brush, and smear some on my finger, rubbing it across my teeth. Not the most hygienic thing to do but at least the stale, rotten taste in my mouth is replaced by a minty freshness. I load everything back into my backpack. I'm ready.

The air is still freezing as I exit the tent. No one is up yet so I rub my hands together and try to run in place to get my blood flowing. I notice Arick who is slumped against his tent with his eyes shut, belting out an occasional snore. So much for keeping watch, I think with a grin. He looks peaceful, his salt and pepper hair falling gracefully across his forehead. I notice small lines shooting out from his eyes and deep indents on either side of his mouth that show his age. His glasses are more than a little askew on his face and are in danger of breaking. I hear a rustling as someone else begins to back their way out of their tent. My eyes go wide as Ian's feet hit the ground and he pushes himself up to stand in front of me.

"Oh," he says in surprise. I want to tell him to be quiet so that he doesn't disturb Arick but I find it hard to speak when I'm looking at his half-dressed body. Ian has his jumpsuit on, but it's only zipped up to his waist, leaving his arms and chest bare in the cold. I try to look away, but I can't as my eyes travel from the bulging muscles in his arms to his broad chest and downward. His skin is smooth, and his muscles are tense. He's built like a guy who goes to the gym every day, maybe even twice a day. At this exact moment I am glad that I decided to partake in the Insta-cloth and toothpaste. And then my eyes meet his eyes and I'm so embarrassed that I want to sink into the ground. He flashes me a faltering half grin. I look away and continue to hop up and down for warmth even though much of the freezing cold has been taken over by the heat that covers my face.

"I'm warm-blooded," he says in response to me ogling his body. "Even in the winter months, I never wear a coat." All the same he shoves his arms into the sleeves of his jumpsuit and zips it up.

"Are you cold?" he asks. He takes a step forward and he's standing in front of me, his face inches away. "Here," he says. He reaches out to cover my small hands with his larger hands. His hands are warm over mine and I can feel the heat sinking into my skin. It feels so good that I wish I could curl up next to him in my tent. He rubs my hands gently with his own and I'm suddenly aware of how close he is to me. I am also very aware of my tousled hair that must look like a raging fire and my disheveled jumpsuit. Thank God for the toothpaste. I breathe in his scent, the musk that is all male with a hint of lavender. He has also taken advantage of the Insta-cloth. Ian smiles down at me as he continues to rub my hands and I chance a shy glance through my eyelashes. The deep blue of his eyes is so intense that I begin to feel my heart race and a tingle begins somewhere near my stomach. All I care about is that he doesn't stop rubbing my hands, that he doesn't stop looking into my eyes. When he suddenly blinks and looks down at our hands sandwiched together, he takes a step back, letting my hands fall.

"Thanks," I say, looking away. 'It's better now."

"Okay." I can feel an awkward moment growing between us. His hands twitch as if wanting to reach out and grab mine again. I want him to. The look that covers his face is once again sad, but only for a second before he turns to face Arick, still fast asleep.

"Do you think we should wake him?" I ask as Arick lets loose a loud snore.

"Let him sleep," he replies. "He'll be up soon enough."

Briar is the next one out of her tent. She gives a hasty hello and begins to disassemble it. I decide to do the same. Taking it down seems much easier than putting it up and I find that I can handle it on my own. I knock gently on Gemma's tent. A messy, blond head pokes out. She vigorously rubs her arms and says, "It was freezing last night!" I nod.

"Maybe it will be warmer tonight." I laugh at her bleary-eyed expression. It's hard to believe that I have laughter left inside of me but seeing Gemma makes me happy.

"Let's go check out the river," I say. "Maybe by some miracle there's drinkable water now." She pulls herself from her tent. Her hair is a wild mess of loose ponytail.

"Turn around," I command as I take her by the shoulders. I remove the rubber band and begin to smooth back her hair with my hands. I catch the loose strands and bring it all together at the back of her head.

"Better?" I ask.

"Yeah, thanks," she says as she turns back to me. She gives me a quick hug and I quickly braid my own hair so that it's out of my face. We take the short walk to the sloping edge of the river and discover that nothing has changed.

"Still nasty," I say with a grimace.

"I really hope that Briar's right and the river is cleaner up north."

"I'm sure it will work out," I reply with a smile. "So how are you, Gemma?" She looks up at me with a shrug.

"I'm okay," she replies. "Tired, I guess, but I really like our squad. I feel safe, you know?"

"Yeah, I do too." I wrap my arm around her, remembering the conversation that I overheard between her and Arick. "You know, you're pretty awesome." She leans her head into me as we walk back.

"Thanks," she replies, and I think that she really believes me.

"Are you ready for breakfast?"

There is movement around the tents as we return to our makeshift camp. Everyone seems to be anxious to get on the move again, everyone except Rory. He sits with his back leaning into his backpack, munching on a granola cake. He throws back a bottle of water in about ten seconds and then crushes the plastic bottle in his fist. I eye him warily and then notice several other empty wrappers crumpled up next to him. Hasn't he heard anything that Briar has said? Briar is just zipping up her pack when she notices me staring at Rory. Her gaze shifts from me to him, her brows furrowing.

"You know that none of us is going to give you any of our food once you run out, right?" she says with irritation. Rory continues to chew as he crumples up the last wrapper and throws it into the pile. He leans forward, threateningly, so that he's closer to Briar.

"Look, I'm hungry, okay? I can't help it," he replies. "You can keep your stinking food. We're all going to die out here anyway. I might as well have a full stomach." He leans back onto his pack again and that's when I see Gemma's backpack, resting against her tent, the zipper wide open. Why would she leave her supplies so unguarded? It looks suspicious and as I take a step closer, I see Rory's eyes follow my path. In an instant, I know why he doesn't seem to care about running out of rations.

"What have you done?" I scream, as I race to Gemma's backpack and pull it open. Everyone stops what they are doing and watches as I unload its contents.

"Gemma, did you eat anything last night after dinner or this morning?" She hesitates. I can see the shock in her face as she shakes her head back and forth frantically.

"No, nothing after dinner," she says in a shaky voice. Briar is watching closely, her eyes narrow, as I continue to remove the granola cakes and meal pouches and begin counting. Rory squirms and pretends to repack his backpack, but I see him watching out of the corner of his eye. There are two granola cakes and one meal pack missing from Gemma's pack. After I replace everything, I turn to face Rory. Ian and Arick have also come closer. Good, I want them to see the kind of kid Rory is. I want them to see that we're dealing with a thief.

"She's three meals short," I say. "Two granola cakes and one meal pack." Briar lunges at Rory and grabs him by the collar of his jumpsuit. His dusty blond hair falls into his face as Briar pulls him from his sitting position. He is drowning in shock as she shakes him viciously.

"You little prick!" Briar yells into his face. "Stealing the food out the mouth of a young girl. You're a selfish bastard!" She continues to shake him, and I think there may be a good chance she'll end up punching him before she's done. Rory looks like he's going to be sick and what great karma that would be. Let him throw up all the food that he's stolen. "Look at her!" screams Briar. "Look at her, she wouldn't hurt a fly and you're stealing her life!" Rory tries to pull away, but Briar has a firm grip.

"She's small," he whines, squirming, trying to keep his face away from Briar's fists. "She doesn't need as much as the rest of us." His voice shakes, and his eyes roam the rest of us, searching, as if asking for help. Briar stops shaking him and puts her face so close to his that their noses are almost touching.

"Listen you little shit. If I ever catch you stealing from any of us again, I'm going old school on you, got it? One finger at a time. I'll start with your filthy little pointer finger and move down the line until all you're left with is a bloody stump." Ian and Arick are moving closer, clearly afraid that Briar will keep her word. Gemma's eyes are filled with hurtful tears and I feel the heat of Briar's anger inside of my gut. I secretly hope that, if the time comes for Briar to make good on her threat, I'll be the one to wield the knife. Briar throws Rory down with disgust, as if he's some kind of slimy thing on the bottom of her shoe. He lands in a heap on top of his backpack, Briar's chest is heaving and, though there is now some distance between them, a killer intensity lingers in her eyes. Arick takes several steps forward and stands between Rory and Briar. He places a hand on Rory's shoulder, causing him to jump back in fear. I'm glad he's afraid. Still, Arick's face is calm.

"It looks like you have a choice to make, Rory," says Arick, as Briar stomps back a few feet. "You can choose to follow the basic rules of human decency: no stealing, no violence," I glance over to Briar and she gives me a look that plainly says, I'll still do it. "And develop a sense of respect for the members of this squad." Briar lets out a sadistic laugh.

"Or?" asks Rory his eyes open wide.

"Or you go out on your own," interjects Ian from behind me. "If you can't follow these few rules, then you can't be trusted." Arick gives a nod.

"Fine," Rory says. "I'm sorry, okay? It won't happen again." He's smoldering with the defiant look of a child. His words have a hollow ring and I know that, given the chance, he will steal from any one of us again.

"Good," replies Arick. "Now there's just one thing left to do."

"What now?" asks Rory in a huff. "I said I was sorry." Arick crouches down to look Rory in the eye.

"You have to replace what you took," he says. Rory's mouth is hanging open and my head whips around to see Gemma wiping tears from her cheeks. This is the least that Rory can do.

"What?" asks Rory. Arick stands and takes a few steps away. The rest of us watch, Briar with a smirk on her face.

"Rory, you have to make it right. The only way to do that, without losing any fingers," he glances to Briar, "is to replace what you took. It's the first step, but it will take time for any of us to trust you again." Rory lets out a grunt and then opens his backpack. He takes out two granola cakes and tosses them at Gemma's feet. He adds one random meal pouch as Gemma bends down to gather them. There is satisfaction knowing that Rory is a meal short. He'll have to go without before Gemma.

"Thanks," she says, more to Arick than to Rory. The drama is over, so we scramble to finish packing our things. "Arick's nice," she whispers, and I agree.

"Let's move out," comes Briar's voice. We leave our little campsite as deserted as it was when we arrived and a little wiser to the threat within our group.

CHAPTER FOURTEEN

Aiden

As we get closer to the structures, they begin to take shape. They are tall pillars of stone, four on one side, four on the other, creating an open pathway of smooth, packed down sand between them. They seem to serve no purpose other than to add decoration to an otherwise sparse landscape. And then I notice that something has changed. The terrain outside of the pillars has become a river of thorny shrubs that go on beyond my vision.

"Well, that's new," says Spencer, stating the obvious. "What do you think?" Standing closer to the pillars, I notice the intricate geometric design carved into their surface. They look old, almost alien and so out of place.

"This is stupid," exclaims Raven, as she inspects the pillars. "Maybe we should try to go around them." She's right. You never know what you're going to find out here and the way that these pillars are placed seems like an open invitation to walk between them. It's too planned out, too obvious.

"Look," replies Spencer. "This is probably just some left over garbage from the end of the world as we knew it. You said it yourself, Raven, the straightest path is the best path to take."

"I don't know," I say, agreeing with Raven. Spencer shakes his head as if the whole thing is ridiculous and takes a firm step onto the pathway. I know that it's a wrong decision immediately and so does he.

"Spencer!" yells Raven as bright red laser beams begin to emit from the pillars creating a crisscross pattern, a huge net along the pathway.

"Spencer, don't move," says Raven. "Shit!" Spencer is still, poised on one foot, his arms outstretched, but I can see him shaking. It won't be long before a limb cuts through a beam, and then what? Raven assesses the situation nervously. She turns to me. "We've got to get him out of there." There's no way. The net is tightly sewn. There's no way out but through them.

"Maybe there's a way to shut down the whole system," I say, glancing along the surface of the closest pillar. I can see small pinpricks from where the beams of light originate but no control panel.

"Dammit!" grunts Raven. "Just hold on Spencer. Give us a minute to think." On cue, I see Spencer's leg begin to wobble and he lets out a cry and topples to the ground, breaking through hundreds of lasers.

"My leg fell asleep," he says, glancing to us innocently. The red light disappears, and all is still as we wait. Spencer gets to his feet gingerly, rubbing his leg. "Maybe..." Raven hears it first, a whistling sound, like a missile heading for its target. Her eyes get big as she shouts,

"Haul ass, haul ass, haul ass!" She grabs my arm and pulls

me into the pathway, pulling Spencer with her other hand. We run, flat out, and then I feel pain, white-hot, enter through my head, cutting a path through every limb of my body. My mind is still working when my body stops. I land hard on my back and I see the blue streaks cut the space over me, lightning pulsating through my cells with fiery anguish. Instinctively I look to my side and see Spencer and Raven sprawled out, blue electric arms probing them. I can't think as the current passes through me, my blood on fire, my organs frying. Every ounce of my energy is consumed with breathing, keeping my heart pumping. The pain is hard and fierce causing my body to writhe and jolt. I feel my eyes begin to roll back as the fire turns to razor blades cutting a path along my spine and then all at once it stops and I'm left panting, concentrating on my heartbeat. *It's over*, I tell myself as the pain slowly subsides. *It's over*. I'm left with a dull throb all over my body and I work to catch my breath. Tears are streaming down my cheeks. I quickly wipe them away. I hear Spencer coughing as Raven gives a long slow groan.

"Dammit!" says Raven as she gingerly rolls over onto her side. "Dammit, Spencer!"

"This is messed up," he replies.

"Well, we're all alive," I say. "But clearly we have to be more careful."

"If this thing was designed to kill us, we'd be dead," says Raven. "We knew what we were getting into coming back here but we can't take anything for granted. We can't take chances." Both Spencer and I nod as we sit together in a circle, digging in our bags for water. "Let's take fifteen minutes and then finish this thing." Raven takes out her tablet which miraculously has been unaffected by the lightning and pulls up the hologram map.

"What I don't get," says Spencer. "Is why this is even here."

"Protection," replies Raven. "We're close enough to the government hubs." I can see a line of fresh perspiration along her brow and loose black strands of hair stick to it.

"A warning from Commander Rob might have been nice," adds Spencer.

"Do you think there's a chance that our officials might have been taken out by this?" I ask.

"I don't think so," says Raven. "It wasn't programed to kill. There's a chance that it could have injured one of them though."

"There's also the chance that they saw it for what it is and decided to find a way around," I add.

"Maybe," says Raven. "That could explain the delay."

"Well, if that's what they did then they should be back at the government hub soon," says Spencer. "And that makes our mission a waste of time." Raven tucks a loose strand of slightly chard hair back into her ponytail and packs up her empty water bottle.

"We have a mission to do, Spencer," she says, looking him square in the eye. "We can't speculate, we can only do what we set out to do and then return back to the hub." Spencer looks away, frustrated. "We're about halfway to the bank. We'll check out that location and if they're not there we can skirt around to the eastern side of the mountains. It will add a few hours but if they did decide to make their way around this electric monstrosity, that's the way they'd go." That plan makes sense. The officials would most certainly consult their map and plan the easiest route.

As we walk to the south, I notice that my limbs move a little more slowly. That trap took a lot out of me even if I don't want to admit it to Raven and Spencer. I hope that Wren's journey will not be as hard as this. I hope that she'll have a strong squad that can carry her if she needs to be carried. I wish I could be with her now. I want to see her fiery hair, run my fingers along her cheek, press my lips to her neck and tell her that I love her. I want to be her hero and make a life together, one where we are working towards the same goal, not like before. I have to keep these dreams. I have to believe that they will happen. As long as I can find her and bring her back safely with me, they will happen. Then we'll start the life together that we should have had before the world exploded.

CHAPTER FIFTEEN

Wren

This day begins much like the day before, walking in the never-ending gray sand with the sun obscured by the heavy haze that covers everything. Too soon it becomes unbearably hot and it's made worse this time by the ache in my legs and feet. Briar leads the way, following the curves of the dry river. Arick and Gemma walk just behind, and I can see them talking quietly. As I wonder what story Arick is telling Gemma, Ian walks up next to me once again. I feel my heartbeat quicken. He matches his pace to mine, glancing back to where Rory walks alone.

"I don't know about that one," he says, nodding back to Rory.

"Yeah, I don't know why Briar agreed to let him stay," I reply. "It's not like any of us can trust him."

Ian gives me a little smile. It's amazing how that smile lights up his face.

"Who knows," he says. "Maybe he can change."

"Well, I guess he better if he wants to keep his fingers." Ian laughs lightly and then his eyes turn to me. He's watching me as we walk, watching my face. It causes butterflies to bat their wings against my ribcage. I swallow hard.

"What?" I ask.

"Nothing," he replies shyly, finally glancing away. "I just wanted to make sure that you're okay. How are your hands? Warm enough?" He reaches down to squeeze my fingers and then lifts my hand to inspect it. He sees my silver ring and runs a finger along the surface stopping at the stone. "That's pretty," he says.

"Thanks," I reply, feeling uncomfortable.

"Does it mean something?" he asks, letting my hand slip from his. "From a boyfriend?"

"It's complicated."

"Oh, okay," he replies.

"What about you?" I ask. "What's your story?"

"I don't have much of a story," he says, and I'm surprised. "I guess I'm just like everyone else, lost in a wilderness of sand."

"What about ...before?"

"Oh, nothing extraordinary," he replies. "When the flare hit, I was able to make it to the cryobank but the rest of my family... well, they never made it."

"I'm sorry," I say.

"Yeah, well, like I said, I'm just like everyone else." While he's looking away, I take a minute to really study his face. He's maybe seventeen, but if he were close to my age, he should look familiar to me. After all we were in the same bank and that means the same sector and also the same schools. Gemma's too young to have been in my circles and Arick's too old. But Ian… He turns and catches me staring.

"What?" now it's his turn to ask.

"I'm trying to see if I remember your face around Sector Three," I say, sheepishly.

"Oh," he replies in surprise. "No, you wouldn't. I grew up in Sector Five. I just happened to be in Sector Three when it all went down. I was lucky there was a spot in the cryobank."

"Oh," I reply. "That makes sense." But it really doesn't. If he's not from my sector how did he know where the bank was? How was he even able to access a cryotank room? How does he know that the rest of his family didn't make it? I decide that Ian must just want to keep his life private. We don't know each other, not really.

The sun is getting higher and the heat is becoming intense again. My feet and limbs are heavy with exhaustion and I know we still have so far to go. What I wouldn't give for a pond or even a stream to soak my feet in. I glance over to the river on my right and see that it is still dry. We've traveled at least five or six miles. How many more until we find a water source. I turn to Ian who has remained quiet.

"Ian?" I ask. "What if this is it?" I extend my arms out indicating the never-ending gray all around us.

"I don't think this is it," he replies, keeping his eyes averted from mine. "Try not to worry too much, Wren."

"Break time." Briar's voice breaks through our conversation. As Arick, Gemma and Briar stop, Ian and I quickly catch up to them. We toss our packs onto the ground and pull out water. Rory has lagged far behind and he looks like he's struggling. Arick walks out to meet him and I'm disgusted. You'd think that after all the extra food he had this morning he'd be out in front. He will drag us all down.

I sit down on top of my pack and try to peer into the distance, hoping to see something to break up the monotony and, at first, I see nothing. And then I think I see a speck on the horizon, a break in the terrain. Briar looks over to me and then follows my gaze.

"What is that?" I ask as I shield my eyes from the sun with my hands. Everyone turns to peer into the distance.

"I'm not sure," says Ian with wonder. "But it is definitely something more than flat sand."

"Okay," says Arick with a clap of his hands. "Something new."

I smile. I don't care what *it* is as long as this sand or ash disappears. We are all smiling, all except Rory. He looks bad. His face is red from the heat and sun and he's breathing heavily. Sweat covers his brow and there are dark stains on the fine material of his jumpsuit, under his arms and down his back. He takes a bottle of water and guzzles it. The water immediately comes back up.

"Slow down," says Ian, handing him a half full bottle of his own supply. Generous, I think. Way too generous. Ian and Briar consult the map again as we all gather around. Ian runs his finger along the path that we have already traveled. I blink back disbelief as I realize how short the distance is behind us.

"I think that may be Sector Two up ahead," says Ian. "We will need to pass through a part of it on our way since the river heads that way too."

"Maybe we'll see something there," chimes in Gemma with excitement. "Maybe there'll be people and supplies."

"Don't get too ahead of the game, Gemma," replies Briar. "No matter what we find, we still need to be cautious." Gemma gives a nod as Arick pulls out the compass. Ian takes it and holds it out toward the spec on the horizon.

"Let's follow the compass north," he says. "Even though we may lose the river for a time.

"But following the river seems safer," adds Briar with a scowl. Ian looks towards the horizon, contemplating. He has an answer quickly.

"Let's do both," he says. "I know my way around some of these areas, not well, but I have done some traveling. We'll pass through Sector Two and if we can find a road north, it will eventually lead to a hub. We'll keep our eyes on the river as long as we can but at some point, we may have to make a tough decision."

"Great," huffs Rory. "Just add another month, why not two? As long as we make it to some hub who the hell cares?" Briar turns on him in an instant.

"At this point you should just feel lucky that we haven't ditched your ass," she says. She looks at Ian and adds, "I trust you."

We gather our packs, ready to find out what the speck is ahead of us.

"It's getting hot again," says Gemma as we walk. I turn to her.

"I have an idea." She looks at me questioningly. "How about the second we find a pool of water; we go for a swim?" Gemma's face lights up. I'm not sure if it's the idea of cooling down or the thought of doing something normal that makes her happy. Probably both. Maybe it's cruel to dangle it in front of her but it's worth it if it helps her go on.

Arick comes up to walk with us. "Count me in too," he says with a smile.

There is nothing good in this empty desolate place, I think

as we walk towards what I hope will be better. Even the smallest things, like food and my comfy bed, seem huge now. I miss my mother and wonder how she dealt with all the disappointment in her life, how she found the strength to drag herself out of such difficult times.

When my Dad left, everything fell apart. I was too young to understand. I woke up one morning and found my mother lying on her bed sobbing. I had never seen her cry like that, a deep, guttural, aching sound. I was so afraid. I climbed into bed with her, curling up in the small space of her arms, clinging to her, stroking her hair with my tiny hands.

"Momma, what's wrong?" She couldn't answer me, so I kept asking but she wouldn't stop crying. Eventually, I left the room and wandered into the hallway and then into the kitchen. I noticed the meal containers had arrived. As I looked long at the unassuming foil containers, it all struck me that it would be up to me, that maybe I could make things better by taking care of her. I made my hands busy by taking out the white linen cloth and spreading it across the table. I retrieved the good earthenware that we rarely used and transferred the morning meal onto them. I filled the drinking glasses with water and put everything out just like a holiday meal. When I went back to her bedroom, I gently pulled on my mother's hand. I'll never forget her eyes, leaking with never-ending tears, red and puffy. She saw me then, really saw me, realizing that I was there, seeing it all and, for a second, something snapped back into place.

"It's time to eat, Momma," I said, softly.

"Wren...I'm so sorry," she replied as she wiped away the tears. "Of course, we should eat." She saw the table and all the work that I had put into preparing the meal and she told me that I had done a good job. Then I noticed a hardness in her eyes, and she didn't mince words in telling me what had happened.

"Your father is gone," she said firmly. "He's decided to live with a new partner now."

Innocently, I asked,

"When will he be home?"

"He won't be coming home. He won't be living here anymore," she replied coldly.

Of course, the explanation came once I met Sonja. Years later it was easy to see the attraction. Sonja had ten years of youth on mom but there was more. She had a real enthusiasm for life, an excitement and spark that come from just being alive. I couldn't help think that my mom would have been more like Sonja had she followed her dreams. I don't think she ever recovered from that heartbreak, not really. She was always a shell of herself, hard but broken.

The speck in the distance grows the further we walk and soon we can see the outline of buildings, some fallen, others tall and strong. The sand beneath my feet becomes more compact and slowly a perceivable color change takes place as the sand begins to disperse, leaving open areas of black concrete. The old roads and sidewalks are mostly hidden under what has burned but occasionally I see reminders of what once was. We enter the city over a small bridge that arches over the riverbed. Still no water. But the buildings tower above us like sentinels of the lost souls that once inhabited it. Our eyes wander, taking it all in greedily. There are so many things here that are reminders of what we've lost. Just having a roof over my head would be awesome, but I also notice the old electric tracks and a lone train car resting on its side, unusable. The parks and trees and grass have disappeared, but several metal benches mark out where they once were, probably full of yelling children at one time. I can imagine a bustling city, full of hover cars and people, living in these tall skyscrapers, working in the many buildings, buildings that now are no more than piles of rubble. Those that survived look out through empty eyes, the windows smashed, the victim of time and disrepair. The grey sand has infringed over everything but has not yet taken over.

"Wow," says Arick. "Some city." I'm not sure if he is being sarcastic because it really is magnificent, even now. I feel encased in its metal structures, somehow rescued from the gray we are leaving behind.

"How could all of this survive?" I ask in awe.

"Maybe the tall structures helped," says Ian. "Possibly the flare was more intense in some areas. There could be parts of sectors left whole."

"Well, let's check it out," says Briar. "But don't get too comfortable. We don't know what's living here."

CHAPTER SIXTEEN

Aiden

The golden sand is slowly turning to gray, a reminder of everything we've lost. We are walking on the ashes of what used to be, homes, trees, people. It's so, so depressing and I have to choke back a lump in my throat. The only comfort I get is knowing that the government banks are located away from populated towns, isolated and protected.

"There it is." Says Raven as she stops to drink some water. I can feel the sweat from the day running down my back and my jumpsuit sticking to my skin. The sun has crossed over us and the shadows of our bodies begin to play on the sand. There's still plenty of daylight, time to figure out what's going on.

"It looks deserted," says Spencer. He looks exhausted, rough around the edges, but it makes me smile. This kid really gives a good effort for being a computer geek. I glance to the structure buried in the sand like a huge alien pod, ancient and weathered with time. The steel shutters still cover the windows and the front entrance is piled with sand.

"Let's find the emergency exit," I say, and we make our way to the back of the structure. This government bank is very similar to ours; a rounded one-story structure reinforced with steel. When all four of our chambers became occupied, the building sealed itself, a kind of built in fortress triggered for added protection. Once our bodies went into revival mode, the emergency exit was prompted, allowing for our escape. The thought of being frozen and thawed like a piece of meat makes me sick, but it saved our lives. Of course, now I know that months before we awoke, there were people watching, getting us ready for what was ahead, leaving supplies and monitoring our vitals. Now I know the truth, but I remember the complete terror of waking up in that tank, the fear of what was outside of that emergency exit door.

"Here," says Raven as she finds the door and grips the handle firmly. She shoves her whole body into it and the metal creeks open readily.

"Whoa," says Spencer as we step inside. The common room is deserted and as Raven closes the door the space feels hollow like I've just stepped into an empty soup can. The room is small but lavish with oversized leather chairs perched around glass tables, all covered with dust. The halo screen hoovers above a round desk in the corner, emitting a green glow. That's encouraging. It means that one of the survivors has activated it and most likely has downloaded instructions to their hub.

Our feet slide over the carpet that is covered with a fine layer of sand. No footprints to indicate that anyone was here.

As if reading my mind Raven says,

"They probably left the exit door open when they left. It didn't seem that latched when I pushed it open." I nod but Spencer looks terrified. I have to admit, the place does give off an eerie feel. "Let's check the tanks," adds Raven as she heads to the far end of the room where the stairway is located. Spencer draws his gun causing Raven to roll her eyes for the millionth time.

"What?" he asks defiantly. "We don't know what's here. There could be wild animals from out there," he jabs the dangerous end of his gun to the exit door. "Anyone could have come in here, set up shop, digging into the supplies." I know he's thinking uncomfortably about the small group of nomads we met on our first time out. Harmless for the most part but incredibly strange. They could be unpredictable.

"First of all," replies Raven. "There are no wild animals *out there*. And who are you expecting to just drop into a cryobank? Other survivors?" She pauses briefly but Spencer doesn't answer. "If other survivors did end up here then good for them," she continues. "Some of those banks are miles and miles away. If they find their way to this bank in one piece, then they deserve to dig into the supplies." The two of them are in a stare off and so I decide to say what's on my mind.

"Listen," I say, "We need to be smart about this. I am certain that we have no idea what some of the survivors have been through. There are limited resources out here and if they have to travel with enough supplies to last weeks, well, that would be close to impossible. I can imagine that if they found a place like this, they would do anything to protect it. Desperation can turn the nicest guy into something unrecognizable. And we all know that there are more than survivors out there." Raven lets out an exasperated sigh.

"Fine," she says. "But no footprints, no disturbances of any kind, the door unlocked? Fine." She pulls her gun from her pack, but I notice that she doesn't take the safety off. Our feet hit the metal stairs, taking us down several floors under ground. I can feel the sudden change in air temperature, and I marvel at the efficiency of the generators, pumping in the filtered air that turns cold as it is protected by the earth. I'd love to get my hands on one of those machines, take it apart and see how it works, maybe even make it better if that's possible. Raven pushes through the doorway leading to the crytank apartments. Just like in our bank there are four, two doors on each side of the hallway, each open exposing the rich decor inside. It is quiet and, although the apartments are adorned with large plush beds and comfortable sitting areas, the place feels like a tomb.

"I'll take this side and you two take that side," says Raven as she enters the room closest. "Check around and see if they left anything behind, papers or something to indicate which direction they went." I let Spencer take the room across from Raven's and I walk down the hallway to the other one. As I enter, the first thing that I notice is the lack of anything personal. There are no clothes piled on the large queen-sized bed to indicate that anyone has changed into the tan jumpsuit. My eyes roam the area and I spy the familiar tan fabric folded neatly on the shelves above the dark marble sink. That's odd. The only reason for there to be a jumpsuit here at all is if someone had activated the cryo-tube. I take a tentative step towards the metal tube that rests on its platform in the corner of the room and peer inside. I don't want to see the frozen limbs or blue lips of a corpse floating in viscous liquid and, luckily, I don't. I search for other signs of habitation. The bed is neatly made but there are tell-tale signs that someone has used it; sheets untucked below the deep brown brocade comforter, a slight indentation in the pillow. My eyes flick to the waste receptacle located next to the sink where I see a glint of sliver, empty food packs along with an empty water bottle. It's clear that whoever was here has made an effort to keep the place looking unlived in. I take a step back from the sink and turn towards the small sitting area, hoping to find something of interest, a note or personal item, and that's when I hear it, a shuffling sound. It's coming from somewhere close. Shit, why didn't I pull my gun out when I had a chance. I turn my back toward the sound and walk to the doorway, feigning my exit. I hear the subtle movement again and this time I'm sure that it's coming from the sink area. As I glance back over my shoulder, I notice the cupboards under the sink. It's big enough to hide under. It would be a tight fit for me but for a smaller person it would be perfect. And the truth is, it doesn't matter how small the person is hiding under that sink, if they have a gun barrel pointed at my head. I have to think fast. Chances are, whoever it is, can't see me, only hear my movements around the room. Whoever is in there will have to react to being discovered and I'll have the advantage of surprise on my side. I remove the safety from my gun as quietly as I can but it still makes a loud click, so I throw open the cupboard door without hesitation, pointing my weapon at the small opening under the sink.

"Get away from me!" I hear the voice before I see the face and I immediately register female. I peer over the counter and see her, small and wild, her slight body curved in a U as she tries to avoid the piping under the sink.

"Get away from me, I said! Don't you speak English?" She

thrusts a sharp-looking weapon towards me but it only cuts through the open air. I lower my gun and sigh with relief, trying to stifle a laugh.

"Do you really think you're going to stab me with that thing?" I ask, looking at the old rusty screwdriver that she holds in her hand.

"I'm not afraid to use this thing," she says, her voice full of fear. I can see her hand shaking, the screwdriver dancing all around. Now I feel bad but also extremely curious.

"Look," I say, more softly now. "The only thing you're going to do with that thing is give yourself tetanus." I hear footsteps and the sound of Raven's voice as she talks with Spencer out in the hallway. Her head peeks around the doorway as she says,

"Find anything?" Her black eyes widen. "Who the hell is that?" We all just stand there, Spencer with his mouth hanging open, Raven glaring in the girl's direction, and the girl, her pale, terrified eyes hopping from each of us in turn, waiting for our next move.

CHAPTER SEVENTEEN

Wren

The city is deserted but for the buildings and the remains of old trains with their depots. The hover cars also sit abandoned and it only takes a few minutes for us to discover that there is nothing to salvage within them. Broken glass, and other debris from lives past, crunch under our feet. It is an eerie place with no sound but the whistling of the wind through open frames. Still, I can't shake the feeling that we are being watched, scouted from one of those apartment buildings that touch the hazy sky. We stay close to the river, gazing up at the steel that at one time had a great view of the water below.

"There's no one here," says Rory as if trying to contradict Briar's previous warnings of caution.

"Shut it, Rory," she hisses in turn. "We've been here a second, it's too soon to know what we're walking into." As we walk deeper into the city's heart, the buildings sit closer together and the wind picks up, rushing down the closed space of the streets like a cyclone, lifting sand and small bits of rubble into our eyes.

I move my backpack to my face to protect my vision when Ian yells, "Let's get inside quickly!" Briar leads us to one of the taller buildings in the center of the block and we follow.

"This place doesn't look too bad," says Arick. I glance around the space. It is open, with a tall ceiling and remnants of what must have been fancy chandeliers dangling precariously above. Everything is covered with layers of dust and much of the interior has faded away. There is a desk near the door and a few chairs scattered across the large sitting area but nothing more, nothing of real value. Suddenly I hear a noise like the hum of a hover car, low and consistent. I hold my hand up.

"Shhh," I say. "Does anyone hear that?" I see Gemma's eyes arch in question while Briar takes a few tentative steps towards the lofty staircase at the back of the room. For a second, I think it must be a generator and my hopes for electricity soar. Then I see it, crouched at the top of the staircase, a mass of muscle and matted black fur. Its face is scrunched up and I can't tell if this is a wild dog or something else, something more deadly. There's no mistaking the sharp fangs slathered with saliva, though, or the protracted claws, ready for ripping. The hum of its growl begins to become louder, threatening. Its yellow eyes scan us as if making the decision for fight or flight. Before I can put a name to it, the creature leaps, soaring down the steps with a snarl that would terrify the dead. Gemma lets lose a scream as I try to follow the thing with my eyes, but it's fast, too fast, and before any of us can react it's on Ian, pulling him by the leg into a dark corner, lashing his body back and forth, teeth digging deep into flesh. I hear him moan in pain as Arick holds Gemma and Rory runs for the door. I stand stock still, shocked, my mind rolling a mile a minute but my body unable to react. An ear-spitting bang erupts through the room, reverberating off the walls and high ceiling. I look to Ian and see the creature fall to the floor, a bullet hole between its eyes, a pillar of dust exploding in its wake.

"Great shot," says Ian with a shaky voice. Behind me stands Briar, steady, feet shoulder-width apart, a small black gun gripped in her hands. She holds her aim as she walks slowly towards the beast that Ian has now tried to kick away.

"Thanks," she replies, her voice as steady as her hands. "Are you okay?" He is covered in perspiration and it appears as if this thing, this animal, has attempted to gnaw off the bottom part of his leg and made some progress.

"I...I'm alive," he sputters. Briar nudges the beast with her shoe, and it doesn't move. Nothing could survive a shot like that.

"What is it?" asks Gemma in a small shaky voice as she continues to huddle in Arick's arms. He leaves her to examine the animal. I notice Rory's head peek in around the doorway. Ian is digging through his backpack with unsteady hands, retrieving his first aid kit.

"I've never seen anything like it." Says Arick as he hunches over to get a better view. "Not even in the cloning labs." Even in death the beast is terrifying, it's yellow eyes wide open with pupils like a wild cat. Its fur is thick, black and stained with blood around its stubby muzzle. Its thick limbs give a hint to the power it has, especially for leaping and running. It's a cross between a giant dog and mountain lion only much more vicious and angrier.

"The canines suggest a dog," says Arick as he lifts the foaming lip of the animal to reveal its dagger-like teeth. My stomach gives a lurch as I watch saliva mixed with Ian's blood ooze out. "But this animal is designed for killing." He pauses, glancing over the rest of the animal, lifting its arms and legs, and examining its underbelly. "It's possible that this could be the result of mutation over time, especially with the radiation that I'm sure was in the atmosphere."

"What, are you some kind of animal geneticists?" asks Briar in awe.

"Yep," replies Arick. "Genetic cloning before all of this."

"Can we eat it?" We all turn to Rory in disgust. He shrugs his shoulders.

"What? It's meat and we need food," he says defensively. Nobody's talking about the real elephant in the room, Briar's gun. We are all thinking the same thing, thank God, as she tucks it back into her pack.

"I think we better wait on a barbeque," replies Arick as he grabs the animal by the front legs. "This guy could be contaminated, rabid. It's definitely a carnivore and it had to survive on something. They'll be other animals out there." He drags it a few feet and then adds, "Here, help me move it outside." Begrudgingly, Rory moves to help pull. Gemma walks to where Ian sits, applying some kind of gel to his injured leg and covering it with a thick flesh-toned bandage. He pulls a packet of red pills from his pack and takes them without water.

"How is it?" she asks, her eyes are full of concern.

"Not bad," he replies with a small smile. "It will heal."

"Can we do anything to help?" I ask, studying his face. I know that he has to be in extreme pain."

"No, I'm good. The medicine will take care of the pain and

infection."

"You sound like you've been bitten by a rabid dog before," I say jokingly.

"First time, believe it or not." He offers me a small smile before wincing as he tries to stand. As Arick and Rory return, Ian continues, "I think we better scout out the building, just in case."

"Yeah," replies Arick. "If they're anything like other canines, I'm pretty sure those mutts travel in packs. I would be surprised if there weren't more. Briar, are you ready?" He turns his head to her, nodding at her gun. I think of my own gun tucked away, but I hesitate to pull it out. I'm not ready, not even for those foul creatures.

"Briar and I will go check out the upper floors," says Arick. "See if you can get those front doors closed and barricaded," he says to Rory. Briar takes the second gun from her pack and hands it to Arick. He takes it readily.

"Thanks," he says in amazement. "What else do you have hidden in there? Because if you've got a turkey dinner, I'm ready for that too."

She laughs. "I wish."

Together, Rory and I are able to close the heavy glass doors. They scream on their hinges and slide jaggedly over years of broken glass and rubble, but they close. We search around and find an old rotting plank of thick compressed wood that has dislodged from the old desk at the entrance and slide it through the handles in the doors. It's secure enough to put me at ease, for now. I check on Ian who seems to be remarkably resilient. He's already up and hobbling around, helping us search the area for other holes and crevasses where animals could hide. Rory pries open the elevator doors revealing a long deep shaft devoid of any cars. It's a death trap.

Suddenly we hear a gun shot from above followed by three more. My eyes meet Gemma's and I see the fear deep within her.

"It's okay," I say soothingly. "It just means they found the rest of them, that's all." She nods in agreement.

"I think we got most of the Mutts. That's what we're calling them due to the obvious. They are definitely a mix of something," comes Briar's voice from the top of the stairs. She stands next to a pile of fur, black, and brown and roan. There are eyes, yellow cat-like eyes staring back at me, crazy, evil mutated eyes that would swallow me up if they could, but they are dead. Arick drags another body from the hallway, adds it to the pile as Briar begins to kick them down the stairs. Their lifeless bodies thump down each stair and leave a trail of blood behind, splattering the carpet with streaks of crimson.

"Get the door," says Briar. It's a command and I follow, pulling the heavy plank from its resting place and helping Rory open one door just enough to get the bodies out. Then we seal ourselves in again, hoping that Briar and Arick really did get them all.

"We found a good apartment on the third floor," says Arick as he wipes his hands on his pants. "It's big and there are beds and maybe some supplies, plus there's a lock on the door."

"Let's check it out," I say, eager to put myself in a smaller space, somewhere that I can feel secure.

"Can you make it up the stairs, Ian," asks Gemma.

"No problem," he replies. I move towards him, offering my shoulder to lean on. Rory is already at the top of the first staircase but has to wait for Briar to show him the way. The irritation shows all over his face.

"Let's go," says Briar as we all reach the top. She leads us to another set of stairs, stairs hidden at the end of the hall that were once used as an emergency exit. We ascend, our footfalls clanking on metal, echoing off concrete walls.

"How high up did you guys go?" asks Ian. "Can we be sure that there aren't more, what did you call them... Mutts higher up?"

"No, we can't be sure," replies Briar. "But we'll hear them coming. They aren't the stealthiest animals."

As we walk down the hallways of the third floor, there is a stillness that envelops us. Dust, urine and a sweet rotting odor accost my nose and I almost gag. There are scratch marks on the walls and parts of the carpeting have been pulled away from the floor in jagged strips. Doors line the hallways, each with a number. Several of them are flung open, rooms torn apart and wasted.

"Here it is," says Arick as we reach the end of the hallway. The digital pad that was most likely used for entry has been ripped from below the door handle, but the door is closed securely. Arick slowly turns the handle and pushes it open. We all hesitate, but then Briar pushes through and we follow. "Not too bad," continues Arick as he sits down on an old worn sofa. It's not bad. The main room is large and though it is covered in dust, at least there is no scent of urine. Tall windows overlook the devastated street below and they are remarkably unbroken. There is a small kitchen that appears to have been ransacked and cabinets with doors thrown open. Still there might be something of value there. The sofa is pale green and is accompanied by matching armchairs with sagging cushions. As I explore the other rooms, I discover three bedrooms, one with two twin beds and the others each with one larger bed all just dirty mattresses on a frame but it's better than where

I was last night. There's one bathroom across the hallway from the bedrooms. Oh, if there was only running water, I think, as I gaze longingly at the large jetted tub. The Insta-cloth scent from this morning has long since worn off. The sound of clanging metal comes from the other room and I walk back to where Arick and Briar sit on the sofa. Ian has taken refuge in one of the chairs, his foot propped up on a small coffee table. It's only the frame, the glass completely gone.

Rory has managed to make an even bigger mess of the kitchen and I join him there just to keep him under control.

"Find anything?" I ask, wiping the dirty countertop with my hand. "Yuck." My reflexes kick in and I instinctively reach to turn on the sink faucet and then stop myself. Rory sees and gives he a scowl. "I guess that was stupid," I say.

"No shit, Sherlock," he replies with disgust. What a jerk. "There's nothing here," he continues as he flips open another cabinet. This time there is something there. A stack of pots and pans.

"We might be able to use those if we do find food," I say, fantasizing about juicy pieces of meat frying up in cast-iron pans. It's strange to think of food that way. I've never cooked a meal in my life. Having fresh meals delivered in foil pans seems like such a luxury now.

"They're too heavy," he replies as if I'm the stupidest person he's ever met.

"You know, I'm just trying to help." I say with irritation. "And they're not all heavy."

"What's this?" he says, ignoring my outrage. He pulls out two large cans. They are heavy and covered in grime. I shake one and hear liquid inside.

"What is it?" asks Briar who peeks into the kitchen curiously.

"I'm not sure," I reply. Rory takes the cans and sets them on the small dining table next to the living space where Ian, Arick and Gemma can see.

"What do you think is inside?" asks Gemma as she tries to whip the coating of dust away. "Look, there's a label." I see the paper sleeve on the can, but it's faded and peeled so that any writing that might have been there at one time is now gone.

"It's probably food," says Rory as he shakes his can gently. I know that there are some foods that come in cans, but I have never seen any. Meals delivered to us fresh by the government, ready to be heated and eaten makes eating something out of a can seems strange. But if it's something good, I'm going for it. Even if it's not something good, I'm going for it. And then I realize that none of us knows how to open the cans and my hopes are momentarily dashed. Briar lets out a sigh of exasperation as she watches Rory bang one of the cans against the table. She grabs it away roughly.

"Watch and learn," she says as she takes a short, thick knife from her bag. Carefully she inserts the tip into the top edge and pushes down until it penetrates the metal, leaving a nice sized slit. Juices spill over the side and she continues this process until she can cautiously lift the lid away. I put my nose over the opened can and sniff. It's something sweet, possibly fruit and I feel my stomach give a rumble. Briar dips a grubby finger into the liquid and pulls out a chunk of something deep orange and brown and pops it into her mouth.

"Peaches," she says thickly as she chews. Tonight we have a treat to go along with our freeze-dried meals. As I take my portion and feel the slimy, sweet flesh coat my tongue, I'm grateful. Who knows how many finds like this we'll come across? We may as well enjoy them when we can.

"We should camp out here for a few days," says Briar. "There might be more food and supplies in some of the other apartments, plus Ian's leg needs time to heal." She smiles at him encouragingly, but I know that she's thinking about how far we still have to go. Gemma and I share the bedroom with the twin beds while Ian and Arick insist that they will be fine sharing one of the rooms. Rory glances to Briar with narrowed eyes.

"I suppose I get the nice soft comfy sofa," he says.

"You're lucky you're here at all," replies Briar as she heads into her bedroom slamming the door behind her.

CHAPTER EIGHTEEN

Aiden

"Now what?" asks Raven, breaking the silence. The girl in the cupboard is still waving the screwdriver frantically but she's not talking anymore.

"What did you guys find?" I ask, completely ignoring her. It's clear that she's not a threat even if I am still curious about her.

"The other three apartments show signs of being used so I'm assuming that's our officials," replies Raven, also deciding to ignore the girl in the cupboard and her flailing screwdriver. "Jumpsuits gone, beds slept in, a few toiletries scattered around."

"I found this!" exclaims Spencer, holding up a small piece of paper with a grin. "It's got Donovan's name on it."

"It's a manifest," says Raven with disgust. "A short one with bios of the three officials. It's basically worthless, the same information that we already have."

"Well, I'm keeping it," replies Spencer. He smooths the wrinkled paper on his chest and folds it into a neat square. Raven looks away, shaking her head.

"Chances are they used the halo screen to print the manifest out along with a map and their instructions," she says. "We can assume that they made a plan and left. These guys are too smart to hang around."

"Who are you?" Her voice is little more than a whisper, but it catches our attention and our eyes snap to the girl under the sink.

"We're survivors, like you," says Raven, an edge to her voice. She's not the maternal type and she won't mess around, not even with a seemingly innocent girl.

"Did you come to rescue me?" Raven looks at me, and I give her a shrug.

"Well, I guess that depends," she replies. The girl begins to dislodge herself from the cramped space, dropping the screwdriver with a clatter. Soon, she is standing before us, short, slight and pale, her white-blond hair flying in every direction around her delicate face. Though she's small, she's not as young as I thought. I can see it in her eyes, confidence in her features that clearly say, *don't screw with me*. Take her out of this fear-driven scene and she might be an asset. Raven sees it too.

"What's your name," she asks, the military tone back into her voice. The girl's pale eyes meet Raven's and she stands a little taller. They are opposites, Raven tall and dark and the girl, slight and pallid, but something snaps into place between them and they seem to come to an understanding. I'll respect you if you'll respect me.

"Jewel, my name is Jewel Marks."

"Where do you come from?" Jewel looks around the room in

confusion.

"From here," she replies. "I mean, this room. This is my cryotank." She blinks twice and I know that she's not being completely honest. Raven doesn't skip a beat.

"How is it that you were fortunate enough to end up in a government bank? Why didn't you leave with the others? Who are your parents?" I can see the wheels turning in Jewel's head. Raven has bombarded her with questions, not giving her a chance to come up with new lies.

"I, I didn't see anyone else," Jewel replies nervously. Spencer takes a seat in one of the large leather chairs and lays his gun down on the glass table with a clank. The sound catches Jewel's attention and her eyes snap to the table. Spencer notices it too and slowly retrieves the gun and sets it protectively on his lap.

"You have to be honest with us," says Raven. "If we can't trust you then you're not coming with us and I'm telling you now, no one else is coming to get you."

"Okay, okay, I'll tell you everything, please just put your guns away." Raven tucks her weapon into the back of her pants and gives Spencer a nod. I return my own gun back into my pack, happily.

"Better?" asks Raven. "Now it's your turn." Jewel takes a deep breath.

"My name is Jewel Marks and I come from Sector Three but I'm assuming that's gone now."

"Go on," says Raven, all business.

"When the flare hit, I was at my grandparent's house in Sector Two. My grandmother had a government connection, an old friend who owed her a favor, I guess, so she brought me here in a government issued car." She spreads her arms wide and adds,

"I guess this is that favor repaid.

"Wow, that connection must have owed your grandmother big time," says Spencer. Jewel is standing with her eyes downcast.

"Yeah," she says softly. "Some favor." When she looks up again, I notice that she is on the verge of tears. I get it; she's the sole survivor and that carries a huge bundle of guilt. We've all felt it.

"When were you revived," asks Raven, ignoring the tears.

"Yesterday." Jewel swats away the tears angrily. "But there wasn't anyone else here. I checked the other apartments and they were empty and then upstairs, there was no one."

"Okay," says Raven. "How about when you arrived at the bank? Did you see anyone else, any officials or adults that looked important?"

"No," she replies solemnly. "When I got here it was chaos outside. I didn't think my car would make it through all the people. It was horrible. Then when I got into the bank all the other apartment doors were shut, only this one remained open. Once I stepped inside, the entire place sealed itself shut and that was it." The same safety measures employed in our bank. "Look," continues Jewel, sadness covering her face. "I don't feel good about this. I survived but I took someone else's life when I walked into this room."

"We all feel that way," I say. "But you can't think about the past."

"Just don't throw away your second chance," adds Raven. "Make it count." Jewel nods and takes a big breath.

"Well, I'm guessing that since you were the last to arrive, you were probably the last to be revived. I think your timetable was probably out of whack since the tank wasn't really yours." Raven's words carry a sting but she's just trying to get the facts right.

"So, what's the plan?" asks Spencer.

"We need to make some decisions," says Raven as she glances around the room. I pull out my tablet and see the bright blinking sequence of numbers indicating the time as well as the hours spent in our mission. We've been in the wild for a little over six hours. Raven catches a glimpse.

"It's getting late in the day," she says. "We've got maybe four more hours of daylight and I don't want to be exposed out there in the dark."

"Agreed," says Spencer a little too enthusiastically. I'm sure he wouldn't mind camping out here for the night. The longer we stay in one place, though, the less chance we have of completing our mission successfully.

"Let's do a quick sweep of the building," says Raven. "Maybe we can find a clue to which direction the officials went, get a handle of where they would be right now."

"Spencer, want to go play around on the halo screen upstairs?" I ask with a smile. Of course he does. "Let's see if you can get a copy of their map and any instructions they were given." He gives a nod. "Raven and I will see if we can hunt down supplies."

"There's a storage room next to the stairs," says Jewel. "I took some things this morning."

"Okay," says Raven. "Let's get to it."

The storage room is loaded with things we already have; foil pouches of freeze-dried meals, additional bottled water, first-aid stuff and toiletries. We each add water to our packs to replace those that are gone and dig into the meal packs, taking a few extra. Jewel is hesitant to take anything so Raven tosses her a backpack commanding her to fill it with enough supplies to last for a few days. Once Raven is done, she takes Jewel to help scour the other rooms while I help myself to as many more meal packs and water that I can carry. The extra food should carry me though for a while once I leave the others behind.

"I got it!" I can hear Spencer pounding down the metal staircase. He bursts into the hallway. "I found the manifest in a corrupt file on the halo screen." He holds up a piece of paper. "It was pretty easy to access. Jewel, your name isn't on the updated list," he adds. "They probably didn't even know you were here." She looks away, casting her eyes to the ground. "I was able to print out the instructions along with a map," he continues. He hands the map over to Raven. "It looks like they were smarter than we gave them credit." Spencer pauses. "Well, I mean, Donovan's a frickin' genius but I don't know about the other two." Raven glances over the map. I come up behind her to look over her shoulder.

"It looks like they've made their own adjustments," she says, thoughtfully. I see it too. The original instructions took them north, just as we suspected, leading them in a direct path to the hub. The new map deviates east, but only slightly.

"They must be planning to skirt the mountains to the east. It takes them totally out of the way for miles," I say. "Do you think they were told about the obstacle?"

"I don't know, but either way, it should be easier to find them now."

"I hope they're okay," says Jewel softly. We all turn our eyes to her small, slender form leaning against the wall. She has no idea what is on the outside, no way of knowing what it will be like once we leave. Will she be strong enough?

"They've been gone roughly seventy-two hours," I say. "They should have plenty of supplies with them."

"Yeah, they'll be okay," echoes Spencer with confidence.

"I think we better head out this afternoon," says Raven. "We can make camp once we hit the mountain. If we keep up a good pace, we should make it there in a few hours."

"Great," says Spencer sarcastically under his breath. Raven's plan works out in my favor, though. When we reach the mountain, we'll head east and that will put me perpendicular to my old sector and closer to Wren.

"I hope we find them quickly," says Spencer as he begins to reorganize his pack. "I'm not looking forward to a night on the cold hard ground." Raven looks up from the map.

"Oh, poor baby," she coos. "Is the little bitty mission getting too hard for you?" Spencer gives her a steely glare, causing her lips to turn up at the corners. "Stop complaining," she adds. "You'll be back in your comfy warm bed soon enough."

CHAPTER NINETEEN

Wren

"So, what should we do today?" asks Rory as he digs into breakfast. We should have saved the peaches for the morning because Mac and Cheese this early is tough. Rory seems okay with it though. We all gather around the small dining table; Gemma's wild ethereal hair is a halo around her head. It was nice sleeping in a bed.

"I say we start searching the other apartments as soon as we can," says Briar. "I'd love to find a few more of those cans." She takes a sip of water. "How's your leg," she adds to Ian.

"It's fine," he replies. "Almost like new." I know that this can't be true when last night, as I watched him change the bandage, the wound was an angry open gash. He's trying to be strong and I admire that.

"I want to search the other apartments too," says Rory. "There's got to be other stuff stashed away somewhere."

"Yeah, more Mutts stashed under the beds," counters Briar.

"So, give me your gun," he says. My eyes flick to Briar as she considers this and then she lets out a laugh, shaking her head from side to side.

"Right," she replies. "Like I'm going to trust you with a weapon. What's going to stop you from shooting all of us to take our food?" Rory gives a huff and looks away.

"I'll go with him," says Arick as he takes his last bite of Spaghetti. He gives a sigh of contentment. "That was excellent! If only I could have Spaghetti again for dinner." He pulls a sad face and then says with mock excitement, "Oh, yeah, that's right, I can!" We all laugh, all except Rory who pushes from the table in disgust.

"Okay," says Ian. "One more night here and then we're off. We've got a long road ahead of us." The idea of sleeping again on a soft mattress makes me smile and I turn to Gemma.

"What do you want to do today?"

"Maybe Arick and Rory will leave this floor for us to explore," she says shyly. Arick hears and rests a hand on her head.

"No problem," he says. "We'll check for Mutts and then you can hunt for something good, maybe more peaches." He smooths the wild wisps of hair from her face just like a father would. "Rory and I may take a short trip outside as well. I want to see where the main road leads."

"Fine," says Briar. "I'm going too." Briar hands over one of her spare guns to Arick once again and they head out the door. While Ian is busy tending to his wound, I pull Gemma aside.

"We have to be careful, okay?" Gemma nods. "If there's any sign that something doesn't feel right, we have to come back." She nods again. I can see the excitement in her face, the idea of a treasure hunt with the anticipation of finding a toy at the end. After she has finished her breakfast and has used some of the toothpaste form her small bag of supplies, we get the all clear from Arick.

"Okay, let's go." I tuck my short knife into the pocket on my thigh, just in case.

The apartment next door is trashed and it's clear that it has been a lair for Mutts at some point. The furnishings are torn apart, pillows devoid of stuffing and the mattresses shredded and full of urine. As we move down the hallway, we stop at a closed door several spaces down from ours.

"Let's give it a try," I say as Gemma turns the door handle. We walk into a dusty but pristine living room suited up with rich, fancy furniture and matching drapes. The dining table is made of glass and light from the filthy windows tries vainly to reflect off its surface. The space has a feeling of wealth. Even the watercolor paintings that adorn the walls are lovely, their bright hues not completely dulled by time and dust.

"Wow," says Gemma as we close the door behind us. "I would love to live here."

"Maybe before the flare," I say. "I think it needs running water at the very least." This gets a laugh and we immediately begin to explore. We hit the jackpot when we find two musty sleeping bags in one of the bedroom closets. They are rolled tight and light enough to carry. At least two of us will be warm. We find other things of interest, a gold-plated box with jeweled rings and silver necklaces. I want to take something from it, but it feels wrong, so I tuck the box back in the drawer where we found it. Everything we find paints a picture of those who lived here. There are clothes still hanging in the closets, but they are elaborate, not like the plain gray clothes that I used to wear and not at all practical for us. A wooden box of toys, story books on a shelf, and a large plush bear indicate a child's room. A halo screen hangs in the family room as well but, of course, it doesn't work. I wonder if this family is somewhere else, perhaps at a cryobank; maybe they are making a similar journey. It certainly looks like they could afford tanks. Gemma and I spend a long time in this apartment, searching through all the personal possessions but there isn't much to take. I think we really stay because the place feels like home, maybe not our home, but someone's.

"Let's go show Ian the sleeping bags," I say as we flip through the children's books. I think we did pretty good.

"Okay," she replies, and we tuck our treasures under our arms.

Ian is asleep when we get back. I spend time looking out of the tall windows, searching the street for anything or anyone. The front door burst open, banging against the wall behind it and jolting Ian from his slumber. Gemma comes running in from the bedroom that we share just as Briar comes rushing in with Arick and Rory behind. They drop a load of something on the floor and slam the door shut, locking it.

"What happened?" I ask with concern. Briar has her back against the wall, hunched over, gasping for breath. I notice the gun handle protruding from her hip pocket.

"Was it Mutts again?" I ask taking a step towards her, searching for visible injuries.

"No, no..." she says as she tries to get enough air into her lungs. Rory has thrown himself onto the floor. His face is bright red and his breaths come quick and sharp. Arick takes a heavy seat in one of the armchairs.

"Not Mutts," he says with wide eyes. "People. We saw people." His words cause Ian to sit up taller as he glances to Arick and then to Briar.

"Could they have been other cryobank survivors?" he asks.

"We don't think so," replies Arick. "They were…different." He casts a glance at Briar and they share a moment of understanding. I don't know why but the way they look at each other makes my stomach tense.

"Tell us everything," says Ian sternly. It's good to hear the authority in his voice. His deep blue eyes spark with intensity and it's attractive, making me feel safe. Briar has finally caught her breath and she moves to sit on the floor by Rory.

"We went down to the second floor and started going through the apartments. We found some good stuff, more canned food and blankets and even rope." She points to the pile next to the door. "Then we decided to go outside and look for the best path out of the city. We made it down the main road wanting to find the river again but then we heard voices. We dashed into the first building we could find and hid. I had a good view from the busted-out windows and that's when I saw them."

"How many?" asks Ian.

"Four," replies Arick. "But it's not so much about how many as what they looked like."

"They were freaks!" hisses Rory. He sits up and wipes the sweat from his brow. "They were…almost not human." I wait for Briar to say he's overreacting, but she doesn't.

"I don't understand," says Ian. Gemma grips my arm and I feel her shaking in her skin.

"I'm telling you," says Rory with conviction. "They looked like something from a zombie movie." There is fear in his eyes and it's real, very real.

"Stop being dramatic." There's what I've been waiting for.

"They weren't zombies but there was something wrong with them. Their faces were mutated, melted almost and their behavior was reckless and loud."

"Are you certain they weren't just another squad heading to their hub?" asks Ian again. "Maybe they've been out here a long time and are injured or, I don't know, trying to make a life here."

"No," replies Arick. "They weren't survivors. They were dressed in different clothes, not jumpsuits."

"They had weapons." Briar's voice is strong again. "But I didn't see a gun. We could take them down if we had to."

"They had the Mutts," adds Rory. "They took one of the Mutts. They're going to eat it." I feel bile course up my throat, and I push it down.

"Possibly they were just passing through, looking for food and will be gone by morning," says Ian calmly.

"Could they be people from the underground caves?" I ask. We haven't really talked about that possibility or brought up the fact that people surviving after the flare might exist. It would make some sense.

"I think that's exactly right," replies Ian. "It could be that there are people living outside of the hubs, existing for years inside the caves, scavenging for food, though I've never heard of any." Mutated by high radiation levels, fighting tooth and nail to exist, and becoming primal again, I think in my head. And then I wonder about Ian's comment. How would he have heard about mutants living in the wild? Who would have told him? I glance at him questioningly and he quickly looks away.

"Well, why didn't our little halo screen message give us more details of what is out here?" asks Briar with frustration. "You'd think that they would give us an idea of the perils we might face, including crazy cave people." She lets out a sigh. "Look, we can't stay here. I say we take our chances and leave in the morning like we planned. At least we know about them now and I'll be ready if we see them." I see Rory's face fall.

"This is stupid," he yells. "Why are we risking our lives when we're perfectly safe here. There's no way they can get through the door and we have food for now."

"It won't do any good to stay," replies Briar. "What happens when you do run out of food? What about water?" Rory is shaking his head in defiance.

"This is so stupid!" he screams. "Why do you get to be the one calling the shots?" He bangs his fist against the ground. Gemma is sobbing now, more from the anger in Rory's voice than from the strangers outside.

"Stop!" comes Ian's booming voice. It shocks all of us and as I look at him he continues, "Briar, I don't suppose that you and Rory will ever be friends."

"You got that right," she replies with a sardonic laugh.

"But this bickering amoung us has to stop." He gives each of them a confirming nod. "Rory, this is not a dictatorship, but this is a democracy and majority rules. You have the right to voice your opinion, but it is the group as a whole who will decide our next move." He turns to Arick as if for conformation.

"Ian's right," he says. "If you can't get along, then just pretend like the other doesn't exist."

"Is there any chance you were seen?" asks Ian.

"No," says Arick. "They were pretty much in their own world. They seemed excited about the Mutt, not at all concerned about how it got dead. My vote is to leave tomorrow," continues Arick, earning him a glare from Rory. "Ian can lead us out and Briar can follow up behind us. Once we get out of the city, we should have an open view of what's around us and whether we need to protect ourselves. Are you ready to travel, Ian?"

"I'm good," he replies. Rory pulls himself up from the carpet and heads to a bedroom, slamming the door behind him.

"He better get over his disappointment quick," says Briar.

"He'll live," I say to Briar, knowing that there's no way he'll chose to stay here by himself.

"He'll live unless I kill him first," she replies with a sneer.

CHAPTER TWENTY

Aiden

We waste no time leaving the bank now that we have a plan. Even Spencer hurries us out the door saying,

"The sooner we get out of here, the sooner we get back to the hub and three-square meals." Jewel's first tentative steps into the wild leaves me remembering my own view of what was left, basically nothing. Her lips quiver and her eyes scan the area in disbelief, but she keeps herself together, glancing at Raven for strength. Her new jumpsuit blends in and she feels like one of us. She asks questions as we walk, and we try to answer them as best we can. Have we met many more survivors? Have any of the sectors come through the flare unscathed? I'm sure that she's wondering about her family but none of us asks her about them. She'll tell us when she's ready.

"So, what are the chances of us finding these guys before nightfall?" asks Spencer as our feet sink into the sand, step after step. We've been walking for over an hour and my neck burns with sweat and grit.

"I don't know," I reply. "I guess it's possible."

"I wouldn't get your hopes up," comments Jewel. "The simple odds of probability are against it."

"What's that supposed to mean?" asks Spencer. His forehead is beaded with perspiration that he takes a swipe at it with his sleeve. His face is bright red and he looks in danger of heat stroke.

"Well," replies Jewel. "You can measure the outcome of an event through a simple probability equation." She glances at Spencer with a smile. "You take the ratio of the number of outcomes that are favorable for an event and compare it to the total possible outcomes."

"Huh?" Jewel gives an exasperated laugh.

"Okay," she says. "There is really only one favorable outcome for your mission: that we find the officials tonight." Spencer nods. "But there are many outcomes that could happen like we won't find them tonight or that they are already back at the hub or even that they're lost somewhere else."

"Great," says Spencer sarcastically. "So, what does that mean in English?"

"It means that statistically, the odds of finding them tonight are slim, not impossible but not probable."

"How old are you, twenty-five?" asks Spencer in awe.

"Fifteen," says Jewel softly, her eyes cast down.

"Man, with a brain like that you should have already been at the university."

"I was," replies Jewel. "I mean I received my letter two weeks before the flare. I chose mathematics as my field of study."

"Impressive," I say. "That must be some kind of record."

"Yeah, I'm one of eleven students that have ever been admitted before the age of seventeen," she replies with pride. Then her face falls. "I guess that doesn't mean much now."

"I don't know," says Raven as she gives Jewel a playful nudge. "You've got a lot to offer. You'll probably end up with a great job affording you anything you want without a university degree." Jewel nods but she doesn't look convinced. I take a good look at her. She's small and shy but also fierce with a screwdriver and smart. Her blond hair sticks to the back of her neck and she struggles to keep up, but she's no different from us.

"Well, there they are," Raven's voice cuts me from my thoughts. I glance up and see the mountains cutting a jagged edge along the horizon. If we were somewhere else, anywhere else, they would be beautiful, majestic even, but not here, not in this wasteland.

"This doesn't feel right," says Spencer as he glances to his feet. "My feet keep sinking deeper into the sand. It feels weird."

"That's what sand does," replies Raven in an exasperated voice.

"No, I mean it. It feels different." Raven picks up her speed.

"Come on, walk faster and your feet won't sink so much." She's about ten yards in front of us when it happens. She lets out a low screech and then just vanishes.

"What the hell," gasps Spencer.

"Oh my God, oh my God..." I hear her voice even though I can't see her. Then I peer down into the sand. Raven's head and one arm is the only thing left of her; the rest is buried in deep quicksand. I can tell that she's struggling to get out, but it seems to only make her sink deeper. Jewel drops to the ground and begins to combat crawl, inching her way out determined to help. I grab her leg and pull her back forcefully, but I can't move her. She glances back over her shoulder in full panic mode and I see that her arms have already vanished in the sand.

"Shit!" This is bad. Could the officials have met with this. This quicksand could be our answer but also our end.

"What are we going to do?" asks Spencer. His voice is desperate.

"I don't know, give me a second." I try to pull at Jewel again but it's no use. I see her back heave with sobs of fear. The rest of Raven is slowly disappearing and, when the sand has finally made it to her lips, I hear a shuffling beside me. Spencer lurches forward like a crazy person, a look of complete determination covering his face. Raven tries to shake her head back and forth trying to tell him to stop but her mouth is in danger of being filled with sand. Amazingly, he reaches her and begins to dig away the sand from her face. He must have done a decent job because I hear Raven shout,

"You stupid idiot!"

"Shut up, I'm saving you." He continues to work frantically, digging at the sand and seems to be making progress until I see his legs sinking below the surface and I know it's a lost cause. I'm the only one left and I have absolutely no idea how to fix this, how to get us all out of this mess. My mind races, trying to land on some idea, thinking about the contents of my pack. Unfortunately, the gun tucked away won't help. I hear a sob escape Jewel's throat as Raven's body is slowly overtaken by the sand and disappears. Her hair trails behind like a black stain on the golden surface.

"No, no, damn it!" yells Spencer. Time stands still as I watch in shock and horror. What a horrible way to die, and like this, out here again on a mission. We worked so hard to get to the hub the first time and it seems like a complete waste. But before I can start to really process everything that I'm about to lose, I hear something, a voice far away.

"It's okay." A hollow sound from somewhere deep inside the earth.

"What was that?" asks Spencer as his chin hits the sand.

"It's coming from down there," says Jewel. "It's Raven, it sounds like Raven."

"Shhh," I hiss.

"It's okay, don't fight it. Just hold your breath. It'll be over in a minute." Her voice sounds otherworldly, like an angel or a spirit deep below the sand, calling us to follow. My heart races as my eyes meet Spencer's and then Jewel's. They're still panicking; Spencer's eyes flashing towards me in fear. As Jewel's head begins to sink below the surface, I see her take a deep breath and scrunch her eyes shut.

"What the hell is this?" Spencer tilts his head back as far as he can to get the words out. My eyes dart around this horrific scene, first scanning the mountain ridge in the distance. There's no one, only more sand. I turn my eyes behind, and I see a groove, a small valley made by four sets of feet trudging through the sand. It's just us out here and no one's going to save us, so I've got to go with my gut on this one.

"Don't fight it, Spence," I say, trying to make my words seem calming. "Try to relax, take a deep breath and I'll see you on the other side." His eyes go even wider but then he takes a deep breath and in an instant he's gone. Now I'm alone. God, I hope my gut is right. Without hesitation, I take the plunge and leap feet first into the slippery sand. The force of my landing pushes my body deep and before I have a chance to think about the fact that this could be a huge mistake, my head goes under and I'm trapped.

CHAPTER TWENTY-ONE

Wren

We spend our last night in the apartment, digging into the supplies that Briar and Arick retrieved on their search. A can of juice that is so sweet it makes me pucker.

"Pineapple juice," says Arick with a laugh. We can't take the food with us, so we have a feast of our normal spaghetti along with small pale potatoes and green beans from cans. The beans are salty and mushy, not like the fresh produce that I'm used to but they're tasty and at least give us all a little variety. Once the cans are devoured, Arick pulls a hidden one from the pile of blankets.

"Who want's dessert?" he asks with a grin. Gemma's eyes

light up as he tosses the can of chocolate pudding to her. Even out of a can, it's awesome and soon we are spooning up the delicious velvety goodness. I shut my eyes tight knowing that it will probably be a while until I taste something so good again. With full bellies, we turn in early and I sleep like I am home in my own bed. It's amazing what good food will do.

We leave our dwelling behind just before dawn and I turn to glance upwards at this tall structure as we hit the street. The Mutt's bodies are gone. Maybe two weeks from now those corpses will look more like Filet Mignon. That's my fear. What will I stoop to for survival, how far will any of us go? I'm learning about myself more and more and I realize that I've never really known how capable I am, how strong I am. Without hesitation, Briar pulls her guns from her pack and hands one to Ian. Rory watches with a sly grin on his face. Ian walks with a slight limp but doesn't appear to be in much pain. The streets are deserted and again, eerily quiet, but for the continuing wind whistling through the broken-down structures. The river is easy enough to find as we make our way to a long bridge that leads out of the city. Still empty and dry. There is something comforting about the river, as if even though it no longer has the element that holds life, it still lives. It winds and moves on its own, burrowing into the earth, refusing to die. We follow it north away from the city toward more unknow places. We find what was once a busy highway that makes the walk easier. The black asphalt overtakes the grey ashen sand more and more as we go, winding away from the river and then back again. From above I'm sure that the road and the river look like two serpents, weaving their way to the same destination but on different paths, meeting and then moving away and then meeting again. The taller buildings have fallen away but I notice old burned out factories and fallen hover train tracks along with dwellings. I am struck with new amazement that there are places and things that have survived. I envision the wild flames of the flare hopping from sector to sector, sparing some while destroying others, like an uninhibited tornado. But nothing is livable and every place we gaze at appears abandoned. These might be hiding places for the strangers that Arick and Briar saw, possibly even their homes if they are keeping a low profile. But we don't see any sign of them as we walk, and the tenseness that I felt when we first left the city begins to relax.

We all walk in silence with an occasional grunt as someone wipes their brow. The heat is bad again, but the sky is tinged with blue today. The haze is still there, but at least the gray is gone. The meal from last night is long gone too and my stomach begins to demand food and water. Not yet.

"What is that?" asks Arick. And we all stop, shaken out of our daydreams. My eyes follow in the general direction that he is pointing. Ian stands next to me shading his eyes from the sun.

"Well, I can't be certain," he says. "We're still too far away to tell for sure, but it looks like a house."

Our pace quickens and soon Ian's suspicions are validated. We leave the highway behind and venture onto a side street, all thought of the heat and the thirst and hunger gone. Even after hours of walking, Rory seems to have a renewed sense of energy and he begins to ramble nonstop about what we might find there.

"Maybe there's a hover car," he says excitedly. We all knock that dream down as quickly as it arrived. Anything mechanical left over from the flare would be long gone, salvaged by the government. If we didn't find anything like that in the city, we won't find it out here.

"Okay," continues Rory. "But there could be other things: tools, water, more canned food, maybe even a way to communicate with the hubs." My lips turn up into an involuntary smile thinking about more cans of food.

"It's possible," replies Arick. "It's also possible that the house is inhabited." I hadn't thought of that: the idea that there might be other people out here, living, surviving, normal non-mutated people who wouldn't even consider eating a dead monster dog.

"Listen, klepto," says Briar as the house looms closer. "If there are people living here, you can't just go in and take whatever you want, got it? This isn't like the city, not until we make sure the place is deserted." Rory's face screws up in a grimace and he glares at Briar. His beady eyes are defiant.

"I'm sure *if* someone is living here, they won't mind helping us," he replies. "I mean, look around. Anyone living out here must know how hard it is to survive."

"I'm saying that you can't expect anyone to help us," says Briar. "It's survival of the fittest. No one's going to give up their life to help a pack of strangers. We shouldn't ask for anything."

"There's also the possibility that whoever is living in that house is watching us right now with a gun pointed at us," adds Rory. "Or that they are the same as the others we saw." I feel my pack bumping against my back as we walk. I think about the gun buried at the bottom. My eyes meet Briar's and she gives me an almost imperceptible shake of the head.

"I've got this," she says as she conceals her gun into a side pocket. The bulge is a dead giveaway, but I know she's thinking the same thing. We don't want to ask for trouble if we don't need to.

As we follow the side streets away from the highway, we see

that the house before us is just one of many. They dot the winding path of the subdivision that looks very similar to the one I grew up in, only the houses are much bigger. Aiden was right about Sector Two. The house that we saw from the highway is the biggest and closest and though the grass is gone, replaced by ashen sand, the yard is vast and must have been green and lush in its day. This place is different from the city. There is a lived-in feel, not the empty feeling of the tall buildings we left behind.

"Wow," says Ian. "This is a pretty big house way out here."

We slow our pace when we are yards away. On closer inspection, the house looks weather beaten, the blue paint chipping away at the edges and the white shutters in danger of falling off. The muted, peeling colors remind me of the passage of time and homes left to themselves.

"Look, there's something out back," says Rory, pointing behind the house. It looks like a shed, painted the same color as the house and just as beaten down.

"Let's go," says Rory, He eyes the bulge in Briar's pocket and stops to let her lead the way, probably as a shield just in case. The rest of us hang back. I sweep back my ginger hair that has become loose from the braid in all the walking and roll it into a knot on the top of my head. It looks like a crown of fire out here in the sun. The back of my neck feels gritty and hot. I catch Ian watching me. We stop at the front porch and Rory turns to the rest of us.

"Well?" he yells. Slowly, Briar advances onto the porch. I can see that the front door is just as worn as the rest of the house and even the porch looks questionable as I take a tentative step forward. I give a small jump and it's sturdy enough. The door is slightly ajar.

"Hey," yells Rory. "Is anyone in there?" He nudges the door with his dusty shoe, opening a bigger gap. The door squeaks on its hinges.

"Are you out of your mind?" hisses Briar. "Are you trying to get all of us killed?" It's like being in a ghost town and, just when I am sure that no one is here, a man's voice comes from somewhere deep within.

"Hello, hello out there!" Briar whips around to look at me, her eyes wide. But before we have a chance to consider weapons, Arick steps in front, edging Rory out of the way.

"Hello," he replies in his kind, soft way. He pushes his glasses up the bridge of his nose and hitches on a smile. We hear heavy footsteps come from inside the house, down the stairs, which are just inside the door. At first, I only notice his clothes, gray canvas pants with a matching tunic, very similar to those I wore before this tan jumpsuit. My eyes travel upward, and I look into the face of an old man. His face is lined with age, and a patch of gray hair is swiped across a balding head. His pale eyes crinkle into a smile as he steps over the threshold of the doorway.

"Well, hello," he says, eyeing us warily. His tall frame blocks the doorway in a gesture of protection, and I see Rory pulling up on his tip toes, trying to get a look inside.

"My name is Arick and this is Briar, Ian and Rory and little Gemma." They all nod to the man. "And this is Wren." The old man looks at me with his pale blue eyes, eyes the color of the sky. His smile falters slightly as he notices that there's so many of us and only one of him.

"Come and sit on the porch for a while in the shade," he says. "I'll bring some cool drinks and you can rest for a bit." He enters back into the house and I see Rory's eyes follow him. The words "cool drinks" play over and over in my mind. Could he possibly have ice? The old man quickly comes back with several cushioned folding chairs and sets them up in a neat row.

"Thank you," says Arick as we all gratefully take a chair. "I don't think we got your name," he adds. But before we get an answer the old man disappears back into his house. I throw my backpack down, relieved by the momentary lightness I feel. It is much cooler on the porch, the shade makes a big difference. If only we would get some real clouds. I can hear noises coming from the house. Rory has taken the chair closest to the door and he leans over to peer in. Even in this new world, even in our own desperation, it seems rude. Briar notices too and says,

"Really, Rory?" He gives a shrug but doesn't turn away. I watch as she surreptitiously tucks the gun into her pack. The man is certainly not threatening. As soon as the old man returns, I see what he's been up to. He carries a large metal tray laden with six glasses and a huge pitcher of what appears to be lemonade. The pale, yellow liquid instantly makes my mouth gush with saliva. Who cares that there are no ice cubs clanking around the glass? He sets the tray onto a bench that is built into the porch and begins pouring out tall glasses for each of us. I take mine eagerly as Arick gives a word of thanks. As the first sip enters my mouth I pucker from the tartness. My tongue explodes from the sweet and tart and cold. The drink brings tears to my eyes. I know it's ridiculous to cry over lemonade but there is nostalgia mixed in with the lemons and sugar. I close my eyes and I can almost be sitting on my own front porch...almost. The silence lingers as glasses clink and eyes close and our thirst is satisfied.

"Thanks for this," says Briar, holding up her empty glass. "You have no idea how amazing it is." I can see from the faces around me that we all have a renewed sense of energy, even Rory. But with him, there is always the dark cover of greed playing in his eyes. That's when I notice something odd. Though the man wears the clothes of my old sector, my eyes linger on his shoes. They are tan and light weight and grippy just like mine. In fact, they are identical to all of our shoes and I know that this means that he has come from a cryobank compound.

"Oh, well, it's no problem," replies the old man with a nod to Briar. "It's just the right kind of day for lemonade." He sits back in his own chair, gazing out to the endless nowhere as if he's watching traffic go by.

"So, how long have you lived out here?" asks Ian with interest. He doesn't answer at first but takes a long sip of lemonade instead.

"It's been some time now," replies the old man vaguely.

"So, you live alone?" asks Rory.

"Hmmm," replies the old man not really giving any information. His hesitation bothers me, and I can see the wheels turning in Rory's tiny brain. Any sense of ease I have is quickly evaporating.

"So, this neighborhood," says Ian. "It looks like it wasn't even touched by the solar flare."

"Oh, well, from what I understand, there are pockets of towns and cities that were left relatively unharmed. I think it must have been the river that saved most of Sector Two but if you walk down a few blocks you'll see a few charred roofs." The man takes another sip of lemonade and I notice his attention shift briefly back through the doorway into the house.

"It sounds like you weren't here during the flare," says Briar. Her eyes peer into the old man, questioning. "Did you escape to the bunkers? You must have been a child." I see her eyes flick to his shoes. Before he can answer, Rory stands up and puts his empty glass on the tray.

"Mind if I look around," he asks. The man shifts in his seat and peers nervously once again back into the house.

"It's okay," says Arick kindly. "We should be on our way."

"What's it going to hurt to just look around?" asks Rory with agitation. "Unless there's something to hide." Just as Arick begins to protest the old man says,

"It's okay, you can look, but please don't touch." A shadow falls over his pale eyes leaving me wondering if he's ready to protect his stuff. Rory wastes no time. He grabs his pack and jumps to his feet, leaping from the porch, heading in the direction of the shed behind the house. Arick and Ian begin to ask the old man questions that might help us as Gemma takes a second glass of lemonade. Has he seen any of the Mutts or wild people in the area? What is the terrain like up north? He doesn't seem to have many answers. I give Briar a glance and we both jump up to follow Rory. Someone's got to keep an eye on him.

CHAPTER TWENTY-TWO

Aiden

The cool sand presses in on every part of me. My mind races as I beg my lungs to hold in the oxygen they have, even if they feel as if they will explode with the effort. I can feel the pulse in my neck beating out my final seconds, the pressure of the earth pressed in tight like a tourniquet around my chest. I can't hold on any longer and I have to let the air in my lungs go, causing more sand to creep in and push my body harder. I'm in real danger of passing out now, my lungs begging for me to take a breath, my pulse frantic. Just when I think it's over, it's lights out, my feet break through and I thrash them wildly. I am falling through the sand, my skin scraping across its rough surface until it's gone, and I land hard on solid ground. I choke and gasp for air all at the same time, trying to fuel my brain with the oxygen it needs, coughing and spitting out sand.

"See if he's okay." I hear Raven's voice and detect a flash of light across my eyes even though they are still closed.

"Hey, tough guy," says Spencer, as he gently pats my back. "That was a rough landing."

"You think?" I reply, wiping grit from my eyes. There they are, leaning against the side of a narrow cave, Raven, Spencer and Jewel, unhurt and alive.

"What the hell," I say as I take in my surroundings. We're not in a cave as I first suspected but in a long dark tunnel, a tube cut into the earth. I reach out and touch the damp floor and then extend my hand to run it along the cool walls. They are rough and as I pull my hand away, I take a handful of soil and stone with me. Raven's flashlight illuminates the small area and I can tell that it would be pitch black without it.

"Thoughts, suggestions, concerns?" asks Spencer as he watches me. He's rubbing his wrist gingerly.

"I mean, wow," I reply, standing and wiping the dirt and sand from my knees. "I don't know."

"Well, I don't think this is something created by the government," says Raven. "The quicksand, maybe, but not the tunnel." She's holding something back; I can tell by the tone in her voice. She knows something.

"Yeah, I think you're right," I reply as I unzip my backpack and rummage around for my flashlight. I add its light to Raven's. I shine it up to the ceiling and see four large openings in the tunnel's structure, clearly where we fell through, but the holes are filling in fast. There's not even a glint of light from above or anything to indicate how far below the surface we are.

We do a thorough search of the area around us and see that in one direction the tunnel narrows while the other opens up.

"I guess we don't have much of a choice," I say. "Is everyone okay? Jewel?"

"I'm fine," she replies.

"Yeah, she had my head to stop her fall."

"Sorry," replies Jewel with a grin at Raven. "And thanks."

Spencer, how about you?"

"I'm good," he says, hitching his backpack back up on his shoulder. "Let's just get out of here."

Our feet step onto soft earth and stumble over dead, decaying roots as we walk. At first, we form a line, Raven taking the lead and me bringing up the rear. But soon the tunnel opens up enough for us to walk side by side. The darkness is oppressive and I'm silently praying that the solar chips in my flashlight were fully charged.

"What if we're trapped in here forever," whispers Spencer. I think the walls are closing in on him. "Buried alive by the very soil we need above ground."

"That's very poetic," replies Raven. "But we're not going to be trapped in here forever."

"But you said that you didn't think this tunnel was a government creation," says Spencer questioningly. Natural erosion underground, created by the complete devastation of everything above, it's not so far-fetched.

"No," replies Raven. "This tunnel, perhaps these tunnels, are definitely man-made."

"Then, by whom?" I ask. "What's your theory.

"I think you know the answer to that," she replies. I think back to this morning and our thoughts about nomads roaming the area, taking refuse in the compound. But could there possibly be enough of those wild people to build a structure like this?

"I don't know," I say with disbelief. "I'm going to have to go with Spencer on this one and say nature created this thing." Raven stops walking and turns to us, the beam of her flashlight skimming our faces.

"Look," she says. "I didn't want to bring this up and now it's probably not the best time to talk about it, but I do have information." Spencer's face goes from calm to terrified in less than a second and Jewel looks on questioningly.

"Maybe you shouldn't say anything," says Spencer. "Wait until we're back above ground in the light, safe and sound." Raven gives a sigh of disgust before she continues.

"Those nomads that we saw the first time out, they're not just random people looking to rough it out in the wild. There's more to the story."

"What?" I ask, not sure where she's going with this.

"They're actual survivors of the flare and I'm not talking about cryotank survivors. These are people who either went through the flare and escaped to the government underground bunkers or descendants of those survivors."

"The underground bunkers," echoes Jewel.

"My guess," continues Raven. "Is that, since the environment isn't hospitable above, they probably added the tunnel system over time.

"But this doesn't make any sense," says Jewel as she drags her hand along the rough, surface of the tunnel wall. "If these people survived, they should have gone to the hubs."

"Yeah," adds Spencer with certainty. "Just about everyone we met in the hub was a survivor or a descendant with or without a cryotank."

"That's true," replies Raven. "The government needed people to maintain the banks, to rebuild, to clean up, but these nomads are different. They're wild, untamed. You remember our encounters. If we hadn't been wielding guns, who knows what they would have been capable of." She's right. The few groups we ran into were scary for a lot of reasons. Even their faces seemed strange and their behavior was loud and unruly. They were harmless to us, but anyone without a weapon would probably be in danger.

"How do you know any of this?" I ask.

"Let's just say that while you two were tucked away getting three squares a day and building up your energy, I was making friends, friends with information." She takes a moment to let her words sink in and I wonder if she's waiting for us to congratulate her on her intel when she continues. "These people are different. They have certain mutations created by the radiation influx."

"I would think that all the DNA left on Earth would have certain mutations," I say.

"Well, from what I was told, these mutations were bad enough for the government to deny them access into the hubs."

"W-why?" stammers Spencer. "Why are you telling us this, Raven?"

"Because, I'm certain that these tunnels were created by those people and you can bet that they are not going to treat four government cryotank survivors well if we come face to face with them. I want you to be prepared. There may be more than a few down here." I get it now. Even in this new world, there will still be divisions. But I have to believe that the government has its reasons for keeping these people out. Perhaps they do have illnesses that could infect those of us who are healthy. An illness like that could wipe out all of us.

"Gosh," says Spencer. "Yet again, another warning from the Commander would have been nice."

CHAPTER TWENTY-THREE

Wren

"We'll be right back," says Briar as we leave the shade of the old warn porch. "And thanks again for the lemonade." The old man gives her a smile.

There is a small deck on the back of the house, but it is not shaded, and it, too, is very worn, the bare wood exposed in places. I notice big heavy metal doors that I know must lead underground, probably to a cellar. I wonder how deep it goes.

"Great! It's locked!" Rory's voice reminds me of why I followed him. He fingers the heavy lock hinged across the shed door.

"Well, what did you expect?" asks Briar, walking up to stand next to him. "Wouldn't you lock up supplies if you were out here by yourself?"

"You think you're so high and mighty," spits Rory, as he turns to us. "Yeah, maybe I was a jerk for stealing from Gemma. She's one of us. But this guy?" He shakes his head in disbelief. "Look at him! He's old, his days are numbered anyway. He can spare some food and water for us."

"Well, that's not your decision to make, is it?" replies Briar with anger. "He's been nice to us so far and, anyway, we know where he lives. If things get really tough, we can come back. He would help us."

"I don't want to have to come back!" shouts Rory. "I want to get this over with. I want to get to the hub and the only way for that to happen is to have enough food and water. Nothing else matters."

"God," replies Briar. "You're such a selfish jerk." I can feel the heat rising inside of me, anger that matches her words. "First you take the food out of the mouth of an innocent girl and now you're willing to starve an old man, a helpless old man."

Rory turns to face us, fire in his eyes, but his next words are low and quiet. "You're a hypocrite," he says. "You said it yourself, survival of the fittest, everyone for themselves. That's all I'm doing, surviving." Quickly, Rory opens his backpack and pulls something out. My eyes widen at the small, sleek black handgun. I instinctively jump back.

"Dammit," hisses Briar. We both left our own packs back on the front porch.

"You were so anxious to get your hands on Briar's gun. Where did you get that?" I ask, and I wonder what else he has in his pack.

"The same place where you got yours," he says with a sneer. "I didn't want to play all my cards at once." His pinched face has taken on a sinister appearance and even though I have inches on him, I can't compete with a gun. Rory's plan becomes crystal clear. Asking for Briar's gun at the apartment building and then again as we left; disarming the enemy, us, so that he can take whatever he wants, just like now.

"What are you going to do now, shoot us?" asks Briar. Her voice is steady.

"I don't want to, but I will if you get in my way. You'll leave me no choice."

I know Rory, at least his type. He's a frightened little boy, probably the boy who was bullied for being chubby or short or for some other reason. I look at his angry face and dusty blond hair that sticks to his forehead with sweat. I can see the boy, maybe fourteen at most. His sharp eyes dart back and forth between Briar's and mine. Having Briar next to me keeps me steady.

"I'm going to get supplies by any means possible. Then we can head out of here and leave the old man in peace." Briar lets out a growl of frustration. "Get in front of me," he commands, waving the gun frantically in our faces. I notice that his hands are shaky. We move but my mind is racing, trying to figure out how we can stop this before he does something stupid, something he can't take back. As we circle back to the front of the house, I hear chatter. Arick is asking questions and the old man is giving answers. There is the ring of laughter that is Gemma and the deep strong voice of Ian. The conversation, just out of my reach, seems so familiar and normal and I don't want it to stop, but as Ian's eyes alight on us, his smile drops. His eyes find the gun that is now pointed at my back and I can see him quickly piece the scene together.

"Where's the key to the shed?" commands Rory. He moves

the gun ever so slightly threatening the old man. Arick and Gemma turn toward us. Gemma let's out a gasp as Ian jumps to his feet.

"Not so fast," says Rory. "I am desperate enough to use this." His voice is steady even if his hands aren't. We are at a standstill, the gun shoved into my back, Ian half out of his seat ready to pounce, and Briar eyeing her backpack on the porch. And then out of nowhere, a woman comes walking out of the house, an older woman dressed in a jumpsuit, a jumpsuit identical to mine, her graying hair pulled back in a braid.

"Stop!" she commands as Rory flashes the gun one more time. The rest of us forget the gun for a second and fix our eyes on the man and woman. Something's wrong about them. Clearly the man doesn't want us to know who they really are, survivors from a compound.

"You're one of us," says Rory, stating the obvious. "None of this belongs to you either."

"Look," replies the man, holding up his hands in submission. The woman moves to stand next to him. "We came from one of the compounds nearly six months ago. We found this place and decided to call it home." Six months ago? How long ago did they start taking people out of hibernation?

"That doesn't seem like the smartest decision," says Ian with concern. "Food, water, supplies..."

"A crazy kid with a gun," adds Briar with distaste.

"We have some supplies," replies the man warily. "There are rumors about what's out there. Terrible things, like your Mutts and worse. We're old. We just wanted a quiet life together."

"Rumors from whom," I ask as Rory continues to shove the gun barrel into the small of my back. I can hear him breathing, a rough rapid sound. He wants to get on with it but knows that we need this information. The man's eyes flick to mine.

"We've had other visitors from other compounds that have been wandering, looking for food and water. There are people out there, terrible brutal people that many believe are survivors from the underground bunkers." So, we were right and now we know that there are more than the small pack from the city. "And I've heard other things, unexplainable things..."

"Enough!" yells Rory. It's getting to him, all the nightmares that may lie ahead, all the terrors that wait just around the corner. It's getting to me too. "Just give me the key to the shed and we'll get the hell out of here." Rory focuses on the man and the woman who begin to move toward the door.

Briar slowly inches her way to her backpack that rests next to her chair on the porch. Rory catches the movement too and says, "If anyone tries to stop me, the old man gets it first." Ian flicks his eyes to his own pack and then back to mine. He must have a weapon too. I'm amazed at how much Briar and I underestimated everyone. We all wait as the old man slowly walks down the porch steps.

"Rory, there's no need for this," comes Arick's calm voice.

"Shut up!" he shouts in reply. "Just shut up!" He waves the gun wildly again and he looks crazy, completely hyped up, beads of sweat forming at his temples. "Now where's the frickin' key?"

"Rory," says Ian. "None of us wants you to do this." Rory lets out a sadistic laugh.

"Please," he says, his words dripping with sarcasm. "Weeks from now when you're all starving, you're going to thank me for having the guts to do what it takes to survive out here." The old man begins to walk slowly toward Rory, his hands held high. "Anyway, I'm sure they have plenty to spare."

"Okay," says the man under his breath. "We can work something out."

"So, now you can put the gun away," says Briar. "You heard him. He's willing to give us supplies."

"No way! What is wrong with all of you? Trust no one, survival of the fittest, no one's going to help us out here. Was that all trash-talk, Briar, because I believed you."

"They are like us," screams Briar. Rory gives her a scathing look and then focuses on the man and woman in front of him. "The key?"

"It's in the house."

"Let's go," barks Rory. The old man turns to enter the house behind the woman as Rory follows. Rory eyes each of us with a warning glare. Gemma cries softly and Ian slowly rises from his chair, his hands out in front of him. The second Rory disappears inside the house we leap from the porch to get some distance away and begin to figure out how to end this.

"We can't leave him in there with those people alone," hisses Briar. She rummages through her backpack that she grabbed as soon as Rory was out of sight.

"I don't think Rory will hurt them," replies Arick. "As long as they give him what he wants."

"How can you be so sure," I ask incredulously. "He's like a caged animal right now, Arick. He's capable of anything if he believes it will ultimately save his life." Arick looks toward the house with some concern. The time to keep calm is over, long gone. As if reading my thoughts Briar pulls out her gun.

"I don't trust that little jerk. I'm going in," she says with determination.

"I'm not sure this is the right way to go about it," says Ian. "Inside of the house Rory will feel even more trapped. He might be more inclined to use the gun."

"Well, what do you suggest? Should we try to reason with him, maybe we can offer up some of our own supplies to quiet him down, maybe give him another lecture on how we expect him to behave?" replies Briar harshly. She gives a huff of frustration. Time is ticking by. Arick bows his head and takes a deep breath, waiting for Briar to end her rant.

"He's going to take out one of them," says Ian. "If we threaten him, he'll react."

"Let's just let him take a few things and leave the couple in peace," says Briar with loathing. "But the first chance I get, I'm taking that gun."

Just as we decide to head back to the shed and face the problem there, the quiet world around us is ripped away by the sound of an explosion. The ground beneath my feet shakes, throwing me up into the air and away from the house. The air is hot, like fire and is filled with so much force that I feel the breath being knocked from my lungs. I hit the ground hard. My shoulder bashes against the ground and I see the sky light up with orange and blue fire followed by immense clouds of billowing black smoke. As my mind tries to rationalize what is going on, I panic at the thought of another solar flare hitting the earth. My eyes sting with soot and smoke and I turn away from the house that is now lit up like a fireball. I've been thrown back fifty yards from where we stood and as I glance around, I can only make out blurs of the others deposited all around me. I wipe my burning eyes hastily with the fabric of my sleeve. To my right, Arick has already rushed to Gemma and holds her head in his lap. To my left, Ian sits rubbing the back of his head while Briar is nowhere to be found. My limbs begin to shake, adrenaline rushing through me, mixing with the panic of the total chaos around me. My ears ring and the heat coming off the burning house singes any exposed skin. I've got to move.

"Ian!" I scream as I turn toward him. He turns and sees me and is on his feet in an instant. He throws himself down next to me, his face full of worry.

"Are you okay?" he asks, his chest rising and falling quickly. His face is covered in black soot.

"I think so." Then I see Briar through the wafting smoke, laid out on her back several feet in front of me. Ian and I rush to her. She is unconscious but breathing.

"What do we do?" I can feel my voice trembling with fear. Ian motions for me to help him drag her further away from the explosion and I quickly grab an arm and begin to pull. My lungs hurt from the effort and I am still shaking terribly but I don't think anything is broken. Arick and Gemma join us a safe distance away from the danger and we wait. Another explosion rips the air and another huge plume of black smoke belches into the sky. There's nothing we can do until the fire extinguishes itself. It is too dangerous to move any closer. I look toward Gemma who is battered and bruised, but whole. Arick tends to Briar, but Ian stays by my side, glancing at me nervously.

"You're bleeding," he says as he reaches out to gently touch my forehead. His fingers hold a hint of crimson as he draws back. "Wren, are you really okay?" I can feel the sting of a long shallow cut across my forehead where shrapnel from the house must have hit me and my back is sore from the hard landing. The foggy feeling in my head is dissipating and there's a slight ringing deep within my ears.

"I'm fine," I reply hastily.

Ian takes an antibiotic wipe from his bag and cleans my wound. I wince from the sting, but his touch is gentle. We sit until the sun begins to dip past the horizon, until the fire looks more like a campfire in the distance than a raging inferno, until Briar opens her eyes and only complains of a headache, and then we walk back to the house. The sun has gone down, and the darkness hinders our search. I'm not sure what we're looking for and I'm afraid of what we'll find. The house looms over us, a dark skeleton with nothing inside but charred remains of possessions. Small fires are scattered all around like lanterns lighting our way. We step over burnt piles of what was once the house, seeing a chair here a table there. Broken glass and piles of singed cloth, that somehow survived, litter the area. Then several yards to the left of the porch rests a long lean figure, still and unmoving. I chance a glance at Briar, and she nods.

"That's the old man," she says softly. "We need to check him out." There is an eerie quiet all around us making my nerves pull tight. I feel Gemma take my arm as we get closer to the old man. Another body, the woman, lies in the distance. Gemma buries her face in the crook of my elbow. I smooth her pale hair back and whisper, "You don't have to see this. Go back with Arick and wait for us." I look to Arick who is standing right beside me listening. Gently, he takes Gemma and wraps an arm around her. I approach the old man's body first with Briar and Ian on either side. I've never seen a dead body. Well, maybe I did on that last day, the day of the solar flare, but I didn't stop to notice. The old man lies on his back, his arms outstretched and burnt. His clothes are almost completely gone, replaced by a thick black sear that might once have been his skin. The acrid odor that the fire has left behind fills my sinuses and leaves me with a bad taste in my mouth so that I almost gag. It is the taste of death. His fingers are curled into black fists and his feet are almost completely gone. All I see in his face is charred remains, nothing of the kind man who offered us lemonade. Ian kneels and places a hand on the old man's burnt out chest and I hear a slight crunch. I recoil but keep watching. The woman's body is no different. Her face is also unrecognizable.

"Should we bury the bodies?" asks Briar. Ian glances up.

"No," he replies.

"But what about any wild animals in the area, the Mutts?" says Briar. "I would hate to think…"

"We can't worry about that," replies Ian as he stands.

"Okay," says Briar. "Fine, let's look for Rory."

CHAPTER TWENTY-FOUR

Aiden

The tunnel begins to slop downwards as we continue walking. It changes, becoming wider, the sides smoother and more refined. The space has a lived-in feel, the sense of running back and forth, leveling out the ground and flattening the walls. We come upon other connecting tunnels, leading off in unknown directions but we stay the course on this main avenue because it is larger than the others. I am now certain that Raven is right, these passageways cannot be a fluke of nature. They were created for a purpose, survival, most likely added to over time. Suddenly, Raven's flashlight goes out and we are left with my fine beam that is dimming by the minute.

"Damn it!" she hisses, smacking the device against her palm in frustration.

"I've got one," says Jewel and she begins to rummage through her backpack.

"What was that?" asks Spencer as we stand huddled together. We are silent and hear the echo of shuffling somewhere in the distance.

"Shut your light off," whispers Raven and I immediately obey. We wait in complete darkness, our ears pricked for any noise, our limbs ready to spring into flight. But where would we run to? Slowly I unzip my backpack, careful to keep it quiet. My fingers graze metal but before they can wrap around my gun, I hear the click of Raven's safety being released. The shuffling ahead is sporadic and comes from deep inside the tunnel. I can sense that it's getting closer.

"Get to the side and press against the wall," commands Raven. "Don't move, don't even breathe." And then I see it, the sweeping of a flashlight's beam. I feel Jewel shiver beside me, and I carefully find her fingers. I squeeze them gently to reassure her. The light falls over the area where we stood seconds ago. Slowly it lifts and makes one big sweep across our faces. Raven launches from the wall, her gun pointed directly in front of her.

"Who are you? State your name," she demands. A low laugh comes from the darkness in front of us and I instinctively flip back on my flashlight to see what we're dealing with. He's an older man maybe in his forties, stocky but strong. My light reveals a lined and pale face covered with the beginnings of a gray beard and dark eyes that seem to be filled with humor. The problem is not the man but the two others that flank him on either side holding rifles.

"State your name," echoes the man with laughter. He shakes his head back and forth in amazement. "We don't go for that military talk here and it seems to me that you're outnumbered…weapon wise." He pauses to give one of the burly men behind him a grin. "But, I'm willing to tell you who I am if you're willing to tell me who you are." Raven gives a quick nod.

"M'name's Samuel," he says simply. "I just happened to be starting the evening watch in tunnels five and six and heard noises and here you are. So, I guess I was right, hey boys?" The words *tunnels five and six* hit my brain like an explosion. I glance back to Spencer. His eyes are wide with disbelief while Raven's eyes are narrow, holding her ground. "I guess it's your turn now," says Samuel.

"Lower your weapons first," says Raven, her hand remaining steady on her gun.

"Lower yours." When it's clear that Raven will not acquiesce, Samuel's men take a step closer, this time pointing their guns at Jewel. "Look, we're not gonna get anywhere like this. You have to understand, I have a community to protect, a community of a lot of people who don't trust government types, not even cryotank survivors like yourselves, not yet anyway."

"A community?" questions Spencer in a shocked voice. I can feel Raven's hesitation now and once again I realize that she must know more about these people than she has shared with us. It pisses me off. After everything we've been through as a squad, after me saving her ass and she saving Spencer's ass time and time again on our first time out, I thought we were tighter than this. I glare at her as she slowly lowers her gun.

"That's good," says Samuel and he gives a wave to his cronies to lower theirs as well. "So, the next question is, what are you four doing here? Get lost?"

"We're not answering any questions," replies Raven. "Not until we know what's going on, who you are and what this tunnel's all about."

"Fair enough," says Samuel. "But before we go any further, I'm going to have to ask you to put that thing away." He nods towards the gun still clenched in her hand.

"How do we know that we can trust you?" asks Spencer.

"Look," replies Samuel. "If I wanted to kill you, you'd be dead already." Raven continues to hold her gun. "Okay," sighs Samuel. "Put the guns away boys. I take full responsibility if these kids get out of hand." Raven gives an indignant laugh at the word, *kids*. None of us are kids, not after everything that we've been through. "Let's go." We gather ourselves together as Raven tucks her gun onto her thigh pocket and we follow.

We have three flashlights guiding us now, Samuel's being twice as powerful as ours. He leads the way, his two men following behind us. It isn't long before I see a glow in the distance and soon we are stepping under an archway into an open space of light. It's an underground bunker. The smooth concrete floor and walls give it away, along with the huge metal doors blocking out other rooms or tunnels. In the center of the room, the United Nations symbol, an intertwining U and N is etched into the stone floor.

"Welcome to our humble abode," says Samuel with a chuckle. "It may not seem like much but it's home." It's easy to feel the hum of activity all around the space as wide eyes scan over us, trying to figure out who we are. Many men and women lean against curved walls chatting or hurry in and out of doors only to disappear behind another. There are several small stainless-steel tables assembled in the center occupied by citizens of this underground community. They are reading actual paper-bound books or writing on thick white sheets with charcoal instruments, pencils. Not one tablet can be seen. Children scurry across the room, chasing balls or playing games. There are others carrying boxes and supplies to places unknown and, as we watch, a woman enters laden with a tray of small cups, each filled with something suspiciously resembling fruit. But that can't be. There is nothing that can grow out here. Spencer gives an audible, "Whoa," as Jewel takes a step forward watching the children run past.

"This is...this is..." I can't even finish my sentence. I don't know what this is. My brain cannot wrap around what I am seeing.

"This is one of the common areas," says Samuel. It's a place where people meet up or read or just hang out. I usually try to make a point of showing up around snack time for the kiddos," he continues with a smile. My eyes travel over the entire space, taking it all in and then stop when I notice the track lighting that lines the perimeter.

"How is this possible?" I ask, pointing to the lights.

"Oh, well, everything is pretty much run on solar power down here. We've got thousands of panels placed in strategic locations," he says. "Kind of ironic, ain't it? The sun giving us something after taking it all away?"

"Yeah," I reply softly.

"Anyway, we've got the hydroponics growing food, fruits and vegetables down in tunnel one and the labs synthesize other products that we need. It's not a bad life and we'd all like to keep it that way." He waves us forward. "Come on, you need to meet the Big Wigs." I follow him, stunned and glance over to Raven. It's apparent now that she's just as shocked as I am.

CHAPTER TWENTY-FIVE

Wren

As we walk back toward Arick and Gemma, away from the bodies of people we didn't have a chance to know, my heart is filled with thankfulness for Arick and his sensitive, comforting arms that encircle my small friend. I'm surprised at how full I feel looking at them, like there is someone else more important than myself. Not even Aiden made me feel this way. I want to fight for things now, work toward things, be better than I am, not just for myself but for those who need me.

"It's okay," I say to Gemma as I lift her face and dry her tears on my sleeve, a sleeve that's getting pretty gross from extensive use. "I think they died quickly and didn't even know what was happening." Arick gives me a quick nod.

"I see something," yells Briar. She is standing next to the shed that is now visible in the dimness of the small fires. It has also suffered. "I think it's Rory."

We don't hesitate. We run to the still figure yards away. His body lies in a heap and he looks terrible, almost unrecognizable. Ian bends down over him, and Rory's face comes into view. It's a mess of black scorch and raw red blistering. I search his body for any sign of life and let out a sigh of relief as I see his chest rising and falling in shallow breathing. The fire and explosion got him bad. His lips are swollen as are his eyes and I immediately become concerned that his vision is gone. My eyes travel down his injured body where huge blisters are forming on any exposed skin. Surprisingly, his jumpsuit is barely damaged. Just a few burn marks but nothing major. Ian rolls him over gently, assessing the situation. Any idea that Briar might have of chopping off Rory's fingers is gone. I can see that only a stump remains on his left hand. His right one seems alright. That's lucky.

I hear Gemma whimpering behind me and then Arick's soft words, "It will be okay. We'll fix him up." Always the optimist.

"Bring me my backpack," commands Ian. Though his voice is calm, there is a tremor beneath it. Briar looks frantically around and spots Ian's pack near what used to be the porch and runs to retrieve it.

"Thanks," says Ian as he unzips it. He pulls a large plastic tub from the bottom that we soon discover holds medical supplies.

"It looks like his leg is broken," he says. I look down to Rory's legs and see the left jetting out at an odd angle. "It's probably better if I try to set the bone before he regains consciousness. Can you help me, Wren?" I nod and bend down to help position

Rory's leg. Ian's face appears years older as he works expertly and quickly, his large hands feeling for the point of the break. I think I see Rory jerk as the bones are brought back together.

"Can someone look around for anything I can use as a brace? A piece of wood, maybe, that hasn't been burned?" I glance to Briar and we begin to comb the area of debris. I walk to the frame of the house that is still standing and climb in. I can see a rubble pile in an area that must have once been the kitchen and I begin to dig through. I pull my hand out sharply when it hits something hot.

"Ouch!" I lift off charred chucks of wood and find a long metal canister with a strange circular valve on top. As my eyes roam the area, I spot several more, one shattered into large pieces. They are tanks, perhaps compressed oxygen or maybe liquefied petroleum, a gas that could be used to cook with. My mind reels with the possibilities of finding a spare cylinder of that stuff but then I realize that we won't find anything like that here, not anymore. I wonder if that's what Rory was after. Then I spy a metal spoon. It's long and sturdy. I try to nudge it with my toe, kicking it away from the pile. I extend one finger to test it and find that it's cooled enough for me to grab it and run it over to Ian.

"Here," I say. "Will this work?" He takes the spoon gingerly and bends it in his hands. The spoon part gives way and he twists it off, leaving the long handle.

"This is perfect, Wren, thanks." As Ian finishes up with Rory's leg, dressing it in a heavy wrap and inserting the spoon handle splint, Rory's eyes flutter.

"Ahhhhhh," he moans. His limbs begin thrashing about as his moans become louder.

"He's going into shock," says Ian. "We need to keep him warm and I need to get medication on his burns." I help to hold Rory down and, when he becomes calm again, we decide to move him away from the area where the air is cleaner. Briar and I walk slowly back to the explosion site. I'm hoping that we might find something of use.

"This is bad," says Briar in a hushed voice. The air is still, like its devoid of any oxygen. The only sounds we hear are the dying fires crackling on any remains. Briar shakes her head. "He just wouldn't listen," she continues. "And now look, he's a bigger liability."

"There's nothing we can do about it now," I say. "We can't just leave Rory here to die." She gives me a sideways glance.

"If it were just me and you, I'd give him a bottle of water and tell him that he's on his own. But Arick..." She trails off, knowing that Arick would never abandon one of us, even Rory.

"I don't think you'd really leave him," I say with confidence.

"You really don't know me then," she replies, darkly.

The sky is beginning to lighten; the black that surrounds us is slowly turning into the day that it will become. We walk around what remains of the shed. The walls have fallen in and the roof is gone but this structure has fared better. We dig through the wreckage and spot melted plastic and curled up foil packaging, a lot of it. Briar lets out an audible, "Whoa". They were hoarding supplies all right, by the looks of what's left, months and months maybe even years' worth of freeze-dried meal packs and cases of water now all spoiled and gone up in flames.

We leave the shed and head back to our small squad. Ian is still tending to Rory, Gemma kneeling next to him. As we get closer, I can see that they have applied several long strips of gel-like pads to Rory's skin. He looks like a mummy all wrapped up in bandages. Even much of his face is covered, though his eyes are left alone. The swelling seems to be a little better. Ian looks up at us.

"Well, he was pretty lucky. He has deep burns on most of his exposed skin, but his jumpsuit saved the rest of him."

"Will he be okay?" I ask.

"I think he'll survive the burns," replies Ian with a reassuring nod. "These pads will cool down the burns and numb them for a while. Rory's body needs time to heal."

"That's good," I say, and I mean it. I know that all that has happened will leave scars, some deeper than his skin. My eyes meet Briar's and we silently agree to not mention the shed. Instead we help Gemma find a place to settle in and offer her a meal pack and a bottle of water. It's been a long night and none of us has had anything to eat or drink in a while. Thoughts of the lemonade come back to me and form a bitter taste on my tongue. I push it away.

I watch as Rory's eyelids flutter and he tries to move. Arick rests a steady hand on the top of his head and whispers,

"You're going to be okay, Rory." He lets out another strangled moan. "Just rest," adds Ian, and Rory seems to drift back into unconsciousness.

"Okay," says Ian, spreading out the map on top of his pack. "I think we have to readjust our timetable. A few days ago, I thought we would be able to reach the hub in a a few weeks at most, but now..." He glances to Rory. "I think it would be better for all of us if we slow down." Briar gives a hiss of frustration. "Obviously, Rory needs time to recover and with the extra work that it will take to pull him, we will be pushing our bodies even harder," continues Ian. Briar gives Rory a scathing glance. No one's talking about the fact that we're almost out of water.

There's nothing left to do but find a place to recover for a few days.

"Arick," says Ian. "Will you help me pull him?" He bends down to pick up a corner of one of the sleeping bags taken from our last stop, a treasure now with Rory is tucked inside. Arick doesn't hesitate, of course, and he steps up to help. Gemma comes to give me a gentle hug as Ian makes sure that Rory is secure and isn't in danger of slipping out while they are pulling him.

"I think he'll be okay," whispers Gemma. I kiss the top of her head and squeeze her tight.

"I think we all will," I reply.

There seems to be a sigh of relief from all of us. We have gone through some bad crap and, strangely, it has erased many of the stresses that we struggled with previously. Hunger, fear, leadership, even contrasting personalities are nothing compared to the idea of being injured or dead. We've gotten through our first taste of that now and I think we all feel a little bit stronger, a little more ready. We leave the burnt remains of the house behind and stroll the sidewalks of the subdivision. The gray sand is still here, patches of it, reminding us that this is not our home anymore. There are several homes that are scorched, many to the point of no return. As we walk, I can almost hear children playing in the yard, smell freshly planted flowerbeds that would have decorated the front of each home. It could be my old neighborhood or Briar's or Gemma's. We turn a corner and are left in a cul-de-sac of three sturdy houses.

"I think this is home for a while," says Ian as he pulls Rory to the house at the end. It's a good location with windows facing away towards the road leading north. We will see anything coming and prepare.

"Ian, let's go check it out first," says Briar. The house is lovely and big, bigger than my old three-bedroom house, and it stands tall like a welcoming reminder of what has been and what might be again. Briar grabs her gun and they jump onto the wide-open porch. The front door is open, and they disappear inside. It doesn't take long before Briar bounds out of the house, a smile on her face.

"It's all clear," she says as Ian appears behind her.

"Let's go have a look," says Arick. I'm slightly disappointed as I stand in the entryway. I don't know what I was expecting, perhaps a clean, put together home with furnishings and a loaded kitchen, not this ransacked room that smells of ash. How stupid to be surprised, especially after the city. For a moment, I seem to have forgotten everything that has happened in the need to see something normal. It's not a bad house, though. There was once furniture, a sofa and chairs that is now a pile of rubble and the long drapes that once hung in the tall front windows are a bunched-up wad of fabric in the corner that looks suspiciously like a nest. The kitchen is bare but for a few pots and several empty plastic water bottles.

"Let's check out the upstairs," I say as I watch Gemma take in the mess around us. "It's probably better."

"It is," says Briar. "Much better." We follow her up the tall staircase and I run my palm along the smooth wooden banister as I go. "Ta da!" says Briar as we reach the hallway of the second floor. There are three bedrooms and they are almost as nice as the last place, clean enough but no mattresses in the bed frames. A night on the hard ground won't be fun but at least we'll be safe and protected. The girls take the largest bedroom while the boys take another. No one wants to be alone. Arick and Ian go slowly, lifting Rory up, one step at a time. The third bedroom has windows that face to the road to the north. We set this space up as a watch tower.

"How long do you think we can stay here?" asks Briar as we try to make the first floor livable by hauling away rubble. Arick has taken several light-weight chairs from the second floor and set them up in a circle in the main room. "I mean, how long until Rory's able to travel?" We can all sense the frustration in her voice and Ian meets her gaze quickly.

"I know this is a tough situation," he says. "I know that we all want to just get to the hub, but we have to be smart about this. It doesn't make sense to go running through the wilderness with one of us so grievously injured, especially when we have a good place to stay for the time being." Briar kicks at an old table that is now nothing more than scrap wood.

"Okay," she replies angrily. "Okay, we'll stay but just to make it clear, if it gets to the point where it's his life or ours, I'm done. I won't think twice about leaving him behind." Arick looks as if he's just been slapped but gives a nod. "We all know that it's suicide to stay in one place too long," she adds.

"How about you Ian?" asks Arick. "Your leg seems to be better." Ian glances down at his leg and gives it a rub.

"Completely healed," he says with confidence. "We'll almost." My eyes flick to Briar's in confusion. I saw the gash that the Mutt made. It was deep.

"That must be some medicine," says Briar, staring hard into Ian's eyes. He looks away and mumbles,

"Guess so."

As we dig into our meal packs, I watch Briar watching Ian with suspicious eyes. But there are other things to worry about and my heart sinks as I notice how low my supplies have become. We'll have to figure something out soon.

CHAPTER TWENTY-SIX

Aiden

We walk through the common space, catching more curious glances, following Samuel. He leads us down a tunnel to the right and we are greeted by another man who stands in front of a closed door.

"Anyone at home?' he asks. "Got a few outsiders." The man who stands guard opens the door and peeks inside. He waves Samuel in and we follow. The space is similar to the common area with smooth concrete walls and track lighting above, but much smaller. Two men and one woman sit around a steel table littered with paper, a tablet in front of them. A halo screen hangs overhead and a renewed wave of shock washes over us.

"Samuel," says one man with a nod. He is younger than the

others, late twenties and not so different from myself, dark blond hair, slim build. "Who do we have here?" The woman stands abruptly as her eyes notice our appearance. Their eyes take us in and try to figure us out wordlessly. The two burly guys behind us quickly reach for their weapons and I see Raven's hand go for her thigh pocket.

"Why don't you boys go and get a cool drink," says Samuel, dismissively. The woman sits down again but there is concern in her eyes as she glances at her two colleagues.

"We don't want to cause any trouble," I say. "We didn't come here on purpose."

"Yeah," adds Spencer. "This is not what we expected to find down here." He gives a nervous laugh earning him one of Raven's scathing glances.

"What's your name?" asks the woman but she's not speaking to me. Her eyes are turned to Jewel. She smiles warmly.

"I'm Jewel," she replies as she takes a step forward. Raven lays a gentle hand on her shoulder stopping her from moving any further. The woman looks away still smiling, her golden hair sweeping in waves to frame her gentle face.

"I'm Lynda," she says. "This is Stephen and Clay. She says the younger man's name last and he nods.

"I'm Raven." She steps forward to shake Lynda's extended hand. "This is Aiden and Spencer."

"Welcome to the Underground," she replies.

"Thank you, but we're not staying," says Raven. "We have a job to do, a job on the outside. Lives depend on it."

"What kind of job?" asks Lynda, eyeing Raven suspiciously. "Maybe we can help."

"You can't help," counters Raven. "It's confidential." Lynda leans back in her chair and glances at Clay and Stephen.

"Are you on your way to a hub?" asks Clay.

"No," replies Raven curtly.

"Your jumpsuit kind of gives you away," says Clay with a grin. "Come on, I know it's difficult when you're first waking up after fifty years..."

"We didn't just wake up and we have other plans right now, other objectives."

"You sound like a military girl," says Lynda. Raven doesn't answer and neither do the rest of us. Jewel looks uncomfortable and, if I didn't know any better, I'd think she liked these people. I'm trying to figure out what their game is buried like they are beneath the ground. Raven turns to glance at Samuel.

"If Samuel could just lead us in the right direction..." I know where Raven's head is at. She's sick of the banter. We've been through enough. She wants to get this mission over with and go back to the life she's dreamed about.Lynda's eyes glance to Samuel's before she says,

"I'm afraid we can't let you leave, not yet." Raven shifts on her feet, noticeably agitated and she's about to start an argument. The woman senses it and stops her. "You seem to have been through a long day. Samuel will make sure that you're comfortable and we can talk again after you're rested." The conversation abruptly ends, and we're escorted out.

"This sucks!" says Spencer, eyeing Raven warily. After traversing other tunnels, Samuel leaves us in our apartment without another word. It's clear who's in charge. The lodging's not bad, one large living area with a few comfortable chairs and a small steel table that we sit at now. There are two bedrooms, each containing two twin beds and a small bathroom. I'm more and more amazed at the ingenuity behind this place. Flushing toilets, running water, even if it is cold. Raven is beyond angry, more so about being told what to do than anything else. That's not her style, being told no. If I'm honest, I'm not ready to leave. I'm hoping that these people may have information about other cryotank survivors, about Wren. Raven drums her fingers against the metal, her brain trying to find a solution.

"So, what's your big plan?" I ask. "It doesn't seem like we have many options."

"What's the big deal?" asks Spencer. "Who cares where we go? It's none of their business." He glances at Raven again and gives her a half smile that he changes to a scowl when she doesn't return it.

"What I don't understand is why they care who knows about them?" I add. "I mean, let them live out their lives underground. They seem happy and no one from the outside is rushing to join them. No one would choose this over the hub and the Capitol. Why would the government interfere?"

"They might," replies Raven in a small voice. She's looking down at her fingers as they continue to drum on the table. I take a deep breath.

"Okay, Raven. I've had enough." I fix my gaze on her as Spencer and Jewel look on. "It's obvious that you haven't told us everything you know. It's not fair especially after everything we've been through. Just be honest." She looks up quickly.

"You mean like how you're being honest with us, Aiden?"

"What's that supposed to mean?"

"I think Spencer and I both know that you have ulterior motives. I mean you nearly jumped for joy when we were sent out again. It doesn't take a genius to figure it out, that you're searching for someone else." She doesn't say Wren's name, but I've told her enough for her to figure it out. I glance at Spencer for confirmation and he gives a shrug and looks away.

"Okay, okay," I stammer unabashed. "I do have plans to set out on my own, but only after our mission is complete. I would never put you two in jeopardy over my own decisions. I know what you both have to lose."

"I don't have the answers," she says in frustration. "Only speculation." She stands and heads for her room.

"I'll talk to her," says Jewel and she says a hasty good night.

I can't turn my brain off. Even as I stretch out in my small bed, listening to the even breathing coming from the bed next to me, I can't turn it off, so I think about the one thing that will make me happy. Seeing her deep green eyes looking back at me, feeling her gentle touch. Around midnight, I drift off into dreams of Wren.

I awake in the morning forgetting for a second where I am. My heart gives a pang of grief as my dreams fall away. Suddenly I hear a knock at the door and as I exit the bedroom, I look over to see Lynda walking through it. Spencer, Raven and Jewel are already up and sitting at the table, so I join them.

"How are your rooms?" she asks. "Do you have everything you need?" Jewel gives a nod and smiles up at Lynda. Raven just shrugs. "May I?" she continues, reaching to pull out a chair and join us. The legs scrape against the concrete floor as she pulls it out and sits down. "I know this may be difficult for you..."

"Difficult?" asks Raven. "You're holding us against our will. We're prisoners so, yeah, I'd say it's difficult."

"I hope you really don't believe you are prisoners," replies Lynda. Raven gives a snort.

"What would you call us then?" she replies with sarcasm.

"For the time being, guests." Lynda's demeaner remains calm but I can tell she's wrestling with something, a decision, possibly how much to tell us. I give her a nudge with my next words.

"Just tell us why," I say. "Why all the secrecy, why all the paranoia?" Lynda glances around the room, looking for an answer that she can't seem to find.

"It comes down to control I guess," she replies.

Her statement causes Raven to say,

"Oh really?" the sarcasm thick.

"Not this kind of control," replies Lynda. "Something much bigger, the control of the world."

"Come on," says Spencer. "Aren't you being a little dramatic. You guys have been down here too long."

"We have been living down here a long time," she says. "Fifty years. And in those fifty years, we have grown, multiplied. I've witnessed marriages, babies being born and death, a lot of death." She pauses and reaches out to place a gently hand on Jewel's. Jewel doesn't pull away. "But the worst thing that I have witnessed is a strong government of the people, turning into something worse than a dictatorship."

"That's not true," says Raven sharply. Lynda raises a hand to silence her.

"What do you believe happened after the flare?" she asks.

"People going crazy, losing their minds, trying to survive. Chaos," replies Spencer.

"I assumed that everyone would storm the bunkers, that they would wait it out and then head to the hubs, once the government had them up and running," I add. "It's clear that a lot of rebuilding has been done, just look at the Capitol."

"Yes," she says. "That's exactly what happened. I was a baby then, not even a year old. My parents took me to the closest hub and then the next hub and then the next because each time, we were turned away."

"That's a lie!" shouts Raven, pounding her fist into the table. "The hubs were set up to help every survivor find refuge. How do you think the city got rebuilt, how did the crops get grown, the soil become fertile again? How did we create new kinds of medicines and vaccines against all of the new viruses out there?" She pauses and looks to each of us pleading for us to believe her. "It took people, survivors."

"Yes," replies Lynda quietly. "Yes, it took survivors but not everyone."

"So, what are you saying?" I ask. "That the government only took in a certain number of survivors, first come, first served?"

"That's exactly what I'm saying only they didn't always take the first to arrive. Survivors from the bunkers were put through a selection process. Those who had any government tie were granted access immediately. Anyone showing a high aptitude for a specific area of expertise where also admitted. They need strong builders, architects, doctors, teachers, scientists and farmers and they had a calculation to decide on how many to take."

"That's horrible," says Jewel. "How could they turn anyone away?"

"So, what you're saying is that the people living in the Underground are the people that the government turned away?" I ask. Lynda nods.

"Mostly, or the descendants of those turned away." My mind turns back to what I already know, the real fact that wanderers are living out here in the wild. But those people are nothing like those that I've seen here. These people seem healthy, intelligent and able bodied.

"But the people here have to be smart and resourceful. You

must have your own doctors and scientists and tech staff. You've got solar power, hydroponics, a whole city under the earth. Surely the hubs would have accepted that kind of brain power."

"They did, but there were people who didn't agree with the selection process. They didn't want to be a part of that kind of government."

"That's nuts?" exclaims Spencer without thinking.

"Is it?" replies Lynda. "We have our own government here. The people vote on everything, including who is in charge. I was voted onto the council along with Stephen and Clay. Every decision is implemented by us through the people. I would rather have a real voice in what happens than to be told what to do and think and say."

"This is bullshit," says Raven. Her voice has been conspicuously silent throughout Lynda's explanation. "You're a hypocrite. You're not giving us a say in anything. We have good jobs to go back to, good lives."

"Let me guess," says Lynda. "Each of you has a government family member, you were encapsulated in a government bank, your time in the wild has been minimal and you will most likely have high ranking jobs that give you access to the Capitol." Right on every count. As I look to Raven, I can see that she feels uncomfortable. "It's not your fault," continues Lynda. "They're grooming you to be a part of the system, teaching you that if you do what they say, you'll be rewarded...but at what cost I wonder. You're young and strong and smart, but you are ignorant to what is going on around you. People on the outskirts of the city are starving. They don't have access to all of the lifesaving things that you do. Life quality is based on a hierarchy."

"I don't want to hear any more!" shouts Raven. "Lies, all lies. The government wouldn't starve the people who grow our food, who supply us with goods."

"Okay," says Lynda, raising her hands in submission. "Okay. But there's one more thing you should know before I leave you in peace. We have it from good sources that the government is planning to shut down the wild once all of the cryotank survivors have reached the hubs."

"What do you mean *shut down*?" asks Spencer. "They can't just shut down open land." Lynda looks at him with surprise.

"Spencer, the wild is just the government's plaything, their chess board. They control just about everything that happens out here and they can do whatever they want when they're done with it. That's why we're secretive. That's why we're paranoid. And we won't let anyone ruin what we have created, not even the government."

CHAPTER TWENTY-SEVEN

Wren

Several uneventful nights pass as we find ourselves getting used to our new home. I'm becoming used to the creaking of the stairs, the sound of tree branches hitting the roof and even the smell of rot. But on the fourth morning I awake to a horrifying sound. At first, I think that it's a part of my dream, the nightmares that I have also become used to. Then I hear it again, howling, high-pitched and close. I sit up quickly, glancing around the bedroom to Gemma curled up next to me on the hard floor. Briar is gone. I scramble out of the room, careful to leave Gemma sleeping and rush to the lookout room. There Briar sits, perched on the window frame looking down at the yard below. I hurry to her side and see the horror of Mutts, three of them, pacing back and forth in front of the house.

"The explosion that Rory caused must have attracted them," comes Ian's voice from the doorway. I turn as he reaches me. He looks good even with his black hair tousled around his face. His skin had browned from the sun and there's a ruggedness about him, a strength. His blue eyes pierce into mine as he continues. "There's only three of them. Arick thinks that they'll wander away when they realize that we don't have anything for them."

"Yeah, "we've got nothing but skin and flesh and blood which spells dinner to these crazy dogs," replies Briar. "And there were only two at dawn."

"What should we do?" I ask as my pulse begins to quicken. Briar turns away from the window.

"We hope that Arick is right."

Rory wakes up an hour later, clearly in pain as he moans and tries to force his brain to figure out what is going on. He's been in and out of it since we settled here.

"I'm glad to see you're awake," says Arick as we approach. "You need to drink some water." Rory doesn't speak, but when Arick unscrews the cap on a fresh bottle of water and places it to his lips, he drinks. "Small sips now." I hear Rory reply,

"Thank you." His voice is dry and raspy, like sandpaper. Arick lays a hand lightly on the top of Rory's singed head and says,

"You're welcome, Rory. Try to rest." Arick moves away to access the situation outside and as he leaves the room, Rory's eyes lock with Briar's. They look long at one another until Briar gives him a look of indifference and Rory looks away. Now that the bandages have been removed, I can see that his face will never look the same. Rory rests his puffy eyes on Ian and then Gemma who both give him small encouraging smiles. As his eyes meet mine, I don't know what to do. I'm not ready to smile so I look away. He's figured out where we all stand, and once again, he closes his eyes. Gemma stays with him all morning, offering him sips of water and making sure he's still alive. Briar and I decide to tear the house apart again, searching for anything that we can take with us while the Mutts continue to circle our house. We score in the bedrooms: tucked high on the closet shelves, we find miscellaneous pieces of clothing, a pair of shorts, random tee shirts and socks. We also come across a small stuffed rabbit that must have once belonged to a child. It's worn and musty but Gemma smiles when she sees it and claims it right away. I discover a box of foil ware pans under the kitchen sink which surprises me. They are reminiscent of the food delivery system back home and are probably a result of someone forgetting to return them for redistribution. I count them and find twenty in total and begin to think of ways to use them. Now with the sleeping bags and blankets from the city, I feel like we're getting somewhere, a small step closer to civilization.

"They're still out there," says Briar as I follow her into the back bedroom where Ian and Arick watch. It's time to think about our options.

"There's more," says Ian. I count eight now and they're getting aggressive. I watch as they growl, barring sharp dagger-like fangs from large evil heads. They are bulky and muscular, just like the Mutts in the city, but there is something different too. They lift themselves up on hind legs to peer into the lower windows and their eyes travel upwards to where we watch, meeting our gaze with a snarl. They are smart and not like gofetch-a-stick smart. They're clever and resourceful, I can see it in their eyes. They're just waiting, gathering in numbers, threatening us but also knowing that eventually we'll have to come out.

"This is messed up," says Briar breathlessly. She sees it too. "We have to take care of this before more come. If they get up to the roof, we'll be trapped. The only way is to take them out." As the last words exit her mouth, one of the beasts lunges upward, its steely claws grasping the window shutter below us. Its hind legs work furiously, trying to make purchase as the rest of the pack watches on.

"Shit!" exclaims Briar. The mutant dog falls, unable to pull its way up but once it hits the ground another dog tries. "Okay," says Briar turning to me and grasping my shoulders firmly. She looks into my eyes. "You're going to have to use your gun," she says. I'm horrified and excited all at the same time. Fear creeps up my back as adrenaline pumps its way into my blood stream. Before I can really think about it, before I can wrap my mind around the fact that I will kill something today, Briar has retrieved my gun and places it into my shaking hands.

"Pull the clip out," she says sternly. She's not messing around. I turn the heavy metal object over in my hands and find the bottom of the handle where the bullets go. "Good," she continues. "Here are the bullets. Load them in and be ready to reload once these are gone. Put the rest of the bullets in your pocket." I do what she says and load in the bullets as she watches. I drop one and it hits the hard wood floor with a clank. My hands are sweaty, and I wipe them on my pants.

"How do I…" She can see the bewildered look on my face and quickly takes the gun from me.

"Cock this back," she says, pulling back the top of the gun

with force. "Aim and fire, that's it." She holds it out to me, and I take it. She tosses her second gun to Ian who smiles roguishly. "Let's go," Briar says with finality.

"Be careful," adds Arick. "If at any time it looks like you're losing the advantage, get off the roof and back inside."

"Will do," replies Briar like a real soldier. That's what we are now, soldiers in a fight for survival.

We open the back-bedroom window to a chorus of snarls and howls. They see us and are watching our every move. Do they know what a gun is? Do they know how much their lives are in danger right now? Briar sits on the ledge, her back to the horde. She reaches up to the overhang of the roof and pulls herself up and over. I can hear her footfalls above me as she scrambles to lock her feet into place on the slanted surface.

"Are you ready?" asks Ian. His face is full of concern and I know that if I told him that I just couldn't do this, he would understand. But that's not who I am anymore. I'm a fighter now and I'm not going to let my fear get in the way of that.

"I'm good," I reply though my shaky voice gives me away.

"I'll spot you," he says as he wraps his hands around my waist, helping me reach the overhang from the windowsill. "You'll be fine." Stupidly, I glance down. All the Mutts are watching us, their eyes drilling holes into my own. If I fall, I'll die. *I cannot fall.* But as I begin to pull my way up, I realize that I do not have the same upper body strength as Briar and I find myself hanging over the edge, my arms scraping the rough roof tiles. I feel Ian grip my ankles and see Briar scooting her way down towards me, but I can't move. A howl and a series of aggressive barks echo up and I glance down again to see the Mutts up on their hind legs ready for dinner. That's enough to get my butt onto the roof. I pull the energy from somewhere deep and inch my body up until my hips are resting on the firm surface of the roof's edge.

"That was scary," I say as I find a holding spot neat Briar. She rolls her eyes and shakes her head, letting out the breath she was holding. Ian joins us and we scoot around the perimeter, ready for our attack. The Mutts sense something's up and they begin to pace all around the house, trying to find a better way up to us.

"Here we go," says Briar and I hear her gun cock back. She aims at the closest creature and fires a loud blast that resonates through my head. "Got him!" she yells. I see the dog fall backwards and land with a deadly thud next to its pack mate. The living Mutt's eyes travel from the dead animal next to it up to where Briar is perched. Its eyes are narrow and there is emotion there, anger and sadness, all in front of a calculating mind. It lets out a long low howl.

"That's right'" says Briar. "It's either me or you. Now what are you going to do?" Ian fires a shot taking it down but, as I look out towards the road, I see figures running, thick, furry, muscular creatures, too many to count.

"Oh no!" I exclaim pointing with my gun.

"Damn it," replies Briar in frustration. "Fire at will!" she yells, and Ian doesn't hesitate. I cock back my gun and aim at the closest beast. I pull the trigger and hear the bang of the bullet leaving. I'm not ready for the force and it pushes me off balance. I yell out and Ian steadies me.

"Careful," he says. I glance at my target, still looking up at me, and aim again. This time I'm ready and I watch it fall to its death. I see a deep bloody hole where its eye once was and my stomach lurches. I gulp the air and feel beads of sweat begin to form on my brow. *I can't do this. I can't do this*. The pack is running full force now and I think that maybe I've misjudged them. How stupid to run towards three rooftop assassins with guns, but there are so many, close to twenty now, jumping and snarling with those dagger-like teeth, ready to avenge the deaths of the others. We have to make quick work of this so we keep shooting. One down, two and then three. Briar stops to reload as I take my next shot.

"Take that, you filthy scum bag!" I yell as I pull the trigger. The bullet hits it in the hindquarters and as it falls, I see something that stops me in my tracks. It's small and furry and cute and not at all like the bulking pile of muscle and fangs that is attacking. A baby. It looks like someone's pet though its huge paws and tiny pointed teeth are signs of what it will become. My heart bleeds as I see it lay its small body on top of what I suspect is its mother. It whines and tries to suckle but the beast is quickly taking its last breath. I feel tears begin to fog my vision and then I hear the bang of Ian's gun and the small creature drops, gone along with its mother, its head blown off. I close my eyes and shake my head free of all the emotion inside of it. Anger, fear, sadness, frustration, and doubt, I push it all down and try to extract my warrior, that small piece of me that I hope is like Briar. As I open them again, there she is, the girl who is fearless. She nods curtly and continues to fire.

The carnage is vast. In less than an hour we've managed to take down more than fifty.

"Do you think more will come?" asks Gemma with concern.

"Not now," replies Briar as we walk through the bodies, our guns still at the ready. The smell of blood, metallic and foul seeps into my skin. Dead eyes follow us while tufts of fur blow by in the breeze. The sky is pale blue, the bodies are black and brown and gray, the blood is crimson, leaking into the bare earth and concrete.

"I think the problem that we face now is attracting other things," says Ian covertly.

"You mean the mutant people," replies Briar nonchalantly.

"Well, we did make a pretty big mess," adds Arick.

"Yes, and created a pretty big disturbance," says Ian. "This along with the explosion and house fire, we've set a target on our location. Anyone would come to investigate, others from the compounds and, yes, the people from the city."

"Can Rory travel?" asks Briar, not bothering to hide the bitterness in her voice.

"Yes," replies Arick softly. "We will have to carry him, but he can travel."

We waste no time in packing up. The thought of being surrounded again by vicious predators plays over in my mind making my hands work faster to stow the foil ware pans, sleeping bag and random clothes into my pack. I see Gemma lovingly tuck in the stuffed rabbit before zipping her own. Ian and Arick load up Rory for the trip while Briar watches on broodily. Rory is noticeably better, though his leg still remains in the splint and his burns remain covered by think gel-like pads; at least he's awake. He doesn't talk to anyone as we bustle about. There's something deeper going on in his head, deeper than just his wounds.

"Let's move out," says Ian as we gather on the front porch an hour later. We'll have to weave our way around the dead to get to the road. "We can continue following the main road and make some distance in the next few hours." We all hope that the river will follow and hopefully produce something soon. This walk is different than days ago. The road is firm under my feet and the gray has all but disappeared into the concrete. The haze lingers at the horizon and the obscure celestial body that was once the sun still burns down, but the sky is blue and pure and adds its hue to break up the monotony. Rory fluctuates between consciousness and sleep which is probably a good thing. Being dragged on concrete with a broken leg and burned skin couldn't feel good. I bet he wishes for the gray sandy moon again.

It has been a little more than a week since we left the safety of the cryotanks, but it feels like months. I can't imagine what several more weeks would feel like. And then, what will happen once we arrive at the hub? I'm afraid to face a new life alone. I miss my mom and I wish Aiden were here. I miss him too. I feel the smooth surface of the ring hugging my finger and the ache in my heart is intense, like claws scraping against my tissue, pulling me apart piece by piece. I miss my friend, my only real friend, but I feel the sting of these thoughts because I know that I hurt him. Our last moments together will always be tainted by that.

I am sweaty and tired as time ticks by. We have been careful to scan the perimeter as we walk, looking for movement of any kind. No one speaks just in case, and I can see the butt of Briar's gun poking out of her pocket. Mine has been relocated from the bottom to the top of my pack and now I know I won't hesitate to use it.

Rory lets out an occasional moan causing Briar to hiss, "Shhhh," and Gemma seems lost in her thoughts as she walks by Arick's side, glancing down to Rory every now and again. I'm happy to leave the house behind and I want to leave behind the memories too, the killing, the death, the fear, but why bother.

There will be many more bad memories to keep them company.

One more hour, then another. And then, something changes. I don't notice it at first but when my foot comes down with a crunch, I feel something that isn't hard and unyielding. I stop walking and look down. As I lift my shoe, I see a small mound of soil with a shoot of thick grass pushing its way through the concrete. It's not green but brownish and blends into the color of the dirt. It's close to death but still, it's grass and there's just enough of a greenish hue mixed with the brown that it couldn't have been dead long. My heart begins to beat faster, and I forget momentarily the sweat dripping down my back as I search frantically for more. I cup my hands over my eyes to shield them from the brightness of the sun. Up ahead, the rest of my squad walks, soundlessly, in their own thoughts.

"Wait," I say, but my throat is dry, and my words sound more like a croak. "Wait!" I say more loudly, and Ian is the first to turn. "Look down!" I point to more small mounds of dirt, breaking through the concrete in front of them, wondering how they haven't noticed. Ian's eyes go wide as he sees the grass, and I see a glimmer of hope flash across Briar's face. More shoots of grass lay ahead of us. They are also brown and half dead, but I notice that as we walk, they become paler and paler until I see true green. We stop, and Gemma sits down next to the grass in the middle of the road and touches each blade with loving hands. Seeing her, I want to cry, not because I'm so happy we have grass, but because a stupid plant can make us all so hopeful. This is the sign that I've been waiting for, an indication of new life ahead, a sign that we have left death behind.

CHAPTER TWENTY-EIGHT

Aiden

"We need to get out of here," says Raven once Lynda has left. "These people don't stand a chance."

"So, you believe Lynda?" I ask.

"No," she replies. "But I believe that she believes it."

"Huh?" asks Spencer.

"I don't think she would make that whole story up," adds Jewel. "Even if ten percent of what she's saying is true, at the very least, the government is corrupt."

"Commander Rob would have told us," replies Raven. "If the wild is their playing field, he would have said something."

"Are you sure?" I ask with skepticism. "If we really are being groomed as Lynda says, then this mission could just be another test."

"No," says Raven firmly. "I refuse to believe any of this. We don't know these people, there's nothing going on here but a group of people living underground by choice." I grab my tablet that rests on the table in front of me. For the hundredth time, I try to activate it, but an error is all a see.

"This is useless," I say, dropping it back onto the table.

"These devices aren't programed to pick up signals below ground," replies Spencer. "And they're barely functional on the outside, at least in the wild."

"Okay," I say. "So getting out of here is going to be a problem. Spencer?" He looks up from the table where his hands are twisting nervously.

"Yeah?"

"If we can get our hands on one of the tablets down here, could you hack it, maybe find a map of this place or surveillance video?" His eyes get bright with excitement.

"Of course," he replies. "But how...?"

"Let me worry about getting a tablet," I reply with a grin. "Let's go back to the common area this morning. Maybe we can meet some of the locals, get a better understanding of what this place is about."

We exit our rooms, glad that at least we're not being isolated from the population, and wander our way back to the large room we visited upon arriving. It's deserted but for a man and woman seated at one of the tables. They talk softly to one another. I notice that they are dressed simply but not in clothes that I've ever seen. The woman wears deep blue slacks and a gray button-down shirt, a striped shawl of crimson and purple over her shoulders. The man wears similar clothes, deep blue slacks and an orange collared shirt. They remind me of the wild nomads that we met on the outside, not torn and soiled, but colorful.

"Not much going on here," says Spencer stating the obvious.

"It's too early," adds Jewel.

"So much for information gathering," says Raven in frustration.

"Maybe everyone's still sleeping." Suddenly, the sound of ringing bells cuts through the silence and I glance up to see a large speaker that I hadn't noticed before. Three bells and then a pause. The pattern repeats several times and then stops. Slowly the man and woman rise from their table and seem to notice us for the first time. The woman takes in our appearance and I see recognition register on her face. She must realize from our jumpsuits who we are.

"It's time for breakfast," she says calmly, approaching us with a smile. I realize that I'm starving and as I look to Spencer, I see a stupid smile covering his face at the mention of food.

"Come with us," the man says kindly. He's older and his brown eyes crinkle at the corners reminding me of my father. I feel a stab of loss but shake it away. "The dining hall is just down the hallway there." We follow them through one of the many metal doors and enter a new tunnel. It's dark, the only light coming from ahead.

"So, how long have you been here?" asks Raven. "I mean at the Underground?" She trying to act nonchalant but she's definitely digging for information.

"Only about a week," replies the woman. "We came here together."

"Came from where?"

"From our cryobank," answers the woman simply.

"But...why?" asks Spencer in awe. "Why not go directly to one of the hubs?"

"It's a long story," replies the man. It's clear that they don't want to talk about it, not now.

I can hear the clatter of plates and cutlery, the chatter of people and can even smell the aroma of something savory cooking as we enter a new space.

"Here we are," says the man. "You're welcome to sit with us."

"Okay," says Jewel before any of us can decline. I scan the area, a sea of color, every old sector represented in grays and crimsons and blues. There are many other colors as well. So many faces look up to us, every age, every ethnicity all contributing to this gathering, all intermingled. It strikes me that all of the divisions are gone here and I let out a sardonic laugh, thinking about how hard I worked to get to the university in Sector Two, how important it was for me to live in the Capitol. And after everything, here we are, Spencer, Raven and I, ready to embark on that dream and none of these people care. To them the city is an evil entity and I would guess that all of them are ready to protect what they have here.

"Come on," says the woman. "Let's get you guys something to eat." There is a familiarity in her face, a face beginning to line with age. My brows furrow as I study her features.

"Just over here," she continues, gesturing us in front of her. We join a long line that forms near the doorway and winds its way into a serving area in the kitchen. As we get closer, I see workers ladle out food, eggs mixed with root vegetables and something that looks like pork.

"Tofu," says the man in explanation. I take my plate and wonder how they can possibly grow enough food to serve hearty meals like this. We find a place to sit at a table that is nearly empty. As I set my plate down and pull out my chair, I glance over to Spencer who seems to be a statue glued to his spot, his mouth hanging open in surprise. I follow his gaze to the other person sitting at the table, a young man with curly dark hair and the shadow of stubble covering his cheeks and chin. He leans back in his chair in a relaxed way, glancing at the tablet in his hand. I narrow my eyes, trying to remember where I might have seen his face until Spencer blurts out,

"Dominick...Oh my God, Dom...Mr. Donovan!" Spencer is unable to move his limbs and he's in real danger of dropping his plate, so I take it from him and place it on the table.

"It's...it's an honor," he belts out before shakily pulling out his chair and sitting. Dominick watches him with arched eyebrows and then gives him a nod of acknowledgement. His food forgotten, Spencer continues, "I've been following you for years. Well, I mean before the flare and everything. Not in a creepy way," he explains. "I mean I've been following your work on the new 3-D messaging with the halo-coded inserts. Amazing stuff!" I dig into my eggs, amused with Spencer's excitement and then stop abruptly as the reality hits me. I glance to Raven who is shaking her head in disbelief. I guess our mission is over, but what I can't understand is why Donovan is here? Maybe he and the other officials are being held like us. I turn back to my food waiting for the opportunity to let them know who we are and how we ended up here. The food is delicious, seasoned with herbs and accompanied with a buttery golden sauce. I glance back to Raven and she gives a nod.

"Are you a tech guy?" asks Dominick with interest, causing Spencer to choke on his meal.

"Me? Oh no nothing like you. I dabble." The goofy look on his face almost makes me feel sorry for him.

Raven gives a roll of her eyes before adding, "Spencer is a tech wizard. He's just embarrassed to tell you because he has a man crush on you." For the first time since I've known Spencer, I see a real blush creep onto his cheeks. He gives Raven a sharp nudge and a dirty glance. "Commander Woodman and Dr. Bell, I presume," she continues, directing her question to the man and woman across the table. Now I see the resemblance from the bio pictures we were given but they look much different now, older maybe. Raven takes a deep breath and shakes her head. "We were sent on a government mission to find you," she says. "This would be the last place I would have looked. What are you doing here?"

They don't answer immediately and seem to be contemplating what to say. Spencer is so busy staring at Dominick that he's forgetting to eat. I give him an elbow to the side causing him to look over. I lift my fork full of eggs and potatoes and motion for him to eat.

"Oh, yeah," he says, taking a bite, his eyes still focused on Dominick. "This is the best day of my life," he says with relish.

"Raven, right?" asks Dr. Bell and Raven gives a nod. "We came here because we helped build this place." I see the shock on Raven's face, the sense that these words don't ring true.

"How is that possible," she says.

"Everything that you're seeing here was done long before the flare hit, but the Underground wasn't created for an end of the world scenario. It was built for a rebellion."

"No," says Raven. "No, that's not true. The bunkers were built by the government. They were built for refuge, a place for protection. These tunnels came after."

"Are you saying that while working at government jobs, the three of you were secretly working against the government?" I ask. "Planning some sort of overthrow?" They don't answer but I can tell that I've figured it out.

"But why?" asks Spencer, his attention drawn back momentarily. "Why would you do that? You guys had great jobs; you still do if you go back with us to the government hub. This makes no sense." Commander Woodman looks up at me with his steely gray eyes.

"The government is corrupt," he says simply. "It's always been corrupt, an entity concerned with its own wellbeing and nothing more."

"No, no,' says Raven. "I know that Lynda said that the hubs turned people away and maybe that's true, but I know they had to have had their reasons. This is a different world now, a harsh world and things are bound to change, hard choices have to be made."

"Let me ask you something," says Dr. Bell. "Before the flare, did you ever visit any of the outlying sectors, Sector Five? Sector Six?"

"No, but those areas were mainly farmland and factories. No one visits those areas."

"Would it surprise you to learn that children as young as ten were working in those fields and factories, that many times there was not enough food to keep everyone alive and healthy. Can you imagine the irony in that? Working all day to provide food for our communities while your children starve?"

"This can't be true," says Raven. "This sounds like the kind of propaganda they're spreading here, not real facts. People will be bitter when they see others have it better." Dr. Bell shakes her head.

"I know it's difficult for you to understand. You're so young. But Lynda has been honest with all of you. We began smuggling people out well before the flare, bring those who lived in the worst conditions here," says Dr. Bell. "And after the flare it became a shelter for all of those turned away from the hubs, but the mission remains the same."

"The government will not change just because a world catastrophe is forcing them to begin again. Unfortunately, we have already seen what the past fifty years have done to many of the people allowed into the hubs," adds Commander Woodman.

"God," spits Raven. "You expect us to believe all of this crap? A conspiracy of a government to hurt its people?" She glances to me and I see fire in her eyes. "I worked hard," she says. "We all worked hard. We did everything that was expected of us and each of us, Aiden, Spencer and I, knew that with hard work we could have a better life. Now we do and that life came right from the government. Your story? Your story sounds like a bunch of slackers who aren't willing to put in the effort and want a better life just handed to them. Well, I don't roll that way and, in the end, you will be the ones to suffer because you have the most to lose by staying here." We are all in fear of Raven's outburst and Spencer's eyes keep wandering back to Dominick who still sits relaxed in his chair watching Raven.

"I don't know," says Spencer softly. "If this place is good enough for Dominick then..."

"Shut the hell up, Spencer," yells Raven, causing the tables around to finally notice us. She quickly stands, causing her chair to fly back with a bang, and marches from the room leaving behind her plate of half-eaten food. That's when I notice that Jewel is missing.

CHAPTER TWENTY-NINE

Wren

"This is amazing," says Briar as she bends down to touch the grass at her feet. There are thick patches all around us, poking out of the hard concrete like strong warriors refusing to be kept under ground. Arick gives a loud, Whoo hoo! I glance at him with arched eyebrows.

"It's grass, not gold," I chide.

"Well, it might as well be gold," replies Briar. "Green anything means water." I bend down and gingerly pluck some of the grass, making sure to get the roots. I press them to my mouth.

"The roots are moist," I say with a smile. We dance around the sparse grass like Natives doing a rain dance, all of us but Ian.

He watches with a smile.

"If the grass continues, and we find patches that are big enough, we can dig deep below and find water even if the river remains dry," I say.

"Yes," replies Ian. "But something tells me that we will find a bigger source soon. Look." He points into the distance and I can just make something out on the horizon. A thin line of green begins to unfold. I squint and concentrate on the green and then I see something more. A layer of black billowy clouds is pushing their way toward us, rolling across the blue sky enveloping it in gray once again.

"Those are trees!" says Arick excitedly, completely ignoring the storm.

"Yeah, but look at those clouds," says Briar with trepidation. Ian looks long, assessing the brewing storm.

"We have time," he replies. I glance down at Rory who is sleeping and then scan the distance to the trees ahead. It doesn't look too far but out here distance is deceiving. "Let's drink some water quickly and head out. Those trees might make a good shelter for a few days, and with a storm comes rain. We can collect it and refill our bottles."

We take hasty sips of our water and head out. We all have renewed excitement for what is ahead. Anything will be better than the bloody carnage we left behind. The further we walk the bigger the green becomes and the closer the storm seems. A few yards in, I notice a swift change in the temperature. The sweat on my neck quickly evaporates as cooler air blows toward us. It feels good…for now, like we've just stepped into air conditioning. I still have thoughts about the chilly night spent at our first camp, but trees mean wood and wood means a fire.

"Do you guys think you can pick up the pace a little?" asks

Ian as he and Arick drag Rory's body ahead of the rest of us.

"Yeah," replies Briar. "Come on, Gemma," she adds as she takes her small hand. Gemma's hair is a mass of pale gossamer in the wind that has now picked up.

We all break into a jog and immediately I feel a cramp in my side. Grit from dirt and sand blowing up at my face coats my lips and tongue just as I feel the first thick drop of rain hit my head. We are running flat into the storm. I hear a clap of thunder in the distance and it's like a whip urging us to pick up the speed. Arick and Ian duck into the forest with Rory. I follow closely with Gemma and Briar close behind. We stop to catch our breath.

"That was close," says Briar as another boom of thunder breaks the air. She bends over, resting her hands on her knees in exhaustion. This time the thunder seems much closer and it's followed by a streak of white lightning. As we gather ourselves, the rain begins in earnest, but the tall trees protect us from most of the downpour.

"Well, this worked out," says Arick as he glances around our little resting place. My feet stand on firm earth. I take a deep breath and notice the sweet scent of pine leaves and soil. It is calming and so familiar and happy, so unlike the gray sand, the city and even the small neighborhood of homes that are behind us. I feel a smile creeping into the corners of my mouth. Ian watches me and smiles back. His deep blue eyes are hypnotizing, and I look away quickly, but I see him continuing to watch me from the corner of my eye.

"We need to find something to gather all of this water in," says Arick as he begins riffling through his bag. We all follow suit as my mind goes over my supplies. My hand passes by the foil ware containers that I have stashed away.

"Here," I say, and I pull them from my pack. "We should be able to collect enough in theses."

"Great, Wren," says Arick. He and Ian venture out into the open downpour. I watch, shaking from the cold wind, as they lay out the containers. I can see the bottom of each container quickly begin to fill, thick drops pinging off the reflective surface. Under the canopy, we are protected from the water pouring out of the sky, but not the lightning and wind and chill that is creeping into my bones. I gather up Gemma and we move close to Briar as Ian and Arick hunch over Rory. His eyes are open now and he's shivering just as bad as I am. I unzip Gemma's pack and take out her blanket, wrapping it snuggly around her.

"Thanks," she says through shattering teeth. Ian takes his out and drapes it over Rory. We are a huddle of trembling leaves in a storm that threatens to wash us away. And then just as suddenly as it began, the rain stops. Arick sees a patch of clear sky breaking through the angry clouds and we are soon left with white billowy puffs and crystal blue skies for miles. Blue, green, white, brown, it's all so amazing. No gray sand, no black char from burning houses, no deep red of blood. It feels like surviving on crackers for a year and then being given a hot fudge sundae. I can almost taste these new colors, fresh and vibrant, as my eyes soak them in.

"Wow," exclaims Gemma as she rolls up her blanket. The chill in the air is subsiding and I walk into a patch of sunlight to warm my arms. I close my eyes tight in contentment as the sun tingles down my arms. The air seems pure now and safe. The forest of pine is the perfect resting place. There is a large open area that is well protected by a wall of tall, thick trunks. The canopy is high enough to be safe for a fire but lush enough to form as a natural roof. I may never want to leave.

"Okay," says Ian as he glances to me. "Why don't you and Briar go and hunt down some dry firewood while we put up the tents."

"Perfect," replies Briar with a hint of sarcasm.

"Come on," I say as I grab Briar by the arm. "It'll be fun. Just a little hike in the woods." I feel something like happiness for the first time. It feels good to be walking on new terrain, to be smelling the pine and to know that we will have a fire tonight. Plus, we have water to fill our bottles.

Briar and I wander deep into the pine forest, our feet crunching over dead leaves that blanket the path. It is darker and the further we get in, the closer the trees become. A dead fallen tree blocks our way and I wonder if the storm has struck it down.

"Here's our firewood," says Briar as she stops to inspect the fallen tree. It looks like a good find; there are many thin branches that will be easy to break off. We get to work and quickly discover that the underside is dry and brittle. We snap off smaller twigs and dig under the forest floor to find moss and debris for kindling. Soon we have a pile big enough to last for more than the night.

"This should do it," says Briar as she adds a final log to our pile. "So, what do you think of this place?"

"I like it," I reply, happily. Briar gives a short laugh.

"Yeah, even without four solid walls, this place feels safe," she says. "But we still have to be on the lookout. A good fire will keep things away but, as you know, it might also bring things to us."

As we sit perched on the old fallen tree, the cooler air forces goose bumps onto my arms.

"So, how are you doing, Wren? How are you really doing?" asks Briar.

"I don't know," I reply. "Okay, I guess. I mean, this isn't fun and yeah, I'd much rather be eating the Endless Ice Cream Bowl at Shonnie's, but otherwise, yeah, I'm good."

"Shonnie's," she echoes with a smile. "Yeah, I like that place too."

"Really?" I say with surprise. The old ice cream parlor was one of my haunts with Aiden. It was one of the few places where you could get a treat outside of the meal delivery service.

"Really," she says with finality. "That place rocks. I used to go whenever I was back from the University; any chance I got for the pistachio sundae." I smile, thinking of her digging into a heaping pile of green. Then my smile falters. Memories of Aiden come rushing back. All those times, sharing ice cream, holding hands, when all along I knew I would hurt him eventually, knew that my dreams would never match up to his.

"God, what I'd give for ice cream now," Briar continues, dreamily. I realize in that moment that I don't know her at all. All I know is the image of her, the Briar I want her to be, strong and a little wild. But except for a few quick conversations over canned peaches and burning houses and firing guns, we've never really talked. She slaps dirt from her hands. "I was a researcher before the flare," she says as if reading my mind.

"Oh," I reply. I'm shocked. She doesn't seem old enough to have a job like that.

"I was on a university team that studies weather patterns. The movement and anomalies of the sun were a part of that research. We never saw it coming, none of us." She looks at me. "The thing is, we were trained to see crap like that." My head snaps up and my eyes search hers. "I don't know," she continues, shaking her head. "I guess we missed it."

"Could it have been something else?" I ask. "Could it have been an attack from outside?"

"No," she replies. "No, we would have seen that coming too. We were constantly tracking the skies. The only activity we saw was right before it hit." Briar looks up and her pale eyes meet mine. She really is beautiful, her dark brown skin contradicting her strange blue eyes and her wild brown curls sweeping at her angular cheek bones.

"I got everyone that I knew to safety but most of them went into the bunkers. A few to their cryobanks."

"What about you?" she asks. My eyes begin to well up and I blink the tears away before they can run down my cheeks.

"There was a boy," I say.

"Ah, Ha!" she shouts. "There' s always a boy." I shake my head.

"It's not what you think. I was leading him on because it was easier to be with him than to be alone. I realize that now." Her bright eyes do not leave my face and I can see that she gets it. "Seriously, Briar, the last conversation we had was an argument over our university decisions. He was angry, he had every right to be, because I made him believe that I'd follow him anywhere. Aiden was a good person, and he loved me, but there was something about him, something I couldn't put my finger on, something that made me hesitate." I lift my finger to show her the silver band. The ruby stone shimmers in the sunlight. "He gave me this ring anyway. I think he always believed I'd change my mind, but I wouldn't have, Briar, I wouldn't have."

"Come on, Wren. You're a smart girl. Do you really think you're the only one who's been in that position?" I shake my head. "Did you ever stop to think that the reason you didn't want to be with this boy is because he just wasn't the one? Maybe it's as simple as he's just not the one for you." Could it be that simple? She gives me a quick hug and I think I'm beginning to feel better. "After all that we've been through," she continues. "We're family, more than family if that's possible." I smile. I don't want to talk about Aiden anymore. I want to tuck his memory away, remembering all the good times because I can already feel him slipping away.

"If it makes you feel any better, I had my own relationship issues before the flare."

"Oh yeah?" I reply a little surprised. "What was his name?"

"Clare, her name was Clare."

CHAPTER THIRTY

Aiden

I glance around the dining area frantically. It's not like Jewel to wander away. And then I see her blond head bobbing among a group of children. I let out a sigh of relief and turn back to Dr. Bell.

"We're all just a bit overwhelmed and confused," I say, trying to explain Raven's behavior.

"I know," she replies softly. "Have a look around. Maybe you'll get a different perspective."

"So, maybe you'd want to hang out?" asks Spencer shyly, his eyes glancing at Dominick. "I mean, later, when you're not busy," he adds. "I mean, I'll get it if you're busy, I just thought, if you weren't doing anything..."

"Sure, Spencer," replies Dominick. "I'll give you a glimpse into that 3-D model you were talking about." I stand to leave, pulling a stunned Spencer with me.

"Easy boy," I whisper. "You don't want to scare him off."

The next few days are filled with new discoveries. The Underground is huge, bigger than I would have thought possible. Samuel takes us on a tour to Tunnel One and I'm honestly shocked to see the enormity of the crops they grow.

"Hydroponics at its finest," says Samuel, holding his arms out wide. Plants hang from man-made cords, laden with fruit. Tomatoes, melons, oranges and many more varieties, ripe and ready for harvesting. There are massive trays of tiny roots dipped in water, green sprouts just beginning to grow along with blossoming cabbages and heads of lettuce. We enter another room at least a hundred yards deep with tall stalks of corn and grain and soybeans all warmed by hanging lights to emulate the sun. It's all mind blowing and makes me think of Wren. She would do well here. Her skill set is perfect for this environment.

We walk by classrooms filled with children, and by an infirmary with shelves filled with medical supplies. There seems to be a job for every inhabitant. Workers are needed to maintain the crops and teachers are needed for the children. There are cooks and doctors and scientists in labs working on new technology. Men and women work in supply rooms, loading shelves or transporting supplies that are needed in other parts of the community. Samuel leads us down one tunnel after another, but we never see an exit or anything indicating a way out. He has shown us so much that I am sure they will never allow us to leave now. We know too much. As we walk back to our rooms, I sense that Raven is thinking this too and I'm sure she's already coming up with an escape plan.

At lunch I find Jewel. Raven has decided to stay in our apartment while Spencer is off somewhere with Dominick so I'm glad when I see Jewel sitting at a table surrounded by others her age. I smile as she scoots over to make room for me.

"This is Aiden," she says to the table at large. I get a few nods before everyone turns back to their conversations.

"You make friends easily," I say as I take a bite of my sandwich. The bread is flat and a little tough but tasty.

"I think this place is good for me," she says.

"How so?" I ask thickly.

"I don't know," she replies. "Before the flare there was so much expected of me, I was the center of everything. I felt like if I failed at anything it would crush my parents, so I worked hard not to fail."

"That's a bad thing?"

"It's a bad thing if you're working hard to please everyone else and you forget about yourself." I nod. "When my university letter came early, you should have seen my father's face. He couldn't stop smiling. But, Aiden, I really didn't want it." I'm shocked to hear this, and I study her face to see if she's being honest.

"What did you want?" I ask in confusion.

"If I could have any dream, it wouldn't be working at some stressful government numbers job. I've always wanted to be a teacher, a math teacher."

"You could have gone to the university and still been a teacher, a professor even," I counter.

"Even if I had, it would have disappointed my parents. I never really had a choice, but now..." She pauses, contemplating what her choices might be. "I've always loved kids. I have a younger sister...had a younger sister, did I tell you?" I shake my head.

"No."

"She was always in my shadow. I always felt bad about that." I take a deep breath because I know all about regrets. "Gemma was sweet and kind and very resourceful, but no one ever saw that in her because they were all so busy looking at me. She didn't deserve that."

"Well, maybe you still can be a teacher," I say, trying to bring her back to the present. She gives me a small smile, but I still see the sadness in her eyes. "You never know, you might have the chance to make it up to her…someday." I hate giving her false hope, but I can't stand the look in her eyes. I add, "You'll make a great teacher, Jewel, but you'll have to dumb it down a little." That gets me a smile. She's right, this place might be good for her.

After lunch, I wander into a tunnel that I have not explored yet. It is lined with doors, all closed but for the one on the end. I peer inside and see Clay working on a halo screen hovering above his desk. This might be a good chance to see if I can get my hands on a tablet for Spencer to hack into. Clay's eyes flick up to meet mine and he waves me in.

"Hey," I say, walking around him to get a better view of the screen. He doesn't stop me. "I didn't think there were halo screen that worked. I guess I'm not surprised after everything I've seen here." Clay gives a soft laugh.

"Yeah, it's pretty impressive."

"So, how does it work," I ask as I take a closer look. The screen shows a live feed from the outside just above a tunnel entrance. A security camera, I'm sure. I wonder if the halo can be used as a communication device from within the Underground and where the central control is located. Surely, there is no way to access the government halo system. Clay types in a code and immediately the video feed changes. I expect to see Lynda's face or Stephen or even the supply room, but I don't see any of those things. What I do see makes my makes my breath catch in my throat.

"What is that?" I ask, glancing from the screen to Clay. I see the familiar jumpsuits, jumpsuits covering several figures all running full out across mounds of gray sand.

"Survivors," he replies. "Cryotank survivors."

"But how?"

"We have a handful of surveillance cameras scattered across the wild as well as parts of the Capitol and beyond." My heart races as he takes something from a small bin on his desk and holds it in his hand for me to see. It's a small piece of plastic, no bigger than my fingernail. "They are light and thin and the adhesive on the back adheres to almost any surface, and the video quality is good as you can see." I take the tiny camera and turn it over in my hand and then turn my attention back to the screen.

"We're keeping our eyes on the survivors," he continues. "We don't want them to get too close, plus it gives us an idea of how many are left. But Aiden, it isn't pretty out there, especially south of Sector Two." I watch the screen, mesmerized by a small squad crashing across the sand, my eyes looking for any trace of ginger, Wren. I wonder how far away they are, who they are, where they came from, and why they are running. And then I gasp because I see what's chasing them, dogs, wild but so much more than that. They are muscular beasts and it's clear that they can't be outrun.

"What the hell are those things?" I ask as I see a squad member, a man, turn and point a gun. Fire erupts form the muzzle and a dog goes down.

"Those are just one of the government's creations," replies Clay solemnly. "Mutated animals designed to kill."

"That's, that's sick," I spit, my pulse beginning to quicken. This can't be real. I feel like I'm crashing, falling off a ledge, my allegiance crumbling around me. Another wild dog lunges at a younger squad member that can't keep up. The boy is dragged away by sharp teeth as he claws at the sand and screams for help. The others stop for a second to watch and then an older man shouts something and they begin to run again. The dogs have stopped their chase for the moment, and I think that the survivors will be okay until I see them thrown back, their bodies soaring through the air as a fiery red explosion lights up the sand. I take a step back in shock.

"What is happening out there," I whisper. The three squad members lay in a heap, unmoving. This scene is nothing like my own experience in the wild.

"This is what your beloved government is doing, Aiden." He leans back in his chair and rubs at his tired face. "I've seen horrors I can barely explain. Earthquakes shaking the ground, pools of acid that sheer the flesh off of the unsuspecting, lightning strikes, sink holes, killer bees, all let lose by the government, all changing to test those still out there."

"But how do you know this is the government's work and why?" I ask. "Why kill the people who will be of value, who will be loyal? Why kill anyone? Let them live out here if nothing else."

"Because," he replies, his strong eyes meeting mine. "Your government only has room for the strongest now, those who will make good soldiers, good leaders. People like you. They won't risk keeping anyone else alive, especially the weak. The government will keep its strong players close, give them whatever they want while keeping the workers in check. A dictator's greatest fear is his people. Once one person decides to fight back, others always follow. That's what we're counting on. Look," Clay continues. He pulls open a desk drawer and takes out a stack of papers, printouts from the halo. I look closer and see lines of computer code. "Donavan has broken through these encrypted codes. They're signal codes that seem to be connected to what we're seeing, all beginning with GH1."

"Government Hub One," I say with immediately understanding. I've seen similar codes in Spencer's work.

"Yes," replies Clay. "See this," He runs his finger under the top line. I read, GH1MA435. "Government Hub One Mutant Animal in section 435 of the wild. They have their eyes on everything and these codes are adjusted daily for new, fresh terrors," explains Clay. My blood is on fire, coursing through my veins, reaching every centimeter of my body. I continue to watch the video as two people approach the newly dead survivors. They are not wearing jumpsuits and seem hesitant to get too close. The man kicks one of the bodies and soon the two are digging into what's left of pockets and packs, looting any belongings they can find.

"Are those your people?" I ask with disgust.

"No," says Clay. "Those are wanderers. There are pockets of them, but they're unstable, wild, unable to join any normal community. They seem to prefer that. We think they're descendants of the many mutations in unsafe locations after the flare. At some point they'll have to be eradicated." I nod in understanding.

"Look, Clay, we have to do something, we have to get out there!" I'm starting to feel true panic as I watch the wanderers pick apart what remains of the squad. She's out there surrounded by all of this. The chances of Wren making it out alive have significantly diminished. "You have manpower. We need to go out and help them, help the survivors get to safety." Clay shakes his head and it's maddening.

"The survivors are scattered all over the place and we only have a handful of surveillance cameras. There's no way of knowing anyone's location at any given time. Going out there would be a suicide mission, not to mention how it would put our people at risk." He pauses watching my reaction grow from anger to fury. "We have a long road ahead of us. We have to conserve what we have."

"Bullshit! This is bullshit," I yell. "People are dying, innocent people, people who will most likely join your cause if they know the truth."

"Look Aiden," he says in little more than a whisper. "We didn't start this. We aren't the ones who sent out mutated animals or created deadly traps. We're just trying to survive like everyone else." I run my fingers through my hair in frustration. I meet his gaze and I can tell that he will stand firm.

"I've got someone out there," I say. "A girl, someone too special to give up on." Clay clasps his hands behind his neck and lowers his head.

"Damnit," he says. Slowly he looks up at me.

"I'm not going back," I say quickly. "I'M NEVER GOING BACK!" I steady myself. "I'll stay here. I'll do whatever you want me to do but I have to find Wren."

CHAPTER THIRTY-ONE

Wren

Briar tells me all about Clare as we gather up the pile of wood. She talks about how quickly they fell in love; how special she was and also how she felt as if she couldn't share their love with anyone.

"She's the only person that I want to see when we get to the hub. She was the first person I took to safety."

"Well, then, I hope she's there," I reply. "What about your parents?"

"They disowned me years ago," she says bitterly." Once they found out about Clare."

"That's crazy," I reply sadly.

"Is it?" she asks. "You know the way the government is set up. We all have expectations put on us, especially after a university education. What do you think the government would say when I hit thirty and still wasn't married, still hadn't produced my one offspring?"

"Would they even know?" I ask incredulously.

"You bet they'd know," she replies. "I'm sure if I had lived out in Sector Six, if I had left my research job and landed on a farm or in a factory, no one would care but my parents wouldn't have that, not their daughter." She looks up at me as she gathers another pile of twigs into her arms. "That's what I should have done. I should have taken Clare into the countryside where no one really cares about stupid things like who you love."

"So your parents forced you to be something you're not." I say sadly.

"Oh they tried to straighten me out, believe me, they did everything they could and more," she answers darkly.

"You know, Briar, it doesn't matter to me who you love." I say it and I mean it. She gives a slight nod and smiles.

The sun is getting lower in the sky and our arms are full of fuel for the fire. Briar glances toward my face as we pick up the remaining twigs to use as kindling.

"That cut on your forehead looks like it might be getting infected." I can feel a slight sting from where the house explosion let loose its rage. I had forgotten about the cut.

"I'm sure there's some ointment in one of the first aid kits."

"Good idea," I reply. "It's going to take more than ointment to treat Rory, though." We haven't even touched on the topic of Rory since the explosion. I wonder how she feels about everything that happened. Briar remains silent.

"You know," I say. "You're going to have to forgive him at some point." Her head snaps from the wood in her arms to me.

"Why," she asks with anger. "He's the one who should beg for forgiveness." She gives her head a disbelieving shake. "Why is it that God always seems to let the selfish, mean jerks live while so many good people die?"

"I'm sure he's got baggage," I reply. "I'm not saying he's a good person. I'm not even saying that we should all be friends. Just remember where we are."

"We better get going," she says with a scowl.

We spy the tents as we enter the clearing, all perched around a circle of stones in the center. Arick lays the final stone as we approach.

"Wow, impressive," says Briar.

"Why, thank you," replies Arick with a bow. "Looks like you did pretty well yourselves." We dump our burden of logs and twigs next to the fire pit. Gemma and Ian sit next to their tents, reorganizing their packs with full bottles of rainwater, while Rory is absent, apparently stowed away in his own tent. Ian gets up, takes the fine kindling, and lights a match to it. It seems like he's done this before. I watch as a small flame begins to engulf the kindling, turning into a full-fledged fire once it hits the wood. As I rest my back against my pack and gaze into the jumping orange and blue flames, Ian comes to sit next to me. He has a tube of something in his hand. Before I can register that it is ointment, he takes a small amount and runs his finger across the cut on my forehead. His touch is gentle, and I feel his breath on my cheek as he leans in, taking a closer look for signs of infection. A hot spark runs down the back of my neck that has nothing to do with the fire, and I feel my cheeks burn.

"Thanks," I say when he's finished.

"You're welcome," he replies with a slight grin. I sense rather than see Briar watching and I pull my head back a little from his face. He gets the message and turns away.

"Gemma's the real doctor here," he says softly as he returns to his seat next to her. "She's been a real help tending to Rory."

"Yes, Gemma," replies Arick. "You seem to really have a knack for medicine. And you're not squeamish, which is a good thing in this case," he adds with a nudge. Gemma nudges him back with a smile.

"Wow, Gemma," I say.

"Impressive," adds Briar. My little Gemma who I have been trying to shield from as much as I can. This slight, blond girl with big blue-gray eyes, who can barely carry herself across this long journey, has found a skill other than building tents. I can't believe that I didn't notice her tending to Rory. I guess my hands were full with evil dogs. She'll be a great asset to the new world that lies ahead.

"We should all eat something," says Arick as he puts a thick log on the fire. My stomach gives a rumble as I pull out a meal pack. As hungry as I am, I almost gag at the sight of mac and cheese again, but it's food and it's limited. We all eat in silence, listening to the crackling fire. Gemma takes it upon herself to feed Rory and to make sure that he is drinking water. He's been awake for a while now and, from the constant moaning I'm hearing, seems to be in a lot of pain. I watch Gemma hold a spoon to his lips through the open flap of his tent.

"Will he be better soon?" I ask with concern, concern not only for him but for us.

"He should be noticeably better in another twenty-four hours, at least physically," says Ian with confidence. Another moan comes from his tent and Briar just gives a shrug as if she could care less. I don't want to look at him. I don't want to see the damage that he did to himself because every time I think about it, I remember the old man and woman and how they needlessly died. I look away from his tent. Maybe I'm just as hard as Briar when it comes to him.

With the green surrounding us and the crackling fire in front of us, I almost feel normal, like we're just getting ready to tell ghost stories. But the stories are real, and the ghosts are all of those that were left behind. Gemma scoots close to me after she has finished taking care of Rory for the night, and I can see the flames dancing in her eyes, as she watches the wood pop and crack. The sun has dipped below the horizon and I begin to feel my fatigue overwhelm me just as the shadows creep from the forest.

"I think it's a good idea for all of us to get some sleep," says Arick. "I'll take the first watch." Ian stands and stretches his limbs, causing the muscles in his arms to flex attractively. I watch, unabashed, completely checking him out. His broad shoulders make him look powerful and I can imagine the rippling physique that I know is there beneath his jumpsuit. I notice that his black hair is beginning to get longer, forming natural waves. It makes him look sexy and a little wild. And then those deep blue eyes, that seem to hold every emotion, glance my way and I force myself to look down.

"I'll take the first watch, Arick," he says. "You need sleep too, even if you are a tough old bird." Arick laughs.

"Who are you calling old?" He gives a shrug. "I suppose to someone as young as you, forty seems ancient." Everyone has a smile now, even Briar.

"Really, Arick," says Ian. "I don't mind taking the first watch. It takes me time to unwind before I can sleep. I'll wake you in a few hours." Arick gives a nod and we all slowly stand and make our way to our tents.

I am ready for a long rest. My feet are worn, and I am zapped of every last ounce of energy. I peel off my filthy jumpsuit in the privacy of my tent. I feel so dirty, as if I will never be clean again. I've never smelled like this before and what's worse is that I think I'm getting used to it. Before I lay my head down, I take out my toiletry pouch and get to work. I use my toothbrush and toothpaste and pull on a fresh tee and shorts that I took from our last stop. They smell musty, but feel smooth and clean next to my skin. I fall asleep quickly and my dreams are filled with endless scenes of sand houses blown away by the wind and my mother calling my name.

I awake several hours later with an image of my mother in my mind. But I can't get a clear picture of her once my dream fades. Her hair, fiery red, just like mine, her eyes mossy green. I can see all of that, but it's the little things that escape me now, the details like the curve of her mouth when she smiles or the slope of her small delicate nose. It's all disappearing too quickly. I shake my head to clear my mind and rub at my tired eyes. It's still dark but I can see the glow of the fire burning strong and, since there is movement, I assume that Arick sits tending the logs. I decide to sit with him for a while, just enough to forget my dreams and hopefully create better ones. As I peek out of my tent, a silhouette comes into view. Strong, broad shoulders, dark hair and tall, even as he sits. It's Ian. I hesitate. He looks beautiful, sitting there, the firelight turning his skin bronze, his hand absentmindedly running through is wavy hair. I feel shy. *He's just a guy,* I tell myself sternly and I leave the safety of my tent to quietly take a few tentative steps forward. He doesn't hear me until I trip gracefully over a log that I can't see in the dark.

"Whoa," I say as I fall face down on a blanket of pine needles. He turns and quickly comes to my aide.

"Are you oaky, Wren?" he asks as he helps to lift me to my feet.

"Just completely embarrassed," I say without thinking. I look up and see a smile dancing on his lips.

"You're still up?" I ask and then regret it. Clearly, he's up. My nerves tingle and my brain seem to be unable to put a logical sentence together.

"Still up," he says with another smile. We sit in silence in front of the dancing flames. I'm afraid to open my mouth and say something stupid. His arm brushes against mine and I instinctively move away.

"Sorry," he says looking away.

"No," I reply. "It's okay." He turns back to me his eyes searching mine. I swallow hard.

"You never did tell me much about what you were doing before the flare," I say, making small talk. It feels good sitting next to Ian, like this, close with no one else around. I can feel the strength of his body, feel his heat. There's a big part of me that wants his arms around me, that wants him to be my protector like Aiden use to be. "Were you at the university?"

"Yeah," he says. "I was." He turns to me and catches me staring. "How about you?"

"That was my plan," I reply, reaching down to retrieve a twig from the ground. I play with it idly, carving shapes into the dirt at my feet. "I wanted to study Botany. I had a whole hydroponics project in secondary school."

"Oh, that's interesting, Wren. You should do really well once we get to the hub." I nod.

"I hope so," I say. "What were you interested in?" I can't help feeling like I'm prying information from Ian, and it's a little annoying.

"Well," he replies. "I worked for a time in a research lab, working on new vaccinations, but it really wasn't for me. I guess I'm better in a physical environment, something where I can be outside." My brows furrow with confusion.

"I thought you were at the university," I say. "Did you graduate?" I see him frown and take in a deep breath before hitching a smile on his face again.

"Oh, yeah, I was able to get an apprenticeship in the lab during the summer last year."

"Oh," I reply. Most apprenticeships happen after graduation but maybe he had connections. We are silent again and I am beginning to feel so uncomfortable that I decide to head back to my tent and see if I can sleep. As I stand, Ian looks up to me.

"Are you leaving?" he asks softly. His blue eyes sparkle in the dim light, so deep and full of emotion. "Stay," he adds as he pulls my arm towards him.

"Okay," I say, surprised by the change in his tone. I return to my seat and he seems to relax.

"It's rough out here," he says. "Rougher than I thought it would be."

"Yeah, it is, but we'll make it."

"When I first saw you at the cyrobank, I thought you were a scared little girl," he says. "Following Briar around like a puppy. I was sure you would never make it this far."

"Thanks," I say a little too roughly, insulted. He laughs and then turns his bright eyes to mine.

"I've been watching you, Wren," he continues. "The way you take care of Gemma, the way you handled those Mutts on the rooftop, the constant optimism you bring, never complaining, it's inspiring." I'm happy for the darkness, hiding the blush that I feel creeping up my neck. It's the most he's said to me and I feel myself wanting to open up. "You're a soldier."

"And so are you," I reply because I don't know what else to say. He reaches down and takes my hand, intwining his finger with mine. When I don't pull back, he lifts our hands to kiss that back of mine. The gesture takes me off guard and my heart begins a rapid beat inside my chest. Aiden's ring catches the light for a second and I feel the familiar pang of loss for my first love. Ian's other hand reaches up to gently stroke my cheek and I lean into him, my lips parted, wanting the closeness of him. He smells like pine and smoke and sweat, a combination of each that is wholly Ian. He leans in and rests his forehead on mine. I want him to kiss me but instead, he lets out a sigh. What the hell's going on? I feel my stomach drop in confusion.

"In a different time, in a different place, this would work," he says. "I'm so attracted to you on so many levels."

"I feel the same way," I say breathlessly, my eyes watching his lips as he speaks. He gives another sigh and lets his hand drop while releasing my fingers.

"Not here," he says. "It won't work here." I feel tears of disappointment begin to sting my eyes and I blink hard. The glow from the fire illuminates his profile, his strong features, and the curve of his chin into his neck where there is a shadow of stubble. His black wavy hair sweeps across his eye and he instinctively combs it back with his hand. I don't know what to say.

"I've been waiting for the right moment, Wren, waiting for my brain to tell me that it's okay, waiting for a time to see that this might work, but I just can't do this," he says, and I know that he sees the hurt in my eyes. Now I'm left with a strong hollow craving for something I didn't even know I wanted.

CHAPTER THIRTY-TWO

Wren

The fire crackles as it begins to die down. Ian stares at the extinguishing flames.

"What's going on with you, Ian?" I ask, softly. I take a deep breath to calm the heat that still pulses through my body from his closeness.

"It's complicated," he says with a slight grin, throwing my words back at me.

"It's complicated," I echo, and then he turns to me, his eyes pools of liquid blue.

"It's okay, Ian," I continue, not able to meet his eyes. "I get it. I'm sure that there is a special girl out there waiting for you, maybe even at the hub. I hope she's there. I really do."

"No," he says, grabbing my wrist sharply. I pull back slightly from his rough touch. "Sorry," he says. "It's just there's no one. I don't want you to think that this is about me waiting for someone else. I've never met anyone who I've felt so connected with and I don't even really know you, Wren. It's crazy, but there's something I feel when I look at you, a strength, a vulnerability, hard and soft all at the same time."

"Then what is it?" I ask. "If you're worried about me…I had a boyfriend, Aiden, but he's gone…" I choke back a sob. "It wouldn't have worked for us anyway. I know that now."

"How?" he asks as his eyes search mine. "How do you know when it's the right person?" I shake my head and look at the fire.

"I think you know when you'd be willing to give up everything for that person, when you have to be with that person at all costs."

"Yeah, I get that" he says softly. He turns his head and gives me a half smile that makes him look mysterious and sexy. And then a shadow passes over his eyes and the smile is gone. "Sometimes what we want isn't what's best for us," he continues. "Trust me, Wren, you should keep your distance." I let out an aggravated, sarcastic laugh.

"Now you sound like you're working some covert dangerous secret mission that's liable to get me assassinated." I'm expecting him to laugh and when he doesn't, I give him a playful nudge. "Come on, Ian," I say. "It's okay. I'm not as innocent as I seem, and I'm not worried about getting hurt if that's what this is all about."

"Maybe you should be," he says darkly. "Maybe you should be worried about getting hurt." We sit in silence watching the fire die down. I'm so confused. There is no denying the strong connection that is beginning to form between us and I want to explore it. At the very least it could be a distraction from all the crap that we have to deal with. Aiden brought comfort and safety, even if I didn't want it, but Ian feels wild and untamed. Why is it so hard for him? I can't shake the feeling that there's more to his story, a lot more.

The golden colors of sunrise are just beginning to reach out over the horizon. The fire dies and then I hear movement across the way. Arick's head pops from a tent.

"You should have woken me," he says to Ian with a yawn. "I could have taken over long ago."

"It's okay," Ian replies. He stretches his arms wide and adds, "Looks like it's time for a nap." He holds out a hand to help me stand but keeps my hand a little longer than he needs to. His eyes look sad, but I also see a question in them. And then he turns away and disappears into his tent.

As I lay, staring at the blank ceiling of my tent, my mind cannot rest. Ian's bottomless blue eyes, his touch, keep me wide awake. Ian is different. He makes my heart race. I wonder what my life would have been like if I had met him before the flare.

Sleep comes, but it's short. When I awake, sun streams into my tent and I hear movement around the fire pit. Everyone must be up and ready to figure out the day. I pull my jumpsuit back on, ready to go exploring and see what, if any, resources are hidden in this green forest.

"Hey, sleepy head." Briar is digging into a meal pack. I sit down next to her and notice that Rory has been moved outside into the open air. Gemma gently replaces his bandages and tends to his wounds. He's awake and he glances toward me, giving me a slight smile that makes his puffy, red face look even more scary. I nod. For as bad as he looks, he doesn't seem to be in much pain now, so I guess whatever Gemma is doing is working. I even see him move his limbs, and his leg that was so badly broken, seems to be better. My eyes scan to Arick who is still tending a new fire and then to Ian who is also awake and perched on a thick log. He glances up and gives me that crooked half smile again. I feel a flutter in my stomach.

"So, what's going on?" I ask Briar. I add water to my freeze-dried pouch and brace myself for more pasta. Our meals are noticeable diminished. We've got maybe a week's supply left if we keep eating like we are. There's no need to talk about it. We all know the reality.

"It looks like we're going to camp here for a few days."

"Good," I reply. "I like it here." I glance across the fire and meet Ian's eyes. He's staring at me again, though this time he looks away when I catch him.

"Yeah," says Briar. "It could be worse. I actually slept pretty good last night. How about you?"

"Not bad," I lie. "We should go check out some of the areas around us. Maybe we can see how far the forest goes or find a fresh water source, make sure there are no Mutts roaming around."

"Sounds like a plan," she replies as she crumples up her meal pouch. "As soon as you're finished, we'll head out." She turns to retrieve her backpack from her tent, and I notice that she's still unable to look at Rory. Hopefully, he'll be able to walk on his own soon, but he'll still slow us down. I quickly finish my meal and decide to take a closer look at him. His beady eyes dart to mine and he holds my gaze.

"So," I say hesitantly. "How are you feeling?"

"It's better," he replies softly. "Gemma's pretty amazing."

"Yeah," I say. "She is."

Rory shifts his gaze to the sky above and we sit in silence

for a moment. Then he says, "I know I'm a fuck up, okay?" His voice is soft and raspy. "I was always the fat kid, the kid with no friends, the kid that nothing comes easy to. It sucked." He shifts his gaze back to mine. "And when we were out here, alone, all I could think about is the fact that I want to live, I want to prove to all those losers who made fun of me that, hey, I'm still here. For some stupid reason, I wanted to show those jerks that I'm finally good at something: at staying alive. I wanted to prove that I could be resourceful, but I never wanted anyone to die." He closes his eyes and silent tears roll down the sides of his face. "I got carried away in that house, my gun went off and I heard the clink of metal. I saw the compression tanks connected to the stove, but there was no time to react." When he opens his eyes again, they look solemnly at me. "I'm sorry, Wren. I'm so sorry. I just want you to know that." I swallow down my sadness and anger as he continues to stare at me, his eyes intense with need. He doesn't just want me to forgive him, he needs me to.

"I don't really know you, Rory," I say. "I don't know what your life was before this, but I do know that we want the same thing now, because I want to live too." He gives me a curt nod and I think that now, we understand each other. It may not have been the forgiveness that he was looking for, but it seems to be enough. I see an unopened bottle of water sitting just above his head.

"Are you thirsty?" He lifts his head as I unscrew the bottle and help him take a small sip.

"Ahhh," he sighs. "That's good." As I begin to screw the cap back on the bottle, he reaches out and touches my hand.

"Wren, I need you to tell me something."

"Okay."

"I can see what's left of my hands, and my leg was in pretty bad shape, but Gemma, she won't give me a straight answer about the rest of me, about my face." He pauses and takes a deep breath, steeling himself. "My face, Wren, how bad is it?" I have to look away before he can read the truth in my eyes. "Tell me," he pushes. "Please." I turn back to him and search his damaged face. His skin is patchy with angry red scars, his lips turn down as if the tissue has melted away. The injuries may heal but will most definitely leave their mark. I tell him the truth.

"It's bad, Rory. It's really bad." He rolls onto his back with a sardonic laugh.

"Well," he replies. "We both know that my face was never going to be my money maker." I can't help myself, and I laugh with him.

"Look, Rory," I say. "It's just the outside that has permanent scars, just the surface. But you can fix the inside, you can be a better person where it really counts."

"Thanks," he replies. "I mean it, Wren, thanks for being honest." Before I can say another word, Gemma appears next to us, two chalky tablets in her palm.

"How are you?" she asks as she patiently hovers over Rory.

"Better," he says. "I think I can actually bend my leg." It's amazing considering how twisted his leg appeared only a few days ago, in fact, it seems impossible.

"I'm glad," she says, handing him the white pills and the bottle of water from next to him. Rory gazes up at her pale oval face. Her white-blond hair sweeps across her sun-kissed cheeks as she bends toward him.

"You do seem to be doing much better this morning. I guess the pills are working." He swallows the tablets down and lays his head back down with a sigh.

"What are they?" I ask. "The pills." She looks up at me and in this moment my little Gemma seems so capable. Maybe it's the confidence that she has in her new role as doctor. Whatever it is, it suits her.

"I took most of the medical supplies in the storeroom at the compound and I've been doing a little research in a book that was there as well." She pulls a small book from her jumpsuit pocket and shows it to me. The writing is tiny and difficult to read but there are hundreds of pictures of many different pills, tablets, and herbs. "This medication helps to mend bones quickly. It travels to areas where it is needed and creates an accelerated growth in cells. It's referred to as a magic bullet drug." She smiles at me and goes on to explain the chemical properties of the medication but it's hard to keep up. She reaches up to touch my forehead.

"Your cut is already healed," she says.

"Oh, yeah?" Unthinkingly, I touch the area but there is no pain.

"That was some ointment," I say astonished. Gemma smiles, knowingly.

"The medications today are amazing. I think I could heal anything." Little Gemma, a doctor. She can't be much older than twelve, and I realize that I have never asked her age.

"Gemma," I say when she is done with the ins and outs of bullet drug capabilities. "How old are you?" She pauses and glances down at the resource book in her hands.

"I'm eleven," she says softly. My eyes flick to Rory's who seems as shocked as I am. He lets out a low, Whoa.

"Wow, Gemma," I say. "You're really smart." I see her cheeks blush with pink. The color is more noticeable on her pale skin.

"I always loved to read," she says. "And I've always been interested in science but it's hard to compete with a sister who is top of the class at literally everything."

"You know, Gemma. I've always thought that I'd rather be outstanding at one thing than good at many things. I think you've found your niche'." She brightens and gives me a smile. "Anyone who can heal a broken leg in less than a week is a real doctor."

"Or a magician," chimes in Rory. She's too embarrassed to respond and instead busies herself with checking Rory's burn bandages. I stand and brush the dried pine needles from my knees. As I head toward Briar who is packing up her backpack, I wonder if Gemma would have ever found her talent had we not needed it so much. I pass by Ian who sits with his legs stretched out in front of him, leaning back on his pack. Out of the corner of my eye I see him watching me. I smile because deep down I like feeling special to someone, even if he does have baggage, even if it won't go anywhere.

CHAPTER THIRTY-THREE

Aiden

"What are you talking about," says Raven in frustration. "Are you actually saying that you believe all of this crap?" The four of us sit together around our small apartment table, three sets of eyes staring at me in disbelief.

"If I hadn't seen it with my own eyes, I would think they were crazy," I say. Raven looks away. I've spent the last twenty minutes filling everyone in on the video footage that I saw in Clay's office. I'm not surprised by Raven's reaction but Spenser questioning me stirs up feeling of anger. "This is the way it is," I say firmly. "I saw innocent people dying from traps set in the wild, vicious mutated animals attacking children. We saw a few of these traps ourselves, the lightening pillars..."

"That was never meant to kill," replies Raven in defense. "And we were out in the wild too. We had it rough, but no one was trying to kill us."

"Are you sure that this video wasn't some sort of propaganda film, spliced together by the Underground?" asks Spencer.

"Yeah," says Raven. "Who do you trust, Aiden? Whose side are you on?" Raven shakes her head while Spencer glances from her to me. I know that there's a part of him that believes me, but there's a bigger part of him that will always be loyal to Raven. I've seen it coming. It may have begun as a simple crush, but my gut tells me it's something deeper now. Jewel is the only one who seems unconcerned as she watches her hands fold a paper napkin into the shape of a swan.

"That's pretty" I say, nodding towards her work.

"Origami," she replies. "Every fold is based on mathematical units." She smiles up at me.

"So now what?" asks Raven, not wanting to be distracted. "Are they going to lock us up? Maybe they'll just shoot us and get rid of us. I'm sure that no one down here wants to be looking over their shoulders wondering when we're going to bring the government down on their little party."

"God, Raven," I say with disgust.

"I don't think they'd do that," says Jewel softly. Her eyes slowly meet mine and I know that she has made her choice. She's already begun to find a life here, one that she's hoped for. I smile, thinking that she will make a great teacher.

"I've made a deal with Clay," I reply, causing Raven's eyes to widen with surprise. They narrow just as quickly and she asks,

"What kind of deal?"

"It has to be approved by the council."

"How deep are you in, Aiden?"

"All the way," I reply with no hesitation. She looks at Spencer, not bothering to hide her revulsion. She's a government girl through and through.

"So, what's the deal?" asks Spencer.

"They're going to let you go back, if that's what you want to do, but I'm staying here. Clay will help me find Wren and in return I'm going to do or be whatever they need." Raven lets out a loud, bark of laughter.

"God, Aiden. Are you really going to sell out for one girl? You better think about what you're doing because there's no going back."

"There's nothing to think about," I reply shortly.

"So, they're really going to let us just walk out of here and back to the hub?" asks Spencer. I can hear the doubt in his voice.

"What do they want from us in return," asks Raven.

"I gave them my word that neither of you will give up the Underground's location or anything that's going on here."

"And?"

"And that you report back to Commander Rob that you located the officials, deceased in the wild. This will allow them to stay here without having to worry about the initiation of new search parties. It will also allow you to finish your mission in Captain Rob's eyes. Make something up. There are plenty of things to choose from." I can't hide the anger in my voice that is so quick to rise to the surface now.

"And what about you?" she asks, her eyes glued on mine.

"I don't care what you tell them about me. Say I died in quicksand or went AWOL, it doesn't matter because I'm never going back." I see a switch happen in her eyes, a sadness as she moves them to Spencer.

“And you?” He takes a deep breath and swallows hard. I see the same sadness mirrored in his eyes.

“I’ll go with you,” he replies half-heartedly. “I’ve learned a lot from Dominick. Maybe I can take some of that knowledge back.” His words tear at me. The thought of Dominick’s ideas being given to the government who he feels betrayed by makes me sick.

“Well, I’m staying here,” chimes Jewel. “I like it here. I like the people that I’ve met.”

“How soon can we leave?” asks Raven as she pushes away from the table. The decisions are made and there’s nothing left to talk about.

“I suppose in a few days once the council clears it. We all need time to prepare. We can head out together.” Raven gives her nod of approval. As Raven turns to the direction of her room I add, “But Raven. You have to be true to your word. You have to keep this under wraps. I’m trusting you.” She looks at me long and then her eyes slip to Spencer and then to Jewel. She must know that if she leaks this information, she’s signing Jewel’s death warrant and my own.

“You have my word,” she replies. She disappears into her room, shutting the door behind her. Jewel gives me a hesitant smile and then goes to check on Raven.

“Are you sure this is what you want, Spencer?” His eyes are pleading with me to understand and I can see the pain on his face. It’s tough to leave a squad member behind, it’s a hard choice to make.

“I can’t let her go back there alone,” he says. “I believe you, Aiden, and that’s why she can’t go back alone.” I give a nod.

“It’s okay,” I say. “I get it.”

Another day passes and then we are called to meet with the

council. Lynda, Steven and Clay question each of us separately and then call us in together. They approve our plan. Raven must have done some fast talking and assured them that they could trust her. Jewel is assigned as a teacher's aide and I'm confident that by the time I return she will have been promoted to full-fledged teacher. Just wait until they realize her math skills.

"You can move out in forty-eight hours," says Clay. "Samuel will go with you. He knows his way around. I'm giving you five days, Aiden, five days to find her but if you come up empty, Samuel has strict orders to bring you back. He'll do whatever it takes." I nod. It's enough time. "Spencer and Raven, you're on your own. Samuel can point you in the right direction but after that you'll have to find your way back to the hub."

"Not a problem." Raven's voice is confident. She stands tall like a soldier taking orders from her commander, only Clay isn't in charge of her and she knows it.

"I hope that you will both keep our secret," adds Lynda. "We're putting our trust in you, our lives."

"Bell, Donovan and Woodman will be safe now. We won't forget your part in this," says Steven, his deep voice booming across the room. "If you ever want to come back, if you ever need to come back, the door will be open." Steven takes something from his pocket and slides it across the table to Raven. It's a tablet, one similar to my own. "Take this," he says. "This belongs to Professor Donovan. It's still loaded with a few files, nothing important but it will be proof that you found him and hopefully that you found him dead." Raven takes it and tucks it into her pocket.

"Well, I guess that's it," says Lynda. "Feel free to take any supplies that you need and, Aiden, be careful out there."

The morning of our departure comes quickly, and I am filled with a string of emotions that range from anxiety to excitement. Today might be the day that I see her again and my heart races at the thought. I can make this right. My hands long to touch her, to wrap my arms around her protectively, guard her fragile heart. Wren is all I have left in this world but she's also all that I need. I'll never give her up again.

"Let's go!" yells Raven from the living room. She's probably been packed and ready since dawn. Spencer looks up at me with humor dancing in his eyes.

"I guess she's ready to go," he says with a laugh. Then his voice turns serious. "Aiden, you understand, right?" I sigh and smile at him.

"You and I are not so different, Spencer. What I need is somewhere out there, but what you need in right through that doorway."

"I'm gonna miss you, man."

"Me to," I reply. "You never know…" He gives a shrug but looks away zipping up his backpack.

"Ready?" I ask.

"Yep." We stand and leave the comfort of our shared space to head out to the most unhospitable place I've ever known.

Jewel waits with Samuel in the common area. Raven walks to her with quick footsteps and takes her into her arms in an uncharacteristic hug.

"Take care of yourself," she whispers into Jewel's golden hair. "You were good out there, a real soldier. Be proud of that."

"Thanks." Jewel is holding back tears and if I'm honest, so am I. This is the last time our squad will be together.

"Okay," says Samuel, clapping his hands together. "We

should get a move on. I'd like to make some distance before sunset. We may see this place again tomorrow with any luck." He gives me a firm pat on the back. We walk down a familiar tunnel that I know connects with tunnel one and the growing rooms. When we turn a corner, taking a tunnel that I've never seen before, I see an open cavern in front of us. Instinctively I know what that open area holds. A ripple of confidence rushes over me when I see them, three hover cars connected to their charging stations.

"Hop in," says Samuel walking over to unplug the first car that is really more like a van, with its three rows of seating.

"Really?" I say in awe.

"You must be pretty special, have something to offer for the council to be so generous," he replies. "But I don't ask questions, I just follow directions." I open the car door, ushering Spencer and Raven in first. As I shut it behind me and strap myself into the front passenger seat, I wonder. What do they see in me? What could I possible have to offer them once I bring Wren back with me? I shake my head to clear away the questions. It doesn't matter. I've made my deal. Once I find the girl that I left behind, nothing else will matter.

CHAPTER THIRTY-FOUR

Wren

Briar is ready to go. I join her at the forest edge.

"You girls be careful," says Arick as he adds small twigs to the embers in the fire to keep it going. Who knows, maybe soon we'll have some meat to throw on the fire. My mouth waters at the thought of sinking my teeth into a huge chunk of juicy sizzling meat. And then I think about the mutants dragging away the dead Mutts and I chase the thought away.

"I think we should explore a new area today," says Briar. She glances up to the sky to navigate the direction. The sun shines down on her skin, illuminating it into a beautiful golden chocolaty hue. Her curls are wild, almost feral, but she looks alive and strong. "Let's go this way," she suggests.

"Okay." I follow behind her silently, listening for any sign of something wild, something that would taste good barbecued. There's no real path and it's slow going as we navigate the pines and debris that cover the forest floor.

"Maybe we should leave some sort of a trail," I suggest. Briar stops abruptly, causing me to walk into her.

"That's not a bad idea," she says. She reaches up to the nearest hanging branch and bends it slightly. "There." As we move forward, Briar continues to leave sighs of our trail; another bent branch, the movement of debris on the ground, a fallen log strategically placed. It should be enough to find our way back or for others to find us if we get into trouble. I feel good. Maybe not happy but good. I inhale the strong scent of pine and listen to my feet crunching over the forest floor.

The sun peeks through the tight canopy with every other step, its warmth hopping over my face and shoulders, leaving its mark. I pray that the rest of our journey will be like this.

Briar and I walk silently for a while. Just when I think that this forest will never end, Briar stops. I start to ask her what she sees, when she hisses,

"Shhhhh." I listen. I don't hear anything, not even the rustling of debris or a breeze blowing through the pines. I turn my head and close my eyes and then I hear it, the thing Briar has stopped for. It could be the wind but it's steadier, like music that loops around continuously, beating out a rhythm. Briar's eyes alight with excitement as we continue to listen. The sound is becoming more familiar and my heart quickens as I realize what we are really listening to. Without hesitation, Briar begins to run, forgetting about the trail and the signs we are supposed to leave behind. Even though I can't be sure what is in the distance, I can't help myself and I follow. Ten yards, twenty yards, thirty yards and the trees begin to spread out to create a clearing. Now I can hear the sound full force as I see the river before me, in all its splendid, wet glory. A liquid snake, clear and blue, jumping its way over a pile of stones and pebbles to one side, leaving a spray of glistening rainbows in the sky.

"Holy shit!" exclaims Briar and I couldn't agree more. This is killer, a natural filtration system for good drinking water and, for once, I feel like I'll finally be clean. We edge our way closer to the bank where smooth stones make it slippery to walk. The widest part of the river is in front of us and, though there is still movement, it is slower at this point. I think it will be safe to swim in if we're careful.

"I wonder how deep it is?" I say. Briar's feet hit the water and she jumps back as the water seeps into her shoes.

"I don't know, but it's cold," she replies with a shudder. Just as the words escape her lips, I feel the icy water seep into my own shoes.

"You're not kidding," I reply with a laugh. Even though the day is warm, the water feels freezing.

"I don't care," says Briar bravely. "I'm going in." The idea of submerging my body in water and scrubbing off days of grime is so appealing that I almost rip off my own jumpsuit and take the plunge. I know I'm going in eventually, cold or not. Briar turns to me.

"Well, it looks like we have just about everything we need here, except maybe wild game. Still there might be fish in the river. We stand for a moment contemplating the river, trying to come up with fishing strategies. Briar bends down and fills her hands with water, splashing the freezing water to my face.

"Hey," I say, wiping it away. Briar laughs and splashes me again.

"So", she says with a glint in her eye. "Let's go tell everyone about our big surprise! It'll be like Christmas, especially for Gemma."

My feet squish the whole way back, but I don't care. I can't wait to see the look on everyone faces and to get the grime off my own body. Gemma's mouth hangs open in surprise as Briar delivers the news and Arick gives a loud whoop.

"We are going swimming!" he says as he gives Gemma a nudge. "Maybe we can let the girls go first. Ian can help me with Rory." I glance around our little campsite and spot Rory sitting in front of his tent, his back resting on his backpack. He looks good. The burns that cover his face are like an angry mask, but he looks more alert and his leg looks straight and strong, stretched out in front of him. The cold water will probably do him some good.

"Sounds good," replies Ian. It's difficult to look at him now and I wonder what he's thinking about me and our moment by the fire. I'm guessing that his words were just a way to let me down easy. I feel the loss for something I never had.

"Let's go, Gemma!" says Briar as she rummages through her backpack. I quickly retrieve the small bar of soap from my tent, something truly worth its weight in gold at this point. Gemma takes several small bottles of shampoo. I'm shaking with anticipation and I can't remember when I've had a proper bath, I guess fifty years ago. What once seemed ordinary, even trivial, is now a monumental event.

"Grab your empty bottles," says Briar and I take two that are lying in the corner of my tent. I don't know what could be better than the idea of being clean and the sudden abundance of fresh drinking water. Maybe a cheeseburger.

Gemma is quivering with her own excitement as we lead her into the forest to our secret spot.

"I can't believe this'" she says as she follows at our heels. Sweat begins to trickle down my back as the heat of the day begins to intensify. The difference is that this time I welcome it. The heat will make the icy water that much more welcome.

"It's going to be just like swimming at summer camp," says Briar as we get close. "Only we should warn you…the water's cold, freezing actually."

"We'll get used to it," Gemma replies happily. "Whoa," she exclaims as she looks out at the moving river. Sunlight reflects off its surface and, if I close my eyes and listen to the happy water moving its way over stones, I can almost be back home, back to the river where Aiden and I sat so many days after school. A twinge of sadness and loss covers my heart, but it's different this time. Acceptance is beginning to set in, slowly seeping into my soul like a stain on my heart that I have to live with.

"Well, I guess we better bite the bullet," says Briar and, with little hesitation she charges into the water, jumpsuit, shoes and all.

"Oh, man!" she yells as she bobs in the water. Gemma and I laugh. Briar looks as if she is walking on hot coals, like she's trying to get away from the water while dunking her body in. I'm certain that it won't take long for all of us to become numb. Gemma and I take off our shoes and let the water slowly seep through our toes.

"Are you coming in?" yells Briar. Gemma begins to slowly walk into the water, letting each part of her body slowly adjust to the cold. I follow suit, but my body cannot adapt to the chill, so I finally take a deep breath and go rushing in. The water feels better once I'm moving around in it. I dip my head under and pop up through the surface out of breath.

"It's better if you tread water," I say to Briar as she swims close. Gemma is almost all the way in, and I can see her teeth chattering. The sun peeks through wispy white clouds and shines down on us. At least when we get out the sun will warm our skin. Briar spends the next twenty minutes swimming around and splashing us like a five-year old. Swimming to shore, I decide to get to work. I take off my jumpsuit and throw it over the rocks on shore, leaving my underwear and tee shirt intact. I take my small bar of soap and lather a good amount in my hands then begin the process of taking off days and days of dirt and grime. I lather the shampoo in my hair and the aroma of wildflowers hits me, bringing back a sense of home. The process feels so good, so normal. I quickly rinse myself and retrieve my jumpsuit, attacking it with the bar of soap. I decide to let it dry on the rocks while I stretch out in my underwear, letting the sun warm me. I watch as Briar gives Gemma a good dunk. The best part of the day is hearing Gemma's laugh, like music, like everything will be okay.

"You better dry off," I yell. "The boys will want their turn." Reluctantly, they swim to the shallow water. Briar pulls Gemma by the hand and helps her lather up her long hair that looks like gossamer in the sunlight. She gently combs her fingers through it to loosen the knots. As I let the sun warm my face, I think that I never want to leave this spot.

I hear a snapping branch and feet shuffling across the ground behind me and I turn my head quickly. Briar and Gemma glance over to where the pines open into our clearing, just in time to see Ian stumbling his way through. I glance down to my half naked body and begin to freak out, lunging myself back into the river. I don't know what I'm thinking other than somehow trying to cover myself from Ian.

"Woah, buddy," says Briar as he takes a tentative step forward. At least they have their jumpsuits still on. I give a scathing glance at mine, draped over the rocks, useless. Dammit, why didn't I put it back on? I turn my gaze to Ian who stands with a stupid smile playing on his lips.

"So, this is it," he says, pretending to ignore me. I'm treading water hard and getting tired quickly. I feel like a fool, I mean, my underwear covers as much as my swimsuit did back home, maybe more.

"You're not supposed to be here yet!" I yell to make sure that he can hear me over the sound of the water.

Ian ignores me and adds, "Nice trail you left, Briar. It was easy to find the place."

"Where is everyone else?" she asks. Some of my panic is subsiding so I swim closer to shore. At least my feet can at least touch the bottom. I can feel an ache creeping into my biceps from my effort to keep myself afloat.

"They're not coming," he replies. "Arick actually got Rory up and walking on his own. You're some doctor, Gemma."

"That's great!" she exclaims. "But it wasn't me, just the medication."

"Well," says Briar. "Maybe now he won't be dead weight for the rest of us." Briar continues to run her fingers through Gemma's hair. They look like two different people, sitting there together on the water's edge, and not just because they're finally clean. It's more than that. It's like they've known each other their whole lives, like I've known them their whole lives.

"Come on, Gemma," says Briar. "Let's go back and dry off a little bit." My heart beats frantically. Are they really going to leave me alone like this, floating helplessly in the water half naked, with Ian? As if reading my thoughts, Briar glances out to me, slyly. She just takes Gemma by the hand and disappears into the forest. I do get a little smile from Gemma as the green pine envelopes them.

"Wait!" I yell feebly. That gets a renewed smile from Ian.

"How's the water?" he yells as he takes a seat on a smooth stone.

"Just turn around," I yell over my shoulder. "Let me get dressed and then the water is all yours."

"Wren, it's not a big deal. It's not like you're naked..." He's right. I'm overreacting. Nothing has happened between us and if anything, it's clear that Ian wants to keep it that way.

"Come on, Wren, can I come in?" There is an undertone of pleading in his voice that catches me off guard. Who am I to deny him a bath after everything that we've been through?

"Okay," I say. "I'm just...I'm not used to boys seeing me in my underwear." He smiles and shakes his head as if I'm being ridiculous and then begins to unzip his jumpsuit. I swallow hard and turn my back to him. This is about to get uncomfortable.

CHAPTER THIRTY-FIVE

Wren

I hear Ian splashing into the water and I turn around. Once I start staring, I can't stop. He's up to his waist in the river but his bare chest is broad and firm and tan from the sun. The large muscles in his arms contract as he is hit by the ice chill of the water.

"That's some seriously cold water," he exclaims, causing me to laugh. "Here goes nothing!" He dunks himself under the surface of the water. For several minutes, he stays below, making me worry that perhaps he forgot to tell me that he can't swim. Then he breaks through the water only a few feet away, sputtering and wiping his wet hair from his eyes. I'm barely staying afloat as my toes skim the rocky bottom of the lake. If I step back, I'll be treading water again.

"This is great!" he says as he gives me a small splash. I splash him back and the battle begins until I give in.

"Okay, you win," I say with one last splash. "I was just drying off and now my hair is completely soaked. Anyway, it's not a fair fight. You've got two feet on the bottom."

"Well, come here, then," he replies. I take a tentative step forward, just enough so that I can stand.

"I should get out," I say, trying not to stare at the parts of his body that are exposed. His muscular arms, his broad shoulders, even the curve of his neck that leads from his ear to his chin makes renewed heat travel up my spine.

"Wait, Wren." He reaches out and takes my hands, pulling me closer. His eyes search mine as our fingers become intertwined. His deep blue eyes are endless, reflecting the water and the sun.

"About last night," he begins. "I'm sorry."

"For what," I reply, shaking his words off. The last thing I want is a replay of the rejection I felt.

"I don't know, for leading you on, for making you feel that there's something wrong with you."

"You didn't lead me on, Ian," I reply, bobbing in the water inches away. "I mean, yeah, I'm attracted to you and I think you're a great leader, and there's something about you that makes me feel safe, but I really don't know you, right?" His eyes flick to an unknown area above my head and he seems like he's wrestling with a decision.

"Let me ask you something," he says. "Do you think that if a person does something, something for a good reason but that unknowingly causes pain to others, could that person be forgiven?" The question catches me off guard.

"Like what?" I ask not fully understanding where he's going with all of this.

"Well, like in a war, soldiers have to kill people, they have to kill people to survive."

"Yeah," I say. "I suppose that there are things that can be forgiven. Why?" He shakes his head a new smile creeping onto his lips.

"I don't know. I guess I just wanted to know if you would be able to forgive certain things, if you had an open mind." I splash the water in front of me, causing ripples to make a path from my body to his.

"I think I'm pretty open-minded," I say. "I guess I believe that everyone has the right to be happy even if their past is checkered. We all make mistakes, Ian." His smile grows and he looks deep into my eyes. I feel the flutter of desire begin to stir and I push it down.

"So," he says. "Tell me three things about you. Any three things."

"Okay." I pause to think for a second. "Well, I'm seventeen. I was planning to study botany in school and..."

"And?" he asks.

"And, I'm freezing right now and need to get out of the water." He laughs and gives me a little splash.

"Okay, I'll keep my back to you if it makes you feel more comfortable." I walk to the shore, looking back over my shoulder to make sure he's keeping his word. When my feet hit the smooth stones, I grab my jumpsuit and throw it on. It clings to my wet skin so I take a seat on the smooth rock where Ian once sat, trying to dry out the fabric.

"I'm good," I yell. As Ian makes his way to the shore, more and more of his spectacular body is being revealed. His dark hair curls around his cheeks, dripping water into his eyes. I watch his muscles ripple as he moves his hand to wipe it away. My eyes scan over his broad chest down to where his abs form defined lines and then lower still. I smile shyly when I raise my eyes and see him watching me. I turn around, giving him the same courtesy that he gave me even though he didn't ask for it. I hear the zip of his jumpsuit and feel him take a seat next to me and I turn around.

"Now it's your turn," I say. "Three things." He scratches his head and thinks for a moment.

"I'm nineteen, I would be happy with a simple life and I've never been in love."

"Really?" I ask.

"Really, which one?"

"Really, you've never been in love?"

"Yep," he replies. He reaches for a handful of pebbles at our feet and begins to launch them into the river. The leap over the water, leaving their small ringed footprints behind.

"How about you?" he asks. "How about that Aiden guy?"

"No, not love, at least not the kind of enduring love that makes you need a person. I loved Aiden but not like that." He smiles as he tosses another stone into the water. "A simple life," I continue. "That sounds nice, especially now."

"Maybe we can find a way to do that together," he says. He studies my face and reaches up to push a damp strand of hair behind my ear. "You're beautiful," he whispers. "You're good and pure and deserve so much better than a guy like me."

"Last night you said that I should be afraid of you," I reply, keeping his gaze. "I'm not afraid of you, Ian. Not at all."

"I know what I said," he whispers, leaning even closer. "I was afraid, afraid of so many things but we're here now, and we have no way of knowing what will happen tomorrow. I would be a stupid idiot if I didn't take a chance on falling in love with you." He pulls back to meet my eyes. "If you don't think you can get there with me, tell me now, Wren." My heart pumps frantically in my chest and the butterflies in my stomach begin to flutter wildly. I don't know if this is just desire or loneliness or something so much deeper, but I have to find out. Without hesitation I lean into him and press my lips gently to his. I hear him gasp at the unexpected kiss and then his hand finds its way into my loose hair and he's pulling me closer, his kiss deeper. A wave of heat shoots through my body and, all at once, I'm starving for him, needing him on more than just a physical level. It's everything we've been through that brings us together, as if the heat of his body is finding its way into my skin, into my bones and becoming a part of me, a part that cannot be severed. As I gently pull away, I see it in his eyes too.

"I've never felt..." I stammer.

"Yeah, he says. "Me, too." His eyes scan every inch of my face, his hand runs down my neck and along my back. And then we hear the crunch of footsteps coming near and we break apart.

"Well, what do we have here?" comes an unfamiliar voice. I quickly glance to Ian. In a flash, my eyes turn in the direction of the bodiless voice. I scan the forest line until my eyes alight on a pair of heavy boots breaking through the opening. My eyes travel upwards, and I jump to my feet in shock as three strangers appear in front of us. A wave of panic begins at the top of my head and travels downward my spine as Ian and I stand together speechless. It's not so much that there are strangers here, even though that alone is shocking. The horror that churns my stomach is their appearance, as if they've been a part of some horrible experiment, their skin blotchy and worn, like leather. They almost don't look real and make Rory's injuries seem petty. The mutants, the people from the city. I chance a glance to Ian and see some kind of recognition in his eyes.

"Cat got your tongue?" asks the older of the two men. He's probably the least scary. He looks ragged and beat-down, his skin mottled, especially on his head that is visible under a few patches of white hair. The woman who is with them gives a hoot of crazy laughter at his words. He immediately turns to her and gives her a hard smack on the head.

"Shut up, Lucy," he says. "Keep it together." She takes a step away, rubbing her head. Her face looks like a mask, as if it might have once been pretty, as if she might peel away the weathered leathery skin to reveal her true face. And there's something else about her, something that chills my bones to the core. Her eyes are merciless and stare holes into me. She's completely crazy.

"Yeah, shut up, Lucy," echoes the second guy. He's younger for sure and scarier still. He's tall and sturdy but one side of his face has seemed to slide down, melted, causing a permanent droopy frown. I don't want to mess with him.

"Who are you?" asks Ian. I can feel him tense behind me.

"Oh, well, we might be asking you the same question," replies the older man. The young guy gives a chuckle, while the girl's eyes dart from us to the older man with excitement. "I guess you didn't know that this here is our river. We set claim to it years ago. Fought pretty hard for it too." It's difficult for me to believe that any one person can actually own a river, but I keep my mouth shut. My eyes flick to the woman who is smiling broadly. She's watching me.

"We were just leaving," I say.

"Yeah," says Ian. "It's all yours." He gestures to the river behind us. This isn't over, I can tell.

"Well," drawls the older man. "The damage has already been done, hasn't it?" He pauses as if thinking what his next move should be, then nods to no one in particular. "But where are my manners?" he continues. "My name is James and this here is Jobias. We call him Big J for short." He pats the younger guy on the back, heartily. "Of course, you already know this is Lucy." At the sound of her name, Lucy gives out another string of laughter.

"Looks like we've got ourselves a couple of prisoners," says Big J with excitement.

"What?" snaps Ian. "We were just leaving. No harm done." I feel the fight or flight impulse knocking on my brain. There's three of them and two of us but Ian is bigger and stronger than either of the two men, even Big J, and I think I could take down Lucy. Before I can decide, James' hand wraps around to his back pocket and comes back holding a gleaming silver gun. We can't compete with that. I feel anger rising inside of my gut but there's nothing I can do about what comes next.

"Tie em up," commands James as he waves the gun at us. I turn to Ian and see my own terror reflected in his eyes.

"This is stupid," he says in a panic, stepping in front of me. "You can have your river. We really don't care. We were already planning to move along." This gets a hollow chuckle from James, echoed by Lucy clapping her hands together and chanting, "Tie em up, tie em up!" Big J whips out a beaten-up package of plastic ties, the kind that I have used many times to anchor hydroponic filling tubes to piping.

"Now this doesn't have to hurt," says James. "Just turn around and put your hands behind your back, slowly. We'll be done in a jiffy." His tone angers me even more than what they're about to do, and I get the feeling that this isn't their first time. In a last-ditch effort attempt, I yell out, "We're not alone!" All three of them look at me, their eyes void of concern.

Ian takes a shot.

"We came here with a group," he says. "And we're tagged by the government. I would rethink your plan." It's a good ploy even if there's no truth to it. James shakes his head as if disappointed.

"Come on now, boy. Do you really think I'm that dumb?" asks James. "We know who you are just by lookin' at your clothes. And I saw the others," he continues. "What? Maybe three or four? We may only be three strong, but I've got old sharpshooter here." He waves the gun once again. "I think that makes up for the difference." I don't know what to do and neither does Ian. I can see him contemplating the best course of action. He turns to face me.

"Just do what they say," he whispers. "They just want supplies. He won't use the gun." How can he know that? James looks pretty confident with his weapon.

"Now, turn around...please." Ian gives me a sad smile and slowly turns around, his hands behind his back. Big J lunges forward and slips a plastic tie around Ian's wrists, pulling it tight. I see Ian jerk as the edge of the plastic digs into his skin.

"Now it's your turn, sweetheart," says Big J with a semi-toothless grin. My eyes flick to the forest, mapping out an escape route. I take a step back, pretending to turn my ankle and then lunge at the gap between Big J and Lucy. As I feel the brush rub against my shoulder, I stumble just enough for muscular hands to wrap themselves around my waist.

"Nice try," says Big J with a growl. My eyes meet Ian's as I turn, giving up my wrists to the bite of plastic. It hurts. As tears begin to well up in my eyes, Lucy approaches. I can see now what her redeeming quality must have been. Her eyes are crazy but they're also beautiful. The irises sparkle with deep emerald, speckled with gold and chocolate brown. They're nothing compared to Ian's deep blue eyes, but they stand out on her tortured face. Slowly she reaches out a shaking hand and I immediately flinch back out of her reach.

"Pretty," she says as she reaches out again to lightly touch my hair. It's as if she's mesmerized by my flaming locks of red. Ian steps between us and even though I am tied up, I feel protected. I search Lucy's hair and notice for the first time how yellow it is underneath the dirt and grime, not blond but yellow. A wig. I can see the line of it just above her forehead. Any real hair must fascinate her.

"Okay, herd em out," says James. We have no choice but to follow.

CHAPTER THIRTY-SIX

Aiden

Samuel steers the car into dark tunnel that I have never seen before. I feel the seat harness dig into my shoulder as the ground becomes bumpy and unstable.

"Hang on," he says as he commands the steering wheel. It's strange to see someone actually driving one of these things. Every car that I have ever ridden in has been programed to take me to a specific destination. Relying on human reflexes is terrifying. The engine hums, occasionally letting out a squeal of protest. The headlights illuminate the road ahead, the glow sweeping out about six feet. I hope that Samuel knows where he's going because I can't see anything else. I lean back in the smooth leather seat and shut my eyes, picturing Wren sitting next to me in the park, our hands clasped, the breeze playing in her hair. *Maybe today*, I think. *Maybe today I will see her again*. When I open my eyes again, I can see a ring of light in the distance, the exit. The traction tires are military grade but when they make purchase with the sand, they begin to spin.

"Woops," says Samuel as he leans over to punch a button underneath the steering wheel. I feel a jolt and immediately we begin to grind over the sand. A spray of gold follows us as we race across the surface, the sun blinding my eyes, the heat already beginning to seep in.

"Here," says Samuel. He hands me a pair of wire-framed sunglasses with silver reflective lenses. I take them gratefully.

"Thanks." I turn back to glance at Raven and Spencer. Raven is already scouting out the area, trying to find the best path back. The mountains lay across the horizon to our left and I'm beginning to get a feel for our location. I glance over my shoulder to the tunnel exit but it's gone, camouflaged from view. If I'm judging our distance from the mountains correctly, we are at least a mile or two from the quicksand where we entered the tunnel. Of course, now I know that the underground network reaches for miles underneath the earth, spreading out in all directions.

"I can take you as far as the east side of the mountain range," says Samuel, raising his voice over the sound of the engine. "But you'll have to make your own way from there."

"Okay," replies Raven with confidence. I can see recognition in her eyes, and she must have her bearings as well. Once they find the path around the mountains, they should be back to the hub by nightfall. It's a strange thought, Spencer and Raven back in their apartments and me out here. Samuel turns the car in a wide arc to head towards the mountains. They become closer and closer as we drive, the engine humming, constantly rejuvenated by the sun hitting its solar panels. I open the window and let the wind rush into me, whipping my hair and the fabric of my jumpsuit. I feel free, for the first time since the flare hit, I feel hopeful.

"This is going to be it," says Samuel as he brings the vehicle to a stop. He shuts off the motor and we step out onto the hot sand. The range looms on one side while endless desert stretches out on the other. Spencer hitches his backpack over his shoulder and leans in to give me a hearty pat on the back.

"Take care of yourself," he says solemnly.

"Yeah," adds Raven. "And just so you know, I'm not going to report you deceased or even that you went AWOL." She gives me a serious glance and holds it. "We lost you," she says. "You went out to scout for water and you never came back. They would believe that we wouldn't risk the mission over one person." She reaches up and puts a steady hand on my shoulder. "Just in case." I nod even though I know that this is probably the last time I will see either of them. Before I can say anything, before I can tell Spencer to stop being afraid of Raven or remind Raven not to trust the government too much, they're walking away and disappear into the distance.

"Here," says Samuel. He tosses me a pile of clothes. "Put these on." I look at him questioningly. "If the Underground can see what's going on out here, you better believe that the government can too. We need to blend in." He's right. My jumpsuit is a target. Without hesitation, I take it off and replace it with a pair of blue cotton pants and a gray tee shirt. "There," he says. "Now we look like a couple of cave dwellers just roaming around for our next meal. Now, where to?" I glance around, trying to decide on the best plan of action. It's like finding a needle in a hundred haystacks, a thousand. At some point her squad will have to navigate the mountains. Still, the images of the video footage remind me that death is a real option out here and the urgency of that races through my veins. I run my hands through my hair in frustration. I think about the lightning trap and the buried explosives I witnessed in the video and am quickly realizing that I don't have a handle on what's really out here. But Samuel does.

"Okay, Samuel. Fess up. What's really out here. What are we dealing with?" He takes a deep breath and walks around to the back of the van, beckoning me to follow. He opens a back panel exposing a compartment.

"We got wild dogs," he says as he pulls out an intimidating riffle. "That's what this is for." He cocks the gun and aims it off into the distance, then returns it to the compartment. "We got crazy people," he continues, pulling out a sleek black device resembling a pistol. A stun gun, military grade. "That's what this is for." He returns it to the compartment and closes it with a snap. "Then we've got things that we're gonna have to figure out as we go. Buried bombs, sink holes, killer insects, all kind of contraptions that we'll have no idea what to do with." I can feel my mouth hanging open in shock and I quickly close it. "So," he says. "Where to?" Part of me thinks that we should just stay here, find our way to the other side of the mountains, and make camp to wait. But thinking of Wren having to have to deal with even one of these nightmares makes me desperate to find her.

"Let's start by doing a sweep," I say, finally deciding on a course of action. "We can follow the mountain line east and west, heading south as we go. If she gets to this open area, we should be able to spot her."

"Sounds reasonable ," says Samuel and he powers up the van

to begin our search. We drive east as far as we can, until the terrain becomes too difficult to navigate. The sand turns to concrete, fractured and uneven, roads broken up long ago. In the distance I see ruins of towering buildings, a city no longer viable, and beyond that more wasteland. Samuel turns the car south and after about five miles we veer west. There's nothing to see out here. Just more sand. On our second sweep, we pass by the government cryobank and I take a minute to step inside. It's possible that there are new inhabitants since we left almost a week ago. But I find it just as it was. Once in a while I see something of interest, the dry riverbed, a line of green on the horizon that Samuel tells me is a forest, but no people. The enormity of what I've taken on is hitting me hard. As the sun begins to dip down, casting long shadows over us, we decide to stop for the night.

"This place is huge," I say as Samuel bring me a folding chair from the van. We place them in the sand.

"It's a big place, alright," he says, taking a seat next to me. "But there ain't a lot out here. Just scraps left over from the flare. Here." He hands me a stainless-steel container that is a little bigger than the foil meal containers that used to be delivered to my home. I take it and notice that it's heavy, the cool smooth surface feels good after the hot day of scouting. I'm assuming it's food but I can't figure out how to open the lid.

"Here," says Samuel as he shows me a small button on the side near the bottom. He pushes it and a tiny light turns red. "Better put it on your lap," he adds. Within a few seconds, I feel the bottom of the container become warm and I lay it on my knees. I wait, watching Samuel. When the light turns green, he slides off the lid and stirs the contents with a metal spoon.

"Leftovers from the Underground kitchen," he says as he

takes a mouthful of what appears to be chunks of beef, potatoes, and brown sauce. I know better. There's no real meat in the Underground, just chickens and those are too valuable to eat. I take a taste and it's delicious. I savor the spices and rich gravy, so much better than reconstituted meal packs.

"Thank you, Samuel," I say as I finish my meal. The container is of great interest to me and now that it's empty, I take a closer look, turning it over in my hands. I notice a separation between the bottom and the main container and assume that this is where the heating element is located. A bit bulky but effective. I wonder if the heater runs on solar power just like everything else out here and I inspect it for the tale-tell solar cells.

"So, that's your thing?" asks Samuel. I glance up to see his watching me closely. "You were some kind of engineer before the flare?" I laugh.

"Hardly. I was just heading to the university, but, yeah, I like taking things apart and putting them back together in a better way."

"I guess I know now why we got access to this beauty," he says, tapping the van lovingly. "It's to protect that brain of yours."

"I don't think the council would know that about me. They never asked me about my past."

"I wouldn't be so sure," he replies. "If the government knows about you then so does the council. If I were to guess, they have some big plan for that noggin' of yours." I wonder if it's possible that they know who I am, who my father was, if they knew about my university plans, how hard I worked to get there. The Commander knew. He would never have given me this mission and my choice of job if he hadn't known what I was capable of. Could Lynda know all of that about me?

"Let's pack up for the night," says Samuel. "Get an early start in the morning."

"Okay," I say, handing him back the container. "But Samuel?"

"Yeah?"

"Nothing seems to make sense out here. No dogs, no traps. I would think that we'd run into something?" He takes my chair and folds it, storing it into the back of the van.

"I wouldn't be too disappointed, Aiden. Tomorrow's another day and if I know anything, I know that this place can change on a dime without any warning. It's how the government tests their participants in this little game, throwing things at you when you least expect it."

"Do you really believe that the government is controlling all of this?" I ask. "I mean, okay, maybe there are mutant dogs and other wild animals out here and I've seen a few traps. But do you really think that the government is actively controlling everything? How could they possibly do that?"

"Oh, I more than believe it, Aiden. I've been out here a long time and I see how things change. They could call out a pack of dogs right now and take us out if they wanted to, but they don't see us as survivors so we're not a part of the game." I look away and out into the dark distance. "Let's get some sleep," he continues. "I've given you too much to think about for one day."

CHAPTER THIRTY-SEVEN

Wren

"Where are you taking us?" I ask, not willing to budge one step until I know, even with the silver gun flashing. The older man, James, looks like he could have been a kid when the solar flare hit fifty years ago.

"It's not so much where we're taking you but where you're taking us," replies James. "How about we go and meet the rest of your group. I'm sure they have something useful to offer up for the pair of you." I chance a glance at Ian again and I can almost see the wheels turning in his mind. Our supplies are so limited. Losing anything will put our lives in jeopardy. I'm sure they'd take a knife or a gun or all of our food. There's no way I'm willing to put another weapon in their hands.

"Lead the way, Madam," says Big J with a shove. I stumble

over my feet but catch myself. I hear Lucy giggling and chanting behind us,

"Pretty hair, pretty hair, braid it up without a care..." She sounds like a preschooler playing a sick game. We shouldn't have let them tie us up. The only plan that I have is simple. Make as much noise as possible as a warning to Briar. She'll waste no time pulling out her gun and will shoot first and ask questions later. We enter back into the forest following the trail set by Briar.

"Which way did we come?" I say way too loudly, trying to sound confused. We have to take our time. Ian takes the hint and replies,

"Let me think...maybe this way." His voice is as loud as mine and I know that as we get closer to camp, we will be heard. We walk on, snapping as many twigs and branches with our feet, kicking logs and dead things, making as much noise as we can.

"Their camp can't be too much further," says Big J.

"They're stalling," answers James. I feel another shove from behind and my skin squirms at Big J's touch.

"Hurry up," he says, this time with an edge of anger, "I'm starving." Clearly food is their goal.

"Relax," says Ian in an authoritative voice. "It's right up here." I decide it's time to ramp things up and I make a ploy of falling. As I hit the ground, I let out a loud yell. I feel pine needles poking into my face and smell the earth that covers the forest floor. As I roll over, I realize that with my hands tied behind my back, it's difficult to get up. Big J grabs me roughly by the elbow and drags me up, causing a sharp pain in my shoulder. The scream that comes out of my mouth is real this time.

"Shut up," yells James, adding to all the noise. We're almost to camp.

"Hey, I see something," says Lucy in her sing-song voice. "Smoky, smoky, smoke!"

"Let's go," says Big J with another push. I see Ian tense and, as I glance to him, his eyes are full of anger and concern.

"Keep your hands off of her," he yells.

"Big J, keep em here for a sec," says James, eyeing me warily. The gun is wavering from Ian's chest to mine. I think of Gemma, now feet away, my maternal instinct kicking in.

"Wait," I say. "Just untie us and we'll get you whatever you want. We have food." James walks slowly toward me, his eyes locking with mine. I can see it, the crazy deep inside. He stops inches in front of me, his face lowering to meet mine.

"I thought I told you to shut up." His voice is deep and low, almost a whisper. Without warning, I see a flash of silver as the guns handle collides with the side of my head. Ian lets out a panicked cry, along with a string of angry obscenities, as pain rips through my head and I fall again to the ground. I see little stars dancing behind my eyelids, and I stay on the ground, trying desperately to regain myself. The world is blurry and a sharp pain travels from my eye to my cheek to my jaw.

"You didn't have to do that!" shouts Ian. I feel him kneel beside me. My eyes flutter open as he glances up to James and adds, "If you go into our camp this will end badly for everyone. I promise you that."

"We'll see," says James. "Keep them quiet."

"You heard him, keep quiet," says Big J. I feel a hand gently resting on my head and, for a split second, I think that Ian has somehow gotten free. The hand begins to run its fingers softly through my loose hair as I lie on the ground, trying to fight off the searing pain rattling around inside my head.

"Get off of her!" growls Ian and, in an instant, I realize who the hand belongs to and I yank my head away with a cry.

"Pretty," coos Lucy as my eyes connect with Ian's. We both know that this is far worse than the Mutts.

Big J and Lucy leave us on the ground and walk closer to the edge of the clearing to get a look at our camp.

"This is bad, Ian, really bad," I whisper. The shooting pain in my head is subsiding but I can feel a huge welt rising on the side of my face.

"Let me see," says Ian. I tilt my head toward him and wait for any indication that I'm in danger of losing an eye. "It's not too bad. Gemma will fix you up."

."Okay," I reply, trying to calm my nerves. I glance up to Ian's blue eyes. "What are we going to do?" He shakes his head.

"I should have never let this happen. I should have fought them instead of letting them tie us up. I'm sorry."

"Neither one of us realized what these guys were capable of," I reply. Ian's eyes look toward Big J and Lucy and then roam the surrounding area as if looking for answers.

"Hey, shut up!" yells Big J, as he walks back toward us. I quickly push myself back with my feet, scooting on my butt as far away from him as I can get, pushing Ian with me.

"Do you think you can stand?" he whispers, and I nod. I roll onto my knees and slowly push myself up. The world tilts as a wave of dizziness rushes through me. I stumble but Ian blocks me with his body to keep me from falling. I rest myself into him, closing my eyes until the world stops moving. Then I hear the unmistakable sound of gunfire and my heart hammers in my chest. Everything that could go wrong, everything that probably has gone wrong, races through my mind. Without hesitation, I take off running, not away from the camp but toward it. I hear footsteps behind me as Ian follows.

"Stop!" shouts Big J. I don't care what he does to me, I have to make sure that Gemma is safe. As I enter the camp, I see them all and come to an abrupt halt. Ian almost runs into me and we both stand, trying to sort out the situation. I'm looking for blood or any sign of a bullet entering flesh. Arick stands with his hands launched in the air, while Briar sits on one of the campfire logs, holding Gemma in her arms. James holds the small silver gun directly at Arick's chest and, as my eyes meet Briar's, I know that we are thinking the same thing. How can she get her hands on her own gun?

"Welcome to the party," says James. Big J and Lucy follow us into camp and stand next to James. Lucy glances at the gun pointed at Arick and has the look of a child finding herself locked in a candy store. She jumps up and down, clapping her hands wildly, a huge creepy smile plastered on her leathery face. It's a real horror movie. We're all about to get butchered by a bunch of mutants. I wonder if they'll rip my heart out of my chest and eat it raw once I'm dead. Maybe they won't wait for me to be dead. I suddenly realize that Rory is missing, and I try to see into his tent behind me.

"Tie the rest of em up," orders James. "Then take what you can find." Lucy lets out a squeal of delight as Big J takes the plastic ties from his pocket. Arick is first to be bound. As Big J walks toward her, Briar's eyes appear wild and, before I can caution her, she lets go of Gemma and launches herself forward, hitting Big J squarely in the shoulder. He falls back but rights himself quickly. She's on him like a wildcat, clawing at his face and ripping at his ragged clothes.

"Get off. Get off!" yells Big J and I can only imagine the damage that she could do with a knife. Suddenly the air is ripped once again by the sound of James's gun, as he fires it into the air.

"Briar! Briar!" I yell. "Please..." The sound of the gun seems to sober her and the fight in her dies out. As she looks at me, I can see anger pulsing through every vein in her body. "Just let them take what they want and then they'll leave."

"Then they'll leave, then they'll leave." Lucy continues to dance around us as if we're playing a child's game.

"That's right," says James. "Listen to the little lady." Big J gives Briar a forceful shove and she lands on her butt, letting out a renewed growl. She stays where she is, letting the plastic tie cinch over her wrists. James motions with his gun for Ian and me to join the rest of our group on the logs surrounding our fire pit. I take Briar's place next to Gemma as Ian moves in next to me. I watch as Briar is pulled to her feet. She looks bad. Her tee shirt is ripped and there is blood dripping from one nostril. Her curly black hair is decorated with twigs and debris. Big J dumps her on the log and turns to Gemma. I grind my teeth and inch a little closer to her.

"She's just a little girl," I say. "She wouldn't hurt anyone."

"She looks pretty scrappy to me," answers Big J.

"Tie em in the front," says James with a nod. "She couldn't hurt a fly." Big J is gentler with Gemma and I notice that the plastic doesn't dig into her skin like the rest of us.

"It's going to be okay," says Arick, softly, trying to console himself more than anything.

"It's not going to be okay, unless we make it okay," growls Briar as she falls heavily onto the log next to Gemma. We are a bunch huddled together as the fire begins to die and the afternoon wanes on.

"I don't want any more trouble," says Big J as Lucy hops over the fire pit and reaches for Gemma's pale hair. She lets the strands of Gemma's ponytail flow through her fingers like silk as the breeze blows them away.

"Leave her alone!" shouts Briar with a lunge at Lucy. Lucy lets out a squeak of fear and runs away. Good, I'm glad she's afraid. She's not the brightest crayon in the box but at least she can figure out who to be afraid of. She'll need that instinct once we free ourselves.

"Okay," says James as he tucks old sharpshooter back into his pocket. "Let's see what we got." He rubs his hands together greedily as Big J rummages through the tents one by one. He drops three backpacks onto the ground in front of James. I turn back to Rory's tent and I can clearly see now that it's empty. He's gone and so is my backpack along with Briar's. He must have his as well. I guess I'd rather have my gun in his hands than in Big J's. As the three strangers dump out the contents, I lean over to Briar.

"What's going on, where is Rory?" She gives me a shrug. Last time I saw Rory, he was stretched out on a blanket, healing. Still, his bones were mended, and it is possible that he took our stuff and went out on his own once the trouble started. That would be just like him; run away when it gets tough. Ian leans into me.

"My ties are loosening," He whispers. "I think we can take them. Tell Briar to work on hers." I gently move my hands back and forth and feel the plastic tie slip slightly. Ian's right. Before I can convey the message, James scrambles out of a tent.

"Well, lookie here." He holds up a foil food pouch and examines it. "I haven't seen one of these in years!" Lucy snatches it playfully from his hand and looks at it like it's some kind of foreign object.

"It's dinner time!"

CHAPTER THIRTY-EIGHT

Wren

Our three unwanted guests perch themselves on logs across from us and begin greedily digging into their meals. My stomach gives a growl as I watch.

"I think I like spaghetti," says Lucy through a gigantic mouth full. I look away and scrunch a little closer to Gemma. She looks up at my face with steady eyes and touches my injury gently with her bound hands before resting them in my lap.

"I'll make it better," she whispers as she lays her head on my shoulder.

Finally, James pats his full belly and throws an empty meal pack into the fire. It crackles and hesitates to light until the small remaining flame goes out with a hiss.

"Better fix that," says James as he leaves to scavenge around for wood. He takes a bundle of twigs to an ember and the fire, thankfully, reignites.

"That was the best meal I've had in a long while," he adds. Briar glares at him.

I search the contents of everything we own, now scattered on the ground. I see first-aid kits and random pieces of clothing along with meal packs all tossed out like trash. No guns. I can see the disappointment on James' face as he tosses aside a pair of Gemma's thick socks. He hasn't discovered the small knife that I tucked into her pack on that first day. It feels like forever ago, the day we first looked out on the gray sand.

As I continue to move my hands, I notice that the plastic is no longer biting into my wrists. I rock my hands back and forth gently and feel the ties give way even more.

"You can loosen the ties," I whisper to Briar and she gives me a quick nod. She's already figured it out. My pulse begins to quicken as I continue to work stealthily.

I glance over and see Briar watching me and then hear Ian hiss, "I'm almost out."

"Find anything good?" asks Big J as he kicks our belongings now scattered around the ground.

"Naw," replies James. "But now we got food to take with us so that's something."

"You're welcome to have our food," says Arick. His voice startles me. It's scratchy and doesn't sound like him. I can tell he's in dire need of water. "Take the backpacks too. Just untie us before you leave."

"If I were you," chimes in Ian. "I wouldn't linger too long. People will be looking for us." It's a threat and James knows it.

His eyes flick to our tents and then our clothes and then to the empty meal packs burning in the fire in front of him. He must realize that we've had access to things that don't seem readily available on the outside.

"Hmmm," he says, rubbing his stubbled chin. "That so?"

He glances over to Big J with a smile and then fixes his eyes back on us.

"Well, I guess I'm willing to take that chance," he says. Lucy stretches out with her legs toward the fire and her back resting on a log at James' feet. She keeps her gaze jumping from me to Gemma. She pulls something from her pocket, a piece of black fur, and drags it along her cheeks as she continues to stare. She smiles and pulls out another tuft of fur, this time it's auburn in color. As she drags the tuft across her face, I realize with horror that these little bundles are not fur, but human hair, strands and strands held together by a length of cord at one end. One black, another auburn, and yet another deep golden, all a foot long, shining in the last of the sun. As I watch, she drags them across her cheek again, closing her eyes this time in contentment. I feel sick and I wonder who that hair belonged to before she got her hands on it. I don't have to wonder long as her eyes return to my flaming locks. She takes the hair and delicately lays each length onto her yellow wig, blending the colors.

"Looks like you almost got enough," says Big J as he settles down next to her in front of the fire. "Two or three more bunches should do it." He gives me a toothy grin. Lucy's plan is all too clear. Well, she'll have to kill me first.

As the sun hits the horizon, casting streaks of orange and red through the sky, I notice Briar sitting still, focusing on nothing but the movement that I see behind her back. All at once, she stops and her eyes flick to mine with a triumphant look. She's free. Lucy begins to rub her eyes and James gives her a nod toward the tents.

"Go have a rest. You're not missing anything." She tucks her pieces of hair back into her pocket, crawls over to the nearest tent, and zips it closed. I feel Gemma squirm next to me as she sees this crazy, wild creature enter her tent.

"It's okay," I whisper. "There's nothing in there to take now." Nothing but Gemma's blankets and we can burn those later. Big J leans his back against a thick log and stares into the fire. The plastic tie is loosening a little more as I work my wrists but I'm beginning to feel the burn of the edges digging in as I move.

"Good food really makes you tired," says Big J to no one in particular.

"Well, we wouldn't know," spits Briar. *No, Briar, not yet*. I try to caution her with my eyes but she's not looking at me. I glance to Ian, warily.

"You don't look like you're wasting away," replies Big J and he runs his eyes over Briar's body. "Yeah, you look pretty healthy to me." I can feel the intensity in his eyes. He's dangerous, more dangerous than I imagined. Briar lets out a sound of disgust. "You might want to think about being nice to me," he continues. "I'm the one with the food now."

"Right," replies Briar sarcastically. "You've tied us all up, taken over our camp and rummaged through our stuff. Yeah, we should be besties."

"That's enough," says James with irritation and then adds, "She's a feisty one, I'll give her that." He lets out a chuckle.

"You don't know the half of it," growls Briar and before any of us knows what's happening, she launches from her seat, leaps over the fire pit, her hands curled like claws ready for an attack.

"You piece of shit!" she screams as she makes contact with

Big J. "You're nothing but a low life mutated scumbag!" She claws at his face, knocking him off balance until they end up in a rolling heap. "I'm gonna rip your stinking eyes from their sockets!" She is a rabid animal and neither Big J nor James is expecting it. Ian gives me a look of shock and I try to motion behind my back to show him that I'm close to becoming free. Ian jumps to his feet as Gemma buries her head deeper into my shoulder, sobbing.

"Briar, stop!" Ian shouts, but it's like he isn't even there. In the commotion, James has been thrown aside. He looks stunned and for a moment seems to forget that he's got a gun. Briar is done talking and only an occasional grunt escapes either of them as Briar's nails dig into Big J's flesh. She's clearly kicking his butt and a moment of pride washes over me as I feel her redemption. Still, in the pit of my stomach, I know this is a battle that she cannot win and I'm angry that she let Big J's words cause such recklessness. He's trying desperately to pry Briar off with little luck. We are all helpless as we watch Big J rip at Briar's hair and kick at any limb he can reach. Blood covers his face and drips down onto his shirt as she balls her claws into fists and begins beating his face where he's most vulnerable. Their bodies roll next to James and he kicks them away, pushing himself back out of danger. Briar finally releases herself from Big J and stands over him like a tower. Slowly she pulls back a leg and swings her foot into his groin with a sickening thud. Big J lets out a howl and rolls himself into a tight ball, panting for air. She uses this moment to launch a fresh attack, pounding his back with her fists in anger. I don't know where she has pulled all of this energy from. Maybe it's years and years' worth of pent-up hurt. Maybe she was always just on the edge of an explosion. It's impressive and scary. I glance over to

James and notice that he's finally remembered Sharp Shooter. Damn it! I want to be reckless myself and rush at him, somehow take the gun away, but I'm still not free. James points the gun wildly out in front of him, not knowing where to aim. My eyes search Ian's questioning if he's free, if we should tackle James before he can use the gun. I can see Ian working frantically to free himself and notice his wrists covered in blood.

"That's enough!" yells James and he shoots the gun into the air. The sound stops Briar in her tracks as her head whips around to make sure we are all still alive. Big J pushes her away and she sits panting on the ground. She looks from the gun in James' hands to Big J and she knows that she's messed up, she let anger eat at her before we had a real plan. She keeps her eyes focused on the ground, unable to meet any of our eyes.

As he comes into the light of the fire, I see that Big J is a mess of swollen eyes, ripped clothes, and various bleeding cuts. She did a good job on him, including a bloody nose that he wipes with the back of his hand. Some of his cuts are deep and look as if they may require stitches. There's barely a new scratch on Briar and I'm betting that Big J wishes that Briar wasn't so healthy now.

"Okay, okay, show's over," says James. Without hesitation, Big J walks over to where Briar sits, her eyes downcast, her chest heaving with new exhaustion. A tight smile begins to form across his downturned lips. He pulls back his leg and shoots a hard kick directly into Briar's stomach. She slumps to the ground, trying to regain her breath. She's suffocating as she tries to pull in air, her hands clutching at her chest. Big J gives a nod of satisfaction. I feel Ian's anger, wanting to run to her and then as quickly feel him stop.

"I said the show's over," repeats James. Big J steps away from

Briar just as she regains control. I see her chest rise and fall as she continues to stay on the ground.

"What are we gonna do with her?" asks Big J. My heart races in a terrified rhythm as Gemma huddles closer to me. She is shaking out of control and, for the first time, I'm not sure that Briar will make it out of this mess alive.

"Don't look," I whisper as I try to move myself to block her vision of this horrible scene. I lift myself off the log. I need to help her, and I feel so helpless.

"No," I hear Ian say and I sit back down, tears streaming down my cheeks.

James walks a circle around Briar's deflated form and then glances to the rest of us. He shakes his head. "I don't want any more trouble from this one," he says to Big J. "Do what you want."

CHAPTER THIRTY-NINE

Aiden

I awake with a start. My head has found its way into a precarious position on the armrest of the back of the van while my legs stretch out across the seats. A shooting pain wraps its grip around my neck and shoulders, and I sit up trying to rub the kinks away. Light streams through the windows, reflecting off the golden sand outside.

"You're up." Samuel leans his head through the front driver's side window. He tosses me an apple with a smile. "Eat up and then we're off." I bite into the apple and let its sweet juice quench my thirst, another product from the Underground gardens. It's going to be a long day sweeping back and forth in our continuous search. Samuel's words continue to ring in my head, *things can change on a dime out here,* and the urgency to find Wren intensifies.

"How are ya doing today?" asks Samuel. "Did ya get any sleep?"

"I'm fine," I reply a little too sharply, regretting it immediately when I see Samuel's look of surprise. "How are you?" I add. Samuel looks long at me, trying to figure out my frustration.

"I'm good, but I'm used to this. What's going on in your head?" I let out a frustrated sigh.

"I just want to get this over with. I just want to find Wren and get back." He nods with understanding and starts up the van. We continue with our sweep back and forth, parallel to the mountain range. It's a clear day, bright and sunny with good visibility.

"What's beyond that forested area?" I ask, trying to think of a new plan. Perhaps a more in-depth search.

"A river and beyond that another sector, Sector Eight, but I don't go there anymore."

"Are there a lot of wanderers out there then?"

"Nah," Samuel replies. "They kill each other off over food and property. Still that small group living in eight is pretty vicious and they don't like outsiders, even of their own kind."

"They could be a problem at some point," I say. I'm not sure what the Underground's plans are long term for these people though Clay alluded that they might have to be taken out.

"Could be, but not today."

After our third sweep we decide to take a break. Samuel tosses me a sandwich, white cheese between two slices of flat bread. It's too monotonous, what we're doing, and I feel like we're moving but getting nowhere. It's frustrating. I'm quiet for too long and Samuel notices.

"Look," he says, finishing the last bite of his sandwich. "I know you want to find this gal. But from what you've told me, she seems pretty smart and self-sufficient. I'm sure she knows what she's doing." I give him a smile, but it's not genuine. Suddenly, I hear a sound in the distance. I stand up and cup my hands over my eyes to get a better view. I don't see anything but then I hear the sound again and it chills me to the bone. Howls, off in the distance directly in front of us, the unmistakable howl of dogs.

"What do you see?" asks Samuel as he quickly throws our chairs back into the van. I'm about to tell him *nothing* but then a dark spec appears on the horizon, quickly changing to many more.

"It's the dogs," I say with certainty. "The dogs are coming!"

"We'll be ready for 'em." Samuel pulls out two rifles from the back compartment of the van. He tosses one to me and then cocks back his own before aiming at the horizon. As the pack gets closer, tuffs of brown, black and tan distinguish them from one another, the atmosphere changes.

"What's going on Samuel?" The sun's rays shoot through an opening in the clouds and I see what was hidden before. A shield, a forcefield shimmers fifty yards away and reaches out both east and west like a blanket dividing us and the mountain from the rest of the wild. The apparition flickers throwing the dogs into a blurry mirage as they continue to run towards us.

"I've never seen anything like this before," says Samuel in awe. He lowers his gun slightly.

"Maybe it's some kind of protection," I offer. The dogs keep running. I count six, ten, twelve, all with yellow steely eyes. I'm not sure we can take them all.

"Maybe, but let's not take any chances." He lifts his gun again and pulls the trigger. The explosion knocks Samuel back slightly and one dog goes down yelping.

"Well, it ain't protection for the dogs, that's for sure." We fire at will, taking down half of the pack but the rest don't seem to notice or care, and they keep coming, quickly approaching the strange barrier.

"Get in the van!" yells Samuel. From the front seat, he aims his gun again, waiting to see what happens. The beasts are a yard from the barrier now and as the first dog leaps through, I hold my breath. Samuel pulls his gun back in and rolls up the window, preparing to punch the pedal. My eyes go wide as the roan-colored dog's front quarters launch through the glistening barrier. As if in slow motion, I see it happen, the fur and muscle change from solid flesh and bone to droplets of liquid that spray across the sand on the other side.

"What the hell?" I ask, my voice wavering. "What the hell was that?" I look to Samuel who shakes his head back and forth in shock. Over and over again, fur and claws and teeth are transformed as each dog leaps through the barrier without hesitation. When they are all just puddles on the sand, I try to stop my pulse from racing. Samuel lays his gun in the backseat and he exits the van to get a better look.

"Samuel!" I yell. "Come on, let's get out of here." The whole thing makes me too nervous, the sudden appearance of something so deadly makes me question everything we're doing out here. It could be too late. For the first time, I allow myself to think that Wren may already be dead.

Samuel inches tentatively to the puddles that have now absorbed into the sand and then looks up to the barrier. He turns fearful eyes to me and yells, "We gotta go!" His voice is filled with trepidation. "We gotta go, now!" He's running full force back to the van when I see the shimmering curtain begin to move towards us. "Start the van! Start the van!" I pummel the start button with my fist and hear the engine begin to hum just as Samuel hops into the driver's seat. He slams the door shut and begins racing to the mountain, a spray of sand engulfing us.

"We can't enter the tunnel the way we exited. That thing is too close." he says in a rush. "But there are other ways in." My pulse quickens and my stomach turns in knots as fear washes over me. Seeing the fear in Samuel's face makes the danger all too real. I throw my head around to see how much time we have left; how close the barrier is to turning us into liquid. It's closing in but we still have time to make it to the mountain and hopefully that will be safe enough. We hit the range at the eastern edge and Samuel pushes the van onto the toughest terrain yet. As the engine protests, we realize that we'll have to abandon it and go on foot.

"There's a way in on the other side. I know a path we can take but we have to hurry. It' will be a hike." Samuel grabs the riffle from the back seat, and I follow him out of the van. "Wait a sec," he says. "Look."

"It's stopped," I say incredulously. A clap of thunder startles me and I look up to see white hot lightning streaking the sky. It reminds me uncomfortably of the pillars and I glance around quickly determining if there is any place to hide. A flash hits the waiting barrier and in an instant it's gone. We both stand, trying to catch our breath, the storm now gone.

"Damnit!" I yell, kicking out at a pile of boulders in anger. "What the hell is going on out here?" I meet Samuel's eyes. "Now what?"

"Look. Aiden. We have three more days until we're expected back. Let's make camp on the other side of the mountain. You're girl's bright. She'll have to get around the mountain to get to the hub. We'll meet up with her there. If something else crazy like this happens, I know a way into the tunnels. It 'ain't the safest way in, but it'll work in a bind." Samuel grabs some essentials from the van including his gun and camping equipment and food.

"We'll have to come back for the van later," he says. "It shouldn't take us more than an hour to get over the ridge."

I follow Samuel as he leads me to a path that is really nothing more than stone that has been worn down to gravel. To my left the mountains loom above, casting a shadow and welcome shade. To the right the ridge slopes down, creating outstretched arms, eventually becoming part of the surrounding rough landscape. We walk in single file, traversing sections of jagged stone, my thigh muscles straining as we climb steep hills only to slope down again. There are patches of moss and other green plants shooting out from small crevices in the mighty stone. They remind me of Wren's eyes and my purpose out here, but also make the path slippery. As we come to the top of a particularly high hill, I gaze out at the landscape below. For an instant, the valley below feels like home. The golden sand, the dots of green, tell me that we are close to the hub. This view was the hope that Raven, Spencer and I felt on our first tine out, when we knew that the journey was almost over. But my feeling of contentment fades when I picture Spencer and Raven back at the hub, knowing that I'll never see them again and still not having Wren in my arms.

"Almost there." Samuel's voice pulls me from my thoughts. We take the slope down cautiously and soon are standing in the valley where the air is noticeably cooler. The mountain seems to envelope us, its gigantic form protective.

"Let's make camp," says Samuel as we inspect a sheltered area within the bend of the mountain's arm. We drop our supplies and Samuel looks hard at me. "This is as far as I go. Won't go too close to the hub. Can't risk that, not even for you." We begin laying out the supplies and assembling our tents.

"What would the government do, Samuel, if you just walked into the hub. If you said that you wanted to stay? Based on what Lynda told me, they'd probably turn you away but is it really that dangerous?" He looks up from the tent pole in his hand.

"They're not turning anyone away anymore," he says darkly. "If you ain't wearing one of those snazzy jumpsuits, you're dead on the spot."

CHAPTER FORTY

Wren

Even through the blood and dirt and blackened eyes, Big J's smile begins to grow. It's a sick, twisted kind of smile, made worse by his mutated face. He looks like the true monster that I know he is, and I'm terrified for Briar, sprawled out on the ground, and for the rest of us.

"Get up'" he commands. Briar's chest still heaves from the exertion of her final attack. I can see her body tense as she braces herself with her arms and slowly glances up.

"No." One world spoken quietly but with so much force and determination. I yank vigorously at the ties around my wrist, insanely, ignoring the jolting pain at every movement, but they will not loosen more. My eyes are glued to Briar who is staring Big J down. I can't lose her. She's my symbol of strength, my reminder that maybe, some day, I can be strong. But right now, I feel so weak. Gemma's sobs become louder and I hush her and tell her again that it will all be okay. Lies. Deep down, I know that it won't be okay.

"I'm going to bed," says James with a yawn. "You're on watch, here." He hands over his gun. Big J gives a nod.

"I'm going to take care of this one first," he says with a wicked smile.

"Hmmm," says James and he stands and stretches. "Don't get carried away, Jobias. If there's any truth to the tales they've been telling, we might be able to use them for some greater trade off down the road." Big J nods but keeps his eyes glued on Briar.

"I'm not taking any crap from anyone," says Big J. "Next time, I won't use my fist, I'll use the gun." He reaches down and grabs Briar under one arm, jerking her upright. She doesn't say a word as he drags her roughly into the tent behind me, the tent where Rory should be. As Briar's face passes mine, I see a fierceness in her eyes. She will do whatever it takes to survive. They disappear behind the screen of the tent and the three of us are left alone for the first time.

"We have to help her," I whisper fiercely. Ian leans into me.

"I'm trying, Wren, but my ties won't loosen anymore. He takes in a deep breath as he continues to work.

"Okay," I reply with a sob. "What about you, Arick?"

"I'll try," he replies softly

"Do either of you have any weapons?"

"No," replies Arick quickly. I look to Ian. He shakes his head but then adds as if just remembering, "I've got my pocketknife." That's good enough. Suddenly a loud guttural scream rips through the night. Gemma looks up at me, tears making a rapid path down her cheeks. No, no, no, not Briar. I grit my teeth and force myself to say the words again that I don't believe.

"She's going to be okay," I whisper. "She's tough. As tough as they get." Another scream and this time it's Big J's voice. Good, fight back, fight back as hard as you can, Briar. My eyes lock with Ian's and we sit like this, trying to glean some comfort from each other's eyes, waiting for it to be over, each of us wanting to break free and rip Big J apart. My chest jerks with sobs that I'm holding in and my eyes burn with tears. We hear scuffles coming from the tent, Briar's screams and Big J swearing, calling her every name in the book. Big J must be backing off because the sounds within die down and soon I see him backing out of the tent. He looks worse than before, fresh cuts on his face resemble the path of fingernails but I wonder what Briar looks like, what damage he has been able to inflict on her. As he leans his back on a log across from us, the world goes silent.

Mercifully, Gemma has fallen asleep on my shoulder, but my eyes are still glued to Ian. My chest is constricted and, no matter how hard I try to breath, I can't get enough air into my lungs. I gasp and choke and I'm seconds away from vomiting from everything that I've witnessed when Ian whispers in my ear.

"Shhhh, it's okay, Wren." I rest my head on his shoulder and concentrate on breathing. Gemma's head falls to my lap, but she continues to sleep. "Shhh," he repeats. "When we get out of here," he continues. "I'm going to make sure that nothing bad ever touches you again. We'll get to the hub and we'll start a new life, together, a simple life." He smiles as his eyes search my face. My breathing has calmed, and I close my eyes, thinking about how nice that would be. "Hey," he says. "Don't forget about that pizza you promised me." I let the thoughts for the future wash over me, thoughts of Gemma becoming a doctor and Ian and I happy and safe. When my mind gets to Briar, I stop. All I can think about is revenge. I look over at Arick who stares at his feet, unseeing, and then we all continue to work at our bindings with the same idea in mind, get free and kill our captures.

As night wears on, Big J begins to snore. My body aches from sitting in one position, my throat is parched from lack of water, and my stomach is an empty hole screaming for food. I spend the next few agonizing hours twisting my wrists back and forth, back and forth until they are raw. The pain becomes too much as dawn approaches and then I finally feel my left hand slip free. My eyes, itching from lack of sleep, blink once and I glance to Ian and give him a curt nod.

"I'm almost there," he whispers. His voice sounds different, hoarse and dry.

The sun streaks the sky with bright gold and orange. Gemma's eyes flutter open and Arick gives her a slight smile.

"Where is Briar," she asks with a small voice.

"We're going to help her, Gemma, I promise. We're going to help her soon." Ian glances over, his expression grim. I eye Big J warily as he sleeps.

"Where's your knife?" I whisper as I wiggle both hands free. Just as I begin to push myself up from the log, Big J begins to stir, stretching out his limbs, yawning. His eyes blink open and he stares at us, all perched in a row, like we're some kind of mirage.

"Well, how's everyone doing today?" asks James as he exits his tent.

"Pretty good," replies Big J. "What about those meals?" James throws one of our precious meal packs over to him as Lucy comes creeping out of a tent. There is still no sound from Briar's tent. I slowly push my hands back through the plastic tie behind my back and wait for my next opportunity.

"So, what's the plan?" asks Big J as James comes walking back.

"There's not much left to do, is there?" he replies. "We got plenty of water, a little more food now." He scratches his scabby balding head, glancing warily to the tent where Briar is kept.

"What about the girl?" he asks. Big J doesn't answer but keeps his eyes glued to his meal. When he's finished, he tosses the empty pouch into the fire and wipes his hands on his dirty pants.

"I don't think she'll be a problem now," he finally replies. James notices the new cuts on Big J's face but nods his head slowly as if he is fully aware of what Big J is capable of. He has no idea of how strong Briar is.

James makes himself busy pawing through our possessions one more time, loading miscellaneous items into packs for them to take when they leave. Everything else gets tossed into the fire. With a sharp pain of sadness, I watch as Gemma's little stuffed rabbit, the toy she lovingly rescued from one of our make-shift homes, goes flying into the flames. Her eyes fill with tears as her reminder of childhood turns to ashes. Lucy makes her way to where we sit. She sees the tears making a path down Gemma's cheeks and tries to snuggle up next to her. It freaks me out and I feel Gemma pushing against me, trying to somehow get away from her. I try to shove her with my shoulder but all she does is reach out to touch my hair, sending goosebumps down my neck. My skin crawls with her touch.

"Freak," I hiss. The sound of feet shuffling comes from somewhere behind me and I turn quickly thinking that maybe Briar has escaped from the tent. I ready myself to rip my hands free, joining her in the fight this time, but she's not there. I sit quietly, listening, ignoring Lucy's presence. I hear the sound again, a rustling of feet over forest debris. There's someone out there, in the forest, possibly watching us. My heart begins a wild beat that floods into my ears. I glance over to Ian and Arick, wondering if they've heard it as well. By the look of surprise on Ian's face, he has. I give him a questioning glance and he shakes his head in confusion. I turn back to Gemma and realize that Lucy is still watching me. I see her eyes flick to the forest behind us and the creepy smile on her face becomes brighter, excited. She quickly stands, steps over the log where we sit, and heads into the forest to explore. Whoever is out there, I hope they take her out. I hope they've been watching. I hope they've heard Briar's screams and seen the blood that I can feel drying around my wrists. I hope they know we're in trouble.

I hear Lucy's light dancing footsteps as she enters the forest and then the snap of a twig. Gemma looks up in wonder. Then all at once, a loud hoot escapes Lucy's throat as she comes prancing back into view. She dances around what's left of the fire just as James tosses in a fresh log.

"I saw him, but he didn't see me," she sings excitedly. "Maybe there's more yummy food!" She turns in a big circle, her arms wide, happily waiting for what might be another Christmas day of surprises. "Maybe they'll be more girls with more pretty hair," she continues to sing. "I will make two new wigs, one red and one black!"

"Who did you see?" says James sharply. The tone in his voice makes her stop abruptly. She looks to James wide-eyed.

"A guy," she says simply. "I saw a guy. Maybe more than one." I feel Gemma sit up straighter and I look at Ian.

Arick, Ian, Gemma and I quickly swing our legs over the log to face the forest.

"Hold on there, you four. Don't get any funny ideas," says

James. "I still got this." He waves his gun around so that we get a clear view. As if we can forget. It's the only thing keeping me from rushing at him and strangling him with my bare hands. James walks away from us as he cautiously enters the forest alone.

My ears feel like they're working on sonar and the smallest sound makes me pause. Just when every nerve is standing on end, the sound of gunfire rips through the air and James re-appears, his face full of terror. He hits the ground before he reaches us. I scurry out of the way, pulling Gemma with me, as Big J comes running. Lucy just sits there, her mouth an open gap of surprise. I cringe in pain as I pull my wrists from their bondage, feeling crusted-over wounds from the plastic ties eating their way through my flesh. I whip my arms around, and my breath catches at the pain of my shoulder joints that have been pulled for so long.

"Where's your knife?" I ask Ian as I lean into him.

"Left hip pocket," he replies. Before I have time to think about anything, before I have time to be embarrassed, I plunge my hand deep into Ian's hip pocket and feel the cool surface of his folded knife. I chance a glance at Big J, worried that he may come after me, but his attention is on James, leaning over his still form, smacking him in the face. His eyes are wide as he glances toward the forest. I quickly flip open the knife and rip it though the plastic ties that bind Ian. This is no time to be gentle and I hear him give a moan of pain. His wrists look as bad as mine.

"Sorry," I say. Ian gives me a nod and I move to Arick, cutting him free. Gemma's already standing in front of me, her arms out. I sweep the area with my eyes and see James' gun several feet away left unmanned on the forest floor. By the time Big

J notices us, it's too late. The weight of the gun feels good in my hand, cool metal, heavy and full of bullets. I raise it up and point the barrel right between Big J's eyes. From behind him a see a figure emerge from the forest, another gun pointed in our direction.

"Rory," I say blankly. He keeps his gun aimed at Big J, his stump of an arm steadying the weapon. He limps slightly as he comes to stand next to me. He looks in good condition, considering. There's a smug look on his face, intermingled with anger.

"Hey," he replies. "Looks like you've got everything under control now." He eyes the gun in my hands. Big J watches us, his hands raised in submission.

"W-who are you?" he asks, fumbling over his words. "What are you going to do? Before I can stop myself, I feel the anger rise from somewhere deep inside of me, traveling up and out into my limbs. I lunge forward, using all of my strength and bash the side of Big J's head in with the good old sharpshooter. He falls to the ground with a thud and lands next to James. Neither one moves.

"Whoa," exclaims Rory, his eyes wide.

"Is he dead?" I ask, pointing to James.

"Don't know," replies Rory. "I was aiming for his leg, but I might have missed. It's not as easy with only one hand." Ian bends down and rests two fingers on James's neck. As I glance at his motionless body, I see the wound on his leg. Rory's got good aim.

"He's still alive, just unconscious," says Ian, looking up at me.

"Tie 'em up," I say in a perfect rendition of James. I bend down and search Big J's pockets, quickly finding the bag of plastic ties. "Make them tight," I add. "And tie their ankles too."

Ian takes the ties from me and begins dragging James into the forest.

"Where is the water." I ask.

"Check the tents," replies Arick as he bends down and loops his hands under Big J's arms. Ian takes his feet, and together they follow Rory into the forest. Without another moment of hesitation, I race to the first tent, the one where James slept. Sure enough, there is our water supply, bottles stashed in a corner. I grab two and dash out. I have to get to Briar. My heart hammers in my chest and my feet can't get there fast enough, but I'm also afraid of what I'll find. I enter the tent quietly, unzipping the front flap and gently pulling the fabric away. There she is, crumpled on a thin fabric floor, pulled into a ball, barely looking human at all. A deep sob escapes my throat and I cover my mouth with my hands. Her hands are no longer behind her back but instead are pinned together in the front with fresh ties. Her knees curl into her chest, her face hidden beneath her wild black curls. Even as I edge my way closer, I can see the deep gashes caused by the plastic digging into her flesh. She has been beaten and is covered in bruises and dried blood. I know that many of her injuries have come from the fight in her, the drive to fight back. She looks so small.

Gently, I push her curls away from her face and see a trace of an eyelid fluttering. She's alive. Of course, she's alive, but her face doesn't look like her anymore. It's much worse than just a few cuts and a swollen eye. Every inch of her face is home to a fresh injury. Dried blood cakes her open wounds and there are too many puffed up bruises to count. *Gemma will fix her*, I think. *Gemma will work her magic and make her look as good as new.* I reach for the pocketknife and cut her free, feeling her flinch a little as her arms and legs are released. I grab a bottle of water and unscrew the cap, holding it to her lips.

"Hey, Briar, I'm here. You're going to be okay." I hear a rustling behind me and turn to see Gemma entering the tent. She has her medical kit, at least what's left of it and she's ready to get to work.

CHAPTER FORTY-ONE

Wren

"How is she?" Gemma asks, her voice serious and small.

"I don't know," I reply, trying to keep the panic from my voice. "But if anyone can help her, it's you, Gemma." The little girl is gone as the doctor takes over. I back away, giving her room to work and notice that my hands are shaking. I take small sips of water, slowing easing my parched mouth and keep my eyes on Gemma.

"She's alive," she says in a hard voice that isn't hers. I nod.

"How is she?" asks Ian as he pops his head into the tent. "Is she okay?" I turn to see Rory and Arick kneeling next to him.

"I need you to leave," I say more harshly than I mean to. "Please," I add. I don't want them to see Briar this way, broken and naked. I know she wouldn't want that either. I don't want them to know what I suspect Big J did to her, much more than beating her black and blue. "I promise," I say. "I'll give you a full report in a little while, once Gemma has fixed her up."

"Okay," replies Ian. He reaches out his hand and runs his fingers across my cheek, carefully avoiding my battered eye. I close my eyes and savor his touch for just a second and then I push him gently away.

"What can I do, Gemma?" She is busy covering Briar's face with the same gel pads that she used for Rory's burns. She cuts them into small strips to make sure that she can heal everything.

"This will help the swelling," she says. "And help to heal any open wounds. Hold this," she adds, and hands me a small jar of blue cream. It smells strongly of something medicinal and stings my eyes a little. She takes a small sponge and begins to apply the cream to all the cuts covering Briar's body, beginning with her wrists and ankles. When she's finished, she adds a dap to my wrists and then takes a box from the kit.

"Help me put these on," she says as she opens the box and removes bandages wrapped in sterile paper. She rips off the paper and pulls out a flesh-toned bandage, adhering it to one of the deeper cuts. Once it's in place it almost looks as if the cut has magically disappeared, replaced by new skin. But I know that the injury is only hidden.

"Will all of this really work?" I ask, unsure. It just seems like there are too many things to heal. Gemma leans back, gathering up the wrapping from the bandages.

"I'm not sure how many scars there will be, but these wounds will heal," she replies with confidence. She pulls something new from her kit, a plastic syringe along with a vial of clear liquid. She inserts the needle into the vial to draw up the medication.

"What's that for?" I ask.

"It's an antibiotic," she replies as she flicks the syringe with her fingers to release any air bubbles. "I don't want her injuries to get infected. There's also medicine to help with the pain." Without hesitation, she inserts the needle into Briar's thigh, avoiding as much of the bruising as she can. "Don't worry," she adds. "I've read all about injection sites and preparing this medication." I reach out and gently smooth the hair from Briar's face. She looks like a mummy, all wrapped up in Gemma's bandages. Gemma packs up the medical kit and leaves the tent only to return with several silvery blankets in her arms.

"She'll sleep for a while," she says quietly. Together, Gemma and I cover her in a blanket, wrapping it tightly like a cocoon. She looks so helpless and I can't stop another sob from escaping my throat. I wonder if Briar will make it through this and what will she look like on the other side of it. My brave, strong Briar. The girl that won't take shit from anyone. How fractured is she now? I feel Gemma's hand on my back, gently pulling me away.

"She's going to be okay." Her voice is steely, commanding. "I'll stay with her for now," she whispers. "Go get something to eat, try to get some rest. I'll let you know when she wakes up." As difficult as it is to pry myself away, I know Gemma is right.

Ian, Arick and Rory sit around the fire, trying to eat. As I exit Briar's tent, Ian looks up expectantly, his eyes full of questions.

"Gemma says she'll be okay," I say softly. "But she's in bad shape."

"What did they do to her?" asks Rory, his voice full of anger, his eyes full of pain. He looks into the fire and shakes his head. "I'll kill him," he says simply. "I'll kill that bastard." Ian grabs his arm to steady him.

"We'll figure out what to do with them before we go," he says. "For now, save your strength. You'll need it."

"Here." he says, handing me a meal pack and a bottle of water. I see the cuts on his own wrists.

"You should have Gemma look at those," I say, taking his hand and examining more closely. He nods.

"And your eye," he says softly. I touch the area around my swollen left eye, gingerly.

"It'll be okay," I say. "The swelling is already going down." My stomach gives a rumble, reminding me how hungry I am, but it's still twisted in knots. I rip off the top of the pouch, not caring what it contains, and pour in some water. As I shovel the first bite of food into my mouth, my eyes wander over our small camp. With shock, I see Lucy, curled in a ball near the forest edge, sobbing.

"What are you going to do with her?" I ask incredulously. She's not as harmless as she seems, especially when it comes to my hair.

"We'll put her with the others," says Rory. He crumbles up his empty meal pack and tosses it into the fire. "I tried to interrogate her to see where they came from, find out if there are others close by. She's useless." We sit for a while in silence, eating, taking long sips of water, listening to the crackle of the fire.

After we finish eating, Rory is true to his word and leads Lucy at gunpoint into the forest while Ian follows along with Arick ready to take the first watch. I am left to scavenger what is left of our supplies. Luckily, Rory saved my backpack, as well as Briar's and his own. I unzip mine and thrust my hand down deep where I feel the cool metal of my gun.

"You thought I took off, didn't you?" says Rory as he comes walking out of the forest. "Hey, I don't blame you. I was a real jerk." I smile up into his face and immediately notice a curious change. His burns are no longer angry and have begun to blend into new skin. It's not the same face that he had in the compound and I know that there will always be scars, but he's no mutant. There is something in his eyes, a spark of kindness, and there is a new confidence when he speaks. Even with his damaged leg that has apparently left him with a limp, he stands taller. The selfish boy seems to have vanished before my eyes, replaced by a soldier.

"I'm sorry," I reply.

"You did a good job in the forest after you were captured, with all the noise, I mean. I knew something was wrong," he continues. "I thought that maybe, this time, I could do something right, so I made the decision to hide and wait."

"Well, you did, Rory, you definitely did something right," I say. "And you look good, strong."

"Briar will heal quickly too." He looks away, unable to meet my eyes.

"When Briar gets better, I think you two have a lot to talk about," I say, and he nods. I zip up my pack just as Ian walks over.

"We should probably consider moving out soon," he says.

"We have to wait until Briar's well enough to travel," I say.

"We have move quickly, now," he continues. "I think she'll be strong enough in a day or so."

"So, we're heading out?" asks Arick as he walks over to us. "Your turn," he adds to Ian as he points in the direction of the forest where I know that James, Big J and Lucy are tied up. "I'm losing my mind with boredom, watching the three of them squirm. Lucy won't shut up."

"It's okay, I'll go back," replies Ian. "I think we can plan on another twenty-four hours and then we can clear out of here. We'll have to figure out what to do with our *friends*." Rory gives a grunt of frustration.

"I know what to do," Rory says. Ian looks him square in the eye.

"It wasn't that long ago that you were making bad choices," he says. "You were forgiven even though the majority wanted you gone."

"Yeah, right, but I didn't hold anyone hostage or beat the crap out of an innocent woman, did I?

"No," replies Ian softly. "But you did cause one man and one woman to lose their lives." Rory looks away, his face filled with shame. "We'll figure out what to do with them in the morning."

"How far do you think it is?" asks Arick. "The hub, I mean." How long has it been since we saw the compound? Weeks? It feels like years.

"I think if we keep heading north, we can make it in a few days, a week maybe, two at the most, barring any more unfortunate circumstances. We can move quicker on this terrain and we've all had ample time to get our energy back." Rory gives a bark of laughter.

"Good luck," he says with sarcasm. "I can't even imagine what else is lurking out there."

My spirits lift at the thought of all of this being over soon. A glimmer of hope sprouts for the chance to sleep in a real bed, eat a real hot meal and not live in constant terror.

"See you in a little while." Ian stands and heads for the forest. "Try to pack up as much as you can carry.

"Wren." Gemma's voice comes from the opening of Briar's tent and I jump to my feet.

"What is it?" I ask, hurling myself into the tent. "What's going on?" As I gaze at Briar's form, resting on the hard ground, I don't need Gemma to answer. Shrouded in bandages, Briar's eyes flutter open and fix on mine. A low moan escapes her throat and I scoot to her side.

"Wren," she whispers.

"I'm here, I'm here, Briar. Everything's going to be okay. You're going to be okay."

"I got him good, that son-of-a-bitch…" Her voice is weak and scratchy, but there's still a ring of fight in it. I hush her softly, combing the dark, wild curls from her face with my hand. Gemma tilts her head up and gives her small sips of water. Briar coughs at first but then drinks eagerly.

"We won't know the extent of scarring until we remove the bandages. Just let her sleep," she says. "In the morning we can check them."

"You need sleep too," I say. "Ian's talking about leaving soon. There's nothing more you can do right now anyway." Gemma doesn't argue and I try to make myself comfortable next to Briar. Her breathing has steadied, and I watch as her chest slowly rises and falls. She's never going to be the same after this, and neither am I.

"Hey," comes a voice from just outside of the tent. Rory pops his head in, a meal pack in hand along with several bottles of water.

"Briar might be hungry when she wakes up," he says in explanation. I nod my approval and give him a smile. I leave, letting him do what he's dying to do, make amends.

By evening Briar is awake and eating though she is still silent. She lets Rory continue to stay with her while Gemma monitors her improvement. Night falls and they decide to take turns in Briar's tent. I can't sleep even though I need the rest. Tomorrow will be a long day. Ian comes to sit with me by the fire. Everything is quiet and calm, and I wonder how Arick is doing with our prisoners.

"I'm sorry," says Ian as he wraps his arms around me. His warmth feels good.

"There's nothing to be sorry about."

"I should have done more, for Briar, I should have protected her."

"Ian, we didn't have a chance." He holds me closer.

"I just want to protect you, Wren, always. You know I'm in love with you, right? I need you to know that now, more than ever."

By the light of the moon, I see Ian for who he is. We have lost the same things, and want the same things, an invisible string pulling us together. Something in this crazy universe, has brought us together and it feels right, more than right. It feels necessary.

"I love you too, Ian," I say, and I feel his breath on my face as he leans in to touch his lips to mine. "When this is all over..." He reaches up to draw a line from just below my ear downward, tracing my jawline with his finger.

"When this is over," I reply, and he kisses me once more.

The next morning is a whirl of activity as we all begin to pack up.

"How is she?" I ask Rory as he exits Briar's tent. My pulse quickens, anxious to know the answer.

"Sometime in the middle of the night she woke up and actually ate something," he says, and I feel the smile creep back onto my face. "Gemma says that she'll remove the bandages this morning and see how everything checks out."

"That's great," I say excitedly. Rory smiles back but I still see fear in his eyes. "What is it?" I ask.

"She'll be okay," he says trying to dismiss me. "She's just not talking very much, she's not the Briar who was ready to kick my ass every other second."

"Breakfast?" asks Ian, giving me a wink.

"I'm going to check on Briar first," I say as I head in the direction of her tent.

"I'll save you a seat," comes Ian's voice from behind. I feel myself blush, so I don't turn around.

As I open the flap of Briar's tent, I'm surprised to see her sitting up, her back leaning against a makeshift pillow of blankets. She's taking small sips of water, her lips working around the bandages. Gemma turns to me and smiles. Briar's eyes slowly lift to meet mine and I see it: the pain and total dehumanization that she feels.

"I'm glad you're awake," I say because that's all I can get out. There's so much more inside of me, so much I want to say. She'll be okay, we'll move forward and forget about this place and what happened, just like the Mutts and the old man. I want her to know that this isn't who she is, that no one thinks less of her, that no one will hurt her again. I swallow hard. "We've all been so worried...even Rory." I attempt a smile, but I know she can see the pain all over my face. "How are you feeling?"

"Okay," her word is barely a whisper and her eyes cast downward.

"Well," says Gemma in her bubbly voice. "I think it's time to check those bandages." As she reaches out to begin the process, Briar pulls away.

"I'm not ready," she breathes, her eyes tearing up.

"It's going to be fine," says Gemma with confidence. "These bandages are like magic. They heal injuries quickly and don't leave much scarring. You'll be okay, Briar, I promise." I reach out and gently take her hand.

"You're one bad-ass chick, Briar," I say. "I know you've been through some sick stuff. I know you've been through more than most people have gone through in a lifetime. You're strong, stronger than you think you are in this moment." Tears begin to stream down her cheeks, making fast wet pathways along her face.

"I'm not," she whispers. "I'm not anymore." My heart aches for her. I know she's in there somewhere, my fighter, my warrior. I have to find her. I need her back, or I'll never make it out of here. I grab her by the shoulders, gently at first, and then sharply. She looks deep into my eyes, searching for the answer of how to go on after all of this.

And so, I give it to her with my words, "Don't let him win," I say sharply. "Don't you dare let that son-of-a-bitch win." I see a small piece of her snap back into place. She gives me a curt nod and turns to Gemma.

"Okay, let's do this," she says, her voice a little stronger. Gemma begins at Briar's forehead, slowly removing the first bandage. Just as she promised, the skin beneath it is smooth and the bruising is gone. I let out a sigh of relief as Briar's eyes jump from mine to Gemma's.

"It looks good," says Gemma. Slowly, she continues to remove bandages, revealing freshly healed skin, soft and new. "Do you want to see?" "Here." She holds out a small mirror to Briar, but she doesn't take it. I begin to help with the rest of the bandages covering her body. I feel renewed shock each time I see that a cut has been healed or a bruise dissipated. A few of the deeper cuts have left light, raised, pencil thin scars, battle wounds.

"I think we should try to get you up and walking," I say, once Gemma has disposed of the bandages and finished inspecting the scars.

Gemma and I each take a side and slowly lift Briar to her feet. She's wobbly at first, but she also feels strong. We take baby steps, shuffling along until her feet touch the forest floor. Rory comes running over. He offers his arm like a true gentleman and Briar takes it with a roll of her eyes.

"I've got a spot for you right over here," he says, leading her to a fat log in front of the fire. Briar sits but her eyes dart around nervously. Rory notices and says in a soft reassuring voice, "It's okay. You're safe."

"How are you feeling, Briar?" asks Ian. "Do you think that you're well enough to travel?"

"I think I have to be," she answers, her voice still rough. She's not even close to a hundred percent. We all know there are decisions to be made. It's hard to think about James, Big J and Lucy tied up somewhere in the forest, still alive, while Briar has suffered so much. I feel like we should talk about it, like Briar should have the final say in what their fate will be.

"So," says Ian. "I think we all agree that the best plan is to move forward and quickly. Briar?"

"Briar," says Rory softly. "You've been through enough. You need more time to heal." He looks over to Ian. "Can't we give her a few more days?"

"I'm ready," Briar replies without hesitation.

"Are you sure?" asks Rory.

"I think Briar can make up her own mind," I say. "If she feels strong enough to make the trek then that's good enough for me."

"What's that?" asks Rory and we all stop to listen. Ian's brows furrow in confusion as Rory turns his head and peers into the forest. Briar and I follow his gaze as the hum grows. Gemma has returned to Rory's tent, our make-shift hospital, to pack up the medical supplies while Rory continues to linger near Briar protectively. And then I see it, a dark fog that is somehow moving towards us in a uniform almost intentional way.

"Gemma," I say softly as my eyes become wider. "Gemma!" I yell as Briar says,

"What the hell?" The fog whips past the fire with deadly precision, sweeping past my face with an internal whine. Before my brain can register what it is, it is over Gemma's tent, whirling and dipping like a bullet towards her gentle face. Her eyes become huge with shock as the attack begins.

CHAPTER FORTY-TWO

Wren

"Bees," I whisper, and I can't get my feet to move. I'm planted like an unyielding monument watching in horror as the mass of black bees continue to shoot at Gemma in an angry assault. Finally, I come to my senses as I feel Briar leave my side and race towards her. Rory is on top of Briar, holding her back by her arms. Arick comes racing out of the forest and sees Gemma struggling. He launches his body on top of hers.

"Let me go!" screams Briar, pulling herself away forcefully. "Get off of me!" I take charge and leap towards the tent, my eyes searching desperately for something to stop what is happening. I grab handfuls of dirt and dead pine needles and throw them at the black mass that has taken over Gemma and Arick's bodies. Arick yells and bats at the bees but they don't let up. I let out a sob, feeling so helpless. I grab anything I can get my hands on, logs, water bottles and more dirt but the bees continue to hum, attached to their prey. I hear a soft moan from Gemma as Arick's shouts stop and I fall to my knees, pressing my hands over my ears. Two strong arms encircle my body and pull me to my feet. I wrestle with Ian, ripping at his arms, jerking my body away, but I can already see that I am too late. Gemma is lifeless on the ground.

"Stop it!" I scream at the top of my lungs. "Somebody stop them!" I scream it over and over until my throat is raw and I see Briar fall to the ground. The bees continue to swarm around the kindest person I have ever met, stinging relentlessly, causing that gently young face to become distorted and swollen. Her pale blue eyes remain open, but she doesn't run, or crawl or scream out. She doesn't move because I know that she's dead, lying beside her protector who has given up his life in an attempt to protect her.

"We have to get out of here," I hear Ian say from somewhere far away. I can't leave her. My heart will break into a million pieces if I leave her. I feel Ian lift me and begin to run, turning me away from the horrible scene.

"No!" I shout. "No!" but I collapse in his arms and begin to sob uncontrollably.

"Into the water!" he roars, and I hear rather than feel myself being carried into the river. I glance over to see Briar flung over Rory's shoulder and am amazed that he has the strength to carry her so far. *Gemma, Gemma.* My heart bleeds, my mind shatters and my internal organs feel that they will no longer work inside of me. How can I go on? How can I possibly live while Gemma is dead? Dead, my little doctor with so much to offer.

"We have to go back," I cry. "We have to go back to Gemma."

"Not yet," says Ian calmly.

"We have to go back!" I yell at the top of my voice. I wiggle out of Ian's embrace and stand in the cold water, shaking from everything. As I slowly begin to walk toward the riverbank, I hear the hum again and stop. I look to Ian who somehow seems to know what's going on.

"Get ready," he commands. I look toward the forest and there they are, the swarm, as if they have hunted us down. We all wade deeper into the river and I dunk my head under just as the fog of bees swarm over us. I hold my breath, pushing my lungs beyond their comfort level, but the panic that I feel makes it difficult to stay under. *Calm down*. I count in my head, ten, twenty, thirty, forty...until I can feel myself begin to fade, until I know that one more second will be the difference between life and death, and then I surface, gasping. Ian's head shoots up next to mine and we both see that the swarm has gone.

"It's over," he says glancing all around us. The sound of moving water is all we hear. "I had a feeling that they wouldn't come far out over the water."

"But they could come back," says Rory. His voice is strong without the quiver of fear. He holds Briar in the water, helping her navigate to solid ground.

"Once they attack, they lose their stingers," says Ian. "That swarm will not be able to hurt us again." My stomach clenches at the thought of all those stingers in Gemma's body. I want to go back and remove every single one of them. I want to hunt down the hive and attack while they are defenseless, killing them with a single shot of my gun. I want to stomp on the hive, tear it apart, burn it and scatter the ashes.

"Let's go," says Ian gently but I don't want gentle now. I want revenge.

The campsite looks just as it did when we left. The fire still crackles in the pit. Why didn't I think of that, fire? I should have grabbed a burning log and beat down the bees with its flame. One burnt hand would be worth a chance at Gemma's life.

"God, I could have done something," I say. "I could have taken a sleeping bag and cocooned her inside. I could have thrown her over my shoulder and run with her to the river, but I did nothing."

"There wasn't time," says Ian. "There just wasn't time." I see them laid out on the ground in front of her tent. The medical supplies are still in Gemma's hands, ready to be handed over to me. Briar rushes to her and takes her still body in her arms. She smooths back her silvery hair as tears drop onto Gemma's ruined face.

"You were the best of us," she sobs. "The very best of us." I join her as Ian and Rory cover Arick's body with a blanket. Gemma looks so small in death, like the child that she really was. My mind is flooded with all the things that she'll never do, all the new things that she'll never see. I wrap my arm around Briar as we continue to hold our little friend, the youngest member of our twisted family. Death continues to follow us, this time it is truly unbearable.

"Can we bury her?" I ask meekly. "I can't just leave her here." We have no tools to dig a deep hole and the thought of turning her body to ash is repulsive. I look up to Ian who stands in silence. "We can't just leave her."

"Let's take her body to the forest," he replies. "We can find a good resting place there." I nod, but inside I make a promise to Gemma. If her family is alive somewhere in this new world, I will find them and tell them about the woman she would have become. I will tell them about her bravery and her strength and her aptitude for medicine. I know that I will not rest until they know the amazing girl that was their daughter. Ian helps me take her body to the forest and we make a clearing deep in the green, a bed of pine for her to rest on. I allow myself a moment to say goodbye and then I force myself to tuck my grief away. There's no time for it out here, no place for it. We lay Arick next to her and together they could be sleeping, a child and her protector. But they're not. Of course, they're not.

"How are the prisoners?" asks Ian, as we meet Briar and Rory back at camp.

"Not happy," replies Rory with satisfaction. Ian gives a nod and heads back into the forest.

Briar, Rory and I scout the area for any last things that we might need to take with us, but my mind is empty, and my focus gone. Then suddenly, I hear gun fire, three shots and my heart begins to race. We all stop momentarily, and I whip my head around just in time to see Ian coming back to us, a gun clutched in his dangling hand. He doesn't look at any of us. He just walks over to Rory, hands the gun to him and zips up his backpack. There is silence between us all, but I glance over to Briar and see a smug smile. Some redemption, I suppose. Now we've all got blood on our hands.

"Let's head to the river," Ian says calmly.

It doesn't take long to retrace the familiar trail back to the rolling water. I gaze out over its moving body and think that I am like the water, pushing, constantly pushing forward. Unfortunately, there is no real visible trail that will keep it in view, so we decide to head back into the forest, following the water with our ears. It's slow at first, as we dodge thick trees and stumble over the twigs and rocks that make up the forest floor. At least it's not hot, not yet, but soon it becomes eerily quiet, a ghost forest. I realize that the eerie silence surrounding us includes the lack of flowing water.

"Stop," I command, clearly jerking each of us from our thoughts. "Listen. Does anyone hear the river?"

"We better go check it out," says Ian.

"Okay," replies Rory, tossing his pack off his shoulders. "There's no need for all of us to go." Briar and I wait patiently for ten minutes, digging in our packs for more water.

"How are you doing?" I ask Briar.

"I'm okay," she replies with a shrug. "I'll be okay." I give her a knowing smile. "Listen, she continues. I want to show you something while the guys are gone." She unzips the front pocket of her pack and pulls out a small black object. I jump back in fear and surprise as I realize what she is holding in her hand.

"Why would you keep that?" I ask in disgust. The sight of the small black bee makes me sick. "Get rid of it!" Briar takes a long deep breath and looks at the object in her hand, the catalyst of death.

"Just look at it," she says in a defeated voice. "It's important." I take a hesitant step closer and peer at the bee, my face contorted in revulsion. It's small but larger than the average bee. Its body is covered in a fine fuzz, the glittering wings projected from either side. As Briar continues to turn the creature over in her hand, something catches my eye, something glinting in the sunlight on its underbelly.

"What's that?" I question. Briar holds the shiny section up for me to get a better look. It's no bigger than the tip of a match. She presses on it gently and it lifts to reveal a tiny chamber inside of the bee's body. I gasp in complete shock.

"Mechanical bees," I say and Briar nods.

"And see the wings?" she asks, turning the bee around for a better view. "I think they're solar panels, used to charge the engine that runs them." I can see it now, the complexity and the design. I marvel at the brilliance of it.

"But how? Why?" I stutter

"Well, I know one thing for sure," she says. "Only the government could have constructed something like this."

"Do you think this is a new technology to help motivate the ecosystem?" She turns the bee over in her hand and then tucks it back in the pocket of her backpack.

"These bees could be an experiment gone wrong, but there's also another possibility." I know what she's going to say before she says it. "They could also be a weapon, an easy way to get rid of the people like James." I let loose a sound of hatred and frustration.

"Well, they targeted the wrong people," I spit. "Great experiment."

"The bees might not have been programed to know the difference." What kind of new world are we walking into? My mind turns to the Mutts. Were they also programmed to kill on sight? But there was blood and guts and carnage as they were picked off one by one on the roof top. Too many questions and not enough answers.

Rory and Ian return, shaking their heads.

"It's gone," he says, simply. "It looks like the river takes a sharp turn west a few yards back. I can't see it beyond that. It's possible that it will turn again and head north."

"This is so frustrating," says Briar. "Can't something just work out? How about just this one time, something goes right." I let out a sigh.

"Well, it doesn't make sense to follow the river anymore," I say. "Who knows how far it goes west. We have to continue north, it's the only direction we have."

"Agreed," says Ian. The fear of losing our only water source scares me but, if Ian is right about the distance, we can survive with the water we have left.

After about an hour of walking, the forest begins to thin, and we find ourselves at the edge facing a vast stretch of grasslands, lush and green. The sun is still rising, and I have a feeling that once we're out in the open it will suck the moisture from our bodies.

"Be careful," I warn. "We have to conserve our water, especially now." I eye Rory nervously. I feel more at ease as I watch him unscrew the cap of his water bottle, take a small sip and the recap it, stowing it back in his pack. He finally gets it. I'm surprised at how good Briar looks. The medication that Gemma gave her must still be working. Even after death, Gemma is here. It makes me smile.

"It goes on forever," I say, as Rory, Ian and Briar sit with me, looking out over the horizon.

"Let's just hope it goes on until we reach the hub," replies Briar. "At least this is an easy walk." I hope she's right because I can already feel pain begin to spread across my back and settle in my feet. I know it's worse for her.

"Okay, let's head out," says Rory. "Unless anyone needs more time." None of us does.

The walking is monotonous and reminds me of the first days, the days of gray sand. I can't forget that morning when we opened the compound door and saw the new gray world and felt the heat of the sun. We've changed, each of us has morphed into something different. I'm not the confused girl I was before the solar flare. I'm strong and I know I can make my own choices now. Of all of us, I think Rory has made the biggest transformation. He's strong too but he's also found a softness, something inside that resembles humility. I trust him with my life now. He's already saved us once.

The hours pass minute by minute, but the walk is easier. The cool thick grass creates some comfort and the sun doesn't feel as hot as fluffy cotton clouds play hide and seek with it. We are vigilant in our search for Mutts, feeling as if we are the first humans to walk this path. Maybe we are. Ian walks next to me, occasionally bumping a shoulder or feeling the sweep of his fingers on mine. His touch sends tingles traveling up and down my arms. Occasionally we talk about what the hub will be like, how many survivors there might be and what we want for our first real meal. He seems to be certain that it will be better than anything we've ever known.

The grass becomes cooler as the sun begins to set and there is a slight chill in the air. Luckily, we spot a clump of trees and decide to make camp. With our tents up and the tree branches hanging over us, we don't feel so out in the open. These trees are not the great pines of the forest but oak or something similar. Their branches spread out wide all around us, their leaves like small hands waving down. The botanist inside of me awakens as I spy acorns nestled in between a branch. I pluck them out and place them gently in my backpack. Wherever I end up, this is the first thing I will plant.

"Let's eat," says Rory in an unceremonious way. "I'm starving." He turns to Briar who sits next to me. "Can I offer you..." He digs in is pack and pulls out a meal pouch. "Mac and Cheese?" She gives him a half smile and snatches the pouch from his hands. "A spoon, my lady?" he continues. She takes the spoon and grumbles,

"I'm no one's lady." Rory chuckles and sits with his meal

already open. No one talks about it, but we are all down to three meals each after we divided up what was left after James took over our supplies.

"I'm thinking a fire's out of the question," says Ian, digging into his meal. "It's too wet anyway," says Rory. He's right. As I dig my hand through the grass and into the soil, it feels moist. There is water somewhere, that's for sure. We eat our meals and take a few sips of precious water and repack our things so that we can get an early start in the morning. We all want to sleep, and we make the decision to not keep watch. It's a dangerous choice but we all need a good night's rest. I think we're all so tired, anyway, that we just don't care if another group of crazy people jumps out of the grass to claim our tree. I've got my gun and I'll be sure that I sleep with it in reach just in case. Ian finds his way into my tent once darkness has fallen. I snuggle up next to him, enjoying the extra warmth on, what's turning out to be, a cool night. Just having him near gives me so much comfort and reminds me what is ahead. I breathe in his scent, a woodiness mixed with sweat and earth. His strong arms encircle me.

"How are you?" he whispers into my hair.

"I'm ready," I reply, lifting my chin to search his sapphire eyes in the dimness.

"Me, too," he says softly. "I'm ready to start a new life."

"Do you wonder who will be at the hub?" I ask. "I wonder if Gemma's family..." My voice is too shaky to go on. Ian cups my face in his hands and kisses my cheeks. His lips trail down my nose and finally reach my lips.

"It's going to be okay," he murmurs. We'll find them if they're there. We have each other now." I feel his breath on my face like a soft breeze and his hand running along my back. I press myself against him and return his kiss eagerly until my heart is hammering out of control. That's what I am in this moment, out of control. There is a deep need inside of me that only Ian can fill. I need to be understood. I need to be accepted. I need to be loved. Every bad thought is wiped from my mind as Ian's hand slips under my shirt and grazes my breast. An explosion rips through my body and our kisses come faster. His body presses into me but it doesn't seem close enough. The hardness of him rubs against me and a moan escapes my lips. He catches his breath and slowly moves away. I reach greedily to pull him back but he just chuckles.

"What's wrong?" I ask. I haven't been with a boy like this before, not even Aiden.

"Nothing," he replies, short of breath, "You haven't done anything wrong." He laughs lightly again and reaches out to run his fingers through my tousled hair.

"We have to slow down," he finally says, but I don't want to slow down, and I reach for him once again.

"Wren," he moans. "I love you, I'm in love with you. I want to be with you this way, believe me." He gently pushes me away. "Just not right now, not here." I roll over onto my back and stare at the top of the tent and the shadows cast by our bodies.

"Okay," I reply, not bothering to hide the disappointment that I feel. I know he's right, but I don't want to die in this never-ending grassland a virgin.

"We have the rest of our lives," he whispers as he encircles me in his arms once again.

"Have you ever…?" I ask, not sure I want to know the answer. Of course, he's been with women, girls. He's hot and funny and I can imagine how smooth he would be with the opposite sex.

"No," he replies simply. "I've dated a few girls but there was never time to get serious, not with all the work I always seemed to have piled on me. Too many responsibilities and then I just never met anyone I felt like being close to." I feel relieved.

"You?" he asks.

"No," I reply.

"Not even with lover boy?" He seems surprised. I laugh softly.

"No, not even with him," I say. That was the missing piece, that deep I'd-go-to-the-end-of-the -earth kind of love. I know this now.

"Hmmmm," he replies. We are both on the edge of sleep. "But you're in love with me?"

"Yes," I reply. "I'm in love with you, Ian."

We sleep soundly and only awake as the morning sunlight streams across the ceiling of our tent. I feel Ian's arms around me, and hope begins to grow from somewhere deep inside. My feet ache and the idea of another day's hike is depressing, but now I believe that there is a great future up ahead and it's getting real, and so close. Ian kisses the top of my head and sneaks out of the tent, not wanting to get caught and have to answer awkward questions from Briar or Rory. Seriously, who would really care? I take a moment to use my little toiletry supplies, making myself as fresh as I can which isn't much. Without the lake to bathe in, it's going to get grimy again fast. I begin to pack up, taking stock of my water supply. I've gone through two bottles, leaving very little left. There's no need to talk about it. We all know what happens next. We skip the morning meal and I notice that Briar seems tired, worn, and thin. Her glorious dark curls have lost their shine and her deep mahogany skin seems to stick to her bones. She notices me watching her and gives a half-hearted smile, looking away quickly. I hope there is still medication in our merged medical kits left for her to take.

We walk again, today with less chatter, each of us over it all, just wanting to get to the end. It all looks the same again, no living creature but four ragged drifters walking in a straight line through the soft grass. I let my head become full of all the possibilities. Ian and I, we might work together, me developing new plant strains for our harsh environment, and Ian possibly working with his hands. We could live in the country away from the noise. It would be a good life. I wonder what the hub will be like. Have they begun rebuilding a community or will it be like the compound that we've left behind?

After walking several hours, I give in and down my last bottle of water, greedily. We give each other side glances of fear, knowing that this is it. Then suddenly Rory and Briar stop walking. My head snaps up, glancing around at the never-ending grass and then I catch it, stretching across the horizon. At first, I think that the dark forms are clouds and that we will have to brace for another storm but, as I continue to look, I see it for what it really is, a wide hugely tall mountain range.

"This is it," says Ian, knowingly. "This is the last thing that stands between us and reaching the hub."

"How can you be sure?" I ask.

Ian frowns for a minute and then replies, "At the bank. I talked with another squad and one of their people gave me insight about the terrain."

This is major, and stupid relief floods through me thinking about how close we are. But the relief is soon replaced with worry as I realize what this means. It's another obstacle and, as I squint, I make out high snow-capped peaks.

"That's massive," says Rory, stating the obvious. "There's no way we're getting over that."

"Dammit!" exclaims Briar, throwing her backpack down in rage. "Can't we ever catch a break! This nightmare just keeps going on and on!"

"It may not be as bad as it seems," says Ian calmly. "Let's just see what's going on."

"I can tell you what's going on, Ian," spits Briar. "What's going on is we have no place to go. We're trapped by this mountain, we're stranded on an endless grassland with no water, and there's no way we're getting to the hub."

CHAPTER FOURTY-THREE

Aiden

Time seems to creep by as I sit and wait for something to happen, for anything to happen that will give me a direction to Wren. I feel like I'm running out of options. I have a general idea of where the hub is from our camping position, and I'm tempted to sneak back in for one of those government cars. I could ditch Samuel and go out on my own, release myself from the time constraint. But I know I can't do this alone, not after what I've seen. Still, the last twenty-four hours have been a waste. Making camp, waiting it out for the chance that Wren might make her way here is so counterproductive that it makes me crazy. If Raven were here, she'd already be back out there, a fresh plan in her head along with no fear.

"How'd you sleep last night?" asks Samuel as he brings me breakfast.

"Okay," I reply shortly. I take the pears that he offers me and eat. I have to take all the fresh food that I can get while we're together. I know deep in my heart that I won't go back to the Underground without Wren. If I'm honest, without her, there's no place for me to go.

"Finish up," says Samuel. "I want to show you something." I glance up to him questioningly. "Come on, finish up." I take bigger bites wondering if he might have more intel or at least another plan that he wants to share, because right now, I'm fresh out of ideas.

"I'm ready," I say as I stand and brush the sand off of my pants.

"Follow me." Samuel leads me past our camp and back to the trail leading to the other side of the mountain. He stops just short and heads east on a new path that climbs over the slopping eastern arm. This trail is rugged with few flat surfaces and I have to find my grip on the stone with every step. It doesn't take long before we find ourselves in a shallow crevasse, almost a basin, tucked into the belly of the mountain's side. I follow Samuel as he slides down the surface ten feet to the bottom. I glance around and see fragments of stone, tan and black and grey littering the surface. There are small pools of cold clear water around the edge where snow from the top has made its way downward in thin carved paths. The horizon on the other side holds the view south, land visible for miles.

"What is this place?" I ask, watching Samuel skirt the edge of the basin with his boot.

"This is what I wanted to show ya. If you ever get lost out

here or get into trouble and need to find a quick way back to the Underground, just look for the mountain and head east to this basin." I watch him questioningly. His boot has found a hole dug deep in the side of the rocky surface. He reaches his hand into the hole, feeling around for something.

"Here we go," he says and I hear a loud click from somewhere deep within. Samuel stands back as the hole begins to expand, sand and stone sliding inward until a larger hole appears, one large enough for a body to fit through.

"Wow," I say as I get a closer look. "The things the Underground have come up with never ceases to amaze me." As I squat down to my knees, I peer into the hole and see that it is lined with smooth metal, a chute or slide buried deep in the mountain.

"Just climb in and this entrance will take you directly to tunnel six. From there you'll be able to find your way to the common areas." I shake my head in disbelief. "No one has used this entrance in a long time. There's no need for anyone to be this close to the hubs but in a bind..."

"You know, Samuel," I say hesitantly. "If you're tired of all of this, you can take this way back and I'll take the time that's remaining and go it alone. It doesn't seem fair to risk your life for my mission." Samuel's no dummy and I knew he wouldn't fall for my ploy, but I had to try. He grins at me, knowingly.

"No chance of that," he says. "I have my orders." I smile. Good old Samuel. He's as loyal to the Underground as Raven is to the government. "Now, I've got an idea." He closes up the entrance and the hole automatically fills itself. There's no way anyone on the outside would ever know it was here. He leads me to the edge of the basin and we climb to the ridge on the other side. Far off in the distance, I can make out the side of the mountain where the van is hidden from view. Beyond this is more sand. I was right in my assumption that the view is vast. My heart drops a little when I realize that there is nothing to see. No people marching across the terrain, no dogs running to get us. I can see the destroyed city to the east and also the forested areas to the west and it does help to get a bird's eye perspective of the landscape.

"I know you've been down, Aiden. This isn't what you expected and we're running out of options. But look out there." He gestures to all of the open land, the endless land that makes me feel the impossibility of finding just one person. He turns to face me, his eyes hard and determined. "She's out there," he continues. "Somewhere in that vast wild, your gal is out there."

"I don't know, Samuel," I reply. "I just don't know anymore." He gives me a nudge with his shoulder.

"Let's head out," he says. "We've got some time left. Let's gather our strength, take today and come up with a plan. Tomorrow morning, let's head out and find her." I meet his gaze and nod. I can see it written all over his face. He wants me to find her, maybe even need me to find her. And I can tell that he's showing me all of this because he knows that even if it takes me months instead of weeks, he wants me to do what it takes to bring her home.

CHAPTER FORTY-FOUR

Wren

As we stand in the looming shadow of the towering creature of stone, hope begins to leak from every pore of my body. It's just an obstacle that's too large to tackle.

The mountain range becomes more defined the closer we get to it. If I didn't have to think about how I was going to get by this massive structure of glistening black and gray stone, I would think it was beautiful. We stop at a row of tall thick pine trees that dot the foot of the mountain. The air is fresh and clear with the scent of pine and a cerulean blue sky touches their canopy. From down here, the mountain is a god, an overwhelming force of nature that will not let us pass. Maybe

Briar's right, maybe we are trapped. There's no visible path leading into the beast and even if there were, the rock is jagged and steep.

"This is amazing," says Ian as he lifts his eyes upwards toward the peaks that are not visible from where we stand.

"Yeah, amazing," chimes in Briar with little enthusiasm." "Now what?"

"Well, at least we can fill our empty water bottles," says Rory with a smile. I follow his gaze and see a small flow of water trickling down from a crevasse in the stone and pooling up into a weathered stone bowl which was clearly created from years of wear. It's not deep enough to thrust my entire body into, but it will supply us with gallons of fresh water, water that was once snow at the top. I dip my hand in and feel the sting of icy coldness. Taking a sip, I close my eyes tight. It is the cleanest, freshest water that I have ever had, made better by the cold temperature. The sound of it trickling over the stone, winding its way into the basin is soothing. We each take turns drinking from the basin and then fill several of our empty bottles. Okay, this is good, it's enough to begin to fill the balloon of hope once again within me.

"Let's see if we can find a way around this bad boy," says Rory. "Maybe there's a trail to climb." He loops his arm through Briar's causing her to snatch it back playfully.

"Briar and I will go this way," he says pointing to the right. "You two head over there. We'll meet back in an hour, okay?" I nod. "We'll let you know if we find a hover car," continues Rory as he lets out a chuckle. Briar scowls as we turn to the left and begin following the ridge of the mountain. There's no evidence of any other life, no trace of an animal or an old extinguished campfire. The land seems completely untouched. After some time, it becomes clear that trying to walk around the mountain will take a great deal of time, more time than we have, possibly weeks. It would also take us far out of our way to the west, adding who knows how much more travel time. I notice little springs popping up all along the side of the rock's surface. At least we'll have water.

"We better head back," says Ian as we round a corner and see another long stretch of rock hulking above us. I nod but walk over to another spring to get a drink and wash my face in the cold, refreshing water. I drench my neck and feel it run down my back like tiny icy fingers. And then I hear something that catches my attention.

"Are you ready?" asks Ian with a smile.

"Shhh," I hiss, putting my finger to my lips. "Do you hear that?" We stand silently until we both hear the sound. The echo of water dripping but is not coming from the spring. It's a deeper sound as if it's coming from somewhere inside. Our ears lead us to a deep vertical fissure in the surface of the mountain, just wide enough for us to squeeze through.

"Careful," cautions Ian. "We don't know what's on the other side." Slowly, I push my body through and step out onto gravely solid ground. Light streams in from other smaller cracks in the mountain side, illuminating a deep cave. There are boulders of stone sitting next to our entrance, chunks of the mountain left over from the hollowing of the cave. Stalactites hang down from the ceiling like daggers reaching toward the water below. Browns, oranges, and greens paint the cave walls as the sunlight reflects off the stones and minerals embedded in the deposits. Now I can see where the dripping sound has originated. Decades of water, trailing from the snow-capped peaks, has traveled downwards, leaving the mineral deposits behind like long, pointed teeth.

"Wow," says Ian as we stand, our eyes drinking in the beauty before us. The gravel that we stand on leads to the lip of a pond of stagnant water, and I edge my way around to get a better look. As I look beyond the water all I can see is a black hole of nothingness.

"I wonder how far back it goes?" I say. We decide to explore as far back as the light will take us, making our way around the pond, watching the light sparkle off the crystals set deep in the stone. Several yards away from our entrance, another noise hits our ears. There is moving water below us but it's hard to gage how deep it is. The sound of it echoes off the cave walls, creating a symphony of sound.

"Here," says Ian, pulling a flashlight from his pack. He shines it toward the darkness, and I gasp as I see what is there. A deeper gorge, a pathway cut deep in the mountain that goes on beyond what we can see. There's no way of knowing how far it stretches or where it leads.

"Look at that," whispers Ian, pointing to the other side of the gorge. My eyes fall upon a wide ledge, wide enough for four people to walk across. I immediately know what he's thinking, and I turn quickly.

"Ian," I say. "That's a death trap." He takes my hand and kisses it gently.

"This is a source of water," he says calmly. "This is protection from the sun and the storms and anything else that might come our way. This is the fastest way to get to the other side and the hub. The water will take us through." I take a deep breath.

"Okay," I reply. "But what if you're wrong? What if this water doesn't go through the mountain and we end up stuck deep inside? What if our flashlights run out of energy and we're plunged into darkness while trying to navigate around the water?" He looks at me hard and I can see the torment in his eyes. We're running out of options. We both know it. It's time to make hard choices.

"We can go slow," he says. "We can use one flashlight at a time. If we get to a place that's impossible to pass, we can turn back."

"Briar's not going to like this," I say.

"I'm not going to like this," he replies. "But if we make this decision then we have to trust in it." He's right and, as we walk back to our meeting spot, I know that I trust his instinct.

"No freakin' way!" Just as I suspected, Briar wants nothing to do with our plan. "We'll never make it. Even if we do somehow stay alive inside that monster. We have no way of knowing where we'll come out, or if we'll come out!"

"I know it seems crazy," says Ian. "But our options are limited at this point. At least come and take a look." Rory stays silent, watching the debate.

"What do you think, Rory?" I ask.

"I don't know," he replies, clearly contemplating our plan. "It won't hurt to have a look." We take them back to the fissure in the mountain wall and the cave within. The light of day is slowly fading, and I'm beginning to become concerned about what might be lurking in the corners once we are in darkness. Briar is completely unimpressed by what she sees, but Rory seems to be swinging to our side.

"I think this might be doable," he says, rubbing his chin with his fingers. The shadows play across his face making the scars there seem more sinister. Only his eyes show the real Rory now.

They seem to sparkle with life. "Great," says Briar. "So, what happens if we don't come out the other side?"

"Then we don't come out the other side," retorts Rory simply. "We're never going to make it trying to climb over, so why not climb through." Briar gives an aggravated sigh.

"Sometimes you just have to trust your gut, Briar. What's your gut say." She looks over to me and holds my gaze. Her steely eyes seem to tell me that she's been through too much, but there's also resolve in them. *I just need to get to the hub and have this whole thing over*, she seems to say wordlessly. But before she can voice her agreement, we hear a familiar sound and my stomach drops to the ground as fear takes over every part of my body.

We hear the growl before we see the black furry mussel of the Mutt as it tries to shove its way into the darkness of our holding cell. If it gets in, there's nowhere to run but onto the precarious ledge and I think the dog would have better chances navigating that. It bares its fangs at us as it tries to force its head and shoulders through the fissure, but its body is too muscular to shove through. The beast growls and howls and scratches at the stone causing some of the edge to crumble.

"Get your guns!" I hear Briar command and I hastily reach into my pack, digging for my weapon. And then the growls are replaced by a single gunshot and I turn to Briar, searching for her gun. We all stand with our packs half opened, no gun in sight.

"That came from out there," says Rory, his eyes wide.

"Get your guns," says Briar again and now we all pull a weapon.

"Check this for me," says Rory as he hands Briar his gun quickly. She pulls out the magazine, making sure it is fully loaded. It clicks back into place with a snap and she returns it to him with a confident nod. We huddle together, waiting. I can hear the crunch of shoes on gravel and then a strange voice echoes into the cave.

"Wow, that was an ugly one." A woman's voice and I can hear her dragging something heavy away, the dead Mutt.

"Let me check," says Ian in a whisper. "Cover me, Briar." He walks slowly to the opening in the mountain and peers out as Briar stalks behind him, her gun held tightly in two hands.

"Can you see anything?" asks Rory. "Are there any more Mutts?"

"No," he replies. "It's just one person, a woman. She's taking it away."

"Does she look…normal?" I ask, not sure how to phrase it.

"Looks like it," he replies. "But she's lighting the Mutt on fire."

"She's probably trying to deter its friends from coming or maybe she's going to eat it," says Rory. He probably wouldn't hesitate. He'll take a chunk of the leg and wash it down with a urine cocktail. I'm starving but not that starving. Not yet.

"She's coming this way," says Ian. "She looks okay."

"I'll keep this out just in case." Briar brings the gun down but tucks it into her pocket to keep it close. Ian takes a step forward into the outside when the woman is a few yards away. She looks up and stops in her tracks. She must have already put her gun away though I see her finger her pack slowly. It's the same pack that we all carry, made of tan fabric similar to her jumpsuit. Her brown eyes are wide with astonishment. Whatever she thought was hiding inside of the mountain, it clearly wasn't people. We wind our way out one by one until we stand in a line before her. Just when I think she will run; a smile begins to creep across her face, and she walks closer.

"I'm Sara," she says, and she extends a hand to each of us. The fire behind her is beginning to release the repulsive odor of wet dog and burning flesh. Sara sees me watching the flames lick at the body, singeing fur, and melting fat.

"Didn't have a choice," she says in a matter-of-fact tone. "They can smell their own miles away. The only way to stop them coming is to burn the bodies."

"It sounds like this isn't your first encounter with the Mutts," says Briar. Sara's eyes flick to the gun handle peeking out of Briar's pocket.

"No, it's not. But this is the first time I've met any other compound people."

"Us, too," replies Rory. He conspicuously leaves out the old man and his wife.

"Let's go make up camp for the night," says Ian. "You better stay with us. It's getting dark."

We set up camp some distance from the cave and the burning Mutt. The stars illuminate the sky like glitter on black velvet. It's beautiful and terrifying all at once, as if the black velvet will suck me in and pull me into the vastness of the night sky.

Sara tells us her story as we sit around a new fire made with pine. She came from a bank from the west heading towards a different hub, but her squad got cut off from their path by the Mutts.

"We had them on us from the moment we left the compound," she says. "They took out Jimmy the first night. Dragged him off leaving nothing but a blood trail. At least we knew what direction they had gone so we went the other way. That led us to the east and we picked up the river for a while." So, her squad must have been close by at one time. "After that we didn't really know what to do. We were so far off track to our hub and supplies were dwindling. We knew it would make no sense to back track. We followed the mountains but couldn't find a way around."

"How long have you been out here?" asks Ian as he leans back on his pack and wraps a protective arm around my shoulders. I see Briar glance over from across the circle that we form and give me a wink. Rory sees and gives her a playful shove. She whacks him back and he rubs his arm, his eyes full of disdain. The fire crackles low in the make-shift pit, bringing some comfort but we are all still on high alert.

"It's got to be close to a month," replies Sara as she takes a sip of water from a bottle that Rory gave her.

"A month?" I ask incredulously. "How is that possible?" Sara bows her head, shaking it and then glances up, her eyes glistening with anger. She looks young, maybe close to Briar's age and the fringe of dark blond hair the frames her face gives her features a softness though her eyes are hard.

"It's been difficult, more than difficult," she says. "Jimmy was the first to go and then Dale and Rita, all taken down by the Mutts. Then it was just me and Koben and I had to kill him myself." My eyes snap to hers and then find Briar's.

"What do you mean you had to kill him" she asks.

"He got bitten," she replies simply. "I didn't have a choice." What does she mean? I think back to Ian's injury on our first clash with the beasts. It was a bad bite, really bad, but it healed. Maybe they didn't have the same medical supplies at their compound, but killing an injured comrade seems harsh at best.

"What?" exclaims Briar. "What do you mean you didn't have a choice?" Sara looks at each of us in disbelief and confusion.

"He was bitten," she says again as if this should explain it all. She notices our confusion and adds, "You know what happens to a person once they're bitten?" I glance to Briar, shaking my head. "They turn into Mutts."

CHAPTER FORTY-FIVE

Wren

We sit in silent shock and confusion until Briar says, "Are you sure that it's the bite that turns them?" I look to Ian who sits stock still, his eyes fixed on the fire.

"I saw it with my own eyes," replies Sara. She lets out a low sigh, shaking her head. "I've been wandering alone for two weeks, trying to find a hub, any hub."

"Well, you're welcome to come with us," says Ian as he rubs the top of my hand with his thumb. He has nothing to say about his own encounter with the Mutts and I'm not sure why. Briar watches him with narrowed eyes and then her gaze flicks to me and she gives me a look of caution.

Night has come and none of us are in a hurry to leave the comfort and safety of the fire. We won't eat tonight, not only because we have nothing to share with Sara but because we all know that we must conserve our last few meals.

"What's your plan," asks Sara as she continues to drink the water that is in such abundance now.

"We're heading into the mountain," says Ian. The shock shows all over Sara's face. "That's our only choice," continues Ian firmly. Sara nods. Ian stands and stretches, offering his hand to me and pulling me to my feet. We wander back to the burning Mutt that is now nothing more than ash and bone. The fire glows orange but is slowly dying.

"So, what makes you so different?" I ask as I watch the embers. He knows immediately what I'm talking about.

"I've been thinking about that," he replies. "There must be some that are immune to the bite, that have the antibodies to fight off the change." He nudges the smoldering ash with the toe of his shoe. "What else could it be?" I smile at him.

"Well, as bad as this might sound, if your theory is correct, I'm glad it bit *you*."

"Wow, thanks."

"You know what I mean. If it had been me or Briar or... Gemma..." He puts a protective arm around me.

"Yeah, I know," he says. He turns me to face him in the low glow. The stars flash above us and smoke billows around in small puffs. "I'm so glad that it wasn't you. I don't think I could go on without you now." He bends down to touch his lips to mine and even though it is a gentle kiss, I feel sparks rush through me. I pull back and glance down at my hands. The silver ring is not visible in the starlight but the red ruby stone sparkles. I smile and inch the ring off my finger, holding it up in front of Ian.

"You don't have to take it off," he says. "Really, Wren, I get it."

"It doesn't mean the same thing anymore," I say. "I want to

leave my old life behind. I don't need this to remember Aiden and the friendship we shared. This ring symbolized something more and that was never going to happen for us," I toss it in what remains of the fire, causing Ian to gasp.

"Wren!"

"It's okay." I say. "I know that wherever Aiden is, he would want me to move on, to be happy." Ian's arms embrace me.

"Me and you," he whispers in my ear. "No matter what?" The question surprises me, and I pull back a little. "No matter what you might discover about me, no matter what happens when we get to the hub, you and me, right?"

"There is nothing that I could discover about you that would make me stop loving you, Ian," I say wondering at his insecurity. "I'm the one who should be worried. You might find some hot babe at the hub, six feet tall and legs for days..."

"No," he replies seriously. "I know what I want, Wren. I know because I feel like I've been searching for you my entire life." He kisses me then, a hot and passionate kiss that reaches down to my toes. It's a kiss with a promise but also one trembling with fear, as if he is afraid that I will evaporate the second the kiss ends. But I'm happy because we both need each other and I'm excited to discover what those needs will look like once we are out of this place.

The following day comes too quickly, and we take our time packing up, wary of what is ahead. The mood is somber but at least we are given a bright sunny day. Hopefully, some of that light will greet us within the cave.

"Ready to go?" asks Ian as he zips up his pack. I give a nod and drink more water to try to fill the empty hole that was once my stomach. I glance back to the small fire and see that the flames are gone. My eyes turn to Sara who stands next to the pile of ash. Something is wrong. She is standing still, too still, her eyes focused on a point in the distance.

"What's with Sara?" I ask Ian but as my eyes travel the distance between the spent fire and her stare, I see exactly what's wrong. Standing several yards away, snarling low and deep, is a lone Mutt. It is contemplating her, crouching down, waiting for the right time, wondering if she has a weapon. My thoughts go back to our house, our slaughterhouse where at least one pack came to their death. They were smart and calculated and that's what I see blazing in its deep yellow eyes now. My mind races with the thought of it and then to the bees made to kill. This place has the stench of dark intent and stealth.

"Gun...gun..." I say breathlessly causing Ian to turn and look. He doesn't hesitate and grabs for his pack. At the same moment that Ian retrieves his gun, Briar comes crawling from her tent followed by Rory from his own.

"Hey," she says as she sees me. Slowly her eyes move from my face to where Sara stands and then to the Mutt on the verge of attack. "Shit!" Briar races to get her own gun. It's too late, none of us are prepared, not even Sara. The shock on her face is gone in an instant and I see her wrap her hand behind her back to pull the gun hidden in her waistband. The creature pounces in a single leap, its strong muscular hind legs propelling it forward. Its teeth are on her, digging deep into her flesh, whipping her body back and forth.

"Shoot it!" I scream and I hear the cock of a gun next to my ear and the fire of a bullet. The animal's eyes turn towards us. It drops Sara and lets loose a howl that shakes my head. Before the call is finished, another bullet penetrates its scull and it drops in mid cry.

"Sara!" I cry, jumping up to race towards her. The Mutt's

snout lies across her body and she pushes it back, scrambling to get away from it.

"Nooo, nooo," she cries, thrusting a hand out to stop me. I can see the blood pooling up under her leg and the gash of a wound that exposes torn flesh and bone. It's bad, worse than bad. I turn to retrieve my medical kit as Ian, Briar and Rory go to move the Mutt away.

"Nooo, get away!" yells Sara again as they drag the dog off her. I turn and look at her long and hard. *She will not turn into a Mutt*, I think. *Ian didn't. She was mistaken*. But I can see it already beginning. Fur, black and thick, spouting out like a spider's web, covering her arms and her face. Her defeated eyes meet mine and time stands still as she thrusts the barrel of her gun into her mouth and pulls the trigger. It's over in a flash of light and it's a mess. I turn away. Ian races to me and covers me in his arms.

"Shhh," he soothes. "She had to do it."

"Why," I choke out through my tears. "Why is this happening?" I feel Briar's hand rest on my back and sense that Rory is here as well. "Why?" is all that I can say, and I know that it's a question that won't be answered yet. Suddenly I hear another far-off howl and I look towards the dead Mutt wondering if it is not dead at all.

"Let's go," says Ian as I wipe my tears away. He pulls me up in one fluid movement and we grab what gear we can and begin to run. The howls become louder as we race to the fissure and the cave. Briar and Rory lag behind and I turn and shout for them to hurry. I see the opening into the mountain up ahead, but I also see the Mutts. They're close and I get my gun ready. Ian fires the first shot, but it misses his target. They are running towards us in one big pack. I count four and then ten and then twelve, all snarling with their exposed razor teeth.

"Come on!" shouts Ian. We can make it. Briar squeezes through the opening just as the first snarling dog reaches us and begins to claw at the stone. It bares its teeth and thrusts its head in but just like before, it is too big.

"Help me close this," says Ian as he runs to take one of the wasted boulders of stone from the ground. "We can't take any chances." We all help, filling the opening with stone, pushing it in hard, making sure to wedge firmly. The clawing continues, successfully crumbling the outer edge of the fissure but not even making a dent in the newly added stone.

"We should leave an opening at the top," says Briar. She looks tired and haggard from the run. "We need some light." After we have encased ourselves into this stony tomb, we rest. In our hurry we did not take the time to refill our water bottles, but we have some stored in our packs.

"I came up with an idea last night," says Ian. He pulls something from his pack, several thick lengths of rope wrapped around themselves and secured in the center with a knot. He unties one, wrapping one end around his wrist, securing it in an elaborate knot that I've never seen him make before. "Rory, I'll tie myself to you and Wren and Briar can use the other cord." He tosses me the remaining length of cord. "Just a precaution," he adds. "The cords will help us find each other if it gets dark in there. Make sure to leave enough slack." I follow what he is doing and secure myself to Briar. We have to walk through the stagnant pond to get to the ledge and, thankfully, it's not too deep. Still, it doesn't stop my shoes from getting soaked. The grippy soles still hold the rock ledge, making me feel safe enough. At first, we make our way easily, following the sound of the rushing water to our left. Though it is dim within the cave, thin beams of light find their way to us through cracks and openings from the outside surface of the mountain. We walk silently. Even if we tried to talk none of us could possibly hear one another over the echoing of the gushing water below. The walls of the cave are damp with the spray, making them slick and glossy. They resemble a watercolor painting of layers of browns and oranges and white. Thank God that the gravel under our feet keeps the surface sound.

"It's not too bad so far," says Ian, taking a sip of water as we stop to take a break.

"No," agrees Rory. "Maybe it'll be okay after all." Briar remains quiet. There's something going on in her head. Maybe she's claustrophobic. I could see how these walls could freak her out and give the feeling of being trapped. Maybe it's something more than that.

"We should get going again," says Ian and we all agree. It hasn't been a difficult hike, but we are all anxious to get to the other side, if that is indeed where we will end up. As we walk the gorge becomes deeper dipping down hundreds of feet to the bottom. I can feel an incline as my thighs begin to ache and then the path levels out. Slowly, almost imperceptibly, the light around us begins to fade. All at once, I notice the deep shadows around me and stop. I can see the gravel ledge beneath my feet, but not much more, and Ian and Rory are quickly disappearing into the darkness. It feels like we are in the heart of the beast, the water its blood rushing past below. There is a chill in the air and a dampness that reaches deep to my bones. It feels like a bad omen.

"Hey!" I shout. "Hey, Ian, Rory!" I can just make out Ian stopping in his tracks and turn. "It's getting too dark!" Rory leads Ian back to us.

"Guess it's time for flashlights," says Ian, pulling his from his pack. "We can use mine first, but we have to stay close now." I can feel Briar shaking behind me and I'm hoping that she's just cold. But when I turn to look at her, I realize that panic has set in. Briar's eyes are wide and dart around her, trying to find another way to go, any way, as long as it gets her out of here.

"Listen up," continues Ian. "Let's make a chain. Rory, hold on to the rope close to my wrist. Wren, grab onto the back of Rory, and Briar get close to Wren. We're going to have to take this slow." We follow his instructions and the flashlight beam shines out in front of us. It will be enough if we just take one step at a time. Briar is grasping onto the back of my jumpsuit and I can feel her hands shaking with every step. A whimpering sound escapes her lips, a sound that I have never heard from her before.

"One step at a time, one step at a time," I repeat over and over again, hoping it will help her. Suddenly, she releases me. I stop and pull Rory back with me.

"What's wrong?" asks Ian in panic.

"Just wait," I reply. "Give me a minute." I can hear the fear and frustration in my own voice. "It's Briar. She needs a minute." I let go of Rory and follow the cord around my wrist several paces back to where Briar sits huddled in a ball, pressed against the mountain wall. The darkness is thick, and I can barely see her face in front of me. I reach out and take her trembling hands. I push the curls away from her face and I touch the tears that are freely falling down her cheeks.

"What is it?" I ask. I feel her rather than see her shake her head violently.

"I can't," she says through her tears. "Wren, I can't."

"What are you talking about, Briar? You can do this. We can

do this."

"It's too dark," she chokes out. "I'm..., I'm afraid, Wren. I'm more than afraid. I don't have it in me to go on." Fresh tears drop onto my hand as I hold her, and I reach up to wipe them away.

"Briar," I whisper into her ear.

"I'm trying, Wren, trying to be that girl but it's too much." She's sobbing now, full on, not trying to hide it, not making excuses. It's not a weak type of crying but a release. "The darkness," she continues. "The darkness makes it all come back, like bad nightmares."

"Big J is gone." I give her hand a reassuring squeeze.

"Not Big J," she says, her voice shaking. "The men, the men who came to get me."

"Shhh," I soothe. "You don't have to talk about it." I'm not sure what she's talking about, what past nightmare she's had or even if it's real. She pulls away slightly.

"I want to talk about it," she replies in a hard voice. "I need to talk about it."

"Okay," I say.

"When my parents found out about Clare, they hired a group of counselors to help me. They were a fanatical, evil, group. Nothing more than hired hitmen ready to beat my differences out of me, beat Clare out of me." I gasp and clamp my hand over my mouth. I reach out and take her hand, feeling it shaking out of control. "My parent's thought it was something in my head, some kind of choice that I wouldn't let go of. They didn't understand...it's not a choice, Wren. They hated me, just me, the real me."

"They were jerks, Briar. They were stupid jerks."

"Those men took me to a dark cellar and left me there for

days. It was pitch black. I've never been so terrified. When they came back, the beating began. There was nothing I could do. I couldn't fight back. They left me there to die but I found my way out and I swore I wouldn't let anyone treat me like that again, I would never let the dark overtake me again." Of course, it's clear now. Big J must have triggered the memory and now in this dark cave, that nightmare must be right on the surface.

"All I kept thinking about that whole time was Clare." Of course. her girlfriend, the love of her life, the girl that was left behind. "Wren, I loved her. I loved her so much, but I made her feel like she wasn't worthy. I hid her away like a secret, a secret I wasn't willing to share with the rest of my life because of how those men made me feel, how my parents made me feel." She begins to sob again. "How could I have treated her that way? How could I have made her feel like that? She was everything to me and she never really knew."

"Briar," I say softly. "You couldn't know what would happen, how much time you had to let her know ...I know you. You would have figured it out, you would have told her all of those things."

"No," she replies strongly. "No, Clare didn't deserve that. She was proud of who she was. She was proud of our relationship. She was who she was without explanation. She was the bad-ass warrior, not me. I should have been more like her. I should have been stronger." She gives a deep sniff. "And now I'm broken. I'm not the same girl I was. I know it may seem like it, but I'm just a shell on the verge of being shattered."

"You're not," I say sternly. "The best part of you, Briar, is here right now." I say. "You are my warrior. You are my bad-ass chick who isn't a quitter."

"No," she says weakly.

"Yes," I retort. "And you're also a loving, caring, gentle soul. You are so many things, Briar, so many things, much more than what people see on the surface." Her tears have stopped, and I sense that she is wiping them away for the last time. "You will not shatter; you only think you will because you're afraid, and Briar, it's okay to be afraid." I can hear her breathing becoming normal again, can feel the shaking subsiding. "You have to get it together, Briar." My voice is pleading with her, not because I think she won't make it but because I think I won't make it without her. She sniffs loudly and lets out a grunt.

"Yeah," she says as if realizing that she's had a moment of insanity. "Yeah, screw it, I'm better than this."

I let Briar walk ahead of me so that she can see the beam of light before us. Several hours pass as we inch our way along. My eyes burn for sleep and my legs protest with the effort, but we all agree to keep going. I begin to feel Briar's released fear creep inside of me like shadows of doubt. But I follow my own advice and keep my eyes focused on the light and on each small step forward that I take. The path has wound its way around, has taken us up hills and down valleys. We now seem to be higher than ever, so high that the sound of the gorge has disappeared. Suddenly Rory's flashlight dies, and we all start bumping into each other. I hear Briar give a gasp as Ian lets loose a few choice words.

"Hold on, hold on," says Ian and I hear him unzip his pack. A new beam of light materializes, and we all give a sigh of relief. We are like zombies, shuffling in a short line as we go. Ragged zombies, with nothing more on our minds then getting the hell out of here. And then out of nowhere a thin ray of light pierces the darkness ahead, mixing with that of our flashlight. I glance to its origins and see a small crack in the side of the mountains wall where morning light is streaming through. An involuntary laugh escapes my lips and I rest my hand on Briar's shoulder.

"We made it," I say. The further we walk, the more light that seeps in. We can walk quickly now. Soon the gorge disappears, and we are left on solid ground of stone and gravel.

"Look," exclaims Rory and he begins a slow jog. I see it before he does, a circle of light. Rory lets out a *Whoop* and we all run, forgetting how tired we are, forgetting our exhaustion. We come to a stop just outside the large opening to-who-knows-where. We are just grateful that it's over.

CHAPTER FORTY-SIX

Aiden

I spend the next twenty-four hours staring at the mountain, looking for any movement. There are no signs of footprints in the sand as I wander closer to the edge, nor is there anything that suggests that anyone has ever been here, at least not is the recent past. The entire area is deserted but it brings me hope that at least she hasn't come this way already, that I haven't missed my chance. I've got two more days, and then I'll have to figure out a way to shake off Samuel, maybe even hijack the van. At least now I know he'll have a way back home. After our trip to the basin, Samuel and I decided that the best plan would be to head to the forest to the west. After checking that area out we're left with heading south back toward my old sector but there's really not enough time to get far, not with this terrain. I wish that I could contact Spencer, see if Wren has somehow made it there already. And then a thought hits me and I feel like an idiot. I grab my backpack and dig around for my tablet. It's not designed to work out here but I may be able to get a simple message through. I power it up and see that it needs to be charged.

"Damnit!" There's a thin green line on the energy icon in the upper right corner, maybe it's enough. I type in a sequence of numbers that are Spencer's access code and a message box opens. I'm able to type in three words, *is Wren there*, before my device shuts down. I lay the device face down in a patch of sun and wait for it to charge.

"Let's go check on the van and head out." I glance up to see Samuel standing over me, his riffle slung over his shoulder.

"Okay. Maybe we'll get lucky today, right Samuel?" He gives me a nod and we set off.

It's a hot, sweaty walk back over the ridge but the van is still there, the sun reflecting off its silver surface.

"That's good," says Samuel. "I was a little nervous a wanderer might have taken it." I pull open the passenger seat door and a cloud of heat and humidity waft out. It's been baking too long out here but its sun panels should be fully charged. Thankfully, once Samuel starts it up, the air conditioner kicks in and in no time, we are ready to venture out.

We stay close to the ridge because neither of us wants to chance another meeting with the evaporating curtain or any other weird crap that might be out there. I suspect that it was our presence that triggered it in the first place.

"We've got plenty of power," says Samuel with confidence. We can make it all the way west to the forest and back by nightfall." I keep my eyes open, once again, for any signs of activity, a left-over foil meal pack, an empty water bottle, anything that shows that survivors have been here. For the first hour we see nothing, but as we move closer to the forest, the hairs on the back of my neck prickle and stand up. It's more of a feeling that I get as I scan the tall grasslands to the south and the lush opening of trees next to the mountain. It's a welcoming space, hospitable, covered with shade and the rich scent of pine.

"If I were out here," I say to Samuel. "This is where I would make camp."

"Yeah," he agrees. "It's nice, but it's a little too close to wanderers for me."

My feet hit the firm ground and I make my way through the cluster of trees and then stop in my tracks as I come to the edge of the mountain.

"Oh my God, Samuel. Oh my God." My heart hammers in my chest as he comes to stand beside me.

"Here," he says, handing me a sleek black device: a taser gun. The entrance of the tan tent flaps in the breeze revealing that it is empty, but there are other indications that people have recently been here. A few scattered empty water bottles, a few medical supplies, and discarded toiletries, all familiar, all identical to those that I carried my first time out. Hastily, I pull open the tent flap to have a closer look, searching for anything that makes a connection to Wren. I turn toward the mountain and spot a backpack laying open against the stone and hurry to it. I snatch it up, dumping its contents unceremoniously on the ground. The contents are also familiar, a water purification kit, a small folded knife, a good supply of water. A folded piece of paper flutters to the ground and I grab it. It's a list of names, probably squad members. My eyes search the list greedily, Sarah Claremont, James Oakland, Dale Roberts and Rita Kim. I crimple the paper in my hand. This pack does not belong to Wren's squad but there is a chance that the two met up at some point. There is safety in numbers out here. I look around and see Samuel examining the remnants of a fire and go to inspect it myself. The stench is horrible even though whatever was burned has turned to ash. There is a thick trail of ash leaving the pit and trailing off into the forest as if something has been dragged away. I kick what remains with my foot and then lay my hand over the coals. To my surprise, it is still warm.

"This is fresh," I say to Samuel. I glance to the west where the mountain's ridge spreads out for miles, cutting off the grasslands and the forest. "It would be a long trek either way and we would have seen them if they headed east."

"Must have gone west then," replies Samuel. I can see the worry in his eyes, and I know that he's thinking about wanderers again. I glance back down to the dead fire and something grabs my attention, something metal catching in the sun. As I reach out to move the ash away, my heart drops. I stare, unwilling to believe my eyes, at a smooth silver ring, a small ruby stone set into the center.

"No," I say in little more than a whisper. I take the ring and turn it over in my hands, rubbing away soot and burn marks. There's no doubt, it's my mother's ring, the ring that I placed on Wren's finger so many years ago. My chest is constricted, my heart tears, my eyes burn. I can't breathe, I can't breathe, and I know in this moment that this is the end of me. I heave out sobs as I feel Samuel's hand on my back. "No, this can't be true."

Now as I search the pile of ash, I see it for what it is, the love of my life, the only thing that matters, the one thing that has kept me going. Samuel allows me a few moments and then he gently pulls me to my feet.

"Come on now, boy. We should get out of here." I rip my arm from his grasp. I am covered in the dust of Wren, my pants, my shirt my hands, all gray with the ash.

"No," I say harshly. I can't just leave her here. I can't just leave her for the wind to blow away into nothing. I look at the ring in my hand thinking about how, at least at one time, this silver was touching her finger. I smile in spite of my sorrow thinking that she wore it, even after everything that I put her through, even after that final day of anger between us, she wore it. She loved me though she could never say the words and knowing that helps a little.

"Come on," says Samuel more gently now. "Let's get back to our camp. We can head back to the Underground in the morning." I glance to him with hardened eyes.

"They did this to her," I say, not hiding the anger and disgust in my voice. "The government did this and I will never forget." He gives me a curt nod before heading back to the van. The ride back is filled with visions of hardships that Wren must have endured, each one igniting a new flame inside of me that will soon explode. I am in a daze as I follow Samuel over the rough ridge. As I approach my tent, I notice my tablet laying there in the sand, a green light flashing indicating that it is fully charged. I walk to it and take it in my hand and see the message icon flashing in the corner. I touch it with my finger and two words flash onto the screen, *not here.* A fresh wave of grief washes over me, and I power off my device, knowing that I can never contact Spencer again. I can't risk putting his life in jeopardy, especially if the government discovers where I've gone. Samuel offers me a meal container and I take it, but I can't eat. Everything is over, there is no meaning in anything, the Underground, the promise of a new life, even the tainted government is meaningless in this moment.

"You've got to eat something." Samuel comes to sit next to me. "This isn't the outcome you wanted," he says. "A lot of us have lost someone. It ain't easy but just remember who's responsible, Aiden. Never forget that."

My grief has exhausted me, but I have to get out of these tainted clothes. Every time I glance down and see the gray smears of ash, I am reminded of my complete loss. I pull back on my jumpsuit and fall asleep. I sleep sporadically through the night, haunted by dreams of Wren and me and us together sitting by the river, talking about our future. The second I awake in the morning a fresh wave of sadness rushes over me, reminding me of what I've lost. Time to pack up, time to go back to the Underground, time to figure out what to do with the rest of my life. As I exit my tent, I see that the day is fresh and clear, the sun bright, the air filled with the scent of cactus flower. I stretch, trying to shake away the fog in my head. My eyes travel up the stony mountain side, taking in one last time the majesty of it, the browns and grays and mossy greens that remind me of Wrens' eyes. It's lovely, this savanna of sand and stone, a place where I could make a home if things were different. Out of the corner of my eye I see movement. High up above on a ledge jetting out from the body of the mountain, something flicks in and out of my vision. At first, I wonder how the wild dogs could have gotten there and then I catch sight of a tan jumpsuit and a flash of red and I feel as if my heart will explode in my chest.

"Samuel," I say in little more than a whisper, my eyes drinking in what I see. "Samuel!" He pokes his head out of his tent and glances at me questioningly. I point upwards and watch as his eyes travel up the mountain and come to rest on the ledge.

"Well, well," he says as a grin begins to spread across my face.

CHAPTER-FORTY-SEVEN

Wren

"Come on," says Ian. "Let's take a look." Tentatively we take the few steps needed to reach the sunlight. We gasp as we gaze upon the most beautiful thing we have ever seen. The mountain stretches out on either side like lovingly now, not the beast that it was. Far below is an ocean of sand, but not the gray moon sand that we knew before. This sand is golden and sparkles. It is laid out before us as an endless sea of oblique beauty. A canyon, formed by the reaching arms of the mountain, stretches out into the distance. The oranges and blacks and tans mix with the golden sand creating a spectacular view. Succulents of varying size and shape dot the landscape; tall and spiky, fat and flowery, all edible, I hope. There are dry wispy plants and barren trees, low to the ground, that cover the sloping side of the mountain. The azure sky meets the sand like a giant umbrella, protecting us, as puffy white clouds roll by creating needed shade.

"Where are we?" I ask in awe.

"It's perfect," replies Ian.

"What's not so perfect is figuring out how we're going to get off of this cliff," adds Briar. That's when I notice where we really are. Ian holds up the rope that is still knotted around his wrist, causing us to stare at him nervously.

"Well, we've just spent twenty-four hours walking along a ledge next to a deadly gorge in the dark," I say. "I'm pretty sure scaling down the side of a mountain will be a piece of cake." I notice Briar giving Rory a tentative look, eyeing his missing hand.

"I've got this," he says with so much confidence I believe he could do anything. I glance over the edge out to the sand, judging the distance down, when my eye catches something, people, standing beside a small camp several yards away. I stare hard, trying to bring the two men into focus.

"Who is that?" I ask softly, shielding my eyes from the sun. Briar and Rory follow my gaze as Ian searches for a strong hold for our rope.

"That looks like a tan jumpsuit to me," says Briar.

"Maybe they're from the hub," suggests Rory.

"Yeah," I say. That has to be it. Still as I watch the tall figure, a boy with a slight build and blond hair, I feel a familiarity in his movements and my heart begins to race. "Let's get down," I say breathlessly. I wrap the rope around and around my legs, pull my knees together tightly, letting my body use gravity to inch my way down. Even Rory manages to shimmy down, though it takes him some time with one hand.

"I'm pretty sure that was the most terrifying thing that I've ever done," he says once his feet hit the bottom. My heart is still beating wildly in my chest and I glance around, looking for the boy in the tan jumpsuit. Suddenly, he stands before me and my eyes drink him in, not believing, not fully comprehending what I see. I feel weak and my legs wobble beneath me, as my eyes open wide in doubt and uncertainty.

"Wren," he says so that I can barely hear him. Aiden stands in front of me, worn and raw, his arms open, waiting to embrace me. But it can't be him. Aiden is dead.

"How," I say softly. "How is this possible? You weren't at the bank, you sent me your car..."

"Wren?" asks Ian warily. "Are you okay? Do you know this guy?" Hot tears begin to streak down my cheeks as Briar, Rory and Ian glance between us, unsure. His soft brown eyes are brimming with his own tears as he shakes his head back and forth, both of us enveloped in this dream, neither of us knowing what to do next. And so I make the first move and take the steps needed to close the distance between us letting Aiden encircle me in his arms. I sob deeply, clutching onto his clothes as my squad watches in shock. He holds me tighter and I feel his lips touch the top of my head.

"I'm sorry," he says. "I'm so sorry." I lift my face up to his, searching for all the familiar things that are Aiden. His high cheekbones, his wavy blond hair that is much too long now, the curve of his chin, all reminders of home and the life we had.

"You saved my life," I say. "You have nothing to be sorry about." He touches his forehead to mine and we stare deep into each other's eyes.

"I was a jerk," he says. "I only ever thought about myself. I know that now. You always deserved better, Wren. You were the best part of us. You are the best part of us." I feel a pang of regret deep in my chest and I cringe at his words.

"That's not true," I say as I take a small step back. I glance over my shoulder and see Ian standing only a few feet behind me, my protector.

"Wren. I've only ever had one plan ...to find the love of my life and be the guy that she deserves. I would have stopped at nothing to find you, to protect you, to be whatever you need in this new crazy world." He reaches into his pocket and pulls something out, holding it in front of me. I gasp at the sight of the ring.

"How did you find it?" I ask, guilt bubbling to the surface.

"In the remains of a fire," he answers. "I thought you were dead, Wren. I thought my life was over, but now I know that it's just beginning again." He takes my hand and places the ring in my palm. "Our lives are just beginning again, if you'll wear it." I glance down at the silver ring and then turn to look at Ian, but he's gone. I sigh deeply as Briar and Rory watch on. I don't know what to do. I don't want to lose Aiden again even though I know in my heart that we can't be together the way he wants us to be. And when I look into his pools of liquid brown, the confusion deepens. As I study his eyes, turning the ring over in my hand, someone else appears behind him and I gasp, taking another step back. In an instant Briar pulls her gun and Rory comes to stand next to me.

"Aiden...who is this?" My words are sharp and full of panic as the man moves forward. It's a mutant, not deformed like James but clearly one of their clan, dressed in similar mismatched clothes that are not from any cryobank. The man has that untamed look of someone living out in the wild and I can't understand why Aiden is just standing here doing nothing.

"Don't move," says Briar, lifting her gun to eye level. Her hands are surprisingly steady. Ian appears again and comes to stand next to Briar. His gun joins hers.

"What kind of game is this?" asks Ian. "What are you doing with this low life?" He points his gun to the man. The man slowly raises his hands into the air as Aiden glances back to him in confusion.

"This is Samuel," he says. "He's a friend, really, he helped me find you."

"A friend?" spits Briar. "He's not anyone's friend. Do you have any idea what people like him are capable of?" Slow comprehension begins to dawn on Aiden's face.

"No, Samuel isn't a wanderer. He's a part of the Underground..."

"Stop talking boy," snarls Samuel. "They ain't gonna believe you anyway."

"Wait," pleads Aiden. "I'm telling you the truth. Samuel is a friend. He won't hurt any of you."

"Well, we're not taking any chances," says Briar.

"Are there more of you?" asks Ian, glancing around the area.

"No, it's just us," replies Aiden, giving Ian a dark stare. "Look, we've been out here for four days searching for you. The government's corrupt, Wren. You can't go to the hub. I'm here to take you back with us. We can have a better life with Samuel, all of you can."

"That's bullshit," says Ian, keeping his gun pointed at Samuel, but I sense a waver in his voice. I know Aiden. All he's ever wanted is to work for the government. I can tell that he believes what he's saying.

"It's okay, Ian." I say, before turning my attention back to Aiden. "There's no way I'm going anywhere with him," I say.

"You have no idea what we've been though, what people like him have done to us." The intensity in my voice catches Aiden off guard. I'm not the same innocent girl that he knew. A small piece of Briar has rubbed off giving me strength that I never knew I had. "We're going to the hub." Aiden's eyes are pleading.

"Wren, come with me. I promise, I'm telling you the truth. I know you've been through hell and back, so have I, but..."

"Stop!" I take the ring and hold it up to Aiden. "You have to choose Aiden. Him or me." His face falls as he looks to Samuel and then back to me.

"Wren." His voice is torn and ragged just like my heart. My mind goes back to our last day together, all those years ago, when I had a choice to make. A flash of anger licks at me as I think about the agony that I went thought choosing between what I wanted and what Aiden wanted. Now it's his turn.

"Choose!" I yell. He takes a step back. When he refuses to say anything, I take the ring and throw it at his feet.

"I don't need this ring to remind me of what I could have had because I already know what I have. My hand brushes against Ian's and I grasp it firmly. Aiden's shoulders slump as he turns and walks back to Samuel. All of the joy and happiness that I felt moments ago is replaced by profound disappointment. I grieve once again for the boy that I lost.

CHAPTER FORTY-EIGHT

Aiden

She's not the same girl. I bend down and snatch up the ring and turn toward Samuel, the sadness heavy on my shoulders. I can tell that he has no idea what to do next. It's up to me. I need to tell Wren everything especially what she'll be walking into if they really do head towards the hub, but I can't do that with Samuel here. He won't like me giving away too much information and they won't listen to me in his presence.

"Go back to the van, Samuel," I say, my voice begging. "Go back and I'll meet you in an hour." He hesitates, his eyes roaming to the guns pointed at him.

"I'm not sure that's a good idea," he replies. "Aiden, they've made up their minds."

"I'll meet you in an hour," I say again. "Samuel, you have to trust me. I have to make sure that they get back safely." He takes a deep breath and then gives a nod, gathering up the camping supplies before making his way to the ridge.

"Where is he going?" asks the injured boy. His face is a tapestry of damaged and healing skin. I can see fear in each of their eyes. Whatever happened to them, it was brutal. My eyes find their way back to Wren. I hold her determined gaze and then fixate on her hand that is clasped with the tall boy next to her, Ian. The sight pushes another knife through my heart and I nearly rush at him to take back what is mine. But she's not mine and she probably never really was.

"I asked Samuel to meet me on the other side of the mountain. I don't have long." I retrieve my backpack and dig out my tablet. I see Ian's eyes go wide when he sees it and a glimmer of recognition plays on his face. "You've seen something like this?" I ask, trying to keep the bitterness from my voice.

"No," he replies. "What are you doing?"

"I'm calling you a ride," I reply as I power it up. I know now with certainty that once I punch in my coordinates, the government will know that I am alive. Once they get here and see that I'm not among the group, they'll have an idea of where I am. Commander Rob is too smart and, for all I know, they could have eyes on me right now. I only hope that Spencer and Raven aren't interrogated too long for information.

"There," I say, tossing the tablet down into the sand. "Now will you please put your guns away and listen?" Briar and Ian do as I ask and all of us take a seat in the sand, Ian putting protective arms around Wren. I look away. I have to give them as much information as I can in the short time I have left.

"We're listening," says Ian. There's something about this guy that stands out from the others, something authoritative, something that reminds me of the recruits back at the hub. He'll be a good addition.

"I woke up at my government back nearly a month ago," I begin. "I went to my father's tank, Wren. He sent a separate car for me. My journey to the hub was short and once there my squad members and I were treated well. We were given a mission to find a handful of government officials who went missing and I used this as an opportunity to search for you." I stop to catch my breath and think about how much I can tell them about the Underground without putting their lives at risk if questioned at the hub. "Along the way we met a group of people, people like Samuel that live out here in the wild. They're not like the wanderers..."

"The wanderers?" asks Wren. "You mean the crazy mutant people who are out for blood?"

"Samuel is not like them," I say calmly defending him. "There is an entire self-sufficient community out here, one that doesn't want to be a part of the government's new world. They say that the hub has turned people away, that those with no government connections are treated like slaves in the outlying areas. There are all sorts of stories about the poor treatment of citizens who requested sanctuary but there's more."

"What, Aiden? What more could there be than you turning your back on your country?" says Wren. I see Ian hold her tighter. I hesitate because I know that what I'm about to tell them is difficult to believe, impossible to believe.

"This," I say spreading my arms wide. "This whole thing, the wanderers, the wild dogs, the booby traps and whatever else you've gone through, it's all done intentionally by a government who wants to assure itself that only the strong survive." I see the shock on Wren's face as she turns to look at Briar.

"The bees," she says softly.

"This is ridiculous," says Ian in anger. He releases Wren and jumps to his feet. "I don't know who you are or where you've been but this whole thing is a lie." I glance at Wren one more time before I stand and dust the sand from my knees. There is a question mark there, a faint glimmer of doubt.

"I have to go," I say even though I don't want to leave her. The officials from the hub will be here soon. "Just give me five seconds, Wren." She nods and walks with me to the rocky path that leads over the mountain. Ian watches warily.

"I know this is a lot to believe, but I can't go back to the hub knowing what I know. I'm a deserter now anyway." I look over the mountains and into the clear blue sky wondering how I will find the strength to leave. "Tell me you believe me, Wren. Tell me that you understand just a little bit, that you know how much I love you." She doesn't pull back when I take her hand.

"I don't know what to believe. Aiden. I just know that my place is not with you anymore." She must see the hurt in my eyes because she adds, "I know that you love me." I smile through the pain and reach out my hand with the ring in my palm.

"Take this," I say. "Not to remember. Take it just in case you need to find me again. It will let the Underground know who you are." I drop it into her hand, and she closes her fingers around it. "I have to go," I say. "Be happy, okay?" She gives me a nod and turns to go. I want her to call me back, I want to forget about everything I've seen and go back to the hub with her, but I can't. It's too big. I can't choose what I want over what is right.

As I navigate the slope down to the other side of the mountain, I see Samuel waiting for me.

"Let's go," I say as I climb into the van. "I've had enough of this place."

I walk solemnly to my apartment once we are back in the Underground, wanting to be alone. I need time to process it all, to figure out what I'm supposed to do next. For a second, I regret leaving my tablet behind and my fingers itch to message Spencer, to see what's going on at his end. But that's over for me. Of course, two minutes after I shut my apartment door, there's a light knock. I let out a frustrated sigh and open it. I'm not surprised to see Lynda on the other side.

"Samuel told me," she says without hesitation. She takes an uninvited seat at the table. "How much did you tell them?" I look at her incredulously, shaking my head. "I know I sound heartless, Aiden, but my community comes before your love life." Her words are like a punch to my gut and I stagger into a chair.

"Nothing," I reply, coldly.

"Nothing?" she asks. "I'm really supposed to believe that?"

"I don't' give a damn what you believe." My anger is rising quickly. "I told them what they needed to know to make their own choice. I told them what they deserved to know. They're not the enemy, Lynda."

"Not yet," she corrects.

"They have no idea where the Underground is," I say. "They know that we exist, and I offered them refuge here if they change their minds, but they wouldn't even know where to look, so you don't need to worry."

"I'm sorry," she says, her voice softer now. "About the girl."

"The girl has a name, it's Wren and she's not dead, she's just confused." Lynda nods, but she's thinking the same thing I am, she might as well be dead.

"When you're ready, we have a job for you. Take your time, go see Jewel. She has her own place now, closer to the classrooms." I nod and think of Jewel and how happy she must be finally able to follow her dream. After Lynda has gone, I take a long hot shower and then stretch out on my bed. The noise in my head won't shut off and I'm filled with a long list of what ifs. If Wren were here, she would be inspecting the green rooms now, marveling at the plants and the produce they yield. This apartment would be ours, my hands would be entwined in her hair, my lips pressing against hers. I know I have to let it all go, but the thoughts are sweet, though they sting. I wonder what she will think of the hub, if she will run into Spencer and Raven, if she'll think about anything I said. I'll never know. For now, I have to push it all down because there's only one job for me to do. There's only one way to fix everything. We have to take the government down. Somehow, we have to build an army strong enough to fight.

CHAPTER FOURTY-NINE

Wren

The sound of a motor hangs in the air as we wait on the hot sand. None of us has talked about Aiden or his words against the government. We all just want this over.

"Hello!" A man's voice reaches us, and we quickly glance to one another, wasting no time to race toward it. I snatch up Aiden's tablet and tuck it in my pocket. It could be important later. A hover car stops several yards away and the man jumps out, wearing a white jumpsuit with some type of military badge on the chest and shoulder. The most amazing thing about him is how clean he looks. I hope that I will look that clean again.

"You better jump in." I turn my head to Ian and smile, and he opens the door for me. We buckle ourselves into white leather seats, so smooth that I worry I will slide off. I'm also terrified of the dirt I'll leave behind. The kind man brings us a treat, thick protein bars that are sweet and crunchy. It reminds me of the oat bars back at the compound. My mouth begins to salivate at the first bite.

"Just you four?" he asks with concern.

"Just us four," replies Ian. The car glides smoothly across the expanse of sand and the only thing missing are windows. I would like to see the landscape, but I'll have plenty of time for that once we're there. Every part of my body aches and I feel more than tired, and dirty so dirty. I think that I could sleep for months.

"I guess you might get that pizza now," I say to Ian.

"I better," he replies with a smile. It's a real smile, a true grin of happiness but there's something dark behind it, something still questioning. Soon the hover car comes to a stop and we are escorted off, stepping out onto a cement docking area. The walls are smooth concrete and several other hover cars sit waiting. The man leads us through a door and into a small white room. A woman enters, dressed in the same white clothes, her black hair pulled back in a tight bun.

"Good morning, Emma," says the man with a smile.

"Good morning, Sergeant Allen. How are our survivors?" She turns her attention to us and doesn't even flinch at the odor we must be wafting in her direction.

"This way," she says before we can answer. She leads us down a hallway dotted with more doors and to a tall gleaming silver elevator. We step inside and she pushes the only button there. My mind is reeling with the possibilities, trying to piece it all together. Ian reaches out to take my hand and Briar gives a huff of aggravation.

"Where to now?" she asks. "A room full of killer bees? How about an arena of Mutts? That'd be entertaining." I give her a warning glance.

We shoot upwards until I feel my ears pop, then the elevator comes to a halt. The doors open, revealing a high-ceiling circular room. The walls are made of tall wide windows and the only light sources are the streams of sunlight from the outside world and the many halo screens that follow the wall around, forming a large circle. Standing in the center is a man dressed in white. He is tall and built like a truck, sturdy. His brown hair is cut short, so short that I detect patches of his scalp and though he smiles, his eyes look hard. He extends a hand and takes a step towards us as we step into the room with Emma.

"Ah, you all look in one piece," he says as he takes my hand first. He has a firm grip like a man in charge. I nod and continue to glance around the room. "My name is Commander Roberts, but you can call me Commander Rob. Everyone does." He gives a light chuckle as he releases my hand. Around us sit close to twenty people, all wearing the white jumpsuits. Each worker is assigned to a halo screen, each busy typing in commands on a keyboard. Commander Rob watches as I step closer to one of the screens. "They are old school, but they do the trick. But don't worry," he adds. "There is a lot of new technology for you all to check out, not just the halo screens from fifty years ago." I nod but quickly lose the thread of the conversation as I watch one of the technicians' type in a code. I glance at the screen and am surprised to see a familiar sight, the burnt-out city, the bridge, and the river and then even the tall building where we took refuge. It dawns on me then, drones. I look to the screen on my other side and see another place, an area by the mountain. It's not the same place, the place where a fissure gave us access inside but it's got to be close by. Even as I watch I see Mutts wandering, sniffing the ground and howling. My eyes snap up and meet Commander Rob's as the elevator doors close, shutting us in.

"What's going on here?" asks Rory as he too scans the room. My heart hammers as it all comes to me in one swift punch in the gut. Aiden's words ring true. But it can't be true, it can't be.

"Surveillance," I say in a dry voice. "It appears as if Commander Rob here has been watching us for weeks." I gesture towards the screen and glance down once again. That's when I see people, men, women and children, all wearing the familiar tan jumpsuit. Ian walks up beside me and I hear him sigh. Briar stands in the center, her eyes narrowed at Ian.

"What is this?" Her question is directed at Ian not Commander Rob and suddenly I realize what she's thinking. Ian is one of them. He's always been one of them.

"No," I say, releasing Ian's hand. "No, you were at the compound, you told me all about your past, before the flare..." My heart hammers when I think about the Mutts and the bite that never turned Ian, the way he stumbled over stories of his past and the recognition on his face at seeing Aiden's tablet. He knew that the mountains signified the end of the wild and he may have even known about the path through them. How much more did he know? Could he have known about the mutants, the Mutts, the bees? I turn on him in anger.

"You!" I spit, jabbing my finger at his chest. "Say it isn't true, Ian! Please, say it isn't true!" He takes a step back but remains silent. "How many words out of your mouth were lies? How many?" I want to ask him about our kiss, about all the moments we shared. The thought of his part in this sick, twisted game burns inside of me, tearing my heart into pieces. He has the decency to look away, though Commander Rob has an amused smile on his lips. Briar walks around the circle of halo screens, stopping to look. When her eyes meet mine, they are on fire.

"Ian is this true?" asks Rory. His voice is calm, but I know he feels the fire too. "Is Wren right?"

"Yes," he replies softly.

"Now come on young man," says Commander Rob with gusto to Rory. "You look strong and healthy even after everything you've had to endure. That's the kind of stuff we're looking for here." He hasn't noticed his missing hand yet.

Commander Rob waves us over to one of the tall windows and I gaze out at the beautiful city. It's amazing and so perfect with its silver skyscrapers and wide walkways. Everything is new, a haven that was promised. There are hovercars winding their way along smoothly paved streets and I can even see elevated tracks like those at home.

"This is the Capitol," says Commander Rob with a flourish of his hand. "Rebuilt from the ashes of disaster." I feel my pulse quicken. So much has been done. And then my eyes glimpse something to the left, a structure. It's massive. Smooth concrete walls climb upwards, construction that reaches far above the city. I walk around the circle of windows, passing by halo screens and come to stand in front of the wall. It goes on and on spreading out over the land for miles and miles. I feel Briar and Rory next to me and glance to Briar who is shaking her head in disbelief.

"What the hell is going on here?" she asks in a staggered voice. "What the hell are you doing?"

"This is..." stammers Rory but he can't even find the words

to describe what this is, so I fill in the blank.

"You're playing God," I bark. "Aiden was right, this is some kind of twisted game for the government?" In an instant I realize that I should have been more careful and not given Aiden's name, but Commander Rob doesn't seem to notice.

"This is the gameboard," says Rory finally able to piece it all together. "We've been inside of it for weeks?" We wait for some explanation, waiting for Ian to tell us we are wrong.

"It's not a game," replies Commander Rob sternly. He walks around to where we are and glances out at the wall. "Do you think it was easy after the solar flare hit the earth?" he asks and then pauses. He looks to each of us, probing our eyes with his. "Well, it wasn't easy," he continues. "Everything was gone, everything. A select group of scientists remained, covered in safety, waiting it out, but you can bet that they had a plan." He walks over to Ian who stands in the center of the room while technicians continue to input data and watch screens and pretend as if everything is just fine. "I was just a boy then," says Sargent Rob. "My father was one of those scientists and Ian's grandfather was as well."

"You're making a mistake," says Rory. "You're risking the lives of people in the cryobanks who have something to contribute, ideas that will help, even without physical strength."

"I don't know that!" retorts Commander Rob. "Fifty years of sweat and blood and planning. My father wanted a better world, one that was filled with new technology, one that would never allow its destruction again." My eyes flick to Briar who is glaring at Commander Rob.

"It takes strong people to build a strong world," he continues. "We had to know what each of the survivors was made of, so we built a testing field." He pauses and gazes out at the massive structure with pride. "The land inside was a damaged wasteland, well beyond repair, the sectors gone and what better use, with all of its tough terrain and desolate cities, and other obstacles." He turns to eye Ian knowingly, but Ian looks away solemnly. "We had to fabricate a few things, but I think it was enough to prove your worth, don't you?" Commander Rob is smiling, actually smiling like a clever little boy who's waiting to be praised. I can feel the tears sting my eyes, not tears of sadness but hot fiery tears of anger.

"You should all be proud of yourselves," he says. "You made it out. Now you can start your new life."

"Who are you?" My eyes are fixed on Ian. "Who the hell are you, Ian?" I hate Commander Rob and I hate what this new world has come to, but I hate Ian even more because he knew all along and could have changed things. "I thought you were one of us, a friend, but you're nothing more than one of them, a group of murderers killing innocent people." I lunge forward, wanting to rip the skin off his face, but Rory holds me back with one strong arm. Ian jumps back, hurt, shame covering his face. Briar races to him and shoves him hard, landing him on the floor.

"Are you out of your fucking mind?" she screams. "What's wrong with you? How can you care so little for Gemma, a girl who loved you like a brother?" Ian bows his head unable to meet her gaze.

"There was nothing I could do, Briar. Nothing."

"You could have protected her! You could have protected me!" Commander Rob steps in front of Ian as Briar balls her fists for another attack.

"He had a job to do," he says. It's a statement void of feeling. "He was sent as a chaperone to your compound, along with others to help lead the survivors to safety but he could not interfere. We would have known if he had and he would have faced severe consequences. His job was to observe only unless his own life was in danger."

"Screw your consequences." My voice is surprisingly calm when I look deep into Ian's eyes and say, "Was it worth it?" He shakes his head. Finally, he finds his voice again.

"It's survival of the fittest," he replies softly, sadness in his eyes. "It's like Briar and Rory have both said time and time again, in this world you have to look out for yourself. It may not seem fair but it's what has to be in the end."

"Don't you dare use my words," hisses Briar. We have had to endure the worst of conditions and the fear of the unknown and the horror of death, examined under their microscope for our strength and will to survive. But they missed so much.

"There are kinds of strength that can't be measured by zombie people and rabid dogs and days without food and water," I say with conviction. "There's the kind of strength that can be found in talents newly discovered. You have killed a girl who would have been a great doctor. She would have contributed to this new world in an invaluable way. You murdered a man who was kind and brilliant and could have been a part of new cloning techniques. But you didn't think about that when you were building your playground, did you? You didn't take into account the strength of the mind and what it could bring to the table." There is silence as Rory stares wide-eyed and Briar continues to glare at the man we mistook for a friend. Ian stands and takes a step forward next to Commander Rob.

"The bees were never meant to kill Gemma," he whispers. "She was in the wrong tent." Slowly his eyes lift and stop to rest on Rory. This time Briar cannot hold back, even with the

Commander in the way. She flings herself at Ian, grabbing him by the shirt, twisting its fabric around her hand until his face is inches from hers.

"You're a piece of crap, you know that, Ian. Rory is worth more than your little finger." Sergeant Rob quickly interferes and pushes Briar away.

"I know this is a shock," he says as Ian staggers back. He won't try to protect himself. He knows he has betrayed us all. "You're not the first group to make it out of there and you won't be the last. I think it's time for you to be escorted back to your rooms." He walks over to the elevator and pushes the silver button. "I have no doubt that in time you will see the importance of this test and perhaps even feel proud of your accomplishment." The elevator doors open. Emma is there waiting along with two other men. I step into the gleaming compartment. Just before the doors close, I look deep into Commander Rob's eyes with all the intensity that I feel. Every emotion that has played in my head, every horror that I have witnessed, every empty feeling that I am left with bores into him in this one small moment of challenge. He is the first to look away. I don't even bother to look at Ian. He might as well be dead.

I am alone, my room eerily quiet. It's a comfortable space, a large bed positioned against one wall, a small table tucked into the far corner, surrounded by two cushioned chairs and tall windows replacing the wall next to the bed. The reality of everything that has happened swims circles in my brain. I can't handle it. My gut is filled with hatred, a deep guttural hatred that will eat me up. Fine, let it bore deep inside of my skin. Let it twist inside of my soul. Let it push me towards the revenge that I know I'll need. I haven't seen Ian for two days. He's keeping his distance. Our last conversation, shortly after the big reveal, involved him pleading for forgiveness. *You and me forever no matter what?* I think about the words he said as we looked up at the stars on our last night together. He must have known that things would go this way, he must have guessed that I would never forgive him once I knew the truth.

I sit on my bed, staring out at the city from my window. Who are all these people, walking in the gardens, getting into hover cars and talking animatedly with one another? Were they also survivors? I don't think so. It would be hard for anyone to live a normal life after what we've been through. Emma has told me that in a few short weeks we will all be given work assignments and that because we are at government status, we can be tested to be placed within government jobs. Apparently, I should be thrilled at this news, we all should be but, of course, I'm not. I think about Aiden with total and utter regret. No matter what we do, we never seem to be able to be on the same page at the same time. If only he were here. If only I had listened. Now what? A small child runs out into the streets below, chasing a toy. The mother and father chase after, laughing, swinging the child by the arms in a playful way. Life is simple for them. Life is good and fulfilling and rich. I want to be that child. I want my innocence back. I want the simple choices and the simple worries back. I lie on my bed and turn on my side, my eyes still gazing out the window and the people below. I picture myself there, walking in the gardens with Ian, holding hands, watching the stars again when the night comes. Even with his betrayal, I still ache for him. My heart begs me to forgive him, after all, he was never really a part of the governments big plan, just a small piece of it. I can still feel his strong arms around me, feel his lips traveling down my neck. It would be so easy to forgive him, to let that soft part of me welcome him back in. But that's not the girl I am anymore. That girl is gone, dead in the ashes of the wild.

As my mind continues to run through all of the different scenarios that my life might take, the different paths that are open, I feel something hard dig into my hip. Rolling over, I reach into my pocket and take out the silver ring. It still glints in the sunlight streaming through the tall windows, it still shines after everything it's been through. Do I? Will I ever shine again?

With a sigh, I sit up and reach for my backpack that sits on the floor by my feet. It's an old, battered remnant of itself and I should probably dispose of it entirely. As I dump it onto my bed, something heavy falls out. I take the tablet into my hands and turn it over, looking for the power switch. I'm not sure what I'm expecting. It's a tablet from the hub, this hub, no longer connected to its owner. But just having it in my hands, knowing that at one time, Aiden's strong fingers grasped its surface, comforts me. Maybe there's something left inside, something of Aiden's, anything to remind me of him, to make me feel closer. The device powers on with a low hum and it takes me some time to figure out how to work it. My heart drops when I see that any information has been wiped away. Even the signal light glows red, indicating that the device is not receiving messages or data. I toss it onto the bed in frustration. I've been such a fool, torn in so many directions, not knowing what to believe and who to trust. I've grown, I've changed and so has Aiden. I saw it in his eyes, a sharp determination, an urgency. We're not the kids we were, we're miles away from our old beliefs. Could it be that for the first time, we want the same thing and that we'd both be willing to fight for that freedom? Is it too late? I feel the tablet vibrate next to my leg and I snatch it up. Where once the red light glowed, a green light has taken its place. My breath catches as I see a message flash across the screen. *Wren, I will be waiting for you, always. Be safe. Aiden.* The letters fade away as quickly as they appeared and for some stupid reason, all I can do is smile.

ACKNOWLEDGEMENT

A big thank you to all of my readers. Without you, I would not be able to do what I love.

Thanks to my editors and reviewers who helped me make the story real and clean. Linda Mayer, Kurt and Deb Christiansen, Marilyn Parolini to name a few.

Thank you Anna De Leon for the amazing editing and for helping Wren become likeable.

For anyone struggling with the learning difference dyslexia, be brave. You can achieve great things, impossible things as long as you believe in you.

Follow Diane Mayer Christiansen

www.dianemayerchristiansen.com

Made in the USA
Monee, IL
18 March 2023

30035034R00236